HALF MOON STREET

By Anne Perry
Published by The Ballantine Publishing Group

HALF
MOON
STREET

Anne Perry

BALLANTINE BOOKS • NEW YORK

A Ballantine Book
Published by The Ballantine Publishing Group
Copyright © 2000 by Anne Perry

This is a work of fiction. Names, characters, places, and incidents either are a product of the author's imagination or are used fictitiously.

www.randomhouse.com/BB/

A Library of Congress catalog card number is available upon request from the publisher.

ISBN: 0-345-44266-0

Manufactured in the United States of America

First Hardcover Edition: April 2000
First International Mass Market Edition: October 2000

10 9 8 7 6 5 4 3 2 1

To
Carol Ann Lee
in appreciation

HALF MOON
STREET

1

THE WRAITHS OF MIST curled up slowly from the gray-and-silver surface of the river, gleaming in the first light from the sun. Over the river the arch of Lambeth Bridge rose dark against a pearly sky. Whatever barges followed the tide down towards the Port of London and the docks were still invisible in the September fog.

Superintendent Thomas Pitt stood on the stormy wet ledge of Horseferry Stairs and looked at the punt which nudged gently against the lowest step. It was moored now, but an hour and a half ago, when the constable had first seen it, it had not been. Not that a drifting boat was of any interest to the head of the Bow Street police station, it was what lay in it, grotesque, like some obscure parody of Millais's painting of Ophelia.

The constable averted his eyes, keeping them studiously on Pitt's face.

"Thought we should report it to you, sir."

Pitt looked down at the body reclining in the punt, its wrists encased in manacles chained to the wooden sides, its ankles apart, chained also. The long green robe looked like a dress, but so torn and distorted it was impossible to tell its original shape. The knees were apart, the head thrown back, mimicking ecstasy. It was a feminine pose, but the body was unmistakably male. He had been in his mid-thirties, fair-haired, with good features and a well-trimmed mustache.

"I don't know why," Pitt said quickly as the water slurped

against the steps below him, perhaps the wash from some passing boat invisible in the coils of mist. "This is not Bow Street area."

The constable shifted uncomfortably. "Scandal, Mr. Pitt." He still did not look at the boat or its occupant. "Could get very nasty, sir. Best you're in at the beginning."

Very carefully, not to slip on the wet stone, Pitt went farther down. The melancholy sound of a foghorn drifted across the water, and from some unseen cargo barges a man's voice called out a warning. The answer was lost in the cloying vapor. He looked again at the man lying in the punt. It was impossible from this angle to see how he had died. There was no apparent wound, no weapon, and yet if he had died of a heart attack, or a seizure, then someone else had certainly had a grotesque part in leaving his corpse in such a way. Some family was going to begin a nightmare today. Perhaps life would never be quite the same for them again.

"I suppose you've sent for the surgeon?" Pitt asked.

"Yes sir. Due any time now, I should think." He swallowed, and moved his feet, scraping his boots a little on the stone. "Mr. Pitt—sir."

"Yes?" Pitt was still staring at the punt scraping its wooden prow on the steps and juggling a little with the wash of another boat.

"Weren't only the way 'e is that I called yer."

Pitt caught something in his voice and swiveled to look up. "Oh?"

"No sir. I think as I might know 'oo 'e is, sir, which is goin' ter be very nasty, an' all."

Pitt felt the river cold seep into him. "Oh. Who do you think it is, Constable?"

"Sorry, sir. I think it might be a Monsewer de Mornay, 'oo was reported missing day afore yesterday, an' the French won't 'alf kick up a fuss if this is 'im."

"The French?" Pitt said warily.

"Yes sir. Missing from their embassy, 'e is."

"And you think this is he?"

"Looks like it, Mr. Pitt. Slender, fair 'air, good-lookin',

2

small mustache, about five feet nine inches tall, an' a gent. Eccentric, by all accounts. Likes a bit of a party, theatricals an' the like." His voice was heaving with incomprehension and disgust. "Mixes with them aesthetes, as they calls 'emselves . . ."

Pitt was saved further comment by the clatter of hooves and the rattle of wheels on the road above them, and a moment later the familiar figure of the police surgeon, top hat a trifle askew, came down the steps, bag in his hand. He looked beyond Pitt to the body in the punt, and his eyebrows rose.

"Another one of your scandals, Pitt?" he said dryly. "I don't envy you unraveling this one. Do you know who he is?" He let out a sigh as he reached the bottom step, standing precariously only a foot above the sucking water. "Well, well. Didn't think there was much about human nature I didn't know, but I swear it's beyond me what some men will do to entertain themselves." Very carefully, he balanced his weight and moved over to stand in the punt. It rocked and pitched him forward, but he was ready for it. He knelt down and started to examine the dead man.

Pitt found himself shivering in spite of the fact that it was not really cold, only damp. He had sent for his assistant, Sergeant Tellman, but he had not yet arrived. He looked back at the constable.

"Who found this, and what time?"

"I found it meself, sir. This is my beat along 'ere. I were goin' ter sit on the steps an' have a bite to eat when I saw it. That were about 'alf past five, sir. But o' course it could 'a bin there a lot longer, 'cause in the dark no one'd 'ave seen it."

"But you saw it? A bit dark, wasn't it?"

"More like 'eard it, bumpin', an' went ter see what it was. Shone me light on it, an' near 'ad a fit! I don't understand the gentry, an' that's a fact."

"You think he's gentry?" Pitt was vaguely amused in spite of himself.

The constable screwed up his face. "Where'd a working bloke get fancy clothes like that dress? It's velvet. An' you look at 'is 'ands. Never done a day's work wi' them."

3

Pitt thought there was a strong element of prejudice in the constable's deductions, but he was probably right anyway, and it was good observation. He told him so.

"Thank you, sir," the constable said with pleasure. He had aims of being a detective one day.

"You had better go to the French Embassy and fetch someone to see if they can identify him," Pitt went on.

"Who—me, sir?" The constable was taken aback.

Pitt smiled at him. "Yes. After all, you were the one alert enough to see the likeness. But you can wait and see what the surgeon says first."

There were a few moments' silence, then the punt rocked a little, scraping against the stone. "He was hit on the head with something very hard and rounded, like a truncheon or a rolling pin," the surgeon said distinctly. "And I very much doubt it was an accident. He certainly didn't tie himself up like this." He shook his head. "God knows whether he put the clothes on or someone else did. They're torn enough to indicate a struggle. Very difficult to do anything much with a dead body."

Pitt had been expecting it, but it still came as a blow. Some part of him had been hoping it was an accident, which would be ugly and stupid, but not a crime. He also hoped profoundly it was not the missing French diplomat.

"You'd better see for yourself," the surgeon offered. Pitt clambered inelegantly into the rocking punt and in the now clear, white light of sunrise, bent to examine the dead man carefully, detail by detail.

He appeared to be in his mid-thirties, very clean and well nourished but without any surplus flesh. He was a trifle soft, fat on his limbs rather than muscle. His hands were fine and soft. He wore a gold signet ring on his left hand. There were no calluses, no marks of ink, but there was a fine scar on the first finger of the left hand, as if a knife or similar blade might have slipped in his grasp. His face was expressionless in death, and it was hard to judge anything of character. His hair was thick and finely barbered, far better than Pitt's had ever been in his life. Unconsciously he put his hand up and pushed

4

it off his own brow. It fell back immediately. But then it was probably six inches longer than that of the man on his back in the punt.

Pitt looked up.

"Be diplomatic, Constable. Just say we've found a body and would like his help in identifying it. There is some urgency."

"Do I tell 'im it's murder, sir?"

"Not unless you have to, but don't lie. And for heaven's sake, don't tell him any of the details. You won't get the ambassador himself, but get a senior attaché, not a clerk. This will have to be handled with some care."

"Yes sir. You don't think, in view o' the . . . the dress, and the like, that mebbe Sergeant Tellman should go?" he asked hopefully.

Pitt knew Tellman very well. "No, I don't," he replied.

" 'E's 'ere!"

"Good. Send him down. And take a hansom to the French Embassy. Catch!" He tossed up a shilling for the fare. The constable caught it and thanked him, hesitating a moment longer in the vain hope that Pitt would change his mind, then reluctantly obeyed.

The mist was lifting off the river. Here and there water shone silver and the dark shapes of barges were no longer softened and blurred but sharp, mounded with bales of goods bound for all the corners of the earth. Upriver on Chelsea reach the parlormaids would be setting breakfast tables, valets and kitchen maids would be carrying bathwater and putting out clothes for the day. Downriver all the way to the Isle of Dogs dockers and boatmen would be lifting, hauling, guiding. The first markets at Bishopgate would have started hours ago.

Tellman came down the stairs, lantern jaw set, hair slicked back, his disgust written already in his expression.

Pitt turned back to the body and started to look more carefully at the extraordinary clothes the man was wearing. The green dress was torn in several places. It was impossible to tell if it had happened recently or not. The silk velvet of the

5

bodice was ripped across the shoulders and down the seams of the arms. The flimsy skirt was torn up the front.

There were several garlands of artificial flowers strewn around. One of them sat askew across his chest.

Pitt looked at the manacle on the man's right wrist and moved it slightly. There was no bruising or grazing on the skin. He examined the other wrist, and then both ankles. They also were unmarked.

"Did they kill him first?" he asked.

"Either that or he put them on willingly," the surgeon replied. "If you want my opinion, I don't know. If a guess will do, I'd say after death."

"And the clothes?"

"No idea. But if he put them on himself, he was pretty rough about it."

"How long do you think he's been dead?" Pitt had little hope of a definite answer. He was not disappointed.

"No idea beyond what you can probably deduce for yourself. Sometime last night, from the rigor. Can't have been floating around the river for long like this. Even a bargee would notice this a little odd."

He was right. Pitt had concluded it would have to have been after dark. There had been no mist on the river the previous evening, and on a fine day, even up to dusk, there would be people out in pleasure boats or strolling along the embankment.

"Any signs of struggle?" he asked.

"Nothing I can see so far." The surgeon straightened up and made his way back to the steps. "Nothing on his hands, but I daresay you saw that. Sorry, Pitt. I'll look at him more closely, of course, but so far you've got an ugly situation which I am only going to make even uglier, I imagine. Good day to you." And without waiting for a reply, he climbed up the steps to the top of the embankment, where a small crowd had gathered, peering curiously over the edge.

Tellman looked at the punt, his face puckered with incomprehension and contempt. He pulled his jacket a little tighter around himself. "French, is he?" he said darkly, his tone suggesting that that explained everything.

6

"Possibly," Pitt answered. "Poor devil. But whoever did this to him could be as English as you are."

Tellman's head came up sharply, and he glared at Pitt.

Pitt smiled back at him innocently.

Tellman's mouth tightened, and he turned and looked up the river at the light flashing silver on the wide stretches clear of mist and the dark shadows of barges materializing from beyond. It was going to be a beautiful day. "I'd better find the river police," Tellman said grimly. "See how far he would have drifted since he was put in."

"Don't know when that was," Pitt replied. "There's very little blood here. Wound like that to the head must have bled quite a lot. Unless there was some kind of blanket or sail here which was removed after, or he was killed somewhere else and then put here."

"Dressed like that?" Tellman said incredulously. "Some kind of a party, Chelsea sort of way? Some . . . thing . . . went too far, and they had to get rid of him? Heaven help us, this is going to be ugly!"

"It is. But it would be a good idea to see the river police anyway and get some idea how far he could have drifted if he went in around midnight, or an hour or two either side of it."

"Yes sir," Tellman said with alacrity. That was something he was willing to do, and a great deal better than waiting around for anyone from the French Embassy. "I'll find out everything I can." And with an air of busyness he set off, taking the steps two at a time—at considerable risk, given the slipperiness of the wet stone.

Pitt returned his attention to the punt and its cargo. He examined the boat itself more closely. It was lying low in the water and he had not until then wondered why. Now he realized on handling and touching the wood that it was old and many of the outer boards were rotted and waterlogged. It had foundered against the stairs rather than simply catching against them. It was obviously not a pleasure boat which anyone currently used on the river. It must have lain idle somewhere for a considerable time.

Pitt looked again at the body with its manacled wrists and

chained ankles, its grotesque position. An overriding passion had driven his murderer, a love, or hate, a terror or need, had made this disposition of the corpse as much a part of the crime as the killing itself. It must have been a tremendous risk to wait long enough to take off whatever clothes the dead man was wearing, dress him in this torn silk and velvet gown and chain him onto the punt in this obscene position, then set the boat adrift out in the water, getting himself wet in the process. Why had anyone bothered?

The answer to that might be the answer to everything.

He stood in the faintly rocking stern, adjusting his balance to keep upright as the wash of a string of barges reached him. Had the murderer brought the green dress and the manacles and chains with him, and the artificial flowers cast around? Or had they already been at hand wherever he had killed him? Certainly he had not brought the boat. That would have been impossible to move far.

Which also meant it had not come more than a few miles at most now.

His thoughts were interrupted by the noise of a carriage up on the embankment, horses' hooves on the stone, and footsteps on the top of the stairs.

He moved across to the bottom step, which was now slimy and well clear of the water as the tide receded. He looked up to see an immaculate and very anxious man, his polished boots gleaming in the early sun, his head bent, his face very pale.

"Good morning, sir," Pitt said quietly, climbing up towards him.

"Good morning," the man replied with scarcely the trace of an accent. "Gaston Meissonier," he introduced himself, deliberately keeping his eyes on Pitt's face and averted from the figure in the boat.

"Superintendent Pitt. I'm sorry to bring you out so early in the morning, Monsieur Meissonier," Pitt replied, "but your embassy reported one of your diplomats missing, and unfortunately we have found the body of a man who answers the description you gave us."

Meissonier turned and stared at the punt. The skin across

8

his face tightened, his lips drawn a little closer together. For several moments he did not speak.

Pitt waited.

The last mist was evaporating from the river, and the far bank was now clearly visible. The sound of traffic increased along the embankment above them.

" 'Unfortunate' is hardly an adequate word, Superintendent," Meissonier said at last. "What an extremely distressing circumstance."

Pitt stood aside, and Meissonier went gingerly down the steps until he was only a couple of feet above the tide. He stopped and stared across at the body.

"That is not Bonnard," he said fiercely. "I am afraid I do not know this man. I cannot help you. I'm sorry."

Pitt studied his face, reading not only the distaste but a certain tension that was not eased by his denial of recognition. He might not have been lying, but he was certainly not telling the entire truth.

"Are you sure, sir?" Pitt pressed.

Meissonier swiveled towards him. "Yes, I am quite sure. The man does bear some resemblance to Bonnard, but it is not he. I had not really thought it would be, but I wished to be certain beyond doubt." He drew in his breath. "I am sorry you were misinformed. Bonnard is not missing, he is on leave. An overzealous junior has not read his instructions fully and leaped to a wrong conclusion. I must find who it was and admonish him for raising a false alarm and—as it has turned out—wasted your time." He bowed courteously and turned to go back up the steps.

"Where has Monsieur Bonnard taken his leave, sir?" Pitt asked, raising his voice a little.

Meissonier stopped. "I have no idea. We do not require such information from junior diplomats. He may have friends here in England, or have gone to visit a place of beauty or interest on his own, or for all I know he may have returned to Paris to his own family."

"But you came to look at the body," Pitt persisted.

Meissonier raised his eyebrows a little, not enough for

sarcasm, just sufficient to indicate that the question was unnecessary.

"I wished to assure myself that he had not met with an accident while leaving for his holiday. It was unlikely, but not impossible. And of course I wished to be courteous to all officials of Her Majesty's government, with whom we enjoy the most cordial relations and whose guests we are." It was a polite but unmistakable reminder of his diplomatic standing.

There was nothing Pitt could do but concede. "Thank you, Monsieur Meissonier. It was most gracious of you to come, and at this hour. I am pleased it was not your countryman." That at least was true. The last thing Pitt wished was an international scandal, and were the body that of a French diplomat, scandal would be almost impossible to avoid, although it would have been his unenviable task to try.

Meissonier gave the same little bow as before and then climbed up the rest of the steps and disappeared. A moment later Pitt heard his carriage move away.

The mortuary wagon came, and Pitt watched as the manacles were removed and the body was lifted up and carried away for the surgeon to examine in more detail at the morgue.

Tellman returned with the river police, who took the punt to safeguard it. It would have to remain on the water, but be moved somehow to sufficiently shallow a place it did not sink altogether.

"Was it the Frenchie?" Tellman asked when he and Pitt were alone on the embankment. The traffic was now heavy and moving in both directions past them. The wind had risen a little and carried the smells of salt and mud and fish, and although the day was bright, it was definitely chilly.

"He said not," Pitt replied. He was hungry and longing for a hot cup of tea.

Tellman grunted. "Well, he would, wouldn't he?" he said darkly. "If he's lying, can we prove it? I mean, if he's French, and he gets all the embassy to cover him, what can we do? We can hardly fetch all Paris over here to take a look!" He pulled his face into an expression of disgust.

10

Pitt had already had his own doubts. The thought was increasingly unpleasant.

"It'll be hard enough to find out who did this," Tellman went on, "without not knowing who he is either."

"Well, he's either Bonnard or he's someone else," Pitt said dryly. "We'd better assume he's someone else, and start looking. The punt, in the state it is, won't have come more than a couple of miles down the river . . ."

"That's what the river police said," Tellman agreed. "Somewhere up Chelsea, they reckoned." He wrinkled his nose. "I still think it's the Frenchman, and they just don't want to say so."

Pitt was not disposed to argue with Tellman's prejudices, at least not yet. Personally, he would very much prefer it to be an Englishman. It was going to be ugly enough without working with a foreign embassy.

"You had better go with the river police and see the sorts of places the punt could have been kept within a mile or two of the Chelsea reach. And see if by any extraordinary chance anyone saw it drifting . . ."

"In the dark?" Tellman said indignantly. "In that mist? Anyway, barges passing upriver of here before dawn will be way beyond the Pool by now."

"I know that!" Pitt said sharply. "Try the shore. Someone may know where it is usually moored. It's obviously been lying in water for some time."

"Yes sir. Where'll I find you?"

"At the morgue."

"Surgeon won't be ready yet. He's only just gone."

"I'm going home for breakfast first."

"Oh."

Pitt smiled. "You can get a cup of tea from the stall over there."

Tellman gave him a sideways look and went, back stiff, shoulders square.

Pitt unlocked his front door and went into a silent house. It was full daylight as he took off his coat and hung it in the hall,

11

then removed his boots, leaving them behind him, and padded in his stocking feet along to the kitchen. The stove was about out. He would have to riddle it, carry out the dead ash, and nurture the last of the embers into flame again. He had seen Gracie do it often enough that he should know the idiosyncrasies of this particular grate, but there was something peculiarly desolate about a kitchen without a woman busy in it. Mrs. Brady came in every morning and attended to the heavy work, the laundry and ordinary housecleaning. She was a good-hearted soul and quite often also brought him a pie or a nice piece of roast beef, but she would not make up for the absence of his family.

Charlotte had been invited to go to Paris with her sister, Emily, and Emily's husband, Jack. It was only for three weeks, and it had seemed to Pitt that it would have been mean-spirited for him to forbid her going or to be so resentful that it would effectively ruin her pleasure. In marrying a man so far beneath her own financial and social status Charlotte would have been the first to say she had gained enormously in freedom to become involved in all manner of pursuits impossible to ladies of her mother's or sister's situation. But the marriage also denied her many things, and Pitt was wise enough to realize that however much he missed her, or would like to have been the one to take her to Paris, the greater happiness of both of them rested in his agreeing to her going with Emily and Jack.

Gracie, the maid who had been with them now for seven and a half years—in fact, since she was thirteen—he considered almost as family. She had taken the children, Jemima and Daniel, to the seaside for a fortnight's holiday. They had all three of them been beside themselves with excitement, fervently packing boxes and chattering about everything they intended to see and to do. They had never been to the coast before, and it was an enormous adventure. Gracie felt her responsibility keenly and was very proud that she should be given it.

So Pitt was left at home with no company except the two

12

cats, Archie and Angus, now curled up together in the clothes basket where Mrs. Brady had left the clean linen.

Pitt had grown up on a large country estate, and for some time his mother had worked in the kitchens. He was perfectly capable of looking after himself, although since his marriage he had lost the knack for it. He missed the comfort of all the small things Charlotte did for him, but these were nothing compared with the loneliness. There was no one to talk to, with whom to share his feelings, to laugh or simply to speak of the day.

And he missed the sound of the children's voices, giggling, their running footsteps, their incessant questions and demands for his attention or approval. No one interrupted him to say "Look at me, Papa" or "What is this for?" or "What does this mean?" or the favorite "Why?" Peace was not peace anymore, it was simply silence.

It took over ten minutes for the stove to begin to draw properly, and another ten after that before the kettle boiled and he was able to make himself a pot of tea and toast some bread for breakfast. He considered frying a pair of kippers as well, and then thought of the fishy smell, and the trouble of washing the dishes and the frying pan, and abandoned the idea.

The first post came, bringing only a bill from the butcher. He had been hoping there would be a letter from Charlotte. Perhaps it was too soon to expect one, but he was surprised how disappointed he was. Fortunately he was going to the theatre that evening with his mother-in-law, Caroline Fielding. After Charlotte's father, Edward Ellison, had died, and a decent period of mourning had passed, Caroline had met and fallen in love with an actor, considerably younger than herself. She had scandalized Edward's mother by marrying again, and mortified her by being apparently very happy. She had also adopted a rather more liberal way of life, which was another point of conflict. Old Mrs. Ellison had absolutely refused to live under the same roof with Caroline and her new husband. As a result she had been obliged to move in with Emily, whose husband, Jack Radley, was a Member of Parliament and eminently more respectable than an actor, even if he

13

had rather too much charm than was good for him and no title or breeding worth mentioning.

Emily suffered her grandmother with fortitude most of the time. Occasionally she was just as forthright back to the old lady, who then retreated into icy rage until she got bored and sallied out for the next attack.

However, since Emily and Jack were in Paris, and taking the opportunity of their absence to have the plumbing in the house redone, Grandmother was once again staying with Caroline. Pitt hoped profoundly that she was not well enough to accompany them to the theatre that evening. He had every cause to be optimistic. The sort of play that Caroline attended these days was not what old Mrs. Ellison considered fit entertainment, and even consumed with curiosity as she might be, she would not allow herself to be seen there.

By late morning Pitt was at the morgue listening to the police surgeon summing up the very little of use he had found.

"Exactly what I said. Hit on the head with something round and heavy, wider than a poker, more regular than a branch from a tree."

"What about an oar or a punting pole?" Pitt asked.

"Possible." The surgeon thought about it for a moment. "Very possible. Have you got one?"

"We don't know where he was killed yet," Pitt protested.

"Of course, it might be floating in the river." The surgeon shook his head. "Probably never find it, or if you do all the blood will be long since washed off it. You may surmise but you won't prove anything."

"When did he die?"

"Late last night, as near as I can tell." He shrugged his thin shoulders. "By the time I saw him he'd certainly been dead five or six hours. Of course, when you find out who he is—if you do—then you may be able to narrow it down better than that."

"What do you know about him?"

"Between thirty and thirty-five, I should say." The surgeon

14

considered carefully. "Seemed in very good health. Very clean. No calluses on his hands, no dirt. No parts of his body exposed to the sun." He pursed his lips. "Certainly didn't work manually. He either had money of his own or he did something with his mind rather than his hands. Or could be an artist of some sort, or even an actor." He looked sideways at Pitt. "Hope I'm not saying that because of the way the dratted fellow was found." He sighed. "Ridiculous!"

"Couldn't he have sat like that himself, and been struck where he was?" Pitt asked, although he knew the answer.

"No," the surgeon said decisively. "Blow struck him on the back of the head. Couldn't have been in the boat unless he was sitting up, and he wasn't—couldn't have been. Those manacles are too short. Ankles spread too wide. Couldn't sit up like that. If you don't believe me, try it! Not enough blood there anyway."

"Are you sure he wasn't wearing that dress when he was killed?" Pitt pressed.

"Yes I am."

"How can you tell?"

"Because there are no bruises that there would have been if he had been held or forced," the surgeon explained patiently. "But there are tiny scratches, as if someone had caught him with a fingernail while trying to force the dress over his head and get it straight on his body. It's damned difficult to dress a dead body, especially if you're trying to do it by yourself."

"It was one person?" Pitt said quietly.

The surgeon drew in his breath between his teeth.

"You are right," he conceded. "I was making assumptions. I simply cannot imagine this sort of . . . lunacy . . . being a mutual affair. There is something essentially solitary about obsession, and obsessive—dear God—this is, if anything in the world is. I suppose some alternative is conceivable, but you'll have to prove it to me before I'll believe it. In my opinion one solitary man did this because of a perverse passion, a love or a hatred so strong that it broke all the bands of sense, even of self-preservation, and not only did he strike that man and kill him, he then was compelled to dress him like a

15

woman and set him adrift on the river." He swiveled to look at Pitt sharply. "I can't think of any sane reason for doing that. Can you?"

"It obscures his identity . . ." Pitt said thoughtfully.

"Rubbish!" the surgeon snapped. "Could have taken his clothes off and wrapped him in a blanket to do that. Certainly didn't have to set him out like the Lady of Shalott—or Ophelia, or whoever it is."

"Didn't Ophelia drown herself?" Pitt asked.

"All right—Lady of Shalott, then," the surgeon snapped. "She was stricken by a curse. Does that suit you better?"

Pitt smiled wryly. "I'm looking for something human. I don't suppose you can tell if he was French, can you?"

The surgeon's eyes opened very wide. "No—I cannot! What do you expect—'made in France' on the soles of his feet?"

Pitt pushed his hands into his pockets. He felt self-conscious now for having asked. "Signs of travel, illnesses, past surgery . . . I don't know."

The surgeon shook his head. "Nothing helpful. Teeth are excellent, one small scratch on the finger, just an ordinary dead man wearing a green dress and chains. Sorry."

Pitt gave him a long, level stare, then thanked him and left.

Early afternoon found Pitt at the French Embassy—after he had eaten a sandwich in a public house, with a pint of cider. He did not wish to see Meissonier again. He would only repeat what he had said at Horseferry Stairs, but Pitt was not convinced that the man in the boat was not the diplomat Bonnard. So far it was the only suggestion he had, and Meissonier had been acutely uncomfortable. There had been relief in his face when he had seen the body more closely, but his anxiety had not vanished altogether. Had it been only because there was nothing that could be traced to him and he was free to deny it was Bonnard?

How could Pitt now question him again? He would appear to be calling Meissonier a liar, which, considering he was a foreign diplomat—a guest in England, as he had pointed out—would be sufficient to cause an unpleasant incident for which Pitt would rightly get the blame.

The answer was that he must find some other excuse to call. But what could that be? Meissonier had denied all connection with the corpse. There were no questions to ask him.

Pitt was already at the door. He must either knock or continue along the street. He knocked.

The door was opened by a footman in full livery.

"Yes sir?"

"Good afternoon," Pitt said hastily. He produced a card and handed it to the footman, speaking at the same time. "One of your diplomats was reported missing, I now believe in error, according to Monsieur Meissonier. However, before I alter the police record I should like to speak to the person who made the original report. It would look better if he were the person to withdraw it. Tidier . . ."

"Indeed? Who would that be, sir?" The footman's expression did not change in the slightest.

"I don't know." He had only just thought of the excuse. He should have asked the constable at Horseferry Stairs, but it had not mattered then. "The gentleman reported missing is Monsieur Bonnard. I imagine it would be whoever he works with, or is his friend."

"That will be Monsieur Villeroche, I daresay, sir. If you care to take a seat I shall ask when he is able to see you." He indicated several hard-backed leather benches, and left Pitt to make himself, if not comfortable, at least discreet.

The footman returned within minutes.

"Monsieur Villeroche will see you in a quarter of an hour, sir. He is presently engaged." He said no more, and left Pitt to make up his own mind if he wished to wait.

As it turned out, Monsieur Villeroche must have finished with his visitor earlier than expected. He came out into the hallway himself to find Pitt. He was a dark, good-looking young man dressed with great elegance, but at the moment he was obviously perturbed. He looked in both directions before approaching Pitt.

17

"Inspector Pitt? Good. I have a small errand to run. Perhaps you would not mind walking with me? Thank you so much." He did not give Pitt time to refuse. He ignored the footman and went to the door, leaving Pitt to follow behind. "Most civil of you," he said as he stepped outside.

Pitt was obliged to walk smartly to keep up with him until they were around the corner of the next street, where Villeroche stopped abruptly.

"I . . . I'm sorry." He spread his hands in a gesture of apology. "I did not wish to speak where I might be overheard. The matter is . . . delicate. I do not mean to cause embarrassment for anyone, but I am concerned . . ." He stopped again, seemingly uncertain how to continue.

Pitt had no idea whether he knew of the body at Horseferry Stairs or not. The midday newspapers had carried the story, but possibly none of them had reached the embassy.

Villeroche lost patience with himself. "I apologize, monsieur. I reported to your excellent police that my friend and colleague Henri Bonnard has disappeared . . . that is to say, he is not where we would expect to find him. He is not at his work, he is not at his apartment. None of his friends have seen him in several days, and he has missed appointments of business as well as social functions at which he was expected." He shook his head quickly. "That is most unlike him! He does not do these things. I fear for his welfare."

"So you reported him missing," Pitt concluded. "Monsieur Meissonier has told us that he is on leave. Is it possible he went without the courtesy of informing you?"

"Possible, of course," Villeroche agreed, not taking his eyes from Pitt's face. "But he would not have missed his duties. He is an ambitious man who values his career, at least . . . at least he would not jeopardize it for a trivial matter. He might . . . er . . ." He was obviously at a loss, trying to explain himself without saying more than he intended, and driven to speak at all only by the most acute anxiety.

"What sort of man is he?" Pitt asked. "What does he look like? What are his habits, his pastimes? Where does he live? What parties were these that he missed?" His mind pictured the man in the punt and the extraordinary green velvet dress. "Does he enjoy the theatre?"

Villeroche was patently uncomfortable. His gaze did not waver from Pitt's, as if he willed him to understand without the necessity of words.

"Yes, he is fond of . . . of . . . entertainment. Perhaps not always . . . what His Excellency the Ambassador would have best approved. Not that he is . . ."

Pitt rescued him. "Did you hear that we found the body of a man in a boat in the river this morning, at Horseferry Stairs? He answers the description of Henri Bonnard. Monsieur Meissonier was good enough to come to look at it, and he said it was not he. He seemed quite certain. But he also said Monsieur Bonnard was on leave."

Villeroche looked wretched. "I had not heard it. I am most sorry. I do hope . . . I profoundly hope it is not Henri, but I am equally sure that he is not on leave." His eyes were steady on Pitt's face. "He had an invitation to attend a play by Oscar Wilde, and to dine with Monsieur Wilde and his friends afterwards. He did not go. That is not a thing he would do without the most abject apology and an explanation to satisfy an examining magistrate, let alone a playwright!"

Pitt felt a sinking in his stomach.

"Would you like to go to the morgue and see if this man is Bonnard, and be certain in your own mind?" he offered.

"The morgue!"

"Yes. It is the only way you will satisfy yourself."

"I . . . I suppose it is necessary?"

"Not to me. Monsieur Meissonier has said Bonnard is not missing. I have to accept that. Therefore it cannot be him."

"Of course. I will come. How long will it take?"

"In a hansom we can be there and back in less than an hour."

"Very well. Let us make haste."

Ashen-faced and deeply unhappy, Villeroche stared at the face of the dead man and said it was not Henri Bonnard.

"It is most like him." He coughed and held his handkerchief to his face. "But I do not know this man. I am sorry for having taken your time. You have been most civil. Please, in no circumstances mention to Monsieur Meissonier, or anyone else, that I came here." He turned and all but ran out of the morgue and scrambled up into the hansom again, directing it back to the embassy so hastily Pitt had to jump after him not to be left on the pavement.

"Where does he live?" he asked, flinging himself into the seat as the cab pulled away.

"He has rooms in Portman Square," Villeroche replied. "But he isn't there. . . ."

"More precisely?" Pitt persisted. "And names of one or two other friends or associates who might know more?"

"Second floor of number fourteen. And I suppose you could ask Charles Renaud or Jean-Claud Aubusson. I'll give you their addresses. They . . . they don't work at the embassy. And of course there are Englishmen also. There is George Strickland, and Mr. O'Halloran." He fumbled in his pocket and did not find what he wanted.

Pitt habitually carried all sorts of things. It had been the despair of his superiors when they saw him more frequently, and even now Commissioner Cornwallis, who had been in the navy before taking up his present appointment, found Pitt's untidiness hard to tolerate. Now he pulled out string, a pocketknife, sealing wax, a pencil, three shillings and sevenpence in coins, two used French postage stamps he was saving for Daniel, a receipt for a pair of socks, a note to remind himself to get his boots mended and buy some butter, two mint humbugs covered in fluff, and a small pad of paper. He handed the pencil and paper to Villeroche, and put the rest back.

Villeroche wrote the names and addresses for him, and when they reached the corner nearest the embassy, he stopped the cab, said good-bye and then ran across the road and disappeared up the steps.

Pitt called upon all of the men Villeroche had named. He found two of them at home and willing to talk to him.

"Ah, but he's a fine man," O'Halloran said with a smile. "But I haven't seen him in a week or more, which is surely a shame. I expected him at Wylie's party last Saturday night, and I would have bet my shirt he'd have been at the theatre on Monday. Wilde was there himself, and what a night we had of it, for sure." He shrugged. "Not that I'd swear I can remember everything of it myself, mind."

"But Henri Bonnard was not there?" Pitt pressed him.

"That I do know," O'Halloran said with certainty. He looked at Pitt narrowly out of vivid blue eyes. "Police, you said you are? Is there something wrong? Why are you asking about Bonnard?"

"Because at least one of his other friends believes he is missing," Pitt replied.

"And they're sending a superintendent to look for him?" O'Halloran asked wryly.

"No. There was a body found in the Thames at Horseferry Stairs this morning. There was a question it might be him, but two men from the French Embassy have both said it is not."

"Thank God for that!" O'Halloran said with feeling. "Although it's some poor devil. Surely you don't think Bonnard is responsible? Can't imagine it. Harmless sort of fellow, he is. A bit wild in his tastes, maybe, all for enjoying himself, but no malice in him, none at all."

"That was never in question," Pitt assured him.

O'Halloran relaxed, but he could say nothing more of use, and Pitt thanked him and left.

The other person willing to see him was Charles Renaud.

"Actually I rather assumed he'd gone to Paris," he said with surprise. "I seem to remember him saying something about having to pack, and he mentioned the time the Dover train left. It was all rather in passing, you know? I made the assumption. I'm afraid I wasn't especially interested. I'm sorry."

Tellman went to the river police eagerly, not because he had any great fondness for them, but questioning about tides and hours was infinitely preferable to trying to extract embarrassing truths from foreigners who were protected by diplomatic immunity. What the man in the punt had been doing that provoked his murder it was beyond Tellman's power, or desire, even to guess. Tellman had seen a great deal of the sordid and tragic sides of life. He had grown up in extreme poverty and knew crime and both the need and the viciousness which drove it. But there were things some so-called gentlemen did, especially those connected with the theatre, which no decent person should have a guess at, far less observe.

Men who wore green velvet dresses were among them. Tellman had been brought up to believe there were two sorts of women: good women, such as wives, mothers, and aunts, who did not show passions and probably did not have them; and the sort who did have them, and who showed them publicly and embarrassingly. A man who would dress up as the second was beyond his comprehension.

Thinking of women, and love, brought Gracie to his mind. Without intending to, he could see her bright little face, the angle of her shoulders, the quick way she moved. She was tiny—all her dresses had to be taken up—and too thin for most men's tastes, with not much shape to her, no more than a suggestion. He hadn't thought he liked women like that himself. She was all spirit and mind, a sharp tongue, all courage and wit.

Tellman had no idea what she really thought of him. He sat on the omnibus going along the embankment and remembered with curiously painful loneliness how her eyes had shone when she spoke of that Irish valet. He did not want to name the pain inside him. It was something he preferred not to recognize.

He would point his mind to what he should ask the river police about tides and where the boat must have started in order to finish at Horseferry Stairs by dawn.

He reported his findings to Pitt in the late afternoon, at Pitt's home in Keppel Street. It was warm and clean, but it seemed very empty without the women in the kitchen or busying about upstairs. There were no children's voices; no light, quick feet; no one singing. He even missed Gracie's orders, telling him to watch his boots, not to bump anything or make a mess.

He sat across the kitchen table from Pitt, sipping at his tea and feeling strangely empty.

"Well?" Pitt prompted.

"Not very helpful, actually," Tellman answered. There was no homemade cake, only a tin of bought biscuits. It was not nearly the same. "Low water was at three minutes past five at London Bridge, and it gets later the higher you go up the river. Like it would be near quarter past six up at Battersea."

"And high tide?" Pitt asked.

"Quarter past eleven last night at London Bridge."

"And an hour and ten minutes later at Battersea . . ."

"No . . . that's the thing, only twenty minutes, more like twenty-five to midnight."

"And the rate of flow? How far would the punt have drifted?"

"That's the other thing," Tellman explained. "The ebb tide takes six and three quarter hours, near enough. The flood tide takes only five and a quarter. He reckoned the punt could go as much as two and a half miles an hour, but on the other hand, on ebb tide there are mud shoals and sandbanks it could get stuck on . . ."

"But it didn't," Pitt pointed out. "If it had, it wouldn't have come off till the flood again."

"Or it could have got caught up by passing barges in the dark, or anything else," Tellman went on. "Caught on the piles of a bridge and then loosed again if something bumped into it . . . a dozen things. All they can say for sure is that it most likely came from upriver, because no one'd carry that extra weight against the tide, and there's no place likely anyone'd keep a boat like that, which is a private sort of pleasure boat, downriver from Horseferry Stairs. It's all city, docks and the like."

Pitt remained silent for several minutes, thinking it over.

"I see," he said at length. "So time and tide don't really help at all. It could have been as far as eleven or twelve miles, at the outside, and as close as one mile, or wherever the nearest house is with an edge on the water. Or even nearer, if anyone kept that punt moored in the open. It'll just be a matter of questioning."

"It would help to find out who he is," Tellman pointed out. "I still think it could be that French fellow and they're embarrassed to say so. I'd disown him if any Englishman did that in France!"

Pitt looked at him with a faint smile. "I found a friend of his who thought he had gone to Dover, on the way to Paris. I'd like to know if that's true."

"Across the Channel?" Tellman said with mixed feelings. He was not very keen on the idea of foreign travel, but on the other hand it would be quite an adventure to go in a packet boat or a steamer over to Calais, and then perhaps even to Paris itself. That would be something to tell Gracie! "I'd better find out if he did," he said hopefully. "If he isn't the body, he might be the one who killed him."

"If it isn't he, there's no reason to suppose he has anything to do with it," Pitt pointed out. "But you are right, we need to know whose body it is. We've got nothing else."

Tellman stood up. "So I'll go to Dover, sir. Shipping company ought to know whether he went over to France or not. I'll go and find out."

2

$T_{HE\ LAST\ POST\ ARRIVED}$ just as Tellman left, and Pitt felt a surge of excitement as he recognized Charlotte's handwriting on a thick envelope addressed to him. He ignored the others and went back to the kitchen, tearing hers open and pulling out the sheets of notepaper as he went. He sat down at the table and read:

My dearest Thomas,

Paris is marvelous. What a beautiful city! I miss you, but I am enjoying myself. There is simply so much to see, to listen to, to learn. I have never been in a place so buzzing with life and ideas. Even the posters on the walls are by real artists, and quite different from anything in London. They have such a flair they invite interest straightaway—even if it might not be of a kind one would be willing to own.

The streets, or should I say "boulevards," for they are all relatively new and very wide and grand, are lined with oceans of trees. Light dances on fountains in all directions. "Or blew the silver down-baths of her dreams, to sow futurity with seeds of thought and count the passage of her festive hours." Elizabeth Barrett Browning said it so well.

Jack plans to take us to the theatre, but one hardly knows where to begin. There are over twenty in the city, so we are told, and of course that does not include the opera. I should love to see Sarah Bernhardt in something—anything at all. I hear she has even done Hamlet! Or intends to.

Our host and hostess here are very charming and do everything to make us welcome. But I do miss my own house. Here they have no idea how to make a decent cup of tea, and chocolate first thing in the morning is horrible!

There is great talk about a young man who is on trial for murder. He swears he was elsewhere at the time, and could prove it, if only the friend he was with would come forward. No one believes him. But the thing which is interesting is that he says he was at the Moulin Rouge. That is a famous, or perhaps notorious, dance hall. I asked Madame about it, but she seemed rather scandalized, so I did not pursue the matter. Jack says they dance the cancan there, and the girls wear no underclothes. A very strange artist called Henri Toulouse-Lautrec paints wonderful posters for it. I saw one when we were out on the street yesterday. It was rather vulgar, but so full of life I had to look. I felt as if I could hear the music just by seeing it.

Tomorrow we go to see M. Eiffel's tower, which is enormous. I believe there is a water closet at the very top, whose windows would have the very best view in Paris—could one see out of them!

I miss you all, and realize how much I love you, because you are not here with me. When I come home I shall be so devoted, obedient and charming—for at least a week!

Yours always,
Charlotte

Pitt sat with the paper in his hand, smiling. Reading her words, written enthusiastically, scrawled across the page, was almost like hearing her voice. Again he was reminded how right he had been to let her go gracefully rather than grudgingly. It was only for three weeks. Every day of it dragged, but it would come to an end. He realized with a start that the time was flying by on wings and he needed to prepare to go out to the theatre with Caroline. He folded up Charlotte's letter and slid it back into the envelope, put it in his jacket pocket and went upstairs to wash and change into the only evening suit he possessed. It was something he had been obliged to purchase when going to stay, on police duty, at Emily's country home.

He worked hard at looking tidy and sufficiently respectable not to embarrass his mother-in-law. He was fond of Caroline quite apart from their family relationship. He admired her courage in seizing her happiness with Joshua regardless of the social risks involved. Charlotte had done the same in marrying him, and he did not delude himself that the costs were not real.

He surveyed himself in the glass. The reflection he saw was not entirely satisfactory. His face was intelligent and individual rather than handsome. No matter what he did with his hair it was always unruly. Of course a good barber could have cut several inches off it and helped a lot, but short hair made him uncomfortable, and he somehow never remembered to make time. His shirt collar was straight, for a change, if a little high, and its dazzling white was becoming to him. It would have to do.

He walked briskly to Bedford Square and caught a cab to the theatre in Shaftesbury Avenue. The street was milling with people, the somber black and white of gentlemen, the brilliant colors of women, the glitter of jewels. Laughter mixed with the sound of hooves and the rattle of harness as carriages fought for room to move. The gaslight was bright and the theatre front had huge posters advertising the performance, the actress's name above the title of the play. Neither meant anything to Pitt, but he could not help being infected by the excitement. It was sharp and brittle in the air, like moonlight on a frosty night.

Everyone was surging forward, all pressing to get inside, to see and to be seen, call to people they knew, take their seats, anticipate the drama.

Pitt found Caroline and Joshua in the foyer. They saw him, perhaps because of his height, before he saw them. He heard Joshua's voice, clear and carrying, with the perfect diction of an actor.

"Thomas! Over to your left, by the pillar."

Pitt turned and saw him immediately. Joshua Fielding had the sort of face perfectly designed for conveying emotion: mobile features, heavy-lidded, dark eyes, a mouth quick to humor or as easily to tragedy. Now he was simply pleased to see a friend.

Beside him, Caroline looked remarkably well. She had the same warm coloring as Charlotte, hair with auburn lights in it touched with gray, the proud carriage of her head. Time had dealt kindly with her, but the mark of pain was there for anyone perceptive enough to see. She had not been unscathed by life, as Pitt knew very well.

He greeted them with real pleasure and then followed them up the steps and around the long, curving corridor to the box Joshua had reserved. It had an excellent view of the stage, quite uninterrupted by other people's heads, and they were at a broad angle so they could see everyone except in the wings on their own side.

Joshua held a chair for Caroline, then both men seated themselves.

Pitt told them of Charlotte's letter, omitting the part about the young man's trial and the question of visiting places like the Moulin Rouge.

"I hope she is not going to come home with radical ideas," Caroline said with a smile.

"The whole world is changing," Joshua replied. "Ideas are in flux all the time. New generations want different things from life and expect happiness in new ways."

Caroline turned toward him, looking puzzled. "Why do you say that?" she asked. "You made odd remarks at breakfast also."

"I am wondering if I should have told you more about tonight's play. Perhaps I should. It is very . . . avant-garde." He looked a little rueful, his face gentle and apologetic in the shadows from the box curtains and the glare of the chandeliers.

"It's not by Mr. Ibsen, is it?" Caroline asked uncertainly.

Joshua smiled widely. "No, my dear, but it's just as controversial. Cecily Antrim would not play in something by an un-

28

known author unless it was fairly radical and espoused views she shared." There was a warmth in his voice as he spoke and a humor in his eyes.

Pitt thought Caroline looked uncertain, but before either of them could pursue the subject their attention was caught by people they knew in one of the boxes opposite.

Pitt settled back in his seat and watched the color and excitement around him, the fashionable women parading, heads high, more conscious of each other than of any of the men. It was not romance which motivated them, but rivalry. He thought of Charlotte in Paris, and imagined how well she would have read them and understood the finer nuances he could only observe. He would try to describe it to her when she came back, if she stopped talking long enough to listen.

The lights dimmed and a hush fell over the auditorium. Everyone straightened up and looked towards the stage.

The curtain rose on a domestic scene in a beautiful withdrawing room. There were half a dozen people present, but the spotlight caught only one of them. The rest seemed drab compared with the almost luminous quality she possessed. She was unusually tall and extremely slender, but there was a grace in her even when motionless. Her fair hair caught the light, and the strong, clean bones of her face were ageless.

She spoke, and the drama began.

Pitt had expected to be entertained, perhaps as much by the occasion as by the play. That was not what happened. He found himself drawn in from the moment he saw Cecily Antrim. There was an emotional vitality in her which conveyed loneliness and a devastating sense of need, so that he ached for her. He became unaware of his own surroundings. For him reality was the withdrawing room on the stage. The people playing out their lives were of intense importance.

The character of Cecily Antrim was married to an older man, upright, honest, but incapable of passion. He loved her, within his own limits, and he was loyal and possessive. Certainly he did not ignore her, and it would have been beyond his comprehension to betray her. Yet he was slowly killing something inside her which, as they watched, was beginning to fight for life.

There was another man, younger, with more fire and imagination, more hunger of the soul. From the time they met their mutual attraction was inevitable. That issue was not what the playwright wished to explore, nor what would occupy the vast majority of the audience. The question was what would each of the characters do about it. The husband, the wife, the young man, his fiancée, her parents, all had fears and beliefs which governed their reactions, inhibitions which distorted the truth they might otherwise have spoken, expectations taught them by their lives and their society. Above all, was there any avenue of escape for the wife, who could not institute divorce, though the husband could have had he wanted?

As Pitt watched he found himself reconsidering his own assumptions about men and women, what each expected of the other and of the happiness marriage might afford—or deny. He had expected passion and fulfillment, and he had found it. Of course there were times of loneliness, misunderstanding, exasperation, but on the whole he could only feel a deep and abiding happiness. But how many others felt the same? Was it something one had the right to expect?

More urgently and far more painfully, had any man the right to expect a woman to conceal and endure his inadequacies as the character on stage demanded of his wife? The audience was intensely aware of her loneliness, of the weight of his inability which was crushing her, but no one else was, except the young lover, and he understood only a part of it. The flame that burned within her was too great for him also. In the end one feared he would be charred by it.

The wife had duties towards the husband, physical duties on the rare occasions he wished, duties of obedience, tact, domestic responsibility, and the need always to behave with discretion and decorum.

Legally he had no such duties toward her—what about morally? Unquestionably he had to provide her with a home, to be sober and honest and to take his pleasures, whatever they might be, with a corresponding discretion. But had he a duty of physical passion? Or was the need for it unbecoming in a decent woman? If he had given her children, should that be enough?

Cecily Antrim, in every movement of her body, inflection of her voice, showed that it was not enough. She was dying of an inner loneliness which consumed her being. Was she unreasonable, overdemanding, selfish, even indecent? Or was she only voicing what a million other silent women might feel?

It was a disquieting thought. As the curtains drew closed and the lights blazed up again, Pitt turned to look at Caroline.

Caroline herself was as deeply disturbed by the first act of the play as Pitt had been, but in different ways. It was not the questions of hunger and loyalty which disturbed her most, at least it was not the answer to them; it was the fact that they should be raised at all. Such matters were intensely private. They were the thoughts one had alone, in darker moments of confusion and self-doubt, and dismissed when common sense prevailed.

She did not even look across at Joshua, embarrassed to meet his eyes. Nor did she wish to look at Pitt. In showing her emotions so nakedly on the stage, Cecily Antrim had, in a very real sense, stripped the decent clothes of modesty and silence from all women. Caroline could not forgive her easily for that.

"Brilliant!" Joshua's voice came softly beside her. "I've never seen anyone else who could combine such a delicacy of touch with such power of feeling. Don't you think so?"

Caroline felt the movement as he looked towards her.

"She is extraordinary," she answered with honesty. She never doubted for an instant that he was referring to Cecily Antrim. No one in the entire theatre would have needed assurance on that. She hoped her voice had not sounded as cool as she felt. He had made no secret of how profoundly he admired Cecily. Caroline wondered now if the regard was personal as well as professional. It brushed by her with a coldness she preferred to dismiss.

"I knew you would love her," Joshua went on. "She has a

31

moral courage which is almost unique. Nothing deters her from fighting for her beliefs."

Caroline made herself smile. She refused to ask what those beliefs were. After watching the first act of the play, she greatly preferred not to know.

"You are quite right," she said with as much enthusiasm as she could manage. She was no actress at all. "I always admire courage . . . more than almost any other quality . . . except perhaps kindness."

Joshua's reply was cut short by a knock at the door of the box. He stood up to reply, and a moment later a man in his late forties came in, tall and slim with a mild, rather austere face. The woman beside him was almost beautiful. Her features were regular, her eyes wide, deep-set and very blue. There was perhaps a lack of humor in her which robbed her of the final magic.

They were a Mr. and Mrs. Marchand. Caroline had known them for over a year and enjoyed their company on many occasions. She was pleased they had called. Without question they would feel as she did regarding the play. In fact, she was surprised they had come to see it. Like her, they could not have known its content.

Their first remarks after being introduced to Pitt proved her correct.

"Extraordinary!" Ralph Marchand said quietly, his face reflecting his puzzlement. He avoided Caroline's eyes, as if he had not yet overcome his embarrassment at the subject and could not easily discuss it in a woman's company.

Joshua offered Mrs. Marchand his seat, and she accepted it, thanking him.

"Remarkable woman," Mr. Marchand went on, obviously referring to Cecily Antrim. "I realize, of course, that she is merely acting what the playwright has written, but I am sorry a woman of such talent should lend herself to this. And frankly I am surprised that the Lord Chamberlain permitted it a license to be performed!"

Joshua leaned gracefully against the wall near the edge of the red, plush-padded balcony, his hands in his pockets. "Ac-

32

tually I should be very surprised if she didn't have considerable sympathy with the character," he replied. "I think it was a part she chose to play."

Mr. Marchand looked surprised and, Caroline thought, also disappointed.

"Really? Oh . . ."

"I cannot understand the Lord Chamberlain either," Mrs. Marchand said sadly, her blue eyes very wide. "He is lacking in his duties that he has not exercised his power to censor it. He is supposed to be there for our protection. That, after all, is his purpose, isn't it?"

"Of course it is, my dear," her husband assured her. "It seems he does not appreciate the harm his laxity is doing."

Caroline glanced at Joshua. She knew his views on censorship, and she was afraid he would say something which would offend the Marchands, but she did not know how to prevent it without in turn hurting him. "It is a difficult decision," she said tentatively.

"It may require courage," Mrs. Marchand replied without hesitation. "But if he accepts the office then we have the right to expect that much of him."

Caroline could understand exactly what she meant. She knew instinctively her concerns, and yet she was equally sure Joshua would not. She was surprised how moderate his answer was when he spoke.

"Protection is a double-edged sword, Mrs. Marchand." He did not move from his relaxed position against the corner of the balcony, but Caroline could see the more angular lines of his body as his muscles tensed.

Mrs. Marchand looked at him guardedly. "Double-edged?" she enquired.

"What is it you would like to be protected from?" Joshua kept his voice level and gentle.

Mr. Marchand moved slightly, only a changing of weight.

"From the corruption of decency," Mrs. Marchand replied, anger and certainty ringing in her tone. Unconsciously she put her hand towards her husband. "From the steady destruction of our way of life by the praising of immorality and selfishness.

33

The teaching of young and impressionable people that self-indulgence is acceptable, even good. The exhibiting in public of emotions and practices which should remain private. It cheapens and demeans that which should be sacred. . . ."

Caroline knew what she meant, and she more than half agreed with her. The Marchands had a young son, about sixteen years old. Caroline could remember when her daughters were that age, and how hard she had worked to guide and protect them. It had been less difficult then.

She looked at Joshua, knowing he would disagree. But then he had never had children, and that made a world of difference. He had no one to protect in that passionate way that demanded all commitment.

"Is self-denial better than self-indulgence?" Joshua questioned.

Mrs. Marchand's dark eyebrows rose. "Of course it is. How can you need to ask?"

"But is not one person's self-denial only the reverse side, the permission, if you like, for another's self-indulgence?" he asked. He leaned forward a little. "Take the play, for example. When the wife denied herself, was she not making it possible for the husband to delude and indulge himself?"

"I . . ." Mrs. Marchand began, then stopped. She was convinced she was right, but not sure how to explain it.

Caroline knew what she meant. The husband's suffering was public, his wife's had been private, one of the many things one did not speak of.

"She is disloyal," Mr. Marchand said for his wife. His voice was not raised in the slightest, but there was a ring of unshakable conviction in it. "Disloyalty can never be right. We should not portray it as such and seek sympathy for it. To do so confuses people who may be uncertain. Women may be led to feel that the wife's behavior is excusable."

The smile stayed fixed on Joshua's face. "And on the other hand, men may be led to question if perhaps their wives have as much need, even right, to happiness as they have," he countered. "They may even realize that life would be better for both of them if they were to understand that women cannot be

34

married and then safely considered to be purchased, for use when desired, like a carpet sweeper or a clothes mangle."

Mr. Marchand looked confused. "A what?"

"A clothes mangle," Joshua replied with a sudden shift to lightness. "A machine for wringing the excess water out of laundry."

"I have no idea what you mean!" Marchand looked at Caroline.

But it was Pitt who interpreted for him. "I think what Mr. Fielding is saying is that one person's protection may be another person's imprisonment; or one person's idea of freedom another's idea of license," he explained. "If we refuse to look at anyone else's pain because it is different from ours and makes us feel uncomfortable—or because it is the same and embarrasses us—then we are neither a liberal nor a generous society, and we will slowly suffocate ourselves to death."

"Good heavens!" Mr. Marchand said softly. "You are very radical, sir."

"I thought I was rather conservative," Pitt said with surprise. "I found the play distinctly uncomfortable as well."

"But do you think it should be suppressed?" Joshua said quickly.

Pitt hesitated. "That's a harsh step to take. . . ."

"It subverts decency and family life," Mrs. Marchand put in, leaning forward over her taffeta skirts, her hands folded.

"It questions values," Joshua corrected. "Must we never do that? Then how can we grow? We shall never learn anything or improve upon anything. Worse than that, we shall never understand other people, and perhaps not ourselves either." His face was keen, the emotion naked now as he forgot his intended moderation. "If we do that we are hardly worth the nobility of being human, of having intelligence, freedom of will, or the power of judgment."

Caroline could see the imminent possibility of the discussion becoming ugly and a friendship being lost.

"It is a matter of how they are questioned," she said in haste.

Joshua regarded her seriously. "The image that has the

35

power to disturb is the only one that has the power to change. Growth is often painful, but to not grow is to begin to die."

"Are you saying everything perishes sooner or later?" Mr. Marchand asked. He sounded almost casual, but there was a rigidity in his hands, in his body, which belied any ease. "I don't believe that. I am sure there are values which are eternal."

Joshua straightened up. "Of course there are," he agreed. "It is a matter of understanding them, and that is more difficult. One must test the truth often, or it will become polluted by ignorance and misuse." He smiled, but his eyes were steady. "It's like the dusting in a good household. It has to be done every day."

Hope Marchand looked puzzled. She glanced at Caroline, then away again.

Mr. Marchand offered her his arm. "I think it is time we returned to our seats, my dear. We don't wish to spoil other people's enjoyment by disturbing them when the performance has begun." He turned to Caroline. "So nice to see you again, Mrs. Fielding." Then to Pitt and to Joshua he added, "And to meet you, Mr. Pitt. I hope you enjoy the evening." A moment later they were gone.

Caroline took a deep breath and let it out slowly.

Joshua grinned at her. The expression lit his face with warmth and laughter, and her fear evaporated. She wanted to warn him how close he had come to confusing and hurting people, to explain why they were afraid, but her anger evaporated, and instead she simply smiled back.

The lights dimmed and the curtain rose for the second act.

Caroline directed her attention to the stage, where the drama continued to develop. It could only end in tragedy. The character played by Cecily Antrim hungered for more passion in life than the society in which she was could either give or understand. She was trapped among people who were increasingly disturbed and frightened by her.

Her husband would not divorce her, and she had no power to divorce him and no justification to leave. Even her misery was from no cause she could explain to anyone who did not share it.

Whether she could ever have behaved differently was a question not yet raised, but Caroline was asking herself even while the scene was playing itself out in front of her. She did not wish to identify with Cecily Antrim, a creature of ungovernable emotions, wayward, indiscreet, allowing far too much of herself to be known, and in so doing betraying the inner thoughts of all women.

Caroline was angry for the sense of embarrassment. She wanted to turn away, as one does if accidentally intruding on someone in a private moment. One says nothing, and both parties pretend it did not happen. It was the only way to make civilized living possible. There are things one does not see, words one does not voice, and if they slip out in a moment of heat, they are never repeated. Secrets are necessary.

And here was this actress stripping the coverings of discretion from her very soul and showing the need and the pain, the laughter and the vulnerability, to everyone with the price of a ticket to watch.

The character of the husband was well acted, but he was there to be torn apart, to evoke anger and frustration, and in the end Caroline knew it would be pity as well.

The fiancée also evoked a certain compassion. She was an ordinary girl who could not begin to fight against the woman, all but twice her age, whose subtlety and fire swept away the man she thought she had won. The audience knew the battle for him was lost before the first blow was struck.

The fiancée's brother was more interesting, not as a character in the play but because the actor who portrayed him had a remarkable presence, even in so relatively minor a part. He was tall and fair. It was difficult to tell his real age, but it must have been no more than twenty-five at the most. He had a sensitivity which came across the footlights, an emotion one was aware of even though he gave it few words. It was an inner energy, something of the mind. He in no sense played to the gallery, but there can have been few in the audience who would not remember him afterwards.

When the second act ended and the lights went up again Caroline did not look at Joshua or Pitt. She did not want to know what they had thought or felt about it, but more than that, she did not wish to betray her own feelings, and she was afraid they would be too readable in her eyes.

There was a knock on the door of the box again, and Joshua went to open it.

Outside was one of Joshua's fellow actors whom Caroline knew slightly, a man named Charles Leigh. Beside him stood a second man of completely different countenance, taller, a little heavier. There was an intelligence in his face and a humor which lit his eyes even before he spoke, but it was his resemblance to her first husband which for a moment made the breath catch in her throat.

"I should like you to meet my visitor from America, Samuel Ellison. Mr. and Mrs. Fielding, and . . ." Leigh began.

"Mr. Pitt," Joshua supplied. "How do you do."

"How do you do, sir," Samuel Ellison replied, bowing very slightly, glancing at the others, but his eyes resting on Caroline. "Pardon me for the intrusion, ma'am, but when Mr. Leigh told me that you were named Ellison before you married Mr. Fielding, I could not wait to meet you."

"Indeed?" Caroline said uncertainly. It was ridiculous, but she felt a nervousness inside herself, almost alarm. This man was so like Edward she could not doubt some relationship. They were of a height, and their features were not at all unlike. The same longish nose, blue eyes, line of cheeks and jaw. She was uncertain what to say. The play had disoriented her until her usual composure had vanished.

He smiled widely. There was nothing overfamiliar in it. Only a most foolish person would have taken offense.

"I fear I am being much too forward, ma'am," he apologized. "You see, I hoped we might be related. My mother left these shores a short while before I was born, a matter of weeks, and I heard my father had married again."

Caroline knew what he would say. The resemblance was too remarkable to deny. But she had no idea of any such person, still less that her father-in-law had had a wife prior to his

38

marriage to her mother-in-law. Her thoughts whirled wildly—had the old lady herself known? Was this going to shatter her world—assuming Caroline told her?

A flicker of anxiety crossed Joshua's brow.

Samuel was still gazing at Caroline. "My father was Edmund Ellison of King's Langley, in Hertfordshire. . . ."

Caroline cleared her throat. "My husband's father," she answered. "You must be . . . half brothers."

Samuel beamed with unaffected delight. "How marvelous! Here am I come all the way from New York to the biggest city in the world, and within a month I have run into you, and at the theatre of all places." He glanced around him. "Who is to say the hand of destiny is not in it? I am happy beyond words to have found you, ma'am. I hope I may have the privilege of making your further acquaintance, in due course, and that I shall conduct myself in such a manner that we may become friends. Relatives can become mighty tedious, but can any person in the world have too many friends?"

Caroline smiled in spite of herself. It was impossible not to warm to his enthusiasm. And mere good manners required that she make a courteous reply.

"I hope we shall, Mr. Ellison. Are you planning to stay in London for some time?"

"I have no plans, ma'am," he said airily. "I am my own master and shall do whatever I wish, as opportunities arise. So far I am having such an excellent time that I could not possibly think of leaving." Again his eyes wandered around the crowded auditorium. "I feel as if the whole world and all its ideas are here, sooner or later, and if I wait I shall see them all."

Caroline smiled. "I have heard it said that if you stand in Piccadilly Circus long enough, everyone who is anyone will pass by."

"I can believe it," he agreed. "But I should probably be arrested for loitering. I had far rather go out and look for people than wait for them to come to me."

"Do you live in New York, Mr. Ellison?" Joshua enquired,

making room for Samuel and Leigh to be more comfortable, allowing Samuel to have his chair.

"I've lived in all sorts of places," Samuel answered pleasantly, sitting down and crossing his legs. "I was born in New York. My mother landed there from the ship, and it took her quite some time to get a start. What with being alone, and expecting a child, life wasn't easy for her. She was a brave woman, and a likable one, and she found friends who were generous enough to care for her when I was born."

Caroline tried to imagine it, and failed. She thought of what she knew of her father-in-law.

Why had Samuel's mother left him? She racked her memory and could recall no mention of her at all. She was certain beyond any question that her mother-in-law had never said a word about her husband's having had a previous wife. Had she run off with another man?

From what Samuel was now saying, she had reached New York alone. Had he abandoned her? Had Edmund Ellison thrown her out for some unforgivable offense?

"It must have been appalling," she said sincerely. "How did she manage? Was there no one to . . ."

"You mean kin, relatives?" Samuel seemed amused. He leaned back a little, relaxing. "Not at first, but so many people were making new lives, beginning again with nothing, it didn't seem so odd. And there were opportunities. She was handsome, and willing to work hard."

"Doing what?" Caroline asked, then blushed at her clumsiness. Perhaps it was not something he was comfortable to discuss. "I mean . . . she had a baby to care for . . ."

"Oh, I was passed around from hand to hand," Samuel replied cheerfully. "By the time I was two I could have said 'Mama' or 'I'm hungry' in a dozen different languages."

"What amazing courage," Joshua said quietly. "You must have witnessed some remarkable events, Mr. Ellison?"

"Indeed," Samuel agreed with feeling. "And history made. But I'll wager, so have you. And heard great ideas discussed, and seen a heap of beautiful things I haven't yet." He looked around. "There's got to be all kinds of life in this city, everything a man has ever thought of. Crossroads to the nations of the earth. Makes me feel like a boy from the backwoods. And here I thought New York was getting sophisticated, after all our adventures."

"Adventures?" Caroline asked with as much real curiosity as good manners.

He grinned. "Oh, New York after the war was something else, ma'am. You never saw a town like it in your life! Not a place for ladies then, but proper civilized now, compared with the past, that is. Mind, if you want the real gentry, maybe Boston is the town to be in."

"Have you traveled farther west, Mr. Ellison?" Pitt spoke to him for the first time.

Samuel regarded him with interest. "I've been some—you mean like Indian country? I could tell a few tales, but a lot of them'd be sad, to my way of thinking. But maybe not every man'd agree with me."

"Who would disagree with you?" Joshua asked with interest.

A shadow passed over Samuel's face. "The march of progress is not always a pretty sight, sir, and it leaves an awful lot of dead bodies in its wake, sometimes the best part of a nation and its dreams get trodden under. I guess maybe the strongest wins, but the weaker can be very beautiful, and their passing can leave you with an emptiness inside there's nothing left that can fill."

Caroline glanced at Pitt. His face was turned away from the light, and the shadows threw his features into relief. In listening to Samuel he had caught a vision of some kind of bereavement, and the mark of it was plain to see.

"You speak with great feeling, Mr. Ellison," Joshua said quietly. "You make us wish to hear more and learn what it is that moves you so deeply. I hope that we shall make your closer acquaintance."

Samuel rose to his feet. "You are very generous, Mr. Fielding. I'll surely take you up on it. But I guess that's my cue to go back to my own box before the lights go down, so I don't inconvenience you all by not being in my seat in time. Quite

41

apart from manners, this is a play no one should miss the end of. I don't think in all my days I've ever seen a woman like that leading lady of yours. She could light a fire just by looking at dry wood!" He turned to Caroline. "I'm delighted to make your acquaintance, ma'am. A man can choose his friends, but not his family. It's a rare blessing to find nature's pick for you coincides with your own." And after bidding them all good evening, he and Leigh turned and went out of the door, closing it softly behind them.

Joshua stared at Caroline. "Can he be?"

"Oh yes!" she exclaimed without hesitation. She turned to Pitt, but it was not really a question.

Pitt nodded. "He bears a remarkable resemblance to Edward Ellison. It is too great to be coincidence." He frowned slightly. "Did you know your father-in-law had an earlier wife?"

"No! I'm astounded," she admitted. "I have never heard a single word about her. I am not even sure if Mrs. Ellison knows." Years of hidden battles with the old lady were sharp in her mind, the criticism, the comparisons of the present with the past, always to the detriment of Caroline and her daughters. She could not help allowing a little bubble of satisfaction to rise inside her as she turned to the stage, ready to watch the drama there reach its climax.

She was immediately drawn into the tragedy again. Cecily Antrim's character was the vehicle for such passion it was impossible to remain apart from it. Even the coming of Samuel Ellison into her life with his revelations was forgotten as the unfolding emotions captured her and she felt the pain and the urgency as if it were her own life.

Part of her resented the laying bare of feelings within herself she would rather not have recognized. Another part found a kind of release in no longer hiding them—and in the amazing knowledge that she was not alone. Other women felt the same hunger, disillusion, sense of having betrayed their dreams and that some part of life was a disappointment they had not known how to deal with, only to deny.

Should such things be said? Was there something indecent

42

in the exposure of feelings so intimate? To know it herself was one thing, to realize that others also knew was quite different. It was being naked publicly rather than privately.

Usually when she visited the theatre with Joshua she looked at him often, wishing to share the laughter or the tragedy with him. It was a great part of her pleasure. Tonight she wished to remain alone. She was afraid of what she would see in his face, and even more what he would see in hers. She was not yet ready to be quite so close, perhaps she never would be. There must be some privacy in even the deepest love, some secrets left, some things one did not wish to know. It was part of respect, the room to be oneself, a wholeness.

When the tragedy was complete and the final curtain descended, Caroline found there were tears on her cheeks and her voice was choked in her throat. She sat motionless, staring at the folds of the curtains. The last bows had been taken again and again, flowers presented, the applause had died away.

"Are you all right?" Pitt asked softly, close to her elbow.

She turned and smiled at him, and blinked, feeling the tears roll down her face. She was glad it was he who had asked, not Joshua. Just at the moment she felt remote from theatre people, actors who could look at this professionally, as an art. It was too real for that, too much the stuff of life.

"Yes . . . yes, thank you, Thomas. Of course I am. It was just . . . very moving."

He smiled. He did not say anything else, but she could see in his eyes that he understood the thoughts it raised as well, the questions and the confusions that would live on long after tonight.

"Superb," Joshua breathed out, his face glowing. "I swear she's never been better! Even Bernhardt could not have exceeded this. Caroline—Thomas—we must go backstage to tell her. I couldn't miss this opportunity. Come!" Without waiting for a reply he moved towards the door of the box, so consumed in his enthusiasm it never occurred to him either of the others could think differently.

Caroline glanced at Pitt.

Pitt shrugged very slightly, smiling.

43

Together they followed after Joshua's already retreating figure. He led them unhesitatingly through a door marked PRIVATE and along a bare passage, down a flight of steps lit only by a single gas bracket, and through another door onto a landing off of which were several dressing rooms, each marked with someone's name. The one with CECILY ANTRIM on it was half open, and the sound of voices came from inside quite clearly.

Joshua knocked, then went in, Caroline and Pitt on his heels.

Cecily was standing by the mirrors and a table spread with greasepaints and powders. She was still wearing the gown from the last act, and her hair was quite obviously her own and not a wig. She was very tall for a woman—Joshua's height—and as slender as a wand, even though at this distance it was possible to see that she was in her early forties, not thirties as she had appeared on stage. Caroline needed only a glance to know she was one of those women to whom age is irrelevant. Her beauty was in her bones, her magnificent eyes, and above all the fire inside her.

"Joshua! Darling!" she said with delight, spreading her arms wide to embrace him.

He walked forward and hugged her, kissing her on both cheeks.

"You have excelled even yourself!" he said ardently. "You made us feel everything and care passionately. And now we have no choice but to think . . ."

She pulled back, her arms still around his neck. Her smile was radiant. "Really? You mean that? You think we may succeed?"

"Of course," he responded. "When have I ever lied to you? If it had been merely good I should have said it was good. . . ." He pulled a slight face. "I should have been exquisitely vague. As to whether it will succeed or not . . . that is in the lap of the gods."

She laughed. "I'm sorry, darling. I shouldn't have doubted you. But I do care so much. If we can only make people see the woman's side." She waved a hand in a wide gesture.

44

"Freddie may be able to get his bill passed in the House. Change the climate, then the law. Ibsen has already achieved miracles. We are going to build on it. People will see there must be rights in divorce for women also. Isn't it marvelous to live in an age when there is such work to be done—new battles—chances?"

"Indeed it is," he agreed, still staring at her. Then suddenly he seemed to remember the others present. "Cecily, you haven't met my wife, Caroline, and her son-in-law, Thomas Pitt."

Cecily smiled charmingly and acknowledged the introductions. There was no question she looked just a moment longer at Pitt than at Caroline. Then she turned back to Joshua.

Caroline looked at the other people in the tiny room. Just behind Cecily there was the man she had indicated as Freddie. He had a powerful face, broad-bridged nose and sensuous mouth. He seemed very relaxed, even slightly amused.

Lounging in the other chair was the young man whom Caroline had noticed in the play. Closer to, he bore more of a resemblance to Cecily, and Caroline was not surprised when a few moments later he was introduced as Orlando Antrim; she gathered from the reference that he was Cecily's son.

There was a couple named Harris and Lydia, and the man so close to Cecily was Lord Frederick Warriner. His presence was partially explained by the reference to a private member's bill before Parliament, apparently to liberalize the divorce proceedings for women.

Joshua and Cecily were still talking, with only the occasional glance at anyone else. Perhaps they did not mean to exclude others, but their exuberance carried them along, and their professional appreciation was on a different level of understanding from that of those who were merely watchers.

"I tried the scene in rehearsal at least three different ways," Cecily was saying earnestly. "You see, we might have played it as near hysteria, emotions crowding to break through, high tones in the voice, knife-edge, sharp, jerking movements." She demonstrated with gestures which somehow excluded Caroline and Pitt, simply because they extended too close to them, as if to a screen on a wall. "Or with tragedy," she went on. "As if in her heart she already knew what was inevitable. Do you think she did, Joshua? What would you have done?"

"Unaware of it," he said immediately. "She was beyond such consideration of thought. I am sure if you asked the playwright he'd have said she was far too driven, too honest in emotion to have been aware of what would happen eventually."

"You're right," she agreed, swinging around to Orlando.

He grinned. "Wouldn't dream of arguing, Mother. More than my role is worth!"

She glared at him in mock anger, then threw her hands up and laughed. She turned to Caroline. "Did you enjoy the play . . . Caroline? Yes—Caroline. What did you think of it?" Her wide eyes were unwavering, gray-blue, dark-lashed, impossible to lie to.

Caroline felt cornered. She would far rather not have answered, but now everyone was looking at her, including Joshua. What should she say? Something polite and flattering? Should she try to be perceptive, explain some of the impressions the play had created? She was not even sure if she knew what they wanted to hear.

Or should she tell the truth, that it was disturbing, intrusive, that it raised questions she thought were perhaps better not asked? That it would hurt, maybe waken unhappiness best left sleeping because there was no cure for it? The play had ended in tragedy. Was it good for life to follow the same path? No one could bring the curtain down on it and go home to something else.

What would Joshua expect her to say? What would he want? She must not look at him as if she were expecting a cue. She did not want to hurt or embarrass him. She was suddenly overwhelmed by how much she cared and how inadequate she was to match up to these people. Cecily Antrim was radiant, so absolutely certain of what she thought and felt. The power of her feeling lent an incandescence to her beauty. It was at least half the reason the entire audience had watched her.

Cecily laughed. "My dear, are you afraid to speak, in case you hurt my feelings? I assure you, I can bear it!"

46

Caroline found her tongue at last, and smiled back. "I'm sure you can, Miss Antrim. But it is not an easy play to sum up in a few words and be even remotely honest, and I don't believe you are looking for an easy reply. Even if you are, the work does not deserve one—"

"Bravo!" Orlando said from the background, holding his hands up in silent applause. "Please tell us what you really think, Mrs. Fielding. Perhaps we need to hear an honest opinion from outside the profession."

There was complete silence.

Caroline felt her throat tighten. She swallowed. They were all staring at her. She had to speak.

"I think it asks a great many questions," she said through dry lips. "Some of the answers we may need to know, but there are others I think perhaps we don't. There are griefs one has to live with, and the thought that they were borne in private is all that makes them endurable."

Cecily looked startled. "Oh dear. A cry from the heart, Joshua?" Her meaning was plain, even as it was also plain she was only teasing.

Joshua blushed slightly. "By heaven, I hope not!"

Everyone else laughed, except Pitt.

Caroline felt her face flame. She should have been able to laugh too, but she could not. She felt clumsy, unsophisticated, conscious of her hands and feet as if she were a schoolgirl again. And yet she was older than anyone else here. Was that what was wrong? Another three or four years older and she could have been Cecily Antrim's mother. For that matter, she was seventeen years older than Joshua. Standing as he was beside Cecily, he must be aware of that.

How could she retain a shred of dignity and not look ridiculous and make him ashamed of her? They must wonder why on earth he had chosen to marry a woman like her anyway, so staid by comparison with them, so unimaginative, a stranger in their world, unable even to pass a clever or witty comment, let alone behave with an air of glamour and a magic as they did.

They were waiting for her to say something. She must not

let them down. She had no wit to invent. There was nothing for it but to say what she thought.

She looked straight at Cecily, as if there were no one else in the crowded room.

"I am sure as an actress you are used to speaking for many people and feeling the emotions of women quite unlike yourself." She phrased it as a certainty, but left it half a question by her intonation.

"Ah!" Orlando said instantly. "How perceptive, Mrs. Fielding. She has you there, Mama. How often do you think of the vulnerable as well as the passionate, those afflicted with doubts or wounds that are better hidden? Perhaps they have a right to privacy?"

The man named Harris looked shocked. "What are you suggesting, Orlando? Censorship?" He said the word in the tone of voice he would have used if he had said "treason."

"Of course not!" Cecily retorted sharply. "That's absurd! Orlando has no more love of censorship than I have. We'll both fight to the last breath for the freedom to speak the truth, to ask questions, to suggest new ideas or restate old ones nobody wants to hear." She shook her head. "For God's sake, Harris, you know better than that. One man's blasphemy is another man's religion. Take that far enough and we'll end up back burning people at the stake because they worship different gods from us—or even the same God—but in different words." She lifted her shoulders exaggeratedly. "We'll be back to the dark ages and the Inquisition."

"There has to be some censorship, darling," Warriner said, speaking for the first time. "Shouldn't shout 'Fire' in a crowded theatre—especially if there isn't one. And even if there is, panic doesn't help. Gets more people crushed in the stampede than burned by the flames." He looked slightly amused as he said it, but the smile did not go as far as his eyes.

Cecily's mood changed abruptly. "Of course!" she said with a laugh. "Shout 'Fire' in church if you must, but never, never in the theatre—at least not while there's a performance on."

Everyone else laughed as well.

Caroline was looking at Joshua.

It was Pitt who spoke.

"And perhaps we should be careful about libel? Unless, of course, one is a theatre critic. . . ."

"Oh!" Cecily drew in her breath sharply and swung around to face him. "My goodness! I didn't realize you had been listening so carefully. I should have paid you more attention. You're not a critic, are you?"

He smiled. "No ma'am, I'm a policeman."

Her eyes widened. "Good God! Are you really?"

Pitt nodded.

"How perfectly grim. Do you arrest people for picking pockets or causing an affray?" She tossed the idea away.

"I'm afraid more often it is something as serious as murder," he replied, the light gone from his voice.

Orlando stood up. "Which is probably exactly what Mrs. Fielding meant about questions we shouldn't ask because we don't want the answers," he said in the silence which had followed. "Freedom of speech has to include the freedom not to listen. I never thought of that until these last few days." He walked to the door. "I'm fearfully hungry. I'm going to find something to eat. Good night everyone."

"A good idea," Cecily said quickly. It was the first time she seemed in the slightest out of composure. "Champagne supper, everyone?"

Joshua declined politely, excusing them, and after repeating their congratulations, they withdrew.

Pitt offered his thanks again and wished them good night. Caroline and Joshua rode home making polite and rather stiff conversation about the play, speaking of the characters, not once mentioning Cecily Antrim herself. Caroline was filled with an increasing sense of being an outsider.

The following morning Joshua left early to see a playwright, and Caroline took a late breakfast alone. She was sitting staring at her second cup of tea, which she had allowed to go cold, when Mariah Ellison came in, leaning heavily on her

49

stick. She had been handsome in her youth, but age and ill-temper had marked her features now, and her sharp eyes were almost black as she stared at Caroline with disfavor.

"Well, you look as if you lost sixpence and found nothing," she said tartly. "Face like a jar of vinegar." She glanced at the teapot. "Is that fresh? I don't suppose it is."

"You are quite right," Caroline replied, looking up.

"Not much use admitting I'm right," the old lady said, pulling out a chair and sitting down opposite her. "Do something about it! No man likes a wife with a sour expression, particularly if she's older than he is in the first place. Ill-temper is displeasing enough in the young and pretty. In those past their best it is intolerable."

Caroline had spent her adult life curbing her tongue in order to be civil to her mother-in-law. This latest rudeness was beyond bearing, because it was so close to the truth. Her self-control snapped.

"Thank you for giving me the benefit of your experience," she retorted. "I am sure you are in a position to know."

The old lady was surprised. Caroline had never been so blunt before.

"I presume it was a bad play," she said deliberately.

"It was a very good play," Caroline contradicted. "In fact, it was brilliant."

Mrs. Ellison scowled at the teapot. "Then why are you sitting here by yourself over a cup of cold tea, and with an expression like a bad egg?" she demanded. "I suppose you have a servant of some sort you can ring for to get a fresh pot? I know this is not Ashworth House, but I assume that the young actor you have elected to live with earns sufficient to afford the basic amenities?"

Caroline was so angry and her sense of hurt so deep she said the first thing that came into her head.

"I met a most interesting and charming gentleman yesterday evening." She stared at the old lady unflinchingly. "From America, over here on a visit and hoping to trace his family."

"Is that supposed to be an answer?" Mrs. Ellison asked.

"If you want some more tea, ring the bell and the maid will

50

come," Caroline replied. "Tell her what you wish. I did not explain that to you because I thought you could work it out for yourself. I mentioned Mr. Ellison because I thought you would wish to know. After all, he is more closely related to you than to me."

The old woman froze. "I beg your pardon?"

"Mr. Ellison is more closely related to you than to me," Caroline repeated distinctly.

"Does this"— she opened her eyes very wide—"person— claim that he is part of my family? You are no longer an Ellison. You have chosen to become a . . . a . . .whatever he is!"

"A Fielding," Caroline said for the umpteenth time. It was part of the old woman's offense that she pretended to forget Joshua's name. "And yes, he does claim it. And his likeness to Edward is so remarkable I could not doubt him."

The old lady sat very still. Even the bell for the maid was forgotten.

"Really? And what manner of man is he? Who does he claim to be, exactly?"

Now Caroline was not so certain how much she enjoyed the revelation. It had not had quite the effect she had expected. However, there was no alternative now but to go on.

"Apparently Papa-in-law was married before . . . before he met you."

The old woman's face remained like stone.

"Samuel is his son," Caroline finished.

"Is he indeed?" the old woman replied. "Well . . . we'll see. You did not answer my question . . . what manner of man is he?"

"Charming, intelligent, articulate, and, to judge by his clothes, very comfortably situated," Caroline answered. "I found him most agreeable. I hope he will call upon us." She took a deep breath. "In fact I shall invite him to."

Mrs. Ellison said nothing, but reached across for the bell and rang it furiously.

3

P*ITT WAS IN HIS OFFICE* in Bow Street early the morning after the play. There was little pleasure in staying at home alone, and there had been no letter from Charlotte in the first post. As soon as he had eaten breakfast and fed the cats he was happy to leave Keppel Street and be on his way.

It was too early to hear from Tellman in Dover, but Pitt did not expect him to find anything conclusive. Was the grotesquely placed body at Horseferry Stairs that of the French diplomat or some other unfortunate eccentric who had indulged one taste too many? He profoundly hoped it was the latter. A scandal with the French Embassy would be most unpleasant, and possibly not one which could be contained so it did not strain relations between the two countries.

The play the previous night had left him disturbed by the power of its emotions. He was not made as uncomfortable as Caroline had obviously been by the portrayal of the hungers of a woman married to a man who did not satisfy her passions or her dreams. He was a generation younger than she, and he was of a different social class, one which felt freer to express its feelings. And he had also grown up in the country, far closer to nature.

Even so, the nakedness of the emotions he had seen on the stage had provoked deep thought in him, and a new perception of what lies behind even the most outwardly serene faces. He wished intensely that Charlotte were home so he could have discussed it with her. The emptiness of the house was like an ache inside him, and he was pleased to return to the problem of the body in the punt.

In the middle of the morning, while he was combing through reports of missing persons, there was a knock on his door and a sergeant came in looking pleased with himself.

"What is it, Leven?" Pitt asked.

"Woman come to the desk, sir, sayin' as 'er employer is missin'. Ain't bin 'ome fer a couple o' days, like. She says it's not like 'im at all. Most partic'lar, 'e is, bein' a professional gent, an' all. Never misses an appointment. 'Is reputation dependin' on it, dealin' with the gentry an' so on. Can't keep lords and ladies waitin', or they won't come again."

"Well, make a note of it, Leven," Pitt said impatiently. "There's not a great deal we can do about it. Tell Inspector Brown, if you think it's serious enough."

Leven stood his ground. "No sir, that in't the point. Point is, she told us what 'e looks like. Matches the poor soul as yer found at 'Orseferry Stairs just about exact. I were reckoning yer'd want ter talk to 'er, an' mebbe even take 'er ter see the poor feller."

Pitt was annoyed with himself for not having understood.

"Yes I would, Leven. Thank you. Bring her up, will you?"

"Yes sir."

"And Leven . . ."

"Yes sir?"

"That was well thought of. I'll tell you if it's him."

"Thank you, sir." Leven went out beaming with satisfaction, closing the door very gently behind him.

He was back in five minutes with a small, sturdy woman, her face puckered with anxiety. The moment she saw Pitt she started to speak.

"Are you the gentleman what I should talk ter? Yer see 'e's bin gorn two days now . . . least this is the second . . . an' I got messages askin' w'ere 'e is." She was shaking her head. "An' I in't got the faintest, 'ave I? I jus' know it in't like 'im, all the years I bin doin' the 'ouse fer 'im, 'e never let nothing get in the way of 'is work. That partic'lar, 'e is. I seen 'im make time

53

fer folks w'en 'e's bin 'alf out on 'is feet. Always oblige. That's 'ow 'e got where 'e is."

"Where is that, Mrs. . . . ?" Pitt asked.

"That's wot I'm sayin'. Nobody knows where 'e is! Vanished. That's why I come ter the po-liss. Summink's 'appened, sure as eggs is eggs."

Pitt tried again. "Please sit down, Mrs. . . . ?"

"Geddes . . . I'm Mrs. Geddes." She sat down in the chair opposite him. "Ta." She rearranged her skirts. "Yer see, I bin cleanin' an' doin' fer 'im fer near ten years now, an' I knows 'is ways. There's summink not right."

"What is his name, Mrs. Geddes?"

"Cathcart . . . Delbert Cathcart."

"Could you describe Mr. Cathcart for me, please?" Pitt requested. "By the way, where does he live?"

"Battersea," she replied. "Right down on the river. Lovely 'ouse, 'e 'as. Nicest one as I does for. What's that got ter do wif 'im not bein' there?"

"Perhaps nothing, Mrs. Geddes. What does Mr. Cathcart look like, if you please?"

"Sort o' ordinary 'eight," she replied gravely. "Not very tall, not very short. Not 'eavy. Sort o' . . ." She thought for a moment. "Sort o' neat-lookin'. Got fair 'air an' a mustache, but not wot yer'd call real whiskers. Always dressed very well. Sort o' good-lookin', I suppose yer'd say. But 'ow will yer know 'im from that?"

"I'm not sure that we will, Mrs. Geddes." Pitt had had to tell people about deaths countless times before, but it never became any easier or pleasanter. At least this was not a relative. "I am afraid there was a man found dead in a small boat on the river yesterday morning. We don't know who he is, but he looks very much as you describe Mr. Cathcart. I'm sorry to ask this, Mrs. Geddes, but would you come and look at this man and see if you know him?"

"Oh! Well . . ." She stared at him for several moments. "Well, I s'pose I better 'ad, 'adn't I? Better me than one o' them society ladies as 'e knows."

"Does he know a lot of society ladies?" Pitt asked. He did

not even know if the man in the punt was Cathcart, but he was interested to learn what he could about him before Mrs. Geddes saw the body, in case she was so shocked she found herself unable to think coherently afterward.

"O' course 'e does!" she said with wide eyes. " 'E's the best photographer in London, in't 'e?"

Pitt knew nothing of photographers except the odd bit he had heard in passing conversation. Someone had referred to it as the new form of portraiture.

"I didn't know that," he admitted. "I should like to learn more about him."

"Real beautiful, they are. Yer never seen anyfink like it. People was that thrilled wif 'em."

"I see." Pitt rose to his feet. "I'm sorry, Mrs. Geddes, but there's no alternative to going to the morgue and seeing if it is Mr. Cathcart we have. I hope it's not." He said it as a matter of sympathy for her, but he realized immediately that it was less than true. The case would be a great deal easier if the body proved to be an English society photographer rather than a French diplomat.

"Yes," Mrs. Geddes said quietly. She stood up and smoothed her jacket. "Yes, o' course. I'm comin'."

The morgue was close enough to walk to, and there was so much noise in the street that conversation would have been difficult. Hansom cabs, omnibuses, wagons and brewers' drays clattered past them. Street peddlers shouted, men and women argued, and a costermonger roared with laughter at an old man's joke.

It was utterly different inside the morgue. The silence and the clinging, damp smell closed over them, and suddenly the world of the living seemed far away.

They were conducted through to the icehouse where bodies were stored. The sheet was taken off the face of the man from Horseferry Stairs.

Mrs. Geddes looked at it and drew in her breath in a little gasp.

"Yes," she said with a catch in her voice. "Oh dear . . . that's Mr. Cathcart, poor soul."

"Are you quite sure?" Pitt pressed.

"Oh yes, that's 'im." She turned away and put her hand up to her face. "Whatever 'appened to 'im?"

There was no need to tell her about the green velvet dress or the chains, at least not yet, perhaps not at all.

"I am afraid he was struck on the head," he answered.

Her eyes widened. "Yer mean on purpose, like? 'E were murdered?"

"Yes."

"Why'd anyone wanna murder Mr. Cathcart? Were 'e robbed?"

"It seems very unlikely. Do you know of anyone who might have quarreled with him?"

"No," she said straightaway. " 'E weren't that sort." She kept her face averted. "It must be someb'dy very wicked wot done it."

Pitt nodded to the morgue attendant, who covered the body again.

"Thank you, Mrs. Geddes. Now I would appreciate it very much if you would take me to his house and allow me to find out whatever I can there. We'll get a hansom." He waited a moment while she composed herself, then walked beside her out of the morgue and into the sunlight again. "Are you all right?" he asked, seeing her ashen face. "Would you like to stop for a drink, or find a place to sit down?"

"No thank you," she said stoically. "Very nice o' yer, I'm sure, but I'll make us a proper cup o' tea w'en we get there. No time ter be sittin' down. Yer gotta find them as done this an' see 'em on the end of a rope."

He did not reply, but continued beside her until he saw a hansom and hailed it. He asked her for the address and gave it to the cabbie, then settled down for the ride. He would have liked to question her further about Cathcart, but she sat with her hands clenched in her lap, her eyes fixed, every now and then giving a little sigh. She needed time to absorb what had happened and come to terms with it in her own way.

The hansom rumbled across the Battersea Bridge and down the other side, turning left along George Street, and stopped outside an extremely handsome house whose long garden backed onto the water. Pitt alighted, helping Mrs. Geddes out. He paid the driver and gave him a message to take to the local police station requesting a constable to come.

Mrs. Geddes sniffed hard, and with a little shake of her head, walked up the long driveway and, taking a key from her pocket, opened the front door. She did it without hesitation. It was obviously a regular thing for her.

The moment he was inside Pitt stared around him. The entrance hall was long and light, with stairs down one side. It was excellently lit from a very large window extending the length of the stairwell. On one wall were several photographs of groups of people—half a dozen ragged urchins playing in the street; beside them society ladies at Ascot, lovely faces under a sea of hats.

"I told you 'e were good," Mrs. Geddes said sadly. "Pour soul. I dunno wot yer wanter see 'ere. There in't nuffink missin', nuffink stole, so far as I can see. 'E must 'a bin set on in the street. 'E didn't never 'ave them sort o' people 'ere!"

"What sort of people did he have?" Pitt asked, following her through to the sitting room, which was surprisingly small for such a house. It was very elegant, with a Sheraton table and chairs in gleaming wood, and a Bokhara rug which would have cost Pitt at least a year's wages.

The windows looked onto a long lawn set with trees, sloping down to the water beyond. A willow made a cavern of green and reflected like lace on the barely moving current. A pergola was covered in roses, its latticed arches white through the leaves.

Mrs. Geddes was watching him.

"Used that a lot, 'e did." She sighed. "Folks like ter 'ave their pictures took in beautiful places. 'Specially ladies. Makes 'em look good . . . kind o' romantic. Gentlemen prefer summink grand. Like ter dress up in uniforms, they do." Her tone of voice conveyed her opinion of people who wore clothes that made them look more important than they were. " 'Ad one daft 'aporth as dressed 'isself up as Julius Caesar!" she sniffed vigorously. "I ask yer!"

"But Mr. Cathcart had no objection?" Pitt tried to imagine it.

"O' course 'e didn't. 'Elped 'im, an all. Then that's 'is job, in't it? Take pictures o' people so they looks like they wanter see 'emselves. Daft, I call it. But that don't matter. I dunno wot yer wanter see 'ere, but this is all there is."

Pitt looked around, uncertain himself what he wanted to ask. Had Cathcart been killed here? The answer to that might matter a great deal. This house was in an excellent place for a punt to float from down as far as Horseferry Stairs. But then so were scores of other houses that backed onto the river.

"Did he entertain here?" he asked. "Have parties?"

She stared at him with total incomprehension.

"Did he?" he repeated. Although the neatness of the rooms in the house he had seen so far made a party in which clothes such as the green velvet dress might be worn seem unlikely, certainly not before Mrs. Geddes had very thoroughly cleaned and tidied up.

"Not as I know of." She shook her head, still puzzled.

"You never had anything to clear up, a lot of dishes to wash?"

"No, I never did, not as yer'd call a lot. Not more'n three or four people'd use. Why yer askin', Mr. Pitt? Yer said as 'e were murdered. That don't 'appen at parties. Wot yer on about?"

He decided to tell her a half-truth. "He was dressed for a party . . . fancy dress. It seems unlikely he was out in the street in such clothes."

" 'Is clients dressed daft," she responded hotly. " 'E never did! More sense, even if 'e catered ter some as 'adn't."

There was probably a great deal Mrs. Geddes did not know about Mr. Cathcart, but Pitt forbore from saying so.

"Does he have a boat, perhaps moored on the river at the bottom of the garden?" he asked instead.

"I dunno." A look of misery filled her face. "You said summink about a boat before. 'E were found in a boat, were 'e?"

"Yes, he was. Did you do any tidying yesterday when you came?"

"There weren't nuffink ter do. Just cleaned as usual. Did a bit o' laundry, like. Same as always ... 'ceptin' the bed weren't slept in, which was unusual, but not like it never 'appened before." She narrowed her lips a trifle.

Pitt read the gesture as one of disapproval.

"He occasionally spent the night elsewhere? He has a lover, perhaps?" Remembering the green dress, he was careful not to attribute a gender.

"Well, I can't see as she murdered 'im," Mrs. Geddes said angrily. "That's not ter say I approve o' carryin's on, 'cos I don't! But she in't a bad sort, that excepted. Not greedy, and not too flashy, if yer know what I mean."

"Do you know her name?"

"Well, I s'pose as she'll 'ave ter be told an' all. 'Er name's Lily Monderell. Don' ask me 'ow she spells it, as I got no idea."

"Where will I find Miss Monderell?" he asked.

"Over the bridge, in Chelsea. I 'spec 'e's got it writ down somewhere."

"I'd like you to come with me through the rest of the house to tell me if anything's different from the way it usually is," he requested.

"I dunno wot you think yer gonna find," she said, blinking hard. Suddenly the awareness of Cathcart's death seemed to have overtaken her again, now that police were walking through his house as if he no longer possessed it. They were going to be looking through his belongings, in his absence and without asking him. "If there's anyfink wrong I'd 'a seen it," she added with a sniff.

"You weren't looking before," he soothed her. "Let us begin down here and work upwards."

"Yer wastin' yer time," she retorted. "Yer should be out there." She jerked her head toward some unknown beyond. "That's where yer'll find murderers an' the like." Still she led the way into the next room and he followed after her.

It was a well-proportioned house and furnished in extravagant taste, as if Cathcart had had an eye to curtains and ornaments he might use in photographs at some future date.

However, the whole created a place of distinction and considerable beauty. An Egyptian cat of clean and elongated lines contrasted with an ornate red, black and gold painted Russian icon.

A minor pre-Raphaelite painting of a knight in vigil before an altar hung on the upstairs landing, curiously highlighting the simplicity of an arrangement of sword-shaped leaves. It was highly individual, and Pitt had a sharp sense of personality, of a man's tastes, his dreams and ideals, perhaps something of the life which had shaped him. Oddly, the knowledge of loss was greater than when he had stared at the body in the boat as it knocked against Horseferry Stairs, or again in the morgue, when he had been thinking more of Mrs. Geddes and the question of identification.

She showed him through every room, and each was immaculate. Nothing was out of the place one would expect to find it, no chairs or tables were crooked, no cushions or curtains disturbed. Everything was clean. It was impossible to believe there had been a fancy dress party there which had indulged in the sort of excesses the green velvet dress suggested, and certainly no violence in which two men had fought and one been killed.

The last room they reached was up a flight of stairs from a second, smaller landing, and it extended the length of the top story, with windows and skylights giving the light an excellent clarity. It was immediately obvious that this was the studio where Cathcart took many of his photographs. One end was furnished as an elegant withdrawing room, one side overlooked the river, and a person seated would appear to have nothing but the sky behind. The nearest end was cluttered like a storeroom with what seemed at a glance to be scores of objects of wildly varied character.

"I don't come up 'ere much," Mrs. Geddes said quietly. " 'Just sweep the floor,' 'e says. 'Keep it clean. Don't touch nuffink.' "

Pitt regarded the conglomeration with interest. Without moving anything he recognized a Viking horned helmet, half a dozen pieces from a suit of armor, uncountable pieces of velvet of an enormous variety of colors—rich reds and purples, golds, pastel cream and earth tones. There was an ostrich feather fan, two stuffed pheasants, a round Celtic shield with metal bosses, several swords, spears, pikes, and bits and pieces of military and naval uniforms. What lay hidden beneath them was beyond even guessing.

Mrs. Geddes answered his unspoken thoughts. "Like I said, some of 'em likes ter dress daft."

A closer examination of the room discovered nothing in which Pitt could see any connection with Cathcart's death. In a large wardrobe there were a number of other dresses of varying degrees of ornateness. But then since Cathcart frequently photographed women, that was to be expected. There were also men's clothes from many historical periods, both real and fanciful.

There were four cameras carefully set up on tripods, with black cloths for obscuring the light. Pitt had never seen a camera so closely before, and he looked at them with interest, being careful not to disturb them. They were complicated boxes in both metal and wood with pleated leather sides, obviously to telescope back and forth to vary the proportions. In size they were roughly a cubic foot or a little less, and on two of them brass fittings shone freshly polished.

There were also a number of arc lights on the floor. There was no gas supply to them, but heavy cables.

"Electric," Mrs. Geddes said with pride. "Got 'is own machine wot drives 'em. Dynamo, it's called. 'E says as yer can't get proper light fer pictures 'ceptin' in the summer, not inside the 'ouse, like."

Pitt regarded the lights with interest. It was increasingly apparent that Cathcart had taken great thought and trouble to make an art of his work. Neither time nor expense had been spared.

" 'E does 'em all 'isself, o' course," Mrs. Geddes said. "Special room 'e 'as fer it, in the basement, like. Full o' chemicals. Smells 'orrible. But 'e never lets me in there, case I 'urts meself wif anyfink. Spill some o' them things an' yer'll never be the same again."

"Did he keep any of the pictures here?" he asked, looking around curiously. "Recent or current ones?"

"In them drawers." She pointed to a large cabinet a little to his left.

"Thank you." He opened it and studied the prints inside, going through them one by one. The first was of a very striking woman dressed in a highly exotic gown with ropes of beads around her neck. By her feet was a beautifully wrought raffia basket, out of which trailed a very live-looking snake. It was an arresting image, not principally for its suggestions of classical Egypt, which was presumably what the subject had intended, but for the lighting of the face, showing its power and sensuality.

In a second picture was a young man posed as whom Pitt took to be Saint George. He was complete with polished armor, sword, and shield. The helmet was balanced on a table beside him. The light caught the sheen on the points and curves of the metal breastplate and reflected in his pale eyes and through his fair hair, making an aureole of it. It was the portrait not of a knight at war but of a dreamer who fights battles of the soul.

A third photograph caught the essential vanity of a face, a fourth the sweetness, a fifth the self-indulgence, although they were so disguised by the trappings of fantasy or wealth as to be hidden from the less-perceptive eye. Pitt had a far deeper respect for the photographer than he had begun with, and a realization that such skill in judging the human character and portraying it so tellingly might earn him enemies as well as friends.

He closed the drawer and turned back to Mrs. Geddes. As he did so he heard the front doorbell ring.

"S'pose I'd better go an' answer that," Mrs. Geddes said, looking at him as if for permission. "Do I tell 'oever it is as Mr. Cathcart's dead, or not?"

"No, please don't do that yet," he said quickly. "But I hope it is a constable from the local station. At least as a matter of courtesy I have to inform them what has happened, and if the murder actually happened here, then it is in their jurisdiction." If he was fortunate, local police would insist on taking over the case. It now seemed quite certain the French Embassy was in no way involved, and there was no reason why Pitt should remain in charge.

It was indeed the local constable, a plain-faced, agreeable man of middle years named Buckler. Pitt explained to him briefly what had occurred so far. Even the more lurid details were necessary, although he excused Mrs. Geddes before describing them. If Buckler were to assist in the further search, he must know what might be relevant.

"Well I'm very surprised, sir, an' that's a fact," he said when Pitt had finished. "Mr. Cathcart was an artist, an' a bit eccentric, like, but we always found 'im a very decent gentleman. Not what you'd call the best standards, no churchman or the like, but good as most gentlemen, an' better'n many. It's a very ugly business, an' that's no mistake."

"Indeed," Pitt agreed, not yet sure whether he believed Buckler as to Cathcart's character. "Mrs. Geddes has shown me through the house and says there is nothing out of place and no signs of any other presence here, except Miss Lily Monderell, whom I believe is Cathcart's mistress."

"Well 'e was an artist o' sorts," Buckler conceded. "You expect that." He glanced around. "D'you think 'e were killed 'ere, then? Although I can't see anyone gettin' around the streets dressed like you say. Not even at night! Most likely it was 'ere, an' 'e were put in the boat an' turned loose. Could easy fetch up any place between 'ere an' the Pool."

Pitt led him back through the house towards the side door to the garden, passing Mrs. Geddes in the sitting room.

"Watch out for that rug," she called after him. "Edge is frayed an' it's easy ter catch yer boot in it. I keep tellin' Mr. Cathcart as 'e should get it mended."

Pitt glanced at the floor. It was smoothly polished and quite bare.

"Mrs. Geddes!"

"Yes sir?"

"There's no rug here."

63

"Yes, there is, sir." Her voice came quite clearly. "Smallish green one wi' red in it. Edge is frayed, like I said."

"No there isn't, Mrs. Geddes. There's nothing on the floor at all."

He heard the sound of her footsteps and a moment later she appeared in the doorway. She stared at the polished floor.

"Well, I'll go to the foot of our stairs! There should be one there, sir. It's gorn!"

"When did you last see it?"

"Now . . . let me see." She looked bewildered. "Yes, the day before Mr. Cathcart . . . got . . . well, the day before. It were there then, because I sort o' nagged 'im about gettin' it mended. I gave 'im the name o' someone as does that kind o' thing. Cobbler 'e is, actually, but stitch anything up pretty good."

"Could Mr. Cathcart have taken it to him?"

"No sir," she said firmly. " 'Cos 'e don't do that kind o' thing 'isself. 'E'd 'a give it ter me ter take. I reckon it's bin stole. But why anyone'd wanna take summink like that I'm blessed if I know." She was staring as she spoke, her brow puckered, but not at the floor, rather at the blue-and-white vase which sat on the jardiniere by the wall.

"What it is, Mrs. Geddes?" Pitt asked her.

"An' that's not the right jar for there, neither. Wrong color. Mr. Cathcart'd never 'a put a blue-and-white jar there, 'cos o' the curtains along at the end bein' red, like. Big red-and-gold jar, 'e 'ad. Twice the size o' that one." She shook her head. "I dunno, Mr. Pitt. 'Oo'd take a great big jar like that, an' then go an' stick the wrong one in its place?"

"Someone who wished to conceal the fact that anything was gone," Pitt replied softly. "Someone who did not realize how good your memory is, Mrs. Geddes."

She smiled with satisfaction. "Thank yer—" She stopped abruptly, her face paling, her eyes wide. "Yer mean as 'e were killed 'ere? Oh my . . ." She swallowed convulsively. "Oh . . ."

"A possibility, no more," Pitt said apologetically. "Maybe you should go and put the kettle on . . . make that tea you didn't have before." He knelt down on the wooden floor and ran his fingers gently along the edge by the skirting board. It was not long before he felt a sharp prick and picked up a tiny sliver of porcelain. He examined it carefully. One smooth side was dark red.

"That it?" Buckler asked, leaning over a little to look also.

"Yes . . ."

"You reckon 'e was killed 'ere, sir?"

"Probably."

"There's no blood," Buckler pointed out. "Did they wash it all out? Not leave even a mark?"

"No, it was probably on the rug that's missing."

Buckler looked around. "What did 'e do with it? 'Ave yer looked in the garden? In the rubbish? I suppose 'e more likely took it away with 'im. Though I can't think why. What difference'd it make? Doesn't tell us 'oo 'e is."

"No, I haven't looked in the garden yet," Pitt replied, climbing to his feet. "If I find something there, I would rather have a local man with me when I do."

Buckler straightened his tunic coat and breathed out gently. "Right, sir. Then we'd better be about it, 'adn't we?"

Pitt opened the side door and stepped out. The autumn trees were still in full leaf, but the chestnuts were beginning to turn gold. The asters and Michaelmas daisies were a blaze of varying purples, blues and magentas, and the last marigolds were still spilling brightly over the edges of the borders. A few roses glowed amber and pink, fading quickly but with a luminous tone richer than that of summer.

Beyond the evergreens the light danced on the river, and as he and Buckler walked across the grass it was easier to see the dark shadow where the willow made a cavern over the bank and about twenty yards of the stream.

They moved more slowly, eyes to the ground, looking for footprints, signs of anyone's passing recently.

"There, sir," Buckler said between his teeth. "I reckon that's 'cos something was dragged. See where it's all bent. Some o' their stalks is broke."

Pitt had seen it. Something heavy had fallen and then been pulled along.

"I expect he carried Cathcart as far as he could, then dropped him here and hauled him the rest of the way," Pitt said. He stepped forward, leading Buckler to the edge of the river. Here the weed was deeply scored, but the tide had risen and fallen four times in the last two days, and the marks were obliterated below the high-water line. There was a post where a boat could be tied, and the ridges worn on its sides made its use apparent.

Pitt stood staring at the water, rippling, dark peat browns reflecting the sun. It was several moments before he noticed the white edge of another chip of porcelain, and then another. It was Buckler who saw the mass of the rolled-up rug half sunken under the willow, brushed by the branches. At first it had looked like a drifting log, and he had ignored it.

Loath to wade into the river, or ask Buckler to do it, Pitt went back up to the garden shed and fetched a long-handled rake, and together they managed to pull the mass ashore. They unrolled it and looked at it carefully, but it had been in the mud and water too long to tell if any of the marks were blood or not.

"It was done in the 'ouse, and then 'e were carried out 'ere and put in the boat," Buckler said grimly. "An' 'ooever done it broke the jar an' threw the bits down 'ere, an' took the rug up 'cos o' the blood. Mebbe they 'oped it'd 'ide the fact 'e were dead, an' we'd think 'e jus' upped an' took off somewhere."

Pitt was inclined to agree with him, and said so. The longer an investigation was delayed the more difficult it was. But this evidence did not answer whether the crime had been spontaneous or premeditated, simply that the killer had been in sufficient possession of his wits to act with self-preservation afterwards.

"Must a' bin quite a big feller," Buckler said doubtfully, "ter carry 'im down 'ere from the 'ouse an' put 'im in the boat."

"Or else he had help," Pitt pointed out, although he did not believe that. There was too much emotion, too much that was violent and twisted, for a collaboration between two people—unless both were affected with the same madness.

"There's nothing more for us here." Pitt looked around at the quiet garden and the fast-flowing river. The tide had risen several inches even while they stood there. "We'd better go back to your station. This is your patch."

But Superintendent Ward had no desire to take the case, and told Pitt in no uncertain terms that since the body had been found at Horseferry Stairs, and Pitt had already started to investigate, he should continue to do so.

"Besides," he pointed out forcefully, "Delbert Cathcart was a very important photographer. Done a lot of high society. This could be a very nasty scandal indeed. Needs to be handled with a great deal of discretion!"

Tellman returned from Dover hot and tired, and after a cup of tea and a sandwich at the railway station, he went to Bow Street and reported to Pitt.

"No sign of him in Dover now," he said with a mixture of relief at not having had to arrest a French diplomat, and disappointment because he had been denied a trip to France. "But he was there. Booked a passage across to Calais, then never turned up to go. I questioned them up and down about that, but they were absolutely certain. Wherever he is, he's still in England."

Pitt leaned back in his chair, looking at Tellman's dour face and reading the anxiety in him.

"The body in the boat wasn't Bonnard," Pitt said. "It's a society photographer called Delbert Cathcart. He lived in Battersea, just across the bridge from Chelsea, where he had a very nice house backing onto the river." He told Tellman about finding the place where Cathcart had been carried down to the punt, and the broken jar and the stained rug.

Tellman sat in the other chair, frowning. "Then where's Bonnard? Why did he take off to Dover and then disappear? Do you suppose he's the one who killed what's his name . . . Cathcart?"

"There's no reason to think they are connected," Pitt said

67

with a wry smile. He knew Tellman's opinion of foreigners. "We'll go and see Lily Monderell this evening."

"His mistress?" Tellman invested the word with considerable scorn. There was a deep-rooted anger inside him against all sorts of things—privilege, injustice, greed, being patronized or ignored—but although he would have denied it hotly, he was a very moral man, and his beliefs on marriage were conservative, as were his ideas about women.

"We have to begin somewhere," Pitt answered. "There were no signs of anyone having broken into the house, so we must presume that whoever killed him was someone he knew and let in himself. He knew of no reason to fear them. Mrs. Geddes says she has no idea who it could be. Perhaps Miss Monderell will know more."

"Other servants?" Tellman asked. "Does this Mrs. Geddes do everything?"

"Apparently. He very often ate out, and didn't care to have a manservant. Someone came in to do the scrubbing two days a week, and there was a gardener, but no one who knew him any better than Mrs. Geddes."

"Then I suppose we'd best go and see this mistress," Tellman conceded grudgingly. "Is there time for a proper dinner first?"

"Good idea," Pitt said willingly. He would far rather find a warm, noisy public house and eat with Tellman than go home to the silence of Keppel Street and eat something alone at the kitchen table. The sight of the familiar room with its polished copper and the smell of linen and clean wood only made him more aware of Charlotte's absence.

Tellman had formed a picture of Lily Monderell in his mind. She would be the sort of woman a man took to bed but did not marry. There would be something essentially vulgar about her, and of course greedy. She would have to be handsome or she would not succeed in her purpose, especially with someone who was an artist of sorts. Without any reason, he had seen her as fair-haired and rather buxom, and that she would be dressed flamboyantly.

When he and Pitt were shown into her sitting room in Chelsea, he was disconcerted, and yet he could not have said why. Apart from the fact that she was dark, she answered his imagined description very well. She was extremely handsome, with bold eyes, a wide, sensuous mouth, and masses of shining, dark brown hair. Her figure was very rich, and the gown she wore displayed it to fine advantage. It was a trifle ostentatious, but that might have been because she had so much to show. On a thinner woman it would have been more modest.

What upset his composure was that he did not find her unattractive. Her face was full of laughter, as if she knew some joke she was waiting to share. From the moment they stepped into the warm room with its rose-shaded lamps, she flirted with Pitt.

"I'm very sorry," Pitt said after he had told her the news of Cathcart's death, sparing her the details.

She sat on the sofa, her rose-red skirts billowing around her. She leaned back a little, more from habit than thought, showing off her generous body.

"Well, poor Delbert," she said with feeling. She shook her head. "I can't think who would want to do something so . . . vicious." She sighed. "He made enemies, of course. That's natural when you're really good at what you do, and he was brilliant. In some ways there was no one to touch him."

"What sort of enemies, Miss Monderell?" Pitt asked. "Professional rivals?"

"Not who'd kill him, love," she said with a wry smile.

Tellman noticed a slight northern accent. He was not sure where to place it, but he thought Lancashire. He did not know much about the cities outside London.

Pitt kept his gaze steady on her. "What sort?" he repeated.

"You ever seen any of his pictures?" She looked back at him without wavering.

"A few. I thought they were extremely good. Were some of his clients dissatisfied?"

Her smile widened, showing excellent teeth. "Well, I daresay you don't know the clients," she answered. "Did you see the lady dressed as Cleopatra . . . with the snake?"

"Yes."

Tellman was startled, but he said nothing.

"What did you think of it?" she asked, still looking at Pitt.

A flicker of uncertainty crossed Pitt's face.

Tellman was fascinated. He wished he had seen the pictures. He wondered fleetingly if the lady in question had been fully dressed.

"Come on, love! What did you think of it?" Lily Monderell repeated. "Tell the truth and shame the devil! Poor Delbert deserves that."

"I thought it was extremely powerful," Pitt replied, the faintest color rising to his cheeks.

Lily Monderell threw her head back and roared with laughter.

Tellman was shocked. Her lover was newly dead, she had heard the news only moments before, and here she was laughing! He tried to frown to convey his disapproval, and found he could not. There was a warmth about her which enveloped him in spite of himself.

She glanced at him, and her mirth died away.

"Don't look like that, love," she said gently. "He wouldn't want anyone standing around with a face like the milk had gone off. He'd expect us to go on . . . me especially. I knew him, you see. You never did."

Tellman could not think how to answer her. She looked like all the images he had in his mind of such women, but inside she was different, more alive, more disturbing, and it confused him.

But she was finished with Tellman. She turned back to Pitt, her face sharp with interest and amusement.

"Powerful?" she said curiously. "How carefully you choose your words, Superintendent. Is that all?"

Tellman watched Pitt, wondering what he would say. He suspected Pitt had seen far more than that in it.

"Go on! Be honest," Lily urged. "What kind of woman is she?"

A half smile hovered around Pitt's mouth. "In the picture—a sensuous, selfish woman," he replied. "Impetuous, ruthless, very confident. A doubtful friend and a bad enemy."

She nodded her head very slowly, satisfaction bright in her eyes. "You see? It's all there in the picture. You look at it once and you know her better than she wants to be known." There was considerable pride in her. "That was his genius. He could do that time and time again. A light here or there, a shadow, something in the setting. You'd be surprised how often people like the sort of thing that shows up their real character. They forget that a photograph is taken in a very private place but the picture, when it's finished, may be shown anywhere."

Pitt leaned forward a little. "What sort of things did he add?"

Tellman could not see any reason for knowing. He thought Pitt was interested for himself.

"Well, the snake, of course," she started to recall. "And I remember some butterflies from one young society woman. She thought they were beautiful . . . which they were. They also reflected her nature rather too well." She was smiling as she spoke. "And a looking glass, knives, fruit, wineglasses, stuffed animals, different kinds of flowers . . . all sorts of things. And where he put the lights made a lot of difference. A face lit from below doesn't look anything like the same one as lit from the side or above."

Pitt was thoughtful. "And he made enemies with this perception?"

"You can't understand how strong vanity is if you have to ask that," she answered, shaking her head at him. "Don't you know people at all? And you are supposed to be a detective."

"As you said before, Miss Monderell, you knew Mr. Cathcart and I did not."

"You're right, love, of course." A sadness filled her for a moment, and Tellman was startled to see tears in her eyes. He did not know why, but he was pleased. A decent person grieved for death.

Pitt suddenly changed his line of enquiry. "Did he inherit his wealth or earn it with his photography?"

71

She looked momentarily startled. "He never spoke about it. He was generous, but I didn't need him for that." She said it quite casually, but Tellman felt she wished them to know it.

Pitt looked down at his hands. "You weren't dependent on him financially?" he said curiously. "Were you lovers or just friends?"

She smiled at him, shaking her head a little, and the tears spilled over her cheeks. "I know what you're saying, and you're wrong. We were lovers. He liked women, and I never imagined I was the only one . . . but with me it was different. It was never a grand affair, but we liked each other . . . he was fun, that is more than you can say of everyone. I'll miss him." She wiped her cheek. "I . . . I'd like to think it was quick . . . that he didn't suffer. . . ."

"I should think he didn't even know it," Pitt replied gently.

She glanced at Tellman. He thought she was afraid Pitt was being kind rather than honest.

"Back of the head," Tellman confirmed. "Probably went out straightaway." He startled himself by wanting to comfort her. She was everything he disapproved of, and as unlike Gracie as possible. Gracie was small and thin with a wide-eyed, quick little face and as spiky a nature as he had ever met. She was careful, sharp-witted, and as brave as anyone he'd ever known. In fact, she was altogether the opposite of the sort of woman he had always been drawn to and imagined one day he would marry. Liking her was reasonable enough, respecting her certainly was, but they disagreed about so many things, important things like social justice and people's place in society, it would be ridiculous to think of anything more than a pleasant association.

Of course it was ridiculous! Gracie didn't even like him. She tolerated him because he worked with Pitt, no more. She probably wouldn't have done that, had she a choice. But she would have given tea and homemade cakes to the devil if Pitt had asked her to and she thought it would help him in a case.

Pitt was still talking to Lily Monderell, asking about Delbert Cathcart's life, his clothes, his trips to the theatre, his parties, the sort of people with whom he spent his time when not seeking clients.

"Of course he went to parties," she said quickly. "All sorts, but he liked theatre best. It was almost part of what he does."

"Did he dress up himself?"

"You mean fancy dress, for society balls and the like? Probably. Most of those folks do." She frowned. "Why? What's that got to do with who killed him?"

"He was . . . in fancy dress," Pitt replied.

She looked surprised, a little puzzled.

"That wasn't usual. He preferred to be . . . ordinary. He said what you picked for fancy dress gave away too much of who you were inside."

"What would he dress as . . . if he did?" Pitt asked.

She thought for a moment or two. "Only time I remember, he went all in black, and he carried a pen and a looking glass. Kind of a clown, I thought he was. What was he wearing when he died?"

Pitt hesitated.

Her face darkened. "What?"

Pitt looked up at her. "A green velvet dress," he answered.

"Dress? What do you mean?" She was obviously at a loss.

"I mean a woman's gown," Pitt elaborated.

She stared at him in disbelief. "That's . . . silly! He'd never wear that kind of thing. Somebody else did that to him . . . after . . ." She shivered and blinked hard.

"I was hoping you might be able to tell us who it might be," Pitt pressed.

Her voice was higher pitched, sharper. "Well, I can't! His friends are colorful, a bit wild, spend a lot on their pleasures, but not to do that! Poor Delbert." She looked beyond Pitt to something within her own imagination, her eyes troubled. "I'd help you if I could, but it isn't anyone of his friends I've met." She focused on Pitt again. "I want you to find him, Mr. Pitt. Delbert didn't deserve that. He was a bit too clever sometimes, and he didn't always know when to keep his observations quiet . . . and that can make enemies. And he saw too clearly . . . but he wasn't a bad man. He liked a good joke, and a good party, and he was generous. Find out who did that to him. . . ."

"I'll do everything I can, Miss Monderell," Pitt promised. "If you would give me a list of Mr. Cathcart's friends, we'll see if any of them can help us also."

She stood up in a graceful movement and walked over to the bureau, skirts rustling, a wave of perfume teasing Tellman, warm and sweet, and confusing him all over again.

4

MARIAH ELLISON WAS NERVOUS. That made her angry because it was something she had managed to avoid for more years than she could remember, and that was now a great many. She had kept control of events so that she was very seldom placed at a disadvantage. It was one of the privileges of age.

This was entirely Caroline's fault. A great deal that was presently disagreeable was Caroline's fault. Imagine marrying an actor! The woman had taken leave of her wits. Not that she had ever had very many. Caroline had seemed sensible enough when she had married Edward, Mariah's only son. Poor Edward. How he would grieve to see what a state his widow had fallen into—taking up with theatrical people and then marrying one young enough to be her own son! Edward's death must have unhinged her mind, that was the most charitable explanation one could offer. Not made of stern-enough stuff, that was her trouble. Mariah had not fallen into pieces like that when Edward's father had died and left her a widow at much the same age. But then she was of a different generation from Caroline, and had a backbone of steel.

Who was this Samuel person Caroline had gone and invited to tea so hastily? Apparently she had written a note this very morning and dispatched an errand boy with it to the hotel where Mr. Ellison was staying during his time in London. The acceptance had come by return. He would be delighted to call upon them at three o'clock.

He could be any sort of a person! Caroline had said he was charming, but then her marriage was witness enough as to her judgment. Heaven only knew what else she might admire these days.

Naturally, Mariah had brought her own maid, Mabel, with her from Ashworth House. That was the least comfort they could afford her. Accordingly it was Mabel who put out her best black afternoon gown—she was a widow and, like the Queen, had refused to wear anything but black for the last twenty-five years.

Mabel helped her dress, to a constant stream of instruction and criticism, of which she took little notice.

"There you are, ma'am," she said at last. "You look very nice—fit to meet anyone."

The old lady grunted and surveyed herself in her glass for the final time, straightened her lace collar and went to the bedroom door.

Who was this Samuel Ellison person? Of course she knew her husband had been married before. She had never told Caroline because Caroline had not needed to know, and it was not a matter Mariah desired to discuss with anyone. She had not known there was a son. It was perfectly possible this man was an impostor, but if he really resembled Edward so closely, then presumably he was genuine. She would know as soon as she saw him.

She opened the door and stepped out onto the landing. There was no need to be disquieted, even if the man was who he claimed to be. If he was, she would be pleasant to him, and the afternoon would pass agreeably enough. After all, he was American; she could hardly be held responsible if he was not socially desirable. She could apologize, disclaim all connection, and not invite him again.

And if he was charming, interesting, amusing, so much the better.

If he was an impostor she would ring for the butler and have him shown out abruptly. It was nothing to be ashamed of. Everyone had relatives they did not care to own. It happened even in the best families.

76

She went down the stairs and into the withdrawing room.

Caroline was standing by the window looking out. As the old lady came in she turned around. Caroline was very handsome for her age, one might almost say beautiful, except that she had a light in her eye and a flush to her cheek which were unbecoming in a mature woman. She should know how to behave with more discretion. And that shade of burgundy was much too rich.

"You are overdressed," the old lady remarked critically. "He will think he has come to dinner. It is barely three o'clock in the afternoon."

"Well, if he looks at you, he will expect baked meats," Caroline retorted. "You seem to be dressed for a funeral."

The old lady straightened to total rigidity. "I am a widow. As are you, or you were—until you went off and married that actor! I would have thought in deference to the fact that this man is apparently a member of our family, and his brother is dead, you might have worn something more in keeping with the occasion." She sat down solidly in the best chair.

Caroline looked at her closely. "You never told us that Papa-in-law had been married previously."

The old lady avoided her eyes. "It was not your concern," she said coldly. "She was a woman of . . ." For once she was uncertain. Dark memories brushed the edge of her mind, and she refused to allow them closer. "She ran away." Her voice grew sharper. "She abandoned him. Went off with some worthless adventurer . . ." That was a lie, but it was easier to believe and to understand. "Naturally we did not speak of it. No one would." That was true.

"Edward might have wished to know he had a half brother," Caroline said quite gently.

"No one knew," the old lady replied, her voice steadier. That also was true. She had had no idea whatever that Alys had been with child. Edmund would not have let her go so easily if he had known. To lose a son would be altogether a different matter.

Mariah deliberately unclenched her hands. They were cold and a little clammy with tension. Memories long forgotten

77

were stirring in her mind, shapeless pain, things denied so long they were only darkness now, no sharp edges, just the ache. Why didn't someone arrive so she did not have to work so hard at not thinking?

There it was. A carriage outside. The footsteps across the hall, the murmur of voices. Thank heaven.

The door opened and the butler announced Mr. Samuel Ellison. He was tall, well built, and dressed in the latest cut of waistcoat and jacket, but all this was nothing to Mariah. Her breath almost stopped in her throat as she saw his face. He was so like her own son a wave of loss overtook her like a physical pain. It was not that she and Edward had been friends, or shared ideas or confidences, it was the bond of years of knowledge, of memories of childhood intimacy, the very fact that he had been part of her. And here was this man of whose existence she had been unaware until this morning, and he had the same eyes, the same shape of head, the same manner of moving.

Caroline was welcoming him in and, before Mariah was ready for it, presenting him to her.

He bowed, smiling at her, his expression full of interest as he looked at her face.

"How do you do, Mrs. Ellison. It is charming of you to receive me with almost no notice at all. But after so long, hoping to meet my English family, I simply could not wait another day."

"How do you do, Mr. Ellison," she replied. It was difficult to say the name, her own name, to a stranger. "I hope your stay in England will be a pleasant one."

"It already is," he assured her with a smile. "And becoming better all the time."

She forced herself to make a civil reply, and they all sat down to exchange small talk of the usual innocuous and meaningless kind. However, almost immediately it took another turn. Caroline had made some trivial enquiry about Samuel's youth, and he replied with a vivid description of New York, where apparently his mother had landed from the ship which had taken her across the Atlantic.

78

"Alone?" Mariah said in amazement. "However did she manage?" Perhaps it was an intrusive question. The answer may not have been one he was willing to give and it was made in disbelief as much as sympathy.

"Oh, there were many in the same circumstances," he replied easily. "They helped one another, as I was telling Mrs. Fielding yesterday evening." He glanced at her with a smile. "And my mother was a woman of remarkable courage, and never afraid to work hard."

Mariah barely heard the continued conversation. Her mind was filled with thoughts of this woman she had never seen, who had been Edmund's first wife and fled to America alone, without a friend or ally in the world, according to Samuel, and carrying Edmund's child. Why had she gone if not with some lover? The answer to that lay like a dark and ugly threat just out of reach, but close . . . far too close.

"And did you remain in New York?" Caroline enquired.

"Oh no," Samuel replied with a wide smile. "When I was twenty, I decided to journey westward, just to go and see it, you understand?"

"And leave your poor mother?" Mariah said with some sarcasm. It gave her a ghost of pleasure to think of Alys by herself again. It served her right.

"Oh, believe me, ma'am, my mother was well able to care for herself by then," he assured her, leaning back more comfortably in his chair. "She had a nice little business going in dressmaking, and employed several girls. She had made friends and knew a great many people. She missed me, I hope, but she did not mind when I packed up and went west, first to Pittsburgh, then up to Illinois."

He continued with marvelous descriptions of the great plains that stretched for a thousand miles westwards to the foothills of the Rocky Mountains.

Mariah began to relax. He was merely entertaining, after all. Like most men, he loved to be the center of attention. Unlike most, he had a great gift for anecdote and a very ready sense of humor. Caroline's face was quite flushed, and she had barely taken her eyes off him since he began.

Tea was brought, poured and passed. This was not so bad after all.

"But you returned to New York," Caroline asked.

"I came back east when my mother was taken ill," Samuel answered her.

"Of course." She nodded. "Of course. You would naturally want to take care of her. She never married again?"

A curious expression crossed Samuel's face, a mixture of pity and something which could have been anger.

Mariah felt the chill of warning shiver through her. It was not over. She wanted to say something to cut off Caroline's intrusive enquiries, but for once she could think of nothing which would not simply make it worse.

"I hope she recovered," Caroline said earnestly. "She must still have been quite young."

"Oh, yes," Samuel responded with a smile. "It proved to be no more than a passing thing, thank heaven."

"You must have been close," Caroline said gently. "Having endured so much together."

His face softened, and there was a great tenderness in his eyes. "We were. Much as I wished to find my English family as well, I don't think I would ever have left America while she was alive. I never knew a person, man or woman, with more courage and strength of will to follow her own mind and be her own person, whatever it cost."

Caroline smiled; there was a sweetness in her, almost a glow, as if the words held great value for her.

"It does cost," she agreed, looking intently at Samuel. "One can be so uncertain, so filled with doubts and loneliness, and the way cannot always be retraced. Sometimes it is too late before you even realize what you have paid."

Samuel looked at her with quite open appreciation, as though she had offered him a profound compliment.

"I see you understand very well, Mrs. Fielding. I believe you would have liked her, and she you. You seem to be of one mind."

Mariah stiffened. What was he talking about? The woman had left her husband and run off to America. He was speaking as if it were some kind of a virtue. How much did he know? Surely she would never have—could never . . . no woman would! The coldness hardened inside her like ice. Old memories of pain returned, things forgotten years ago, pushed into the oblivion at the edges of her mind.

She must do something, now, before it was too late.

"I suppose you were there during that miserable war?" she said abruptly. "It must have been most disagreeable."

"That hardly begins to describe it, Mrs. Ellison," Samuel said gravely. "Any war is dreadful, but one among people of one nation who are even known to each other, perhaps brothers, fathers and sons, is the most terrible. The violence and the hatred have a bitterness which does not fade."

Mariah Ellison did not understand, nor wish to.

He perceived it quickly, and his expression changed. The sense of tragedy was wiped away; compassion and a wry humor replaced it.

He told them of events as he had perceived them.

"Sometimes it's the silly things that hold you together," he said, his voice dropping even lower. "If you'd ever been really sick with fear till your stomach knotted up like a fist, you'd understand that."

A wave like a prickle of heat swept over Mariah's skin as memory washed around her in a tide, old memory she'd buried years ago, followed by a chill that left her shaking as if she had swallowed ice. How dare he make her feel like this? How dare he arrive out of nowhere and awaken the past?

It was Caroline who cut across the silence and jerked her back to this pleasant, modest room with its well-worn, comfortable furnishings, the afternoon light streaming in through the windows onto the carpet.

"You speak of it with such passion we can feel something of what you know," she said softly.

Samuel turned to look at her and moved momentarily as if he would have put out his hand to touch her, had he not remembered in time that it would be too familiar.

"What did you do after the war?" she asked. She heard the

81

hard edge in her own voice, but it was beyond her control. "You must have made a living at something!"

Mariah wondered if he had ever married, and if not, then why, but she did not wish to detain him any longer by asking, nor did she have any desire to appear interested.

"What about your mother?" Caroline said gently, and Mariah could have kicked her.

Samuel's face filled with a softness which changed him profoundly. For the first time the confidence was gone, and in its place one saw for a moment a more vulnerable man, one with more knowledge of his own need and the understanding that much of his strength came from another source. Mariah wanted to like him for it, and could not because she was afraid of what he was going to say.

"My mother cared for herself, ma'am," he answered, and he could not keep the pride out of it. "And for a good many others also. She had all the courage in the world. She never thought twice about fighting for what she believed to be right—win or lose." He lifted his chin a little. "She taught me all I know of how to face an enemy, no matter how you feel or what you fear the cost will be. I've often thought, in my worst moments, how I'd like to be worthy of her. I daresay there's many a man the same."

Mariah felt the misery tighten inside her, like an iron band, never to be escaped again. Damn him for coming! Damn Caroline for letting him. It's easy to talk about courage and fighting when the battle is an honorable one and everybody understands. When you aren't so ashamed you could die of it!

Was that what he was talking about? Did he guess—even know? She stared at his charming, humorous face, so like her own son's in its features, but she could not read it. There was no one she could turn to, certainly never Caroline. She must not know, ever. All those times they had quarreled, the times over the years, even more often recently, when she had told Caroline what a fool she was . . . marrying a man two-thirds her age instead of retiring decently into widowhood. It was bound to end in disaster, and she had told her that. It was no less than the truth. It would be unbearable now, unlivable with, if Caroline were to know all her long-buried darkness. She would rather be dead and respectably buried somewhere . . . even beside Edmund. That was probably what they would do. It was what she had told them she wanted—what else could she say?

But one did not die merely of wanting to. She knew that well enough.

They were talking again. The noise buzzed around her like a jar full of flies.

"Was New York very different after the war?" Caroline asked. She was bent forward a little, the soft burgundy silk of her dress pulled tight across her shoulders, her face intent. She was very individual, the intelligence and will in her, the unusual shape of her mouth. The old lady had thought her beautiful in the beginning. Now they were too familiar for her to think in such terms. And beauty belonged to the young.

"Changed beyond belief," Samuel was answering. A curious expression crossed his face, laughter in his eyes and something which could have been excitement, and both sadness and distaste in his mouth. "The war had left everything in a flux." And he proceeded to describe its color, violence, corruption and excitement. He told of it so enthrallingly even the old lady listened, begrudging every vivid moment.

"I'm sure you could not imagine, Mrs. Ellison, being a young man recently returned from the fear and hardship of war, and the strange tragedies of victory which were far more bitter in the mouth than any of us had foreseen."

He moved from the city life to his adventure westwards.

"The men and women who took the wagon trains through were among the finest and bravest I've ever known," he said with fierce admiration. "The hardships they endured, without complaint, were enough to make you weep. And they were all sorts: Germans, Italians, Swedes and French, Spaniards, Irish and Russians, but so many from right here. I came across one group of English people who were pushing all their worldly possessions in handcarts, women walking beside, some with babes in arms, going all the way to the Salt Lake Valley. God knows how many died on the way."

83

"I cannot imagine it," Caroline said softly. "I don't know how people have the courage."

Caroline watched Samuel and thought of the previous evening at the theatre, and how utterly different that had been. She could see perfectly in her mind's eye Cecily Antrim's vivid figure illuminated on the stage, her hair like a halo in the lights, her every gesture full of passion and imprisoned despair. She wanted so much more than she had. Would that woman ever conceive of what it would be like to struggle simply to survive?

Or were the emotions much the same, only the object of the hunger different? Did one long for love, for the freedom to be yourself, unrestrained by social expectations, with the same fierceness as one hungered for religious or political freedom, and set out to walk on foot into a vast and unknown land inhabited only by an alien race who saw you as an invader?

Cecily Antrim was fighting a complex and sophisticated society in order to win the freedom to say anything she wished. Caroline felt threatened by her. Sitting here watching Samuel and less than half listening to him, she could admit that. She was used to a world where certain things were not said. It was safer. There were things she did not want to know—about others and about herself. There were emotions she did not want to think others understood. It made her naked in a dangerous way, and far too vulnerable.

Cecily Antrim was very brave. Nothing seemed to frighten her sufficiently to deter her. That was part of what Joshua admired so much; that, and her beauty. It was unique, not a prettiness at all, far too strong, too passionate and uncompromising for that. Her face had a symmetry from every angle, a balance in the smoothness of the bones, the wide, unflinching eyes. She moved with extraordinary grace. She made Caroline feel very ordinary, sort of brown and old, like a moth instead of a butterfly.

And the worst thing of all was that it was not merely physical. Cecily had such vigor and courage to fight for whatever she believed in, and Caroline was increasingly unsure of what she thought was right or wrong. She wanted to agree with

Joshua that censorship was wrong. The only way to freedom and growth, to the just equality of one person's faith with another's, was for ideas to be expressed and questions to be asked, comfortable or not. And for laws to be changed, people's emotions had to be awoken, and their sympathies for passions and beliefs outside their own experience.

That was what her mind told her. Deeper, woven into her being, was the conviction that there are things that should never be spoken, perhaps not even known.

Was that cowardice?

She was quite certain Cecily Antrim would think so and would despise her for it, though that hardly mattered. It was what Joshua thought that would hurt. Would he also find a gulf opening up between them, between the brave of heart and mind, those strong enough to look at everything life had to offer and those like Caroline, who wanted to stay where it was safe, where ugly things could be hidden away and denied?

Samuel was still talking, but he was looking mostly at Caroline. Mrs. Ellison sat straight-backed, her black eyes fixed, her face set in lines so rigid one might have thought she was battling some kind of pain.

For the first time Caroline wondered how much the old lady had known of the first Mrs. Ellison. She must have been aware that she had had a predecessor. There would have been legal necessities, and perhaps religious ones also. What kind of a woman was Samuel's mother that she had bolted from Edmund Ellison, from England altogether, and gone across the Atlantic by herself?

Socially a disaster. In England in 1828 it had been a crime for a woman to leave her husband, whatever he had done or failed to do, whatever she had wished. The law, had he chosen to invoke it, could have brought her back to him by force. Presumably he had not wished that. Perhaps he had even been glad to be relieved of her, though from all that Samuel had said, she had been an excellent mother, and his love for her shone in his face every time he spoke of her. Perhaps he knew nothing of the circumstances? Or perhaps whatever she had told him had been the facts as she saw them, but less than the truth?

85

He was watching Caroline now as he spoke of his journey in the steamship across the Atlantic and of his docking in Liverpool, and later his first sight of London. His eyes were dancing with it, and she could not help smiling in return.

His company was remarkably pleasant. He was most interesting to listen to; he had seen so much and recounted it vividly and with a generous spirit. Yet she did not feel threatened as she had yesterday in Cecily Antrim's dressing room. She was sufficiently experienced in the difference between good manners and friendship to be certain that he liked her, and it was a most pleasing feeling. There was admiration in his eyes as he regarded her, and it was like warmth after a sense of deep chill. He would not find her boring or conventional in her ideas. She did not feel left behind by more daring minds, quicker and more agile and—she said the word to herself at last—younger.

Was that at the core of it, not just sophistication and physical beauty, but age? She was seventeen years older than Joshua. It was like poking at an unhealed wound just to say it to herself. Perhaps the old woman, with her vindictive, all-seeing eyes, was right, and she had been a fool to marry a man she was absurdly in love with, who made her laugh and cry, but who in the end would not be able to protect himself from finding her boring.

That would be the ultimate pain—loyalty through pity.

". . . and of course at the theatre my host told me of his acquaintance with Mrs. Fielding," Samuel was saying. "And that she had been Mrs. Ellison until her recent marriage. You can imagine how delighted I was! Well . . . no, you can't," he amended. "I feel as if in a sense I have come back to my beginnings, a homecoming."

"I am glad you find London so entertaining," Mariah said rather curtly. "I am sure your new friends will wish to show you all manner of things: the Tower, the parks, riding in Rotten Row, perhaps Kew Gardens? There are all sorts of sights to see, not to mention society to meet. I am afraid we no longer know anyone." She gave a sideways look at Caroline, then back to Samuel. It was a dismissal, and so phrased as to

86

make it clear he need not look to return in the near future. Duty had been satisfied.

Caroline was furious and unreasonably disappointed. Damn Mrs. Ellison. She turned a radiant smile on Samuel as he rose to his feet.

"Thank you so much for giving us one of the most delightful and interesting afternoons I can ever recall," she said warmly. "It has been a journey into another land without the dangers and inconvenience of travel. I know you must have a thousand things to see, but I do hope you will come again. We may lay some superior claim to you, since we are family, and we must not lose each other now."

"Don't be ridiculous!" The old lady swiveled around to glare at her. "Mr. Ellison has called upon us, which is all we could possibly expect of him. We cannot suppose that a man who has fought in a war and ridden with savages will find himself entertained taking tea with old women in a withdrawing room."

"I do not judge people by their age, Mrs. Ellison," he replied immediately. "Some of the most interesting people I have ever met have been on the upper side of seventy, and have learned wisdom far greater than mine. It is a mistake of the young to assume that only they have passion or beauty, and I am far too old myself to fall into that error anymore. I hope I shall be invited to call again." He glanced at Caroline, then away. His meaning did not need elaboration.

Mrs. Ellison's face pinched, her lips tightened, and she said nothing.

Caroline rose also and moved towards the door to accompany him at least as far as the hall when he had bidden them farewell. "And as for being invited," she said warmly, "please consider that you are always welcome."

He accepted instantly, and after wishing each of the ladies good-bye, he took his leave.

When Caroline returned to the withdrawing room her maid informed her that the old lady had retired to her room, and she did not reappear all evening, or send further word.

5

IN THE MORNING Pitt and Tellman returned to the area of Battersea near Cathcart's house. It was a gray day with a fine mist swirling in from the river, and Pitt had turned his coat collar up against it. Tellman trudged along with his head down, his face set in lines of disapproval.

"I don't know what you think we can find," he said morosely. "It was probably some time in the middle of the night when all decent folk were asleep anyway."

Actually Pitt agreed with him, but Tellman's perversity was irritating and he refused to let him win.

"This is the neighborhood where Cathcart lived," he replied. "Since we don't know exactly when he was killed, and we certainly don't know why or by whom, can you think of anything better?"

Tellman grunted. "How's Mrs. Pitt getting on in Paris?" he asked in retaliation. He glanced sideways at Pitt's face, then away again. He read him too well.

"Enjoying it," Pitt answered. "Says it's a beautiful city and very exciting. The women have a flair for dress and are extremely elegant. They look as if they achieve it without any effort at all. She says it's infuriating."

"Well, they're French, aren't they?" Tellman asked reasonably. "One would expect them to be infuriating," he added.

In spite of himself Pitt grinned.

"If Cathcart was half as clever as that woman said he was,"

Tellman said, returning to the subject at hand, "then he probably got above himself with someone, and maybe tried a touch of blackmail. I daresay photographers are like servants, and they get to see a lot of things. Maybe people think they don't matter, and speak in front of them. He moved around in a lot of big houses, sort of there but not there, if you know what I mean? He might have found it out only by accident, but took his chance."

The road was wet underfoot, heavy dew glistening in the hedges. The mournful sound of a foghorn drifted up from the water.

Pitt pushed his hands hard into his pockets. "That leaves us a pretty wide field," he said thoughtfully. "I'd like to know how much he earned with his photography, and what he spent."

Tellman did not bother to ask why.

"And how much of that house and its furnishings he inherited," Pitt went on, thinking of the works of art he had seen and trying to make some mental assessment of their value.

Tellman was looking at him. "Worth a lot?" he asked. He knew forgery of banknotes and letters of credit, and the disposal of ordinary household goods and silver, but not art of that quality.

Pitt had not doubted that what he had seen in Cathcart's house was genuine, probably even the vase which had been smashed, and almost certainly the once-beautiful rug that they had fished out of the river.

"Yes . . ."

"More than you'd earn taking photographs of the gentry?"

"I wouldn't be surprised."

Tellman's chin came up a little. "Right!" he said more cheerfully. "Then we'd better see what we can find out about Mr. Cathcart."

They parted company, Tellman going to the local shops and generally asking around. Pitt returned to Cathcart's house and, with Mrs. Geddes looking on proprietarily, made what assessment he could of the value of the works of art he could see. Then he went through Cathcart's desk, looking at such bills and receipts as were there. They covered approximately the last three months. It seemed Cathcart did not stint himself for anything that took his fancy. His tailor's bills were enormous, but all receipted within days of being presented. His appointments diary noted several trips to various other cities within a comfortable train journey: Bath, Winchester, Tunbridge Wells, Brighton, Gloucester. There was no indication whether he was going on business or pleasure.

Pitt leaned back in the elegant chair and read the list of clients Cathcart had photographed in the previous six months. He made notes of those for the last five weeks. It seemed Cathcart worked hard on preparation before he finally made his portraits. He spent time to learn about his subjects and to suggest several possibilities to them.

Next he went through Cathcart's professional receipts for photographic materials, which were surprisingly expensive. The margin for profit was not nearly as large as he had supposed. And then there were all the pieces of stage dressing he used, not to mention the generator for the lights.

He must find out if Cathcart had inherited this house and its beautiful carpets, pictures, furniture, vases and so on. Even if he had, it seemed he must live to the limit of his income, unless there was another source.

He should also find out if Cathcart had left a will. He certainly had much to bequeath. Pitt searched the desk again to find out who was his man of affairs, who would surely know.

He found it only just before Tellman returned, looking less than pleased.

"Didn't shop much around here," he said, sitting down gingerly on a Sheraton chair as if he were afraid he might break its beautiful legs. "Mrs. Geddes seems to have bought most of the household necessities. Sent his stuff out to be laundered, linens, clothes, all of it. Expensive." He grunted. "Still, I suppose keeping a staff would cost a bit too, and it may be he preferred not to have anyone around too much."

"What's the gossip?" Pitt leaned back in the desk chair.

"Not a lot," Tellman replied. "Beyond the impression that he's got money and is a bit odd. Some have a less-charitable word for it, but it comes to the same thing. Local chap comes in twice a week and does the garden, but seems Cathcart liked it all overgrown and artistic, like. Can't bear rows of things, and can't be bothered with vegetables or anything useful."

"Perhaps in his profession flowers are more use?" Pitt suggested. "Roses on the arches and pergolas, the willow trailing over the water."

Tellman refrained from comment. "You find anything?" He had always resented calling Pitt "sir," and for some time now had abandoned it altogether, except when he was being sarcastic.

"He went through a lot of money," Pitt replied. "More than he earned as a photographer, unless his books are fiddled. But I need to know if he inherited the house and the things in it . . . which are probably worth more than it is."

Tellman looked around, his brows drawn together. "Reckon he was killed for it? People have killed for a lot less, but not dressed them up and chained them like that. That's . . . personal."

"Yes, I know," Pitt said quietly. "But we need to find out all the same."

"Now what?" Tellman asked, his eyes going surreptitiously to the Chinese vase on the mantelpiece and then across to a blue plaque with raised white figures of dancing children on it, which Pitt guessed to be Italian Renaissance, either Della Robbia or a good copy. He had seen something like it once recovered from a burglary.

"Is it really worth a lot?" Tellman asked.

"I think so. We'll find out if he inherited it. And who inherits it now." Pitt folded up the paper he had been writing on and put it in his pocket, along with the usual variety of things already there, and stood up. "We'll go and find Mr. Dobson of Phipps, Barlow and Jones. He should be able to answer both questions for us."

* * *

Mr. Dobson was a mild-mannered man with a long, distinguished face which fell very naturally into lines of the gravity appropriate to his calling.

"Police, you say?" He regarded Pitt's untidy figure dubiously. Tellman, he seemed to have no doubt of.

Pitt produced his card and offered it.

"Ah!" Dobson let out a sigh, apparently satisfied. "Come in, gentlemen." He indicated his office and followed after them, closing the door. "Please be seated. What can I do for you?"

"We are here regarding Mr. Delbert Cathcart. I believe he is a client of yours," Pitt replied.

"Indeed he is," Dobson agreed, sitting down and inviting him to do the same. "But of course his business is confidential, and to the very best of my knowledge, completely honest, and even praiseworthy."

"You are not aware of his recent death?" Pitt asked him, watching the man's face closely.

"Death?" Dobson was clearly taken aback. "Did you say death? Are you perfectly sure?"

"I am afraid so," Pitt replied.

Dobson's eyes narrowed. "And what brings you here, sir? Is there something questionable about the manner of it?"

Obviously the newspapers had not yet been informed that the body from Horseferry Stairs had been identified, but it could only be a matter of time. Briefly Pitt told him the essentials.

"Oh dear. How extremely distressing." Dobson shook his head. "In what manner may I assist you? I knew nothing of it, nor do I know anything which would seem to be relevant. It must be some madman responsible. What is the world coming to?"

Pitt decided to be completely frank. "It happened in his house, Mr. Dobson, which would make it probable it was someone he knew."

Dobson's face expressed misgiving, but he did not interrupt.

"Did Mr. Cathcart inherit his house in Battersea?" Pitt asked.

Whatever Dobson had been expecting, his face betrayed that it was not this. "No. Good heavens, why do you ask?"

"He purchased it himself?"

"Certainly. About, let me see, eight years ago, August of '83, I think. Why? There was nothing irregular in it, I assure you. I handled the matter myself."

"And the objects of art in it, the furnishings?"

"I have no idea. Are they . . . questionable?"

"Not so far as I know. Who inherits them, Mr. Dobson?"

"Various charities, sir. No individual."

Pitt was surprised, although he had not seriously thought Cathcart had been killed for property, any more than Tellman did. But it cast a new light on Cathcart's income that he had purchased both house and works of art himself. Pitt was aware that Tellman was shifting uncomfortably in his chair.

"Thank you." He sighed, looking at Dobson. "Did he receive any bequests that you are aware of—from an appreciative client, perhaps? Or a deceased relative?"

"Not so far as I know. Why do you ask, sir?"

"To exclude certain possibilities as to why he may have been killed," Pitt answered somewhat obliquely. He did not wish to tell Dobson his suspicions as to Cathcart's sources of income.

There was little more to learn, and five minutes later they excused themselves and left.

"Do you think they could be stolen?" Tellman asked as soon as they were in the street. "If he goes into the houses of all those fancy people and talks to them before he takes their pictures, he'd be in an ideal position to know what they had and where it was kept."

"And when they came to his studio to be photographed they'd be in an ideal position to see it again," Pitt pointed out, stepping around a pile of manure as they crossed the road.

Tellman skipped up onto the curb on the far side and grunted acknowledgment. He had to stride to keep up with Pitt. He was used to it, but it still annoyed him. "I suppose those sort all know each other."

"Probably," Pitt agreed. "Couldn't take a risk, anyway. But

I suppose we should still check if there've been any robberies. I've got a list of his clients."

But the enquiries produced nothing, as he had expected. Nor were there reports from anywhere else of objects of art or furniture missing which answered the descriptions of any of the pieces he had seen in Battersea. He was drawn back to the conclusion that Cathcart had a second, and probably larger, source of income other than his photography, excellent as that was.

He ate a good dinner at the nearest public house, but with little enjoyment, and went home to sit by the stove at the kitchen table for a while. There were no letters from Paris. He went to bed early and was surprised to sleep well.

He and Tellman spent the following two days further investigating Cathcart's life and visiting his clients listed for the six weeks prior to his death.

Lady Jarvis, whom Pitt called on in the middle of the afternoon, was typical. She received them in a heavily ornate withdrawing room. Brocade curtains fell almost from ceiling to well below floor length, gathered up in the rich swathes that demonstrated wealth. Pitt thought with some envy that they would also be excellent at keeping out winter drafts, even if now they also excluded some of the golden autumn light. The furniture was massive, and where the wood showed it was deeply carved oak, darkened by generations of overpolishing. The surfaces were cluttered with small photographs of people of various ages, all posed solemnly to be immortalized in sepia tint. Several were gentlemen in stiff uniforms, staring earnestly into space.

Lady Jarvis herself was about thirty-five, handsome in a conventional way, although her eyebrows were well marked, like delicate wings, giving her face rather more imagination than a first glance betrayed. Her clothes were expensive and rigidly fashionable, with a very slight bustle, perfect tailoring, big sleeves full at the shoulder. Pitt would have dearly liked to buy Charlotte such a gown. And she would have looked better in it.

"You said it was about Mr. Cathcart, the photographer?"

she began, obvious interest in her face. "Has somebody brought a complaint?"

"Do you know who might?" Pitt asked quickly.

The chance to savor a little of the spice of gossip was too pleasant for her to pass by, even if it was dangerous.

"It could be Lady Worlingham," she said half questioningly. "She was very offended by the portrait he took of her younger daughter, Dorothea. Actually I thought it caught her rather well, and she herself was delighted with it. But I suppose it was a trifle improper."

Pitt waited.

"All the flowers," Lady Jarvis went on, waving her hand delicately. "A bit . . . lush, I suppose. Hid her dress until its existence was left to the imagination . . . in places." She almost laughed, then remembered herself. "Has she complained? I wouldn't have thought it was a police matter. There's no law, is there?" She shrugged. "Anyway, even if there is, I don't have any complaint." A look of wistfulness crossed her face, just for an instant, as if she would like to have had, and Pitt glimpsed a life of unrelenting correctness where a photograph with too many flowers would have been exciting.

"No, there is no law, ma'am," he replied quietly. "And so far as I know Lady Worlingham has not complained. Did Mr. Cathcart take your photograph?" He let his glance wander around the room to indicate that he did not see it.

"Yes." There was no lift in her voice. Apparently this was not a matter of flowers. "It is in my husband's study," she answered. "Do you wish to see it?"

Pitt was curious. "I should like to very much."

Without saying anything more she rose and led the way out across the chilly hall to a study perfectly in keeping with the somber grandeur of the withdrawing room. A massive desk dominated everything else. A bookcase was crammed full of matching volumes. A stag's head hung high on one wall, glass eyes staring into space, a bit like the military photographs on the table in the other room.

On the wall opposite the desk hung a large photographic

portrait of Lady Jarvis dressed in a formal afternoon gown. Her features were lit softly from the window she was facing, her eyes clear and wide, her winged brows accentuated. There was no furniture visible, no ornaments, and the shadow of the Georgian panes fell in a pattern of bars across her.

Pitt felt a sudden chill inside him, an awareness of Cathcart's brilliance which was both frightening and sad. The picture was superb, beautiful, fragile, full of emptiness, a creature just beginning to realize it was imprisoned. And yet it was also no more than the portrait of a lovely woman in a manner which might be intended only to strengthen the awareness of the character in her face. One might see the deeper meaning or miss it. There were no grounds for complaint, only a matter of taste.

He felt a pervading, quite personal sense of loss that Cathcart was dead and could no longer practice his art.

Lady Jarvis was watching him, her face puckered in curiosity.

What should he say? The truth? It would be intrusive and serve no purpose. Could she and Cathcart have been lovers? The murder definitely sprang from some form of passion. He turned to the portrait again. It was not the picture a man created of a woman he loved. The perception was too sharp, the compassion impersonal.

"It's remarkable," he said tactfully. "It is unique, and very beautiful. He was an artist of genius."

Her face lit with pleasure. She was about to reply when they both heard the front door close and footsteps across the hall. The door opened behind them. Automatically they turned.

The man standing there was slight, of medium height, and at this moment his pleasant, rather bland face was filled with alarm.

"Is something wrong?" he demanded, turning from one to the other of them. "My butler says you are from the police! Is that true?"

"Yes sir," Pitt answered him. "I am here regarding the death of Delbert Cathcart."

"Cathcart?" Jarvis's face was blank. Certainly there was no guilt or dismay in it, no anger, not even comprehension. "Who is Cathcart?"

"The photographer," Lady Jarvis supplied.

"Oh!" Enlightenment came in a word. "Is he dead? Pity." He shook his head sadly. "Clever fellow. Quite young. How can we help you?" His face darkened again. He did not understand.

"He was murdered," Pitt said boldly.

"Was he? Good heavens. Why? Why would anyone murder a photographer?" He shook his head. "Are you sure?"

"Certain." Pitt did not know whether to bother pursuing the matter. He had never seen anyone look less guilty than Jarvis. Yet if he did not, there would always be the faint, prickling knowledge that he had left something undone. "You didn't happen to see him last Tuesday evening, did you?"

"Tuesday? No, I'm afraid not. I was at my club. Stayed rather late, I'm afraid. Got into a game of . . . well, a game." He stared at Pitt with wide eyes. "Was playing, you see, and suddenly looked up and realized it was gone two in the morning. Freddie Barbour. Too damned good. Certainly didn't see Cathcart. Not a member, actually. Old club. A trifle particular."

"I see. Thank you."

"Not at all. Sorry to be of no use."

Pitt thanked him and left. It would be easy enough to check, if he ever needed to, but there was no doubt in his mind that Jarvis had neither cause nor passion to have murdered Cathcart.

It was growing late, and Pitt was happy to return home and leave the rest of the client list until the following day. He was tired, he did not really believe that he would learn anything of value, and there might be another letter from Paris waiting for him.

He opened the door trying not to expect too much, squashing down the hope inside himself in case there was nothing. It was only two days since the last letter. Charlotte was enjoying herself in a strange and exciting city. She should make everything of it that she could. She would have little time for writing

97

him, especially when she would certainly tell him everything when she returned.

He looked down. There it was; he would know her exuberant writing anywhere. He was grinning as he picked it up and tore it open, pushing the door closed behind him with his foot. He read:

Dearest Thomas,

I am having a marvelous time. It is so very beautiful along the Bois de Boulogne, so desperately fashionable and terribly French. You should see the clothes!

[She went on to describe them in some detail.]

Which brings me to the Moulin Rouge again [she continued]. One keeps hearing whispers of terrible gossip. The artist Henri Toulouse-Lautrec goes there often. He sits at one of the tables and makes sketches of the women. He is a dwarf, you know—at least his legs have never grown, and he is terribly short. Apparently the dance that the chorus girls do is inexpressibly vulgar and exciting. The music is marvelous, the costumes outrageous, and they have no undergarments, even when they kick their legs right over their heads—or so I'm told. That is why Jack has said we absolutely cannot go. No decent woman would even mention the place. (Of course we all do! How could we not? We simply don't do it in the hearing of the gentlemen—just as they don't within ours! Isn't it all silly? But we have nothing else to do but play games. The less we have to do that matters, the more complicated the rules become.) Reputations are made and lost there.

I think of you all so often, wonder how you are, how is Gracie managing at the seaside and are the children enjoying it? They were so keen to go. I hope it is living up to all their dreams. My trip is, in every way. Best of all because I shall be ready to come home when the time arrives.

I sit here at the end of my long day and wonder what you are doing with your body in the punt. I suppose all cities have their crimes and their scandals. Here everyone is talking about the case I mentioned to you before—the young gentleman who is accused of murder, but swears he was somewhere else and so could not be guilty. But the trouble is that the "somewhere else" is the Moulin Rouge—at the very hour when La Goulue, the infamous dancer, was doing the cancan. No one else is willing to say they saw him because they dare not admit they were there. I suppose most people know it, but saying it is different. Then we "ladies" cannot pretend not to know, and if we know of course we have to react. We cannot be seen to approve, so we have to disapprove. I wonder how many situations are like that? I wish you were here to talk to. There is no one else to whom I could say exactly what I think, or who will tell me what they think so honestly.

Dear Thomas—I miss you. I shall have so much to say when I get home. I hope you are not too bored staying in London. Dare I wish you an interesting case? Or is that tempting fate?

Either way, be well, be happy—but miss me! I shall see you soon,

With my true love,
Charlotte

He folded the last page, still smiling, and held on to the letter as he went along the corridor to the kitchen. She must have stayed up very late writing that. He did miss her terribly; it would probably be foolish to tell her how much. And in a way he was pleased she had gone. It was good to realize how much he valued her. The silence of the house was all around him, but in his mind he could hear her voice.

And sometimes when parted one would write the deeper feelings one did not express in words when the daily business of living intruded. Certainly that had been so lately.

He left the letter out on the table as he stoked up the stove and put the kettle on to make himself a pot of tea. Archie and Angus were both purring and winding themselves around his legs, leaving hairs on his trousers. He spoke to them conversationally, and fed them.

* * *

He did not bother to meet with Tellman before going to see Lord Kilgour, another of Cathcart's clients.

"Yes! Yes—it's in the newspapers," Kilgour agreed, standing in the sunlight in his magnificent withdrawing room in Eaton Square. He was a handsome man, tall and very slim, with delicate, aquiline features and a fair mustache. It was a fine-boned face but without real strength; however, the lines of humor were easily apparent, and there was intelligence in his light blue eyes. "Happened five or six days ago, so they say. What can I tell you of use? He took my photograph. Wonderful artist with a camera. Don't imagine it was professional rivalry, do you?" A quick smile lit his face.

"Do you think that is possible?" Pitt asked.

Kilgour's eyebrows rose sharply. "I've never heard of photographers murdering each other because one was better than the rest. But it would certainly cut down the competition. I suppose anyone who wants a portrait in future will have to go to Hampton, or Windrush, or anybody else they like. Certainly they cannot go to Cathcart, poor devil."

"Was he the best?" Pitt was curious as to Kilgour's opinion.

There was no hesitation. "Oh, undoubtedly. He had a knack of seeing you in a particular way." He shrugged, and the humor was back in his face. "No doubt as you would most like to see yourself—whether you had realized it or not. He had an eye for the hidden truths. Not always flattering, of course." He looked at Pitt quizzically, assessing how much he understood.

Having seen Cathcart's portrait of Lady Jarvis, Pitt understood exactly. He allowed Kilgour to perceive as much.

"Would you like to see his picture of me?" Kilgour asked, his eyes bright.

"Very much," Pitt answered.

Kilgour led the way from the withdrawing room to his own study, threw open the door, and invited Pitt to view.

Immediately Pitt saw why the portrait was hung there and not in one of the reception rooms. It was superb, but bitingly perceptive. Kilgour was in fancy dress, if one could call it such. He wore the uniform and robes of an Austrian emperor of the middle of the century. The uniform was ornate, magnificent, almost overpowering his slender face and fair coloring. The crown sat on a table to his right and half behind him. One side of it was resting on an open book, so it sat at a tilt and looked as if it might slide off altogether onto the floor. On the wall beyond it was a long looking glass, reflecting a blurred suggestion of Kilgour, and the light and shadows of the room behind him, invisible in the picture. There was an illusory quality to the whole, as if he were surrounded by the unknown. Kilgour himself was facing the camera, his eyes sharp and clear, a half smile on his lips, as if he understood precisely where he was and could both laugh and weep at it. As a photographic work it was brilliant, as portraiture it was a masterpiece. Words to describe it were both inadequate and superfluous.

"Yes, I see," Pitt said quietly. "An artist to inspire passionate feelings."

"Oh, quite," Kilgour agreed. "I could name you half a dozen others he did just as fine as this. Some people were thrilled, but then they were not the sort who would have done him any harm were they not. I suppose that is self-evident, isn't it? It is the ones with flawed characters who would think of killing him for his revelations, not the charming or the brave, the funny or the kind."

Pitt smiled. "And his rivals?" he pressed.

"Oh, I'm sure they hated him." Kilgour moved back out of the study into the hallway and closed the door. "I keep that picture where I work. I have enough sense of the absurd to enjoy it, and when I get delusions of my own importance it is a very salutary reminder. My wife likes it because she does not see my weaknesses and has not a very quick eye to understand what Cathcart was saying. But my sister understands, and advised me to keep it out of general sight." He shrugged ruefully. "As if I couldn't see it for myself! But then she is my elder sister—so what may one expect?"

They returned to the withdrawing room and spoke a little

longer. Pitt finally left with several names written on a list, both clients and rivals of Cathcart.

He spent the rest of the day visiting them, but learned nothing else that furthered his knowledge of Cathcart's life.

In the morning he met with Tellman, and over a cup of tea in the kitchen they discussed the matter.

"Not a thing," Tellman said dismally. He kept glancing at the door as if he half expected Gracie to come in any moment. He heard the marmalade cat, Archie, come trotting along the passage and look up hopefully at Pitt, then seeing he was unresponsive, go over to the laundry basket and hop in as well. He curled up half on top of his brother and went to sleep.

"Nor I," Pitt replied. "He was brilliant, and I saw one of his competitors who acknowledged as much, but he was doing well enough."

"You don't murder someone because they've got a talent you haven't," Tellman said gloomily. "You might spread lies about them or criticize their work." He shook his head, staring at his half-empty cup. "But this was personal. It wasn't a matter of money, I'd swear to that."

Pitt reached for the teapot and refilled his cup. "I know," he said quietly. "Someone who merely wanted him out of the way wouldn't do this. But I couldn't find anything in his life to provoke this sort of emotion. We aren't looking in the right place."

"Well, I've been all around this day-to-day business," Tellman said defensively, straightening his shoulders a little. "He lived pretty high! He's got to have spent a lot more than he made taking pictures. And he bought that house, we know that. Where'd the money come from? Blackmail, if you ask me."

Pitt was inclined to agree. They had already investigated the possibility of theft, using Cathcart's knowledge of art and of the possessions of his clients. But none of the clients admitted to any losses.

"You must have talked to enough people." He looked up at Tellman. "What did they say about him?"

Tellman reached for the teapot. "Spent a lot of money but paid his bills on time." He sighed. "Liked good things—the best—but he wasn't awkward to suit, like some folk. Always pleasant enough to the few that saw him, that is. Sent for a lot of things, or had them on regular order. Seems he worked pretty hard."

"How hard?" Pitt asked, his mind turning over the clients he knew of from Cathcart's list.

Tellman looked puzzled.

"Hours?" Pitt prompted. "He only took about one client a week, on average. Visited them maybe twice or three times, then had them to his studio for the actual photograph. That's not ten hours a day, by any means."

"No, it isn't." Tellman frowned. "Doesn't exactly account for the time he seems to have been away, and people assumed he was working. Perhaps he wasn't? Could have been doing anything. Wouldn't be the first man that said he was working when he wasn't."

"Whatever he was doing, it made him money," Pitt said grimly. "We need to know what it was." He drank the last of his tea and stood up. "It's about the only thing we've got."

"Unless it was really the Frenchman and not Cathcart at all," Tellman answered, standing as well. "That would explain everything."

"Except where Cathcart is." Pitt poured a little milk for Archie and Angus, and made sure they had food. Angus smelled the milk in his sleep and woke up, stretching and purring.

"Well, if it is Cathcart, where is the Frenchman?" Tellman continued. "He didn't go on the boat from Dover, he came back on the train to London, but he's not here now."

"And as long as the people at the French Embassy maintain that they know where he is, that is not our problem." Pitt made sure the back door was locked. "Let's go and see Miss Monderell again. Maybe she knows where Cathcart spent the rest of his time."

The door was opened to them by a startled maid who told them very firmly that Miss Monderell was not yet receiving visitors and if they cared to come back in an hour she would enquire whether Miss Monderell would see them then.

Tellman drew in his breath sharply, and only with difficulty waited for Pitt to speak. It was quarter to ten. In his opinion, plain already in his face, anyone who was not ill should have been out of bed long ago.

A flicker of humor hovered around Pitt's mouth. "Will you please inform Miss Monderell that Superintendent Pitt would like to speak with her in the matter of Mr. Cathcart's death, and unfortunately I cannot afford the time to wait upon her convenience." His tone of voice made it clearly an order.

The maid looked startled; his mention of the police, and a death she now knew to be murder, robbed her of all argument. However, she left them to wait in the hall, not the withdrawing room.

Lily Monderell came down the stairs twenty minutes later, dressed in a beautiful morning gown of russet red trimmed with black braid, which showed off her extremely handsome figure to full advantage. The sleeves were barely exaggerated at all, and the skirt swept back to a slight bustle. It reminded Pitt of the fashions Charlotte had described in her letter. There was not the slightest crease or blemish in it, no sign of wear at all, and he wondered if it was new.

"Good morning, Mr. Pitt," she said with a dazzling smile. She looked at Tellman, to his renewed discomfort. "Morning, love. You look as if you've been rode hard an' put away wet. Have a cup of tea and a sit-down. Cold outside, is it?"

In spite of himself, Pitt stifled a laugh at Tellman's expression of conflicting fury and dismay. He plainly wanted to be outraged, and she had denied him the chance. She refused to be intimidated or offended, she refused to see his disapproval. Instead, she swept around the bottom of the stairs and led the way to the dining room with her back to him, her silk skirts rustling, a waft of perfume filling the air.

The dining room was quite small but extremely elegant. It was papered entirely in warm yellow with a golden wood floor and mahogany furniture which could have been original Adam, or else was an excellent copy. There were tawny bronze

104

chrysanthemums in a vase on the sideboard, and the maid was already laying two extra places at the table.

Lily Monderell invited them to sit down. Tellman accepted gingerly, Pitt with interest.

The maid came in with an exquisite Georgian silver teapot, gently steaming at the spout. She set it down admiringly, and Pitt had the strong impression that it also was new.

"There now," Lily Monderell said with satisfaction. "Looks real good, doesn't it!"

Pitt realized that one of the pictures he had noticed while waiting in the hall was new since they had been there before, or else moved from a different room. But did one keep pictures of that quality in a room not seen by guests? Lily Monderell was doing very well for herself since Cathcart's death. And yet she had not been mentioned in the will. Did she know that? Was she spending on credit and expectation? It was ridiculous to feel sorry for her, and yet he did.

He looked at the teapot. "It's very handsome. Is it new?" He watched her face closely to see the shadow of a lie before it reached her lips.

She hesitated so slightly he was not sure if he saw it or not. "Yes." She smiled, reaching for it to pour.

"A gift?" He kept his eyes on hers.

She had already decided what to say. "No. Unless you count a gift to myself?"

Should he say something, rather than allow her to buy herself into debt on false hopes? It was none of his business. And yet where she obtained her money might very well be his business. If Cathcart had blackmailed his clients, or anybody else, then perhaps she knew of it. She might even have shared the information and have taken over since his death. It was Pitt's duty to prevent a crime, whether it was continued blackmail or another murder. And the thought of Lily Monderell's lying grotesquely, half naked, in a punt drifting down the cold Thames in the morning mist was peculiarly repellent. Whatever she had done, or was doing, to provoke it. She was so vital it would be a denial of life itself to destroy her.

He sipped the tea she had given him. It was fragrant and

very hot. "I have been to see Mr. Cathcart's man of affairs," he said almost casually.

"To find out when he bought the house?" she asked.

"Among other things," he replied. "Also to see how he had bequeathed it, and his works of art, and whatever money he had."

She lifted her cup and drank delicately. Hers too was very hot. "Charity," she said after a moment. "At least that's what he always said he would do."

He felt a wave of surprise, and then relief. He should have been disappointed. Her spending was not based on any expectation of profit from Cathcart's death, at least not by inheritance. There was still blackmail.

She was watching him now, waiting.

"Yes, exactly," he replied. He let his gaze rest on the teapot. "That's a nice new watercolor of cows that you have in the hall. I've always liked pictures of cows. They seem so supremely restful."

Did he imagine the tightening of her shoulders under the silk?

"Thank you," she answered. "I am pleased you like it, love. Would you care for some toast? Have you had any breakfast, or have you been walking around the streets asking questions all morning?" Her voice was warm, rich, as if she was really concerned for them.

Tellman cleared his throat uncomfortably. He was almost certainly hungry, and equally certainly did not want to accept her hospitality. He would find it confusing to be obliged to her, even for so small a thing.

"Thank you," Pitt accepted, because he would like it, but primarily because it would give him an easy excuse to remain here talking to her.

She rang a small crystal bell on the table, and when the maid came, she requested toast, butter and marmalade for all of them. Tellman's discomfort amused her, it was there in the curve of her lips and the sparkle in her eyes. By the standards of the day, she was not beautiful, her features were too large, especially her mouth. There was nothing modest or fragile about her. But she was one of the most attractive women Pitt had ever met, full of laughter and vitality. He admired Cathcart for his taste with regard to her even more than for the beauty of his house.

"We haven't learned very much," he said thoughtfully. "We've spent several days asking questions and discovered almost nothing . . . except that Mr. Cathcart spent a great deal more money than he earned in his art." He was watching her eyes for the smallest flicker, and even so he was not certain whether he saw it or not. And then he did not know how to interpret it. Had she loved him? Was her emotion grief, or only a decent distaste for the violence and waste of his death? Surely she had been fond of him. She had liked him, whether she had loved him or not.

She lowered her eyes. "He was very clever. He wasn't just a photographer, you know, he was a real artist."

"Yes, I do know." He meant that every bit as much as she did. "I've seen several of his portraits. I don't think *genius* would be too powerful a word."

She looked up quickly, smiling again. "He was, wasn't he?" There were tears in her eyes.

Neither like nor dislike should overrule his judgment.

"He had a gift I've never seen equaled for catching the essence of a person and symbolizing it in an image," he continued. "Not only what they would like to have seen in themselves, but a great deal they could not have wished shown so clearly. I saw not only faces portrayed, but the vanity or emptiness inside them, the weaknesses as much as the beauty or the strength."

"That's portraiture," she said softly.

"Perhaps it's also dangerous," Pitt observed. "Not everyone wishes to have their character stripped so naked to the eyes of strangers, and perhaps still less to the eyes of those they love or to whom they are vulnerable."

"You think he was killed by a client?" She seemed startled.

"I'm sure he was killed by someone who knew him," Pitt answered. "And who felt passionately about him."

She said nothing.

"Had you thought it was a crime of greed?" he asked her. "It was hardly self-defense. Unless he was blackmailing someone . . ." He stopped, waiting to see her reaction.

Her eyes widened so little, the moment after he was not sure he had seen it at all. Why? She should have been startled, even offended. He had just suggested her friend was guilty of one of the ugliest of crimes.

"Over what?" she asked, measuring her words. "What makes you think he knew anything about . . . anyone?"

"Did he?"

"If he did—he certainly didn't tell me. . . ."

"Would he have?"

She was definitely uncomfortable now. It was very well hidden, only a tightening of her hand on the delicate porcelain of the cup, a very slight shaking so the tea in it dimpled on the surface. She must know he was working his way towards asking if she knew the secret which had cost Cathcart his life, and if she was also using it the same way, which might in the end cost her her life also.

"I don't know." She made herself smile. "He didn't. But then I don't know for sure if there was anything to tell."

Was that true? Where had his money come from? Where had she suddenly found sufficient to purchase the painting in the hall and the silver teapot? It was a great deal of money to spend in the space of one week. Had she acquired a new and extremely generous lover?

Or had she been back to Cathcart's house and abstracted a few keepsakes, with or without Mrs. Geddes's knowledge? It could even be that with no heir to be particular, Mrs. Geddes had collaborated, keeping a few small things herself. Would anyone know? Probably not, unless Cathcart kept a list of his possessions somewhere, and from what Pitt had seen of his life, that was unlikely. Certainly there had been no such list among his papers.

He did not wish to think of Lily Monderell's going in among Cathcart's possessions and taking what she fancied.

He could understand it well enough, but it was still not a pleasant thought.

His silence bothered her.

"Like some more tea, love?" she asked, reaching for the beautiful pot.

"Thank you," he accepted, looking at the light gleam on the pot's satin surface. It was almost as if she were provoking him into the very questions she least wanted.

"Have you been back to his house since he was killed?" he asked.

Her hand clenched, and she had to reach up the other hand to steady the pot.

He waited. Even Tellman sat motionless, toast and marmalade halfway to his mouth.

"Yes," she admitted.

"What for?"

She poured his tea, and some more for Tellman also, and lastly for herself, until she had delayed all she could. She looked up again and met Pitt's eyes.

"He promised me some of his pictures that he was going to sell. I went to get them. That's where the money came from."

"You sold them already?"

"Why not? They were good. I know where to go."

She was nervous. He did not know why. He was not sure if she was telling the truth, but her story was reasonable enough. She had been Cathcart's mistress. Men gave gifts to their mistresses, often very expensive ones. Pitt had been surprised that Cathcart had not bequeathed her anything in a more formal way. He had no dependents, so there was no reason, legal or moral, why he should not have. It would be logical enough that the pictures in question would be her legacy.

Why was she nervous? What were the pictures? The means of his blackmail? Had she sold them back to the victims? Or kept them as further source of income? Most people would do the latter. It was an ugly thought.

But Lily Monderell needed to survive, and her looks would not last indefinitely. She had no husband to care for her,

109

probably no skills but those of a mistress, certainly none which would keep her in the manner she now enjoyed and had become accustomed to.

And all of those arguments were excuses, not reasons.

"Pictures of whom?" he asked, not expecting an honest answer, only to see something in her face.

Her eyes did not flicker. She was prepared for the question, he could see it unspoken in her.

"Artist's models," she replied. "No one you would know, I should think. They were just beautiful pictures. He used them as practice for when he was going to do a client . . . to get the costume and lighting right. But people like them . . . they're so well done they're worth a lot." She sighed and glanced at the teapot again.

Should he ask her whom she had sold them to? And if she told him would he follow up to make sure it was the truth? Could he? It might have been the sort of cash transaction of which there was no written record, a quick profit in the works of a man now dead.

Or on the other hand, she might have sold them back to the people Cathcart had blackmailed, and any written record would be worthless.

Or she might simply have collected more blackmail money. Probably he would never be able to prove any of those possibilities.

"Miss Monderell," he said gravely, "you were close to Cathcart, perhaps he trusted you with intimate knowledge of his business, even of his clients. He was murdered by someone who hated him in a very personal way and with an intensity beyond their ability to control."

The color drained from her face.

"Be careful, Miss Monderell." He lowered his voice even further. "If you have any knowledge about his death, any at all, you would be very unwise not to tell me what it is . . . as fully as you are able. I don't want to be investigating your death next week . . . or the week after."

She stared at him in silence, her bosom rising and falling as she strove to control her breathing.

110

He stood up. "Thank you for your hospitality."

"I don't know anything about his death." She looked up at Pitt.

He would have liked to believe her, but he did not.

6

WHILE PITT WAS TRYING TO LEARN more about Delbert
Cathcart's life, Caroline had invited Samuel Ellison to call
again, and was delighted when he accepted. This much was
obvious to Mariah as Caroline came into the room with
Samuel almost at her heels. She looked pleased with herself.

"Good afternoon, ma'am," Samuel said to the old lady, in-
clining his head a little. "I'm glad to see you looking well. It's
very kind of you to receive me again so soon."

It was soon, far too soon, in the old lady's opinion, although it would be unacceptable to say so. However, she
could not let her displeasure go entirely unmarked.

"Good afternoon, Mr. Ellison," she replied coolly, looking
him up and down with a flutter inside she could not suppress.
He was so like her own son, Edward, it was almost as if his
ghost had returned to her. Perhaps more disconcerting at the
moment, he was also markedly like his father. He could not
know that, but she did. It was as if parallel with this autumn
afternoon in 1891 there were hundreds of other afternoons in
other years when Edmund Ellison had walked in, courteous
as this man, sounding as he did now, with heaven knew what
going on in his mind.

"I daresay you wish to make the most of whatever time you
have in London," she continued. She must leave him in no
doubt that he could not keep coming here. "There must be
many calls upon it. And then you will go back to America. No
doubt you have obligations there."

"Not an obligation in the world," he said airily.

"Please sit down," Caroline invited. "Tea will be served in half an hour or so."

He took the chair she indicated, crossing his legs comfortably and reclining. The old lady thought he looked offensively at ease.

"It is unfortunate you could not have come when Mr. Fielding was at home," she said sharply. She wished to make Caroline sensible of a certain disloyalty to her husband in inviting Samuel, who was far nearer her own age and much too obviously found her attractive, at an hour when Joshua was out doing whatever it was he did. She did not know what he occupied his time with, and had never thought to ask. It was probably something she would prefer not to know. Men should keep their indiscretions to themselves, and a woman with the least sense did not ask. "I am sure he also would have liked to see you," she added, to prevent its being obvious she was not pleased to see him. Criticizing Caroline was one thing; she did not wish to appear rude, if it could be avoided.

"I had hoped he would be," Samuel replied with a quick smile. "I thought the afternoon quite a good time. It seems I misjudged."

There was a slight flush on Caroline's cheek. "Usually it is. He has gone to see a friend who is writing a play and wants his advice on stage directions."

Samuel's face lit up with interest. "What a fascinating thing to do! To know what instructions to give to create the perfect illusion and draw in people's emotions and understanding, to form a world which lies open to observation and yet is perfectly contained within itself. Do you know the play?"

It seemed that Caroline did. She answered with a detailed description of the setting and the plot. Mariah sat back in her chair, still upright, but in a sense, by her posture, expressing her exclusion from the conversation. They were discussing the theatre again, and she did not approve. Certainly marrying an actor was a social catastrophe no decent woman would even consider. But now that Caroline had made her bed, she

113

must lie in it. She owed Joshua some loyalty, and sitting there smiling and hanging on every word of Samuel Ellison was disloyal.

Samuel was talking about Oscar Wilde, of all people. Caroline was listening intently, her eyes alight. Mariah's mind raced over what she could do to get rid of Samuel before he said something which woke Caroline's suspicion and she started to think, to ask.

She had already tried hints so direct any decent man would have taken them. It was perfectly obvious to anyone, except a fool, that he was attracted to Caroline, and she was thoroughly enjoying it. It was intolerable.

"I've just read *The Picture of Dorian Gray*, and I was fascinated," Samuel said with enthusiasm. "The man is truly brilliant. But of course meeting him would be the real thing."

"Really?" Mrs. Ellison said icily. She had not meant to join the conversation, but this was too much to allow to pass. "I would not have thought he was the sort of person any respectable man, and any woman at all, would care to associate with. I believe 'decadent' is the term applied to him and his like."

"I believe it is," Samuel agreed, turning away from Caroline to face her. "I'm afraid my desire to experience as much of life as I can has led me to some very questionable places, and most certainly into some company you would not approve of, Mrs. Ellison. And yet I have found honor, courage and compassion in some places you would swear there was nothing good to see . . . maybe not even any redemption to hope for. It's a great thing to see beauty in the darkness of what seems to be lost."

There was a kind of light in his face which defied her to go on disapproving. He was so like Edward it was deeply disturbing, and also unlike him, and that disturbed her as well, because it was inappropriate, and yet it was also kind. She wished with a fierceness that nearly choked her that he had never come.

Caroline saved her the necessity of replying.

"Please tell us the sort of thing you mean," she asked ea-

114

gerly. "I shall never go to America myself, and certainly even if I did I would never go westwards. Is New York like London . . . I mean now? Do you have theatres and operas and concerts? Do people care about society and fashion, who is being seen with whom? Or are they beyond that sort of silly concern?"

He laughed outright, then proceeded to tell her about New York society. "The original 'four hundred' is superb," he said with a laugh. "Although the word is now that there are at least fifteen hundred, if one were to believe all those who claim to be descendants."

"I don't see how that bears any resemblance to us," Mariah said acidly. "I don't know anyone at all who claims to have arrived on a ship from anywhere. I cannot imagine why they should wish to." She fervently desired him to change the subject away from America and ships altogether. If she could freeze him out of it she would.

"William the conqueror!" Caroline said instantly.

"I beg your pardon?"

"Or, I suppose, if you want to be even grander and older still, Julius Caesar," Caroline explained.

Had they been alone, the old lady could have disclaimed all knowledge of what she was talking about, and indeed of the conversation at all. But ignorance was not a satisfactory riposte to Samuel Ellison. He would only believe her, and then she would have to explain, probably at length.

"I have no idea whether my ancestors came over with William the Conqueror, or Julius Caesar, or were here before either of them," she replied, drawing in a deep breath. "Half a dozen generations should be sufficient for anyone."

"I agree with you wholeheartedly," Samuel said with great feeling, leaning towards her a little. "It is who a man is that matters, not who his father was. Good men have had bad sons, and bad men good ones."

Mariah wanted to say something to end this subject before it became catastrophic, but suddenly her throat was too dry to speak.

Caroline was regarding Samuel with gentleness and concern.

115

She had caught a deeper note of meaning in what he said, or else she had imagined it. Mariah shivered. This was appalling. What did he know? How much was possible? Anything! Everything! What would a woman tell her son? A decent woman, nothing at all. How could she? It was unspeakable—literally—beyond the power of being put into speech. She must get rid of him! Out of the house forever. Caroline must be made to see the unsuitability of this—immediately.

But for now, she must make her heart calm down, cease choking her. This was all unnecessary. His choice of words was unfortunate, but it was accidental, no more. Face him down.

Caroline was talking again. "Bicycles!" she said with delight. "How interesting! Have you ridden on one?"

"Of course! They're wonderful, and incredibly fast," he enthused. "Naturally I'm speaking of gentlemen's machines."

"I'm sure ladies' could be very fast as well, if we wore the correct clothing," she countered. "I believe they are known as bloomers."

"Bloomers are hardly 'correct clothing' for anything at all!" the old lady said. "Really! What will you think of next? As if your theatrical antics are not sufficient, you want to dress like a man and career around the streets on wheels? Even Joshua would not allow that!" Her voice rose sharp and high. "Presuming you care what Joshua likes? You used to be besotted enough upon him, I think you would have jumped off Brighton Pier into the sea if you thought he wished it."

Caroline looked at her with wide eyes, perfectly steady and unblinking. For a moment the old lady was quite alarmed at the boldness of them.

"I think that might be a pleasant thought on a hot summer afternoon—a tedious one when everybody is gossiping and talking essentially nonsense," Caroline replied deliberately. "Not to please Joshua, to please myself."

That was so outrageous, so perfectly idiotic, that for a moment the old lady was robbed of a reply adequate to the occasion.

Samuel was only too apparently entertained by the notion,

and that Caroline should not only think it but say it. But then he did not have to live with her.

Then the perfect answer sprang to her tongue.

"If you act to please yourself, Caroline"—she glared at her former daughter-in-law—"then you may very well end up pleasing no one else. And that, for a woman in your situation, would be catastrophic." She pronounced the last word with relish.

She was rewarded by a look of startling vulnerability in Caroline's face, almost as if she had seen an abyss of loneliness opening in front of her, yet the old lady did not feel the satisfaction she had expected to feel. This was nearly victory, and yet isolation, inadequacy, guilt and the burning sense of shame were too familiar, and she wanted to put them behind her forever, so far behind she would never see them or think of them again, not in Caroline, not in anyone. It was intolerable that Caroline, of all people, should remind her.

"It is vulgar to speak so much of oneself," she said quickly. She turned to Samuel. "How long do you intend to remain in London? You will surely wish to see the rest of the country. I believe Bath is still very attractive. It used to be. And highly fashionable. Anyone who had the slightest aspirations to be anyone would take the waters, in the right season."

"Oh yes." He must have been aware it was dismissal, but he refused to go. "Roman baths, aren't they?"

"They were, yes. Now they are entirely English, if anything can be said to be."

"Please tell us more of your own country." Caroline poured more tea and offered the sandwiches again. She seemed oblivious to decency. "How far west did you go? Did you really see Indians?"

A sadness came into his face. "Indeed I did. How far west? All the way to California and the Barbary Coast. I met men who panned for gold in the Rush of '49, men who saw the great buffalo herds that darkened the plains and made the earth tremble when they stampeded." His eyes were very far away, his face marked with deep emotion. "I know men who made the desert blossom, and men who murdered the old inhabitants and tore up what was wild and beautiful and can't ever be replaced. Sometimes it was done in ignorance, and sometimes it was done in greed. I watched the white man strengthen and the red man die."

Caroline drew breath to say something, then changed her mind. She sat silently, watching him, knowing it was not a time to intrude.

He turned and smiled at her.

The understanding between them was tangible in the quiet room.

"Caroline, will you pour me more tea!" Mariah demanded. How could she make him leave? If she claimed a headache she would have to retire, and he might well be gauche enough to remain even so—alone with Caroline. And she was stupid enough to let him. Couldn't see a foot beyond the end of her own nose. Ever since poor Edward died it had been one disaster after another.

"Of course," Caroline said willingly, reaching for the pot and obeying. "Samuel, would you care for another sandwich?"

He accepted, although he was doing far more talking than eating or drinking. He was showing off, and enjoying it thoroughly. Could Caroline not see that? He probably did the same to every woman who was fool enough to listen. And there was Caroline, simpering and hanging on his every word as if he were courting her. Joshua would be disgusted—and then she would lose even what little she had, which now she had let the world know about it by marrying him, was at least better than nothing. Then where would she be? A disgraced woman! Put out for immorality—at her age—with no means and no reputation.

Caroline was looking at Samuel again.

"The way you speak of it makes me feel as if there is much tragedy attached. I had always heard of it as brave and exciting, filled with hardship and sacrifice, but not dishonor." She sensed in him a real wound, and she wished to understand, even to share a fraction of it. There was an emotion driving her she did not realize, but there was a need for reassurance, to find her own balance and certainties, and she was drawn to Samuel's pain. If one could not gain comfort, one could at least give it. And she could not remember when she had liked anyone so quickly and easily before, except perhaps Joshua, and that was not something she wished to think about just at the moment.

She watched his face for an answer, avoiding Mariah's eyes. The old lady was in a strange frame of mind, even for her. If Caroline did not know such a thing was impossible, she would have said she was afraid. Certainly she was angry, but then Caroline had never known her when there was not an underlying emotion in her which she realized now was a kind of fury. She had always been quick to find fault, to criticize, to strike out, as if hurting another person released something within her.

But today was different. Was it loneliness, the grief she referred to every so often because she had been a widow so long? Did she really mourn Edmund still? Was she angry at the world because they went on with their own lives regardless of the fact that Edmund Ellison was dead?

Caroline had loved her own husband, but when he died her grief was not inconsolable. Time had not robbed her of the need for affection. Occasionally she still missed him. But shock had certainly healed, as had the momentary numbing loneliness without him.

Now, of course, there was Joshua, and that was a whole new world: exciting—sometimes too much so—exhilarating and threatening, full of laughter deeper than any she had known before, and disturbing new ideas—perhaps not all good ones, not ones she could keep up with, or wanted to.

She liked Samuel Ellison very much. Was it for himself or because he reminded her of everything that had been good in Edward, and of a past which was so much less threatening, less dangerous to her safety, her self-esteem, to keeping the ideas and values she had grown accustomed to?

Samuel was talking to her, his face puckered with concern, perhaps because he knew she was not really listening.

". . . all about land," he was saying. "You see, Indians don't see land as we do, to be owned by one individual or another. They hold it in common to the tribe, to hunt, to live on and to preserve. We didn't understand their way of life and we didn't want to. They didn't understand ours. Their tragedy was that they believed us when we said we would feed and protect them in return for allowing us to settle."

"You didn't?" she asked, knowing the answer already from his face.

"Some would have." He was not looking at her but somewhere into the distance of his memory. "But more moved west, and then more again. Once we saw the rich land we were greedy to keep it, put fences around it, and let no one else in. The story of the Indians is a tale of one tragedy after another."

Caroline did not interrupt as he recounted the betrayal of the Modoc tribe. She did not know whether Mrs. Ellison was listening or not. She sat with her black eyes half closed, her mouth thin and narrow, but whether it was the Indian Wars which she disapproved of, or Samuel Ellison, or something else altogether, it was impossible to say.

Caroline was startled, and deeply moved, to see tears on Samuel's cheeks. Without thinking she stretched out her hand and touched him, but she said nothing. Words would have been pointless, a mark of failure to understand, an attempt to communicate the incommunicable.

He smiled. "I'm sorry. That really wasn't a teatime story. I forgot myself."

"This is not an ordinary teatime call," Caroline said instinctively. "If one cannot speak to one's family of things that matter, then who can one speak to? Should it be strangers, so we don't have to think of it again, or live with those who know what we have said and felt?"

Mariah Ellison ached to agree, the words throbbed inside her, but fear held them in. It would be too much, too precipitate. Once out they could not be withdrawn, and they might give her away.

Samuel smiled. "Of course not," he answered Caroline. "But I do speak too much."

"It is customary in England to talk of less personal things," Mrs. Ellison said with emphasis. "Not to disturb people, or cause them embarrassment or distress. Teatime is supposed to be pleasant, a small social interlude in the day."

Samuel looked uncomfortable. It was the first time Caroline had seen him disconcerted, and she felt instantly protective.

"And criticism of other people's behavior or remarks is an excellent thing to avoid," she said sharply.

"As is family unpleasantness," the old lady retorted. "Disrespect," she went on. "Or any form of unseemly behavior, overfamiliarity or clumsiness." She did not look at Samuel but at Caroline. "It makes people wish they had not come, and desire to leave as soon as they decently may."

Samuel glanced from one to the other of them uncertainly.

Caroline did not know what to say. Even for Mrs. Ellison this was extraordinary behavior.

The old lady cleared her throat. She was sitting rigidly upright, her shoulders so tight they strained the black bombazine of her dress. The jet beads hanging from her mourning brooch shivered slightly. Caroline was torn by conflicting loathing and loyalty. She had no idea what emotions raged inside the old woman. She had known her for many years and never understood her except superficially, and they equally disliked each other.

"Thank you for coming to see us, Mr. Ellison," Mrs. Ellison said stiffly. "It is good for you to spare us the time when you must have many other commitments. You must not rob yourself of the opportunity to go to the theatre and see the sights of London, or wherever else you may care to go."

Samuel rose to his feet. "It was my pleasure, Mrs. Ellison," he replied. He turned to Caroline and bade her farewell, thanking them both again for their hospitality, then took his leave.

When he had gone, and before Caroline could speak, the old lady stood up also, leaning heavily on her cane as if she needed it to support herself, and half turned her back. "I have a fearful headache. I am going to my room," she announced. "You may have the maid bring my dinner upstairs to me. You would be well advised to spend the rest of the afternoon considering your behavior and your loyalties to the husband you have elected to marry. Not that you ever took advice. But you have made your bed . . . you had best learn to lie in it before you fall out and have no bed at all! You are making a complete fool of yourself. In the privacy of your own home is one thing, but if you throw yourself upon him like this in public, you will cause scandal—and rightly so. A woman who has lost her reputation has lost everything!"

She lowered her voice and stared at Caroline intently. "You had better hope that your husband does not learn of it. Consider your situation!" And with that as a parting shot she stumped out of the room and Caroline heard her heavy footsteps cross the hall to the stairs. She felt cold inside . . . and angry.

There was nothing to say. Not that she was sure what she would have said, were the old lady listening. Actually she was glad to be alone. The words stung precisely because she realized she was thinking all sorts of things which a few days ago had seemed unquestionable, matters of loyalties and beliefs and a sense of belonging.

She half turned and caught sight of herself in the glass over the mantel. At this distance she was handsome, dark hair with a warmth of color in it, only a little gray, slender neck and shoulders, features still almost beautiful, perhaps a trifle too individual to please the strictest taste. But closer to she knew she would see the telltale signs of age, the fine lines around eyes and mouth, the less-than-perfect sweep of jaw. Did Joshua see that every time he looked at her as well?

He would not be home until that evening. He was performing onstage, and she was going alone to dine with the Marchands. She did not feel in the least like going out and making pleasant conversation about trivia, but it would be better than staying there alone and wondering about herself, about Joshua, and how he saw her compared with someone like Cecily Antrim.

Had she really made as big a fool of herself as the old woman said? Would it all have been better, easier, far more honest if she had married someone her own age, with the same memories and beliefs, someone even like Samuel Ellison?

She hadn't! She had fallen in love with Joshua, and believed it when he had said he returned her feelings. She had wanted it so much, it had been the most important thing in the world to her. Was she utterly blind, like a schoolgirl, as Mrs. Ellison said? Could she lose everything?

She turned away from the glass impatiently and went upstairs to her room to consider what she should wear for dinner. Nothing would make her feel beautiful, charming or young.

The Marchands greeted Caroline with great pleasure. They were charming, supremely civilized people who would never wittingly have made any guest less than welcome, but it was impossible not to see the genuineness of their feelings.

"How very nice to see you," Mrs. Marchand said, coming forward from where she had been standing near a small table of flowers in the withdrawing room. The evening was not cold, but there was a fire burning in the grate and the room was warm with the glow of flames reflected on the copper fender and scuttle and the brass-and-copper fire tongs. The heavy curtains were old rose and the furniture massive and obviously comfortable. Embroidered cushions and samplers and an open book of cards and scraps gave it a look of having long been the heart of a family home, albeit a very orthodox one.

"I'm so glad you were prepared to come even without Joshua," Mr. Marchand added from in front of the largest armchair, where he had obviously risen to his feet. He was smiling broadly. He was a shy man, and this was an unusually outspoken remark for him.

Caroline felt enfolded by familiarity and its comfort. It was people like these she had known and understood all her life. There was no need to make any pretense with them, any effort to keep up with bright conversation or forward-thinking opinions.

"I really am very happy to come," she answered, quite honestly. "It is so relaxing to be able to converse without wondering when the theatre bell will go or who else one really ought to speak to."

"Isn't it!" Mrs. Marchand agreed quickly. "I love the theatre, and concerts and soirees and so on, but there is nothing like the quiet company of friends. Do come and sit for a little while and tell us how you are."

Caroline did as she was bidden, and they spoke for a little while of fashion, gossip, mutual acquaintances and other agreeable and unimportant things.

A little before dinner was served the door opened and a youth of about sixteen came in. He was already tall and lean, as if outgrowing his strength. He had his mother's wide blue eyes and dark hair. His skin was still soft; it would be some time before he needed to shave. He was composed, but his slightly awkward silence, the uncertainty what to do with his hands, betrayed his shyness. That much at least was sharply reminiscent of his father, and Caroline could so easily imagine Ralph Marchand at the same age.

"How do you do, Mrs. Fielding," he replied when they were introduced. She wanted to engage him in conversation so he would not have to search for something to say to her. What manner of subject would interest a boy of his age? She must not seem condescending or intrusive, or make him feel as if he was being examined.

He looked at her steadily because he had been taught it was rude not to meet people's eyes when you spoke to them, but she could see he was highly uncomfortable doing so, only waiting for the moment he could disengage himself.

She smiled. Complete candor was the only thing that came to her mind.

"I am very pleased you joined us, Lewis, but at a loss to know what to say to you. I'm sure you are not the least interested in the latest births, deaths and marriages in society, or the fashions either. I do not know sufficient of politics to discuss them with anyone except in the most superficial manner.

I am afraid I have become rather singular in my interests lately, and that may make me very tedious."

He drew in his breath to make the denial courtesy called for, and she cut him off. "Please don't feel the need to be polite. Instead, tell me what you would most like to speak of, were you to initiate the conversation and not I."

"Oh!" He looked startled and a little flattered. A warm color flushed up his cheeks, but he did not seek to move away.

"Papa tells me Mr. Fielding is an actor. Is that really so?"

"Are you still being courteous?" she said, teasing him very gently. "You really would wish to speak of the one thing I am obsessed with myself? Or are you trying to make me feel at ease, just as I am with you? If so, you are remarkably sophisticated for one so early in his career. You will be an enormous success in society. Ladies will love you."

He blushed scarlet. He opened his mouth to say something and quite obviously could think of nothing adequate. His eyes were shining, and it was a moment before she realized he was making an intense effort to look only at her face, not even for an instant to allow his gaze to slide as far as her neck or shoulder, let alone the smooth skin above her bosom.

Mr. Marchand cleared his throat as if about to speak, then said nothing.

Mrs. Marchand blinked.

Caroline was aware of an oppressive silence. The sudden crackling of the fire was almost explosive.

"Yes, he is an actor," she said more abruptly than she intended. "Do you like the theatre? I expect you are studying plays in your schoolwork?"

"Oh yes," he agreed. "But mostly Shakespeare, I'm afraid. Nothing very modern. That is all very . . . well, some of it is outrageous. Oh! I'm sorry. I didn't mean to imply that Mr. Fielding . . ."

"Of course you didn't," she agreed quickly. "I expect Shakespeare was considered outrageous in his time, at least by some."

"Do you think so?" He looked hopeful. "It all seems so . . .

historical! Sort of . . . safe . . . the histories happened . . . and we know they did."

She laughed. "I expect even Mr. Ibsen will be a classic one day, and perfectly 'safe' as well." She knew that was what Joshua would have said. "And we don't know what really happened in the histories, only what Shakespeare told us for the sake of his drama."

He was surprised. "Do you think it wasn't true?" It was obviously a new thought to him. "I suppose it doesn't have to be, does it? Maybe there was no one to stop libel and blasphemy then." He was frowning. "Only it wasn't, of course . . . I mean, not Shakespeare. Maybe all the things that were have been stopped . . . either by some censorship, or because we learned they were untrue, so we didn't watch them anymore."

"I should think it is more likely we became so used to them, we now believe they are the truth," she replied, and then instantly wondered if perhaps she was speaking too freely. He was only a child, after all. "You may well be right," she amended. "In the long run we are fairly competent judges of what is good." She hoped Joshua would forgive her for such arrant nonsense. "What are you studying?"

"Julius Caesar," he said instantly.

"Marvelous!" she responded. "My favorite . . . except that all the characters that matter are men."

He looked surprised.

"How about Hamlet? You would appreciate that, and perhaps understand him." She was certain he would be familiar with the great scenes, if not with all of it. "And one must surely feel a terrible pity for Ophelia?"

He was startled, then embarrassed, and there was a fleeting moment when she thought she saw revulsion in his eyes, then it was gone again. "Oh . . . yes." But he looked away, the blood pink in his cheeks. "Of course." He struggled for something else to say, away from a subject that apparently disturbed him.

Ralph Marchand moved very slightly.

Caroline sensed she was treading on ground full of unknown

fears and assumptions, far too dangerous to continue when she knew him so little.

"Perhaps in the future," she said lightly. She turned to Mrs. Marchand. "I hear there is a new political satire. I am not sure whether I wish to see it or not. Sometimes they are so obvious there is no point, and other times they are so abstruse I have no idea what the point is."

The tension dissipated. They talked for a few minutes longer on harmless subjects. Lewis, having paid his respects to the visitor, excused himself, leaving the adults to go in to dinner.

It was a very traditional meal, unsurprising but excellently cooked. It took Caroline into the safety of the past, when so much had been familiar with all the reassurance of the knowledge that she understood it, that she knew the questions and the answers and was certain of her own place. Now there were countless situations where she had to think harder, weigh her responses. She seemed to spend half her time struggling to say something appropriate, trying to keep her balance between being true to her beliefs and yet not sounding insensitive, old-fashioned and exhibiting precisely that bigotry her new friends despised. Although it was Joshua who really mattered. How much did she disappoint him? He was too innately kind to look for fault or to express criticism where it could do no good. The very knowledge of that brought a sudden closing of her throat, and she rushed into speech to drive it away.

Mrs. Marchand was talking about censorship. Behind her, her husband's face was dark, his body tense as he listened.

". . . and we have to protect the innocent from the darkness of mind which can so easily injure them permanently," she was saying.

"Darkness of mind?" Caroline had not heard the beginning and did not know to what she referred.

Mrs. Marchand leaned forward a little across the table, the pearl embroidery on her gown catching the light. "My dear, take that play we saw the other evening, just for one example. It is amazing what can become acceptable if one sees it often

127

enough, and in public. There are ideas which you and I would find appalling and which undermine all the values we most cherish, and if we were among our trusted friends we would all feel free to express our outrage when they are mocked or violated." Her face was creased with earnestness. "And yet when it is done with wit and we are made to laugh, it feels different. No one wishes to seem without humor, to be pompous or out-of-date. We all laugh. No one looks at anyone else. No one knows who is really embarrassed or offended. And sooner or later we become used to whatever it is, and it no longer offends us. It becomes more and more difficult to say anything. We feel isolated, as if the whole tide of what everyone thinks has moved on and left us behind, alone."

Caroline knew precisely what she meant. She was correct. One grows less sensitive to vulgarity, to coarseness of thought or perception, even to witness of other people's pain. The initial shock wears off. Anger finally dies.

And yet she heard herself saying what she knew Joshua would have were he there.

"Of course it does. That is why we must constantly explore the boundaries and find new ways to say things, precisely so people will not become used to them and no longer care."

Mr. Marchand frowned. "I am not sure that I follow you. What new things must we say?"

Her husband set down his wineglass, his expression tightly controlled, his eyes very steady. "I admit to being old-fashioned. I believe the ideals of my father and grandfather were high, and I have no desire to see them questioned, let alone flouted," he replied. "They believed a man was bound by his honor, and his word, once given, was unbreakable." His voice warmed. "They held duty sacred, thought of others before self, service the highest calling. They treated all women with gentleness, and those of their family they were not only bound to protect from all violence, coarseness of thought or word, or vulgarity, but it was their pleasure as well. Surely that is what love is, the desire above all things, no matter at what cost to oneself, to protect and make life joyous and rich

128

and safe for them?" He looked at her earnestly, his blue eyes unclouded.

Caroline thought of Edward, and of Samuel Ellison, and heard Joshua's voice in her ears. Oddly enough, she also heard Pitt.

"It is a kind of love," she answered gently. "Is it what you would wish for yourself?"

A shadow crossed his face. "I beg your pardon?"

"Is it the kind of love you would wish extended towards yourself?"

"My dear, our circumstances are entirely different," he said patiently. "It is my place to protect, not to be protected. Women are uniquely vulnerable. If they become coarsened by what is violent and destructive in life, what devalues innocence, reverence for the beautiful and precious, for intimacy and the finer emotions, they pass it on to our children, and then what is there left for anyone? There must be some hallowed place where there is no mockery of the sacred, no belittling of tenderness, no willingness to injure or take advantage, where the spiritual always outweighs the carnal."

Caroline felt a strange, painful mixture of shame and frustration, and at the same time, of comfort.

"Of course there must," she agreed wholeheartedly. "I wish I knew how to keep it without at the same time closing my eyes to everything that is uncomfortable or questioning. How can I keep innocence and yet also grow up rather than remain a child? How can I fight for what is good if I have no idea what is evil?"

"You should not have to fight, my dear," he said with intense feeling, leaning toward her, his face very earnest. "You should be protected from such things! That is society's duty, and if those whose charge and whose privilege it is were honoring their callings, then the question would never arise. As it is, the Lord Chamberlain is gravely remiss, and there is all manner of dangerous—deeply dangerous—material around." He stared at Caroline, faint spots of color in his cheeks.

"You can have no concept of how terrible some of it is. I

pray God you never do!" His face tightened. "The damage is irreparable."

"He certainly does not do enough," Mrs. Marchand agreed, turning to him with a pucker between her brows. "I think you should write to him, my dear, say that many of us are deeply concerned about the openness of very private emotions expressed on the stage, which may suggest to susceptible minds that women in general may be possessed of the kind of . . . of appetites indicated by Miss Antrim's character—"

"I already have, my dear," he interrupted.

She relaxed a little, her shoulders easing, a slight smile returning to her lips. "I'm so glad. Think of the kind of effect, the fearful notions, that could place in the minds of young men . . . like . . . like Lewis! How could he, or they, grow up with the tenderness and respect towards their wives and daughters, not to say mothers, that one would desire?"

Caroline understood only too easily what she meant. It was not herself she thought of, but her own daughters. She remembered with grief, even now, so many years afterwards, how Sarah had suffered, before her death, the fear and the disillusion in her husband because of his behavior. Any censorship at all was better than the misery they had endured then.

"Of course," she concurred, but there was a small voice nagging at the back of her mind, one that condemned cowardice and told her she was sacrificing honesty for comfort. She quelled it and continued with her dinner, although she was aware that Mrs. Marchand had been far more easily reassured than her husband. He had been gentle with her, wanting to give her a comfort he himself could not share.

When she arrived home, Joshua was in the withdrawing room, sitting in the large chair he liked best, a book open in his lap and the gaslight turned high so he could read. It caught the few strands of silver in his brown hair and the shadows of weariness around his eyes. He closed the book and smiled at her, rising to his feet slowly.

"Nice evening with the Marchands?" He came towards her

and kissed her lightly on the cheek. She felt the warmth of him and the very slight smell of stage makeup, and that indefinable odor of the theatre: sweat, excitement, fabric, paint. Ten years ago it would have been as alien to her as a foreign land. Now it had familiarity, a host of memories of laughter and passion. She realized with a rush of confusion how much she was still as sharply in love with Joshua as if she were a girl and this were her first real romance. It was absurd, ludicrous in a woman of her age. It made her unbearably vulnerable.

"Yes, very pleasant," she answered, forcing herself to smile brightly, as if it were all quite casual. "I met their son for the first time. A very shy boy." She walked on past him towards the fire. It was not really cold outside, but she was shivering a little. And she was unprepared for the intimacy of retiring to bed. Her mind was still busy with conflicting thoughts, Edward and the past, Samuel Ellison's smile, his stories, Hope Marchand's fear of the depiction of new ideas, the passion to protect the young from the intrusion of violence and degradation of things they needed to believe in as pure, and Ralph Marchand's longer sight and far deeper fear of things to come. He was right in believing that when you lost the ability to feel reverence, you lost almost everything.

She thought of her own daughters when they had been young. Joshua would not understand that; he had no children. The need to protect was so deep it was far more elemental than thought or reason, it was at the core of life. And it was so much more than merely physical . . . it was a need to nurture all that was of beauty in the heart, that gave happiness. Who wanted her child alive but incapable of faith in the essential value of love, honor or joy?

"Caroline?" There was an edge of anxiety in Joshua's voice. He had sensed the distance she had placed between them.

She swung around to face him, and emotion overtook her. She saw confusion in him also, and tiredness after the mental and physical effort of a performance, and yet his concern was for her. She felt utterly selfish. What did the issues of censorship, or what the Marchands thought about it, matter tonight?

"Silly dinner conversation." She dismissed it with a smile, stepping forward into his arms. It was still easier to hold him than to meet his eyes. She felt his slightness and his strength. He was very gentle. It was far too late to wonder about whether she had made the right decision in marrying him, whether she was absurd or not. She could either go with her heart or deny it. Nothing would change the commitment inside her.

But in the morning censorship mattered very much. She saw it in Joshua's face even before her eye caught it in the newspapers.

"What is it?" she asked, a lurch of alarm inside her. "What has happened?"

He held up the paper. "They've taken off Cecily's play! Banned it!" He sounded stunned, defeated. There were pink spots of color in his cheeks.

She did not understand. "How can they? The Lord Chamberlain gave it a license . . ." She stopped. She did not understand the details of the process, but the principle was clear. Something in his face held her. "What?"

"It isn't quite . . . like that." He bit his lip. "He would never have given it a license," he admitted. "Because it would raise questions, make some people uncomfortable." He shrugged very slightly. "There are ways around that—submit the script late and hope he'll not read it carefully . . . that seldom works because he's clever enough to suspect anything presented that way and read it extra carefully. The other is to perform a new play under the title of an old one that already has a license. That's what they did this time. . . ."

"But they'd all have to know!" she protested. "The theatre manager in particular!"

"They do. Bellmaine is as keen as Cecily. He's prepared to take the chance, pay the fine if he has to. It's worth it to say the things you really believe in, to ask the questions, shake the damnable complacency! If we could stir public opinion, we could reform all manner of laws that are antiquated, unjust." He leaned forward a little, the flush in his cheeks deepening. "More than that, alter the attitudes that are beyond the

132

law, the prejudices that wound . . . and cripple. Can't you see how . . . how terrible this is? Some censorship is absurd. Did you know we aren't even allowed to represent a clergyman onstage—at all. Not even sympathetically! How can we question anything?"

"Will it change Lord Warriner's bill?" she asked quietly.

"Ever the practical," he said with a rueful little smile. "Do you want women to be able to institute divorce for neglect or unhappiness?" His face was unreadable, wry, humorous, sad, uncertain.

"I don't know," she said honestly. "I never even thought about it until I saw the play. But surely that's the point. I should have."

He stretched across the table and laid his hand lightly over hers, barely touching her. "Yes, it is the point. And yes, it probably will affect it. Warriner may well lose his nerve. Too many of his friends will lose theirs. They will have felt which way the wind blows, and retreat."

"I'm sorry," she said quietly, raising her head and closing her fingers over his. She remained like that for a moment, then withdrew and picked up the newspaper from where he had left it.

Farther down on the page from the article on the closure of the play was a letter from Oscar Wilde, eloquent, witty and informed, with the same outrage Joshua felt. He wrote of censorship as an act of oppression of the mind, performed by cowards who were as much afraid of what was within themselves as anything others might say.

"The thing I resent most of all," Joshua said, his eyes still on her, "is not the restriction in what I may or may not say, but what I may or may not listen to! What monumental arrogance makes the Lord Chamberlain believe he has the right to dictate whether I shall listen to this or that man's views on faith and religion? I may find I agree with him! Where does the whole concept of blasphemy come from?"

"From the Bible," she replied quietly. "There are many people to whom it is a very real offense to speak mockingly or vulgarly of God."

"Whose God?" he asked, searching her eyes.

For a moment she was at a loss.

"Whose God?" he repeated. "Yours? Mine? The vicar's? The man next door? Anybody's?"

She drew in her breath to reply, thinking she knew exactly what she was going to say, then realized like a shaft of light in darkness that she did not. There were probably as many ideas of God as there were people who gave the matter a thought. It had never occurred to her before.

"Isn't there . . . some sort of consensus . . . at least . . ." She tailed off. They had never discussed religion before. She knew his morality but not his faith, not the deep, unspoken part that governed his heart. They had never even discussed his heritage of Judaism, even though he made little outwardly of it now. But perhaps it was still part of him if you touched a nerve?

As if reading her thoughts, he looked at her with a twisted smile. "Didn't they crucify Christ for blasphemy?" he said softly. "I would have thought as a Christian you would have a certain tolerance towards blasphemers."

"No, you wouldn't," she contradicted him, a little catch in her voice. Suddenly they were speaking of such fierce reality. "You know better than that; we have almost no tolerance at all. We are perfectly happy to burn one another for a difference of opinion, let alone outsiders of a different religion altogether."

"You are more likely to burn each other than outsiders," he pointed out. "But new ideas do find their way in every now and then, through the bloodshed, the smoke and the fury. It used to be a sin unto death for ordinary people to read the Bible; now we are encouraged to. Somebody had to be the first to challenge that monumental piece of censorship. Now we all accept that the whole concept of denying God's word was monstrous."

"Well . . . perhaps I don't mind about blasphemy," she said reluctantly, thinking of the Marchands again. "But what about obscenity? As well as the good that new ideas can do, what about the harm?"

Before he could answer her the door flew open and the old lady stumped in, banging her cane on the floor.

Joshua rose to his feet automatically. "Good morning, Mrs. Ellison. How are you?"

She drew in her breath deeply. "As well as can be expected," she replied.

He pulled out her chair and assisted her to be seated before returning to his own place.

Caroline offered her tea and toast, which she accepted.

"What harm are you talking about?" She reached for the butter and black cherry preserve. Her appetite was excellent, although this morning she did look a little paler than usual.

Joshua's eyes barely flickered to Caroline before he answered. "There is an article about censorship in the newspapers—" he began.

"Good!" she interrupted, swallowing her toast half eaten in order to speak. "Far too much is said without regard to decency these days. It never was when I was young. The world today is filled with vulgarity. It degrades all of us. I am glad I am at the end of my life." She reached for the butter and helped herself. "At least someone cares enough to fight for standards of a sort."

"It is a protest against censorship," Caroline corrected her, and then instantly wondered if it would not have been a great deal wiser to have allowed the subject to drop.

"Some actress, I suppose." Mrs. Ellison raised her eyebrows. "There seems to be nothing women will not say or do these days, and in public for all to see." She looked at Caroline meaningfully. "Morality is on the decline everywhere— even where one would least expect."

"You agree with censorship?" If Joshua was angry he masked it so well no one would have guessed it. But then acting was his profession, and he was very good at it. Caroline reminded herself of that quite often.

The old lady stared at him as if he had questioned her sanity.

"Of course I do!" she responded indignantly. "Any sane and civilized person knows there are some things you cannot

135

say without corrupting our entire way of life. Where there is no reverence for things which are sacred, for the home and all it embodies, no safety for the mind, then the entire nation begins to crumble. Did they not teach you history wherever you come from? You must have heard of Rome?"

Joshua kept his temper superbly. There was even a shadow of amusement in his eyes.

"London," he replied. "I come from London, the other side of the river, five miles away from here. And certainly I have heard of Rome, and of Egypt, and Babylon, and Greece and Inquisitorial Spain. So far as I know, Greece had the best theatre, although Egypt had some excellent poetry."

"They were heathens." The old lady dismissed them with a flick of her hand, perilously close to the milk jug. "The Greeks had all sorts of gods who behaved appallingly, if the stories we hear are to be believed. And the Egyptians were worse. They worshipped animals. If you can imagine such a thing!"

"There was one pharaoh who set up his own new religion believing in and worshipping only one God," Joshua told her with a smile.

She looked startled. "Oh . . . well, I daresay that is a step forward. It didn't last, though, did it?"

"No," he agreed. "They accused him of blasphemy and obliterated everything he had done."

She glared at him. It was a moment before she recovered her thought. "You weren't talking about blasphemy. You said 'obscene.' "

"That's a matter of view as well," he argued. "What is beautiful to one may be obscene to another."

"Nonsense!" Her face was flushed pink. "Every decent person knows what is obscene, intrusive into other people's private lives and feelings, and where it is unforgivable to trespass, and only the most vulgar and depraved would wish to."

"Of course there are—" he began.

"Good!" The word was like a trap closing. "Then that is the end of the subject. My tea is cold. Will you be good enough to send for some more." It was a command, not a request.

136

Caroline rang the bell. She could see the anger inside Joshua, barely suppressed by a thin veneer of courtesy because of the old lady's age, and because she had been Caroline's mother-in-law and she was a guest in their home, however unwillingly.

Caroline found herself saying what she knew Joshua wished to. "Everybody agrees there are things which should not be said, the disagreement is as to which things they are."

"All things that flout morality and disregard the decent sensibilities of men and women," Mariah Ellison said flatly. "You may have lost sight of what they are, but most of us have not. Ask any of those who used to be your friends. Thank God the Lord Chamberlain knows."

Caroline held her tongue with difficulty, and only because she knew the pointlessness of arguing any further.

The maid came and was sent for fresh tea. Joshua rose and excused himself, kissing Caroline on the cheek and wishing the old lady a pleasant day.

Caroline picked up the newspaper again and looked at an article about Cecily Antrim. Above it, there was a sketch of her from a playbill, looking beautiful and intense. It was that which first caught her attention.

Yesterday Miss Cecily Antrim protested vigorously against the Lord Chamberlain's censorship of her new play, *The Lady's Love,* which is not now to be performed, because of its indecency and the tendency to degrade public morality and cause distress and outrage.

Miss Antrim marched up and down the Strand carrying a placard and causing a nuisance, until the police were called to oblige her to desist. She claimed afterwards that the play was a valid work of art questioning misconceptions about women's feelings and beliefs. She said that refusing to allow it to be performed was to deny women the freedom granted men to explore a far better understanding of those sides of their nature which are profound, and often the wellspring of controversial acts.

Mr. Wallace Albright, for the Lord Chamberlain's office,

said the play would be likely to undermine the values upon which our society is founded, and it would not be in the public good for it to be performed.

Miss Antrim has not been charged with affray, and was permitted to return to her home.

Caroline sat staring at the page. She was filled with an unreasonable anger, but it was confused, veering one way and then the other. Why should one man be able to decide what people may see or not see? Who was he? What manner of man? What were his prejudices and secrets, his fears or dreams? Did he see threat where there was simply intelligent enquiry, a challenge to bigotry and to one person's dominion over another's thoughts and beliefs?

Or was he protecting the young or vulnerable against the assaults of pornography and violence, the coarsening effects upon sensibility of seeing abuse of others portrayed as acceptable, the eroding of values because they were mocked and made fun of, until it took more courage to espouse gentleness and reverence than it did to deny it?

She looked across the table at the old lady's face, set in lines of bitterness, and saw also something she thought for a moment was fear. It was profoundly disturbing; it aroused in her fears of her own, and something far too like pity.

7

THE CONSTABLE STOOD in front of Pitt in his office, very much to attention.

"Yes sir, that's wot 'e said."

It was early morning, the sun hazy gold outside, warm on the walls and the stones of the street, only a little dimmed by the smoke of countless chimneys. The air was dry and mild, pungent with the smells of the city.

"He saw Orlando Antrim and Delbert Cathcart quarreling the day of Cathcart's death," Pitt repeated. "You are sure?"

"Yes sir, I am. That's wot 'e said, an' seems there were no shaking 'im from it."

"Presumably he is acquainted with both men, this . . . what's his name?"

"Hathaway, sir. Peter Hathaway. I dunno, sir, 'cept I reckon 'e must be, or 'ow would 'e know 'oo they are? Two gents quarrelin' could be anybody."

"Precisely. Where do I find this Mr. Hathaway?"

"Arkwright Road, sir, 'Ampstead. Number twenty-six."

"And he reported this to Bow Street?" Pitt was surprised.

"No sir, 'Ampstead. They told us . . . by telephone." The constable lifted his head a little higher. He was proud of new technology and had great hopes of its use in catching criminals—even in preventing crime before it occurred.

"I see." Pitt rose to his feet. "Well, I suppose I had better go and talk to Mr. Hathaway."

"Yes sir. Maybe this Mr. Antrim is our man, sir, seein' as

139

'ow they was quarrelin' real violent, like." He looked hopeful, his eyes wide and bright.

"Perhaps," Pitt agreed with a sharp sense of disappointment. He had admired Orlando Antrim; there was something likable about him, a sensitivity, an acuteness of perception. But it would not be the first time Pitt had liked someone who was capable of killing another person. "Inform Sergeant Tellman where I've gone, will you?" he said from the door.

When Pitt reached Arkwright Road he was told by the housemaid that young Mr. Hathaway was not at home. It was a fine day, and he had gone out with his camera, no doubt to his club, and if the gentlemen were on a field trip, that could be anywhere at all. However, after a little probing, she gave him the address of the place where they met, and the doorman there in turn told him that today the members of the club had taken a trip to the nearby heath in order to practice photographing natural scenery.

"Very big on natural scenery, they are," he added approvingly. "Take some lovely pictures. Fair lifts yer spirits to see them."

Pitt thanked him and walked back towards Hampstead Heath to begin the search for the camera club and Mr. Peter Hathaway. Of course, whatever Hathaway had seen was only indicative. People could quarrel without its leading to violence of any sort, let alone to murder. But Cathcart's death was a melodramatic crime, one perpetrated by a person of high emotion and a great deal of imagination, and presumably a familiarity with art, to mimic Millais's painting of Ophelia so closely. Unless that had been accidental, not a copying so much as another person with the same passion expressing it in the same, fairly elemental way.

It was pleasant walking in the sun over the dry, springy grass, the wind barely rustling the leaves, the smell of earth in the air instead of smoke and manure and dusty stone. There were birds singing, not the ever-present sparrows but what sounded like blackbirds, their song high, persistent and sweet.

He saw a young man and woman half lying on the ground, her skirts billowing around her, a picnic basket near them, as yet unopened. They had been laughing together, she flirting, he showing off a little. They stopped and looked up as Pitt approached them.

"Excuse me," Pitt apologized. He would far rather have been doing as they were, savoring the last echoes of summer, enjoying the moment with no thought of yesterday or tomorrow, than caring who killed Delbert Cathcart, or why.

When Charlotte came home from Paris he would take a day off, and the two of them would go out into the country sunshine, just wander around doing nothing in particular. It would not be difficult, and trains were cheap if you did not go too far.

"Yes?" the young man asked, politely enough.

"Have you seen a group of men go past carrying cameras?" Pitt enquired.

It was the girl who answered. "About half an hour ago. Ever so serious they was, all talking together."

"Which way did they go?"

She looked at him to see if he was carrying a camera as well, and was puzzled when there was none visible.

"I'm looking for a friend," Pitt said somewhat lamely. "Which way did they go?"

She was not sufficiently interested to pursue her curiosity. "That way." She pointed across the swell of grass towards a clump of trees, gnarled roots writhing above the earth in intricate and beautiful form.

"Thank you." He nodded briefly and set off as directed.

It took him twenty minutes longer, and he was hot and out of breath when he saw the group of a dozen young men dressed in jackets, waistcoats, trousers, and all but two in bowler hats as well. Every one of them had his share of equipment, including a variety of leather cases and boxes from less than a cubic foot in size to ones large enough to have carried clothes for a weekend, and boots to go with them. Tripods straddled the grass with a strange, angular kind of elegance.

141

Cameras balanced on top of them with lenses pointing intently at a bough or a branch, or some interesting formation of wood and leaf.

"Good morning," Pitt interrupted their concentration.

No one answered.

"Excuse me!" he tried a little more loudly.

The nearest young man turned, startled by the intrusion. "Sir!" he said, holding up his hand as if to stop traffic. "Unless you are in urgent need of assistance, pray do not interrupt this moment. The light is just so."

Pitt looked to where they all seemed to be staring, and indeed the rays of the sun shone through the leaves of a great oak with a remarkable luminescence, but he doubted it would translate into anything so spectacular without the green and gold of reality. How could mere sepia tint be worth anything after what the eye had seen? Nevertheless he waited while twelve cameras clicked and squeaked and generally recorded the instant.

"Yes sir," the young man said at last. "Now, what may we do for you? Do you wish your photograph taken? Or you are perhaps an enthusiast yourself, and you wish to join us? Bring us some of your work, and we will make our decision. We are very generous, I assure you. We desire only to increase our art, enlarge the boundaries of what may be achieved. Colors will be next, you know." His voice rose excitedly. "I mean real colors! Reds—blues—greens—everything!"

"Will they?" For a moment Pitt's mind was taken with the idea. First he thought of the beauty of it, then hard on its heels he thought of the police use. If photographs could be taken of things shown in the color they really were, then the possibilities were limitless, not just to identify people, but to trace stolen goods—paintings, works of art, all the sort of things in Delbert Cathcart's home. Verbal descriptions never did justice to them. Police constables were not meant to be poets. "That will be marvelous," he agreed. "But I came to speak to Mr. Hathaway. He is a member, I believe?"

"Oh yes, very good, he is; in fact, most talented." He very nearly asked what Pitt wanted, and curbed his inquisitiveness only just in time. He inclined his head towards a young man with rather long fair hair who was still gazing with rapt attention at the light on the branches. "That's Hathaway over there."

"Thank you," Pitt acknowledged, and strode off before he could be further drawn into enthusiasm for the photographic inventions of the future.

Hathaway looked up as Pitt's shadow fell across his camera.

"I'm sorry," Pitt apologized. "Are you Peter Hathaway?"

"Yes. Is there something I can do for you?"

"Superintendent Pitt, from the Bow Street station," Pitt explained, handing him his card.

"Oh!" Hathaway looked serious. He swallowed hard. "Is it about that report I made to the local police? Look, could we discuss it a little farther off?" He gestured rather wildly with his free arm. "Would you mind fearfully pretending it is a business matter or something? It is sort of . . . well . . . delicate. I don't want people to think I'm some kind of busybody who goes around repeating everything he knows. It's just that . . . well . . . with Cathcart dead, and all that . . . you know?" A flicker of distress crossed his face. "He was a damn decent photographer. Almost the best, I'd say. Can't let him be killed and do nothing about it . . . not when I saw the quarrel."

"Tell me exactly what you did see, Mr. Hathaway," Pitt encouraged him. "First of all, where did this happen? Set the scene for me, if you like."

"Ah . . . yes. Well, it was the Tuesday before he was killed, as I said." Hathaway thought hard, re-creating it in his mind, his eyes almost closed. "We were by the Serpentine, trying to catch the early light on the water, so we were there about eight o'clock. A bit inconvenient, certainly, but one has to follow nature, you can't lead it. We did some excellent work, really excellent." He looked away quickly. "You've no idea how blind one can be to the glories of light and shade, the intricacies of form, until you see them through a lens. You really do see the world through a new eye. Pardon the obvious, but it's true. You should take up photography, sir, you really should! Bit expensive, I suppose, but most pleasures are, and without the artistic merit or the truly spiritual uplift of catching a moment of nature's glory and immortalizing it to share with all mankind." His voice increased in enthusiasm. "It's a window in time, sir. A kind of immortality."

Pitt could not help catching a glimpse of what Hathaway meant. It was true, a photograph far more than any painting caught the moment and made it, if not eternal, at least of unimaginable duration. But Delbert Cathcart had been a great photographer, and an ordinary, mortal man, and he was dead. It was Pitt's duty to find out how and why, and by whose hand. There might be time for thoughts of capturing beauty later on.

"It is marvelous," he agreed. "I don't suppose you took any photographs of Mr. Cathcart and Mr. Antrim while they were there?"

For a moment Hathaway's face fell with disappointment that Pitt should think of something so mundane, but he was too much of an enthusiast to miss the point. Interest flared up in his eyes and his face brightened. "Oh, if only I had! What a wonderful thing that would be, wouldn't it? Unarguable evidence. It will come, sir! It will come. The camera is a witness whose testimony no one can doubt. Oh, the future is full of wonders we can barely imagine. Just think of—"

"What was Mr. Cathcart doing at the Serpentine?" Pitt interrupted. Speculation on the marvels of the future could go on indefinitely, and fascinating as it was, it was a luxury he could not afford now.

"Er . . . I don't know." Hathaway sounded surprised. "Actually, when I think of it, it was quite odd. As far as I know, he only takes portraits. He wasn't there to teach us . . . which would have been marvelous, of course. But he didn't speak to us at all. I imagine he was looking at places to use for backdrop. That's all that would make sense."

"But you did see him?"

"Oh yes, quite clearly."

"Did you speak to him?"

"No. No, it would have been . . . intrusive. He is a—was a—very great man . . . something of an idol to an amateur

144

like me." He flushed slightly as he said it. "It is a most awful thing that he should have been killed, an act of barbarism. That's what makes it so hard to understand. But great artists can be volatile. Perhaps it was over a woman?"

"Maybe. What was Orlando Antrim doing here? Is he an amateur photographer?"

"Oh yes, really quite good, you know. Of course he also prefers figures, but one would expect that. After all, drama is his art."

"Tell me exactly what you saw, Mr. Hathaway."

A couple of young men walked past them carrying their cameras and tripods and talking to each other excitedly, their voices raised, trying to gesticulate with arms weighed down by their equipment. The bowler hat of one of them had been knocked to a rakish angle, but he seemed quite unaware of it. They disappeared into the shade of a tree, propped their tripods and began looking at the area with interest.

"I saw them arguing," Hathaway answered, frowning. "Antrim seemed to be pleading with Cathcart, trying to persuade him of something. He appeared very emphatic about it, waving his hands around."

"Did you hear what he said?"

"No." His eyes widened. "No, that's the odd thing. Neither of them raised their voices at all. I knew they were quarreling because of the furious gestures and the anger in their faces. Antrim was trying to persuade Cathcart to do something, and Cathcart kept refusing more and more vehemently, until finally Antrim stormed off in a rage."

"But Cathcart remained?"

"Only for a few moments. Then he picked up his camera and snapped his tripod closed and went off as well."

"In the same direction?"

"More or less. But then they would. It was towards the road and the natural way out."

"Did anyone else observe this exchange?"

"I don't know. One does tend to get rather absorbed in what one is doing. I'm afraid I have lost a few friends because of my obsession. I noticed them because I was at that moment casting my eye around for a particular pattern against which to take a picture of one of my friends, a young lady with fair hair. I imagined clothing her in white and having her stand looking—"

Pitt smiled, but interrupted his explanation.

"Yes, I understand. You have been very helpful, Mr. Hathaway. Is there anything else you can tell me about this encounter? Have you seen the two together on any other occasion? Do you know either of them personally—as members of the club, perhaps?"

Hathaway lifted his shoulders in a shrug. "I'm so sorry. I've only been a member a short time. I know perhaps three or four of the other fellows: Crabtree, Worthing, Ullinshaw, Dobbs, that's about all. Dobbs has the most wonderful knack with light on stones and fences and things, and he's so good with birds." His voice rose again with excitement. "He's the first one who showed me film on a roll, rather than plates. It was absolutely marvelous. You have no idea! A Mr. Eastman in America invented it. Twenty feet long." He gestured with his hands. "All wound up so you can take a hundred pictures one after the other. Imagine it! One after the other . . . just like that. They are round, almost two and a half inches in diameter."

"Round?" Pitt said quickly. All the pictures he had seen in Cathcart's house had been rectangular, as had been the portraits in the houses of his clients.

"Yes." Hathaway smiled. "Of course that's amateurs. I know the professionals use the square ones, but these are pretty good, you know. When they are all done you send the whole camera back to them and they process the film and return you the camera reloaded. It all costs about five guineas." He looked a trifle uncomfortable. "As I said, it is rather expensive. But I'd rather do that than any other pastime I can think of." He jutted his chin out defiantly, daring Pitt to say he was wasting money.

"That is most interesting," Pitt said quite sincerely. "Thank you for your candor, Mr. Hathaway, and your instruction. If anything else occurs to you, please let me know. Good day."

Pitt spoke to every other member of the camera club, but no one else could help. One young man had seen the quarrel but could only describe the participants, he did not know them by name.

"Oh yes," he agreed vehemently. "Very heated. I thought at one moment they would come to blows, but the taller young man stalked off, leaving the other very red in the face and mighty uncomfortable."

Nothing Pitt asked could elicit anything more, except numerous details on the marvels of photography, the newest technical advances, the miracle of Mr. Eastman's roll of film—although it could apparently be used only outside and in natural daylight, which explained largely why Delbert Cathcart, who frequently worked in subdued light or inside a room, still worked with the old plates.

The club members were all male, and it had not occurred to them as worthy of comment that there were no women among them, but they were ardent in their admiration for female photographers, and not the least hesitant in accounting them great artists in their field, and indeed possessing an excellent and comprehensive grasp of the techniques involved as well. Their thoughts did not advance Pitt's detection in the slightest, but in spite of himself he was interested.

From Hampstead, Pitt went to seek Orlando Antrim. The next necessary step would be to ask him what the quarrel had been about and where and when he had last seen Cathcart. Pitt was dreading the moment when he might have to accuse him of the murder. But some confrontation was unavoidable.

He found Orlando at the theatre rehearsing his part in *Hamlet*, which he was due to play within a week.

Pitt was required to explain himself to the doorman and prove his identity before he was allowed in.

"They're in rehearsal," the old man said, fixing Pitt with a gimlet eye. "Don't you go interruptin' 'em, now! You wait till yer spoke to. Mr. Bellmaine'll tell you when it's your turn. Mustn't upset actors, isn't fair. Plainer than that, it isn't right."

Pitt acknowledged the stricture and obediently tiptoed along the dusty passages as he had been directed. After a few false starts, he eventually ended up in the wings of the huge stage, bare except for two embroidered screens and a chair. A tall lean man stood towards the front, perhaps a couple of yards from the orchestra pit and a little to the left. His cadaverous face was fired with emotion and he held one arm high as if hailing someone in the distance.

Then Pitt saw her, coming from the shadows of the wings opposite him into the light of the stage: Cecily Antrim, dressed in very ordinary gray-blue, a simple blouse and skirt with a slight bustle. Her hair was caught up untidily in a few pins, and yet it was extraordinarily flattering. It looked casual and youthful, full of energy.

"Ah, my dear!" the tall man said warmly. "Ready for Polonius's death. From the top. Where's Hamlet? Orlando!"

Orlando Antrim emerged from the wings behind his mother. He too was dressed in the most ordinary of clothes: trousers, a collarless shirt and a waistcoat which matched nothing. His boots were dusty and scuffed and his hair tousled. A look of fierce concentration darkened his face.

"Good. Good," the tall man said. Pitt assumed he was the Mr. Bellmaine the doorman had referred to. "Hamlet, from the right. Gertrude, you and I from the left. This is the arras in question. Let us begin." He led the way off the stage, his footsteps echoed across the boards, then he turned and walked back beside Cecily.

" 'He will come straight,' " he began. " 'Look you lay home to him . . .' " His voice sounded no more than a conversational level, and yet it filled the stage and the auditorium beyond. " 'Pray you, be round with him.' "

" 'Mother, Mother, Mother!' " Orlando called from the wings.

Cecily turned to Bellmaine. " 'I'll warrant you: Fear me not—withdraw, I hear him coming.' "

In a single, oddly graceful movement for one aping age, Bellmaine slipped behind the screen.

Orlando came onto the stage. " 'Now, Mother, what's the matter?' "

" 'Hamlet, thou hast thy father much offended,' " Cecily answered, her voice carrying the same considered music.

Orlando's face was strained, his eyes wide and dark. There was a harshness in him of emotion so tightly held in, and yet so tormented, he was at the edge of breaking. " 'Mother, you have my father much offended.' "

Pitt watched in fascination as people he had seen in totally different characters took on the roles familiar to every generation for nearly three hundred years. He had studied *Hamlet* in the schoolroom on Sir Arthur Desmond's estate. He had read the soliloquy himself with Matthew and pulled it apart to its separate elements. Yet in front of him it now became a story of people with lives as real as his own. He watched the queen's guilt, Polonius's death, Hamlet's torture, all created with voice and gestures on a bare stage and then shattered in an instant as the actors stopped, threw parts aside, and became themselves again.

"Too quick," Bellmaine criticized, looking at Orlando. "Your accusation blurs the words. Hamlet is in fury and indignation, but the audience still needs to hear the substance of his charge. You are too realistic."

Orlando smiled. "Sorry. Should I hesitate before 'heaven's face doth glow'?"

"Try it," Bellmaine agreed with enthusiasm. He turned to Cecily. "You are pleading. Guilt is angrier. You are trying too hard to win the audience's sympathy."

She shrugged an apology.

"Again," he ordered. "From Hamlet's entrance."

Pitt watched them go through it a second time, and a third, and a fourth. He marveled at their patience, and even more at the emotional energy that invested them with passion each time, picking up halfway through a scene, with its changing moods, and throwing themselves into it. Only twice did anyone need prompting, and then continuance was immediate. They seemed able to create the illusion of an entire world by

149

the power of their own belief, and yet to remember someone else's words and speak them as if they were their own.

Finally Bellmaine allowed them some respite, and for the first time Pitt noticed that several other actors and actresses had appeared, ready to rehearse their parts. He tried to imagine them in the costumes of a far earlier period, and see them as they would be in character. A young woman with fair hair and a high forehead he thought to be Ophelia, and as soon as the recognition came to him, he saw Delbert Cathcart obscenely splayed out in the punt, dressed in the green velvet gown in parody of ecstasy and death.

He rose to his feet from where he had been sitting on a pine box.

"Excuse me . . ."

"My dear fellow," Bellmaine said straightaway. "I can't be doing auditioning now. Go and see Mr. Jackson. He'll talk with you. If you can be prompt, come and go exactly as you are told, stay sober and only speak when you are spoken to, a guinea a week and you have begun your career on the stage." He smiled, and his whole countenance was illuminated with sudden charm. "You never know where it will lead. Tour with us in the provinces, get a small part and we'll pay you up to twenty-five shillings . . . thirty-five in time. Now be a good chap and go and look for Jackson. He's probably around at the back somewhere, scenery and lighting, don't you know."

Pitt smiled in spite of himself. "I'm not looking for a career on the stage, Mr. Bellmaine. I am from the Bow Street police station . . . Superintendent Pitt . . ."

Cecily looked up from the edge of the stage where she was sitting. "My goodness, it's the policeman friend of Joshua's. Polonius is alive and well, I assure you!" Since Bellmaine was standing between them, that was incontestable.

"I should hardly arrest Hamlet, ma'am," Pitt promised. "The nation would never forgive me."

"The world would not, Mr. Pitt," she answered. "But I am delighted you have such an excellent sense of priorities. We fluffed a few lines but our performance was hardly a crime." She sat back a little, hugging one knee. "What brings you here? Not my protest against the Lord Chamberlain, surely? Now, if you read my mind as to what I would like to do to the wretch, that may well be arrestable."

"I cannot arrest you until after you have done it, Miss Antrim," he pointed out, trying to hide his amusement. It was not a time for it, and yet it rose unbidden within him.

She understood far too quickly. Her face broke into a lovely smile. "How very kind of you. Thank you so much!"

Bellmaine stepped between them. "You have come for something, sir. Pray what is it? We cannot afford to stop for long. This may not appear much to you, but it is our living, and far harder than it seems."

Pitt turned to him. "It seems extremely hard, Mr. Bellmaine," he said honestly. "I have to speak to Mr. Antrim. I shall keep it as brief as possible. Is there a scene you can rehearse without him?"

"*Hamlet* without the Prince? You jest, sir? Ah . . . I suppose so. A little. Laertes, Ophelia! Come! We have no time to idle. Scene three. From the top, if you please. Begin . . . 'My necessaries are embarked' . . . pay attention!"

Pitt walked across the boards towards Orlando, his footsteps loud and solitary for a moment until the arrival of Laertes and Ophelia muffled them, and the drama began instantly with well-schooled voices and passion lit as if the whole story leading to it were barely dismissed the moment before.

"What is it?" Orlando asked with a frown. "Is it to do with the censorship thing? I protested, but quite peacefully."

"No, Mr. Antrim, it has nothing to do with censorship at all. As far as I know, you have broken no laws in this matter." He walked beside Orlando farther into the wings and behind the stage, where bare brick walls stretched up into the darkness out of sight and huge painted backdrops for a dozen different worlds hung or were stacked in layers.

"Then what?" Orlando faced him, standing with grace so deeply learned he did it without thought.

"Do you belong to a gentlemen's camera club near Hampstead?" Pitt asked.

"What?"

Pitt began to repeat the question.

"Yes!" Orlando interrupted. "Yes, I do . . . at least, I go there occasionally, not very often, but I do belong. Why?"

"Did you join them near the Serpentine last Tuesday quite early in the morning?" He watched Orlando's face, and was not sure in the uncertain light whether he saw him pale or not.

"Yes . . ." Orlando said guardedly. He swallowed and coughed. "Yes, I did. Why? Nothing unusual happened, so far as I am aware."

"You met a Mr. Delbert Cathcart there, and had a heated disagreement with him."

"No." He looked startled, as if the question had taken him completely by surprise. "You—you mean the photographer who was killed? If he was there I certainly didn't see him."

"But you were there?"

"Yes, of course I was there. It was an excellent morning, clear early light with a sort of whiteness to it, and not many people about. I didn't have to rehearse and I hadn't been too late the night before. Who told you Cathcart was there?"

"Do you know him?"

"No." The answer was very quick. Orlando's eyes did not leave Pitt's and they were unnaturally steady. But then he knew Cathcart had been murdered. Any normal man would be nervous. "No, I don't," he repeated. "He was a professional, one of the best, so everyone says. I am completely amateur. I just enjoy it. But I think I'll have to give it up. I haven't time."

Pitt could believe that without the slightest difficulty. He could not even imagine the amount of mental and emotional energy needed to play a role like Hamlet, let alone the physical endurance.

"You quarreled with someone that morning and left in some heat. If it was not Cathcart, who was it?" he asked.

Orlando flushed. He hesitated several moments before replying, and when he did so he looked away first.

"A friend," he said a touch defiantly. "A fellow I've known for a little while. I'd rather not get him concerned in this. It was a simple disagreement, that's all. I daresay it looked more violent than it was. There was no ill will, just a . . . a difference of opinion as to what was right. Not the sort of thing you would lose a friendship over, let alone come to blows."

Pitt disliked what he had to do, but to omit it would be irresponsible, even though he half believed Orlando.

"Others have identified the man as Cathcart, Mr. Antrim. If it was not he, then I need to verify that. The name of your friend?"

Orlando hesitated again, then his face set. "I'm sorry." He waited for a moment to gauge Pitt's reaction. He must have seen no yielding. "Actually he is out of town anyway, and I couldn't get in touch with him. So there would be no point in my giving you his name . . . or address."

"If he is out of town, Mr. Antrim, there would be no harm either, would there?" Pitt resumed.

"Well, yes there would. It might do his reputation some damage, and he would not be there to protect it."

"Mr. Antrim, all I wish to do is confirm that it was he you quarreled with the morning of the day Mr. Cathcart was killed, no more than that."

"Well, you cannot, because he is not here. But surely if a man of Cathcart's standing and reputation had been at the camera club, of all places, some other member would be able to confirm it?"

That was unarguably true. It was also true that they ought to be able to tell him the identity of the man Orlando Antrim had spoken with so passionately. Why should he wish to hide it?

"Then I shall have to ask there," Pitt accepted, looking very directly at Orlando. "No doubt they saw you as well, and if he is a member they will know his name. It would be a great deal easier if you were to tell me, but if I must draw it out by questioning other members, then I will do so."

Orlando looked acutely unhappy. "I see you are not going to let it go. It has no bearing on your case, I swear. It was a diplomat with the French Embassy . . . the situation is delicate . . ."

"Henri Bonnard," Pitt supplied.

Orlando stiffened, his chin jerking up a little, his eyes wide, but he did not speak.

"Where is he, Mr. Antrim?"

"I am not at liberty to say." Orlando's face set, hard and miserable, but completely resolute. It was apparent that he was not going to say anything further, no matter how hard he was pressed. "I have given my word."

Nothing Pitt said would change his mind.

Bellmaine was apparently through with the scene to his satisfaction, or else was no longer prepared to remain in ignorance as to what Pitt wanted with his principal actor. He came around the corner into the cluttered space where they were standing, his face sharp, his eyes going first to Orlando, then to Pitt.

" 'Art is long and life is short,' Superintendent," he said with a wry half smile. "If we really can be of help, then of course we are at your disposal. But if, on the other hand, it is not a matter of urgency or importance, perhaps we could now continue with *Hamlet*?" He looked very carefully at Orlando, perhaps to assess if he were in any way disturbed sufficiently to damage his concentration. He seemed moderately satisfied with what he saw. He turned back to Pitt, waiting for his answer.

Orlando seemed vaguely relieved that Bellmaine had come. Perhaps unconsciously, he moved a step closer to him.

Bellmaine put a hand on his shoulder. "Work, my prince," he said, still facing Pitt. "If the superintendent will allow?"

There was nothing further to be gained. He was breaking their rhythm of creation for no good reason.

"Of course," he yielded. "Thank you for your time."

Orlando shrugged it off.

Bellmaine spread his hands in an eloquent and graceful gesture, then led the way back to the stage, where everyone was waiting for them. Pitt took one last look at the actors as they took up their own world again and lost themselves in it, then he turned and walked away.

* * *

154

He saw Tellman briefly and told him what little he had learned.

"That embassy's hiding something," Tellman replied, sitting in the chair at the other side of Pitt's paper-strewn desk. "I still think it's got something to do with them. There's only Mrs. Geddes that says the body was Cathcart. Maybe it isn't? Maybe it is the Frenchman. The whole thing looks more like actors and foreigners anyway."

"It looks more like passion than greed," Pitt answered. "But all sorts of people are capable of that, not only Frenchmen and eccentrics."

Tellman gave him a look of silent disdain.

"We'll go back to the embassy in the morning," Pitt conceded. "We need to know what happened to Henri Bonnard, even if it is only to exclude him from the investigation."

"Or what happened to Cathcart," Tellman added.

"I think we know what happened to him," Pitt said sadly. "He was murdered in his own house, and then sent down the Thames on a last, obscure journey. What I don't know is by whom, and exactly why."

Tellman did not answer.

However, Monsieur Villeroche was just as adamant as he had been the first time they saw him, only on this occasion he managed to conduct the meeting in the privacy of his own neat office.

"No! No, absolutely!" he repeated. "He has not returned nor sent any word, so far as I know, and I am at my wits' end to know what has happened to him." His face was pink, and he waved his hands jerkily to emphasize his distress. "It is now well over a week and there is no account of him at all. His work is piling up, and I am simply told not to worry. I am worried sick! Who would not be?"

"Have you been in contact with his family in France?" Pitt asked him.

"In France? No. They live in the south—Provence, I believe. He would hardly go all the way there without telling me. If a crisis arose it would be simple enough to ask for leave. The ambassador is not unreasonable."

Pitt did not pursue it. Tellman had already ascertained that Bonnard had not taken the packet boat across the Channel but had returned from Dover to London.

"Could it be a romantic affair?" he said instead.

Villeroche shrugged. "Then why not simply say so?" he asked reasonably. "He has not taken a normal leave of absence, a holiday, that is certain. What kind of a man pursues a secret romantic affair by abandoning his position, where he is trusted and respected, and disappearing into . . . God knows where? . . . and without a word to anyone?"

"A man who is pursuing someone he should not be," Pitt said with a slight smile. "A man in the grasp of a passion so intense he loses all sense of propriety or duty towards his colleagues."

"A man who does not desire to keep his position," Villeroche responded. "And thus be in a situation to afford to marry this secret love." He bit his lip. "So I suppose we must speak of an illicit affair, a woman who is already married or is the daughter of someone who does not find him an acceptable suitor. Or, I suppose, a woman of low class he could not marry? Or . . ." He did not name the last alternative, but both Pitt and Tellman knew what he was thinking.

"Is that likely?" Pitt asked, avoiding Tellman's eye. The green velvet gown was sharp in his memory.

Villeroche frowned. "No!" He was obviously surprised that it should even be considered. "Not in the least. I know that one seldom understands a person as well as one imagines, but Bonnard seemed as natural a man as any I know." He shook his head slightly. "But I wish you could find him. He was distressed before he left, laboring under some . . . some difficulty, some pressure, although I have no idea what. I am afraid some harm has come to him."

Pitt obtained a list of clubs and other places Bonnard frequented, and where he would almost certainly call were he in London. Then he thanked Villeroche and he and Tellman took their leave.

"Well, what do you reckon, then?" Tellman said as soon as they were out in the windy street again.

An omnibus clattered past them, women on the open top deck clasping their hats. A man on the footpath jammed his bowler on more firmly.

A newspaper seller shouted headlines about a government bill and the forthcoming visit of some minor royalty to London, doing his best to make it sound interesting. An elderly man smiled at him good-naturedly and shook his head, but he bought a newspaper and tucked it under his arm.

"Bless yer, guv!" the seller called after him.

Tellman was waiting, his face keen.

"I think we've got to look a great deal harder for Bonnard," Pitt said reluctantly. "It may be a romance that for some reason he had to keep in complete secrecy."

"You don't believe that!" Tellman looked at him with scorn. "Villeroche is his friend. He'd know if there were something like that going on. Anyway, what kind of a man just drops everything and goes off after a woman without telling anyone, however he feels? He's not a poet or an actor—this is a man supposed to deal with governments. I know he's French, but even so!"

Pitt agreed with him, but there was no reasonable alternative. Together they set off to visit the places on Villeroche's list, asking questions as discreetly as possible without being so vague as to be meaningless.

No one knew where Bonnard was or had heard him make any mention at all of leaving London. Certainly no one knew of any romantic interest in particular. He had given them all the impression that he enjoyed the company of a number of young ladies, more than a few of whom were of questionable reputation. Marriage was the last thing on his mind at the moment. Romantic pleasure was something that lay far in the future.

"Not Henri," one young man said vehemently and with a slightly nervous laugh. "He's far too ambitious to marry badly, let alone chase after another man's wife, and when he's on foreign soil as well. Oh no." He glanced from Pitt to Tellman and

157

back again. "He was—is—the sort of man to enjoy himself, perhaps not always with the discretion one would wish in a diplomat, but only . . . convivially, if you like? Temporarily . . . I don't really know how to put it . . ." he trailed off.

"He likes to wine and dine but make no commitment," Pitt interpreted.

"Precisely," the other man agreed. "A man of the world . . . or perhaps I should say a man of the city, the bright lights and the music, and yet not so worldly-wise as might be."

Pitt smiled in spite of himself. They were all trying so hard to avoid the blunter way of expressing Bonnard's indulgences. "Thank you. I believe I understand. You have been very helpful. Good day, sir."

They visited several more of the people whose names Villeroche had given them, but no one added anything new. By the middle of the evening they had begun to call in at the various clubs he was known to frequent.

It was half past nine; they were tired and discouraged when they came to Ye Olde Cheshire Cheese, in an alleyway next to a tailor and a barber's shop.

"Is it worth it?" Tellman protested, wrinkling his nose in distaste as they stood together on the step, the gaslight making their shadows long across the stones.

"Probably not," Pitt answered. "I'm beginning to accept that he's either gone into the country somewhere after a romance which he managed to keep so well hidden even his closest friends didn't know about it, or he is involved in something darker, perhaps illegal, perhaps even Cathcart's murder, although I don't see any connection. Come on, we'll make this the last place. The fellow is probably in a warm bed somewhere with someone unsuitable, and thoroughly enjoying himself, while we tramp around half London wondering what's happened to him." He turned and pushed the door open, and was immediately inside a warm, close atmosphere smelling of wine and tobacco smoke. A score of young men and a few older sat around in groups with glasses or tankards at their elbows, many talking eagerly, others listening, leaning forward to catch every word.

Pitt must have looked a trifle Bohemian with his untidy clothes and hair seriously in need of a barber's attention, because no one questioned his presence. He was not sure whether that pleased him or not. He was certain it would not have pleased his superiors.

Tellman drew a few glances, but since he was obviously with Pitt, he was suffered to pass without question. He took a deep breath, ran his fingers around inside his collar, as if it were too tight and restricted his breath, and plunged in.

Pitt passed the first table, the conversation being so earnest he thought interrupting it would earn him no favor. At the second, where the company was far more relaxed, he saw a face he thought in some way familiar, although he was not sure from where. It was heavyset, with thick, dark hair and dark eyes.

"Lesser men will always criticize what they do not understand," the man said vehemently. "It is their only way of feeling that they have in some way made themselves masters of the subject, whereas in truth they have only displayed their failure to match it. It is a ceaseless source of amazement to me that the greater the fool, the more he is compelled to acquaint everyone with his shortcomings."

"But doesn't it anger you?" a fair young man asked, his eyes wide and bright.

The darker man raised his eyebrows. "My dear fellow, what would be the point? For some men, another man's work of art is simply a mirror. They see a reflection of themselves in it, according to their obsession of the moment, and then criticize it for all they are worth, which admittedly is very little, because they do not like what it shows them. So Mr. Henley believes I am advocating the love of beauty above all things, precisely because he has no love for it. It frightens him. It is clear, yet ungraspable, it taunts him by its very elusiveness. In attacking *The Picture of Dorian Gray*, he is in some way of his own finding a weapon to attack his personal enemy."

Another of the company seemed fiercely interested. "Do you believe that, Oscar? You could reduce him to pieces if

159

you wanted to. You have everything with which to do it, the wit, the perception, the vocabulary . . ."

"But I don't want to," Oscar argued. "I admire his work. I refuse to allow him to turn me into something I do not wish to be . . . namely, an artist who has lost sight of art and will descend to criticizing in public, for retaliation's sake, what he truly admires in private. Or even worse, to deny myself the pleasure of enjoying what he has created because he is foolish enough to deny himself the enjoyment of what I have made. That, my dear friend, is a truly stupid thing to do. And when an ignorant or frightened man calls me immoral it hurts me, but I can tolerate it. But were an honest man to call me stupid, I should have to consider the possibility that he was right, and that would be awful."

"We live in an age of Philistines," another young man said wearily, pushing back a heavy quiff of hair. "Censorship is a creeping death, the beginning of a necrosis of the soul. How can a civilization grow except with new ideas, and any man who suffocates a new idea is a murderer of thought and the enemy of the generations who follow him, because he has robbed them of a little of their life. He has diminished them."

"Well said!" Oscar applauded generously.

The young man blushed with pleasure.

Oscar smiled at him.

"Excuse me, Mr. Wilde . . ." Pitt seized the lull in the conversation to interrupt.

Wilde looked up at him curiously. There was no hostility in his eyes, not even a guardedness as to a stranger.

"You agree, sir?" he asked warmly. He looked Pitt up and down, his eyes resting a moment on Pitt's untidy hair and on his crooked shirt collar, less well cared for than usual in Charlotte's absence. "Let me assay a guess. You are a poet whom some narrow and grubby-minded critic has censored? Or are you an artist who has painted his view of the reality of the soul of man, and no one will hang it in public because it challenges the comfortable assumptions of society?"

Pitt grinned. "Not quite right, sir. I am Thomas Pitt, a policeman who has misplaced a French diplomat and wondered if you might know where he is."

Wilde looked thunderstruck, then he burst into a roar of laughter, thumping his fist on the table. It was several moments before he controlled himself.

"Good heavens, sir, you have a dry sense of the absurd. I like you. Please, sit down and join us. Have a glass of wine. It's dreadful, like vinegar and sugar, but it cannot dampen our spirits, and if you take enough of it, it will no longer matter. Bring your lugubrious friend as well." He waved his arm towards an empty chair a few feet away, and Pitt drew it up and sat with them. Tellman obeyed also.

A pale young Irishman, addressed by his fellows as Yeats, stared moodily into the distance. The newcomers' inclusion seemed to displease him.

"Take no notice at all." Wilde gave them his full attention. "Personally or professionally, may one ask?"

Pitt felt vaguely uncomfortable. He knew Wilde's reputation, and he did not wish to be misunderstood.

Tellman was quite obviously confused, and it showed in the pinkness of his cheeks and the stubborn set of his mouth.

"Professionally," Pitt replied, keeping his eyes steadily on Wilde's.

"Will any French diplomat do?" the young man with the quiff asked, then giggled cheerfully. "Or do you want a particular one?"

Tellman sneezed.

"I would like a particular one," Pitt replied. "Henri Bonnard, to be exact. One of his friends has reported him missing, and it seems that if he does not reappear soon he may be in jeopardy of losing his position, which makes me fear he has met with harm."

"Harm?" Wilde looked from one to the other of them around the table. He turned back to Pitt. "I know Bonnard, slightly. I had no idea he was missing. I confess, I haven't seen him in . . ." He thought for a moment. "Oh . . . a couple of weeks, or nearly as long."

"He was last seen nine days ago," Pitt said. "In the morning near the Serpentine. He had an altercation with a friend and left rather heatedly."

"How do you know?" Wilde asked.

"It was observed by a number of people," Pitt explained. "There was a camera club out taking pictures in the early light. Both men were members."

Tellman shifted uncomfortably in his seat.

"I prefer my visions in words." Yeats lost interest and turned away.

"A poetry of light and shade," the man with the quiff observed. "An enormous number of pictures in black-and-white and shades of gray. Better than Whistler, what?"

"But not as good as Beardsley," someone else said sharply. "A photograph will catch only the obvious, the outside. Beardsley's drawings will catch the soul, the essence of good and evil, the eternal questions, the paradox of all things."

Pitt had no idea what the man was talking about. From the look on Tellman's face, he was no longer even trying to understand.

"Of course," the man with the quiff agreed. "The brush, in the hands of a genius with the courage to draw whatever he wants, and no bigoted, frightened little censor to stop him, can mirror the torment or the victory within. Anything you dare to think, he can show."

Someone else leaned forward enthusiastically, almost knocking a glass of wine off the table with his elbow. "The immediacy of it," he declaimed, looking at Wilde. "Your *Salome*, his drawings, the ideas of black, gold, and red were brilliant! Bernhardt would have adored it. Can't you just imagine her? We would have broken into a new age of the mind and of the senses. The Lord Chamberlain should be shot!"

"The man's a policeman!" a handsome man warned, waving at Pitt, then banging his fist on the tabletop and making the glasses jump.

"He won't arrest you for expressing a civilized opinion," Wilde assured him, glancing at Pitt with a smile. "He's a good fellow, and I know he goes to the theatre because I remember now where I saw him before. When that wretched judge was

162

murdered in his box—Tamar MacAuley was on the stage, and Joshua Fielding."

"That's right," Pitt agreed. "You actually supplied me with the pieces of information that indicated the truth."

Wilde was obviously delighted. "I did? How marvelously satisfying. I wish I could help you find poor Henri Bonnard, but I have no idea where he is or why he should have gone."

"But you do know him?"

"Certainly. A charming fellow . . ."

"Here or in Paris?" the man with the quiff enquired.

"Did you know him in Paris?" Pitt asked quickly.

"No, not at all." Wilde dismissed Pitt's question with amusement. "I just went for a short trip. Visited around a little. Superb city, lovely people . . . at least most of them. Went to see Proust. Awful!" He waved his arms sweepingly. "He was late for our appointment at his own home—and it was the ugliest house I ever saw. Dreadful! I don't know how anyone could choose to live in such a place. Anyway, Bonnard didn't come from Paris. I think his family is in the south somewhere."

"Have you any idea why he might suddenly leave London?" Pitt looked around the table at each of them.

Tellman straightened to attention again.

Yeats frowned. "Could be anything from a woman to a bad debt," he answered. He seemed about to say something more, then changed his mind.

"He had plenty of money," the man with the quiff said, dismissing that idea.

"Not the sort of man to throw up everything on a romance either," someone else offered.

"How sad," Wilde murmured. "There should always be at least one thing in life for which one would sacrifice everything else. It gives life a sort of unity, a wholeness. And then you spend your time soaring and plunging between hope and terror that you never have to. To know that you will not—it would be as dreadful as to know you will. Have a glass of wine, Mr. Pitt." He picked up the bottle. "I'm afraid we can't help you. We are poets, artists, and dreamers . . . and occasionally great political theorists—of the socialist order, of

163

course—except Yeats, who is tangling his soul in the troubles of Ireland, and that has no names an Englishman could pronounce. We have no idea where Bonnard is or why he went there. I can only say I hope he returns safe and well, and if you have to go and look for him, that it is somewhere with an agreeable climate, people who have new ideas all the time, and the last censor died of boredom at least a hundred years ago."

"Thank you, Mr. Wilde," Pitt said graciously. "I wish I could begin in Paris, but I'm afraid we know he did not take the Dover packet he was booked on, and I regret I have something uglier and more urgent to attend to than pursuing this any further."

"Another judge?" Wilde enquired.

"No, a man found dead in a punt at Horseferry Stairs."

Wilde looked sad. "Delbert Cathcart. I am very sorry. When you find who killed him, don't forget to charge him with vandalism as well as murder. The unwitting fool destroyed a genius."

Tellman winced.

"That kind of vandalism is not a crime, Mr. Wilde," Pitt said quietly. "Unfortunately."

"Did you know Mr. Cathcart well, sir?" Tellman spoke for the first time, his voice sounding a little hoarse and very different from those of the group around the table.

They stared at him in amazement, as if one of the chairs had spoken to them.

Tellman flushed, but he would not lower his eyes.

Wilde was the first to recover his composure.

"No . . . only saw him once, at a party somewhere or other. But I've seen quite a lot of his work. You don't have to meet a man who is an artist in order to know his soul. If it is not there in what he creates, then he has cheated you, and worse than that, he has cheated himself." He was still holding the wine bottle. "Perhaps that and cruelty are the greatest sins of all. I never spoke to him—or he to me—in the sense you mean."

Tellman looked confused and crestfallen.

Pitt thanked them again and, finally declining the offer of wine, excused them both.

Outside in the dark alley, Tellman drew in a deep breath and wiped his hand over his face.

"I heard he was odd," he said quietly. "Can't say I know what to make of him. Do you think that lot have anything to do with Bonnard and Cathcart?"

"I don't even know that Bonnard and Cathcart have anything to do with each other," Pitt said grimly, and pulled his coat collar up as he turned along the alley, Tellman's footsteps sounding hollowly after him.

8

THE NIGHTMARE WAS SO REAL that even when the old lady woke up the room around her seemed to be the one in which she had spent her married life. It was a moment before her vision cleared and she realized there was no door to the left leading to Edmund's room. There was no need to be afraid. It would not open because it was smooth, patterned wall. She could see the light on the paper, unbroken. But it was shades of deep rose pink. It should be yellow. She was used to yellow. Where was she?

Her feet were cold. There was light coming through a crack in the curtains. She heard footsteps outside, quick and firm. A maid.

She grasped the covers and pulled them up to her chin, hiding herself. She saw the hands on the sheet, knuckles swollen and clenched, an old woman's hands, blue veined, thin skinned with dark patches on them, the thin gold wedding ring slipping around easily. They had once been slim and smooth.

The past receded. But where was she? This was not Ashworth House.

Then she remembered. Emily and her husband were away in Paris, gadding around again. They were having the plumbing altered in Ashworth House and she was obliged to stay with Caroline. She hated being dependent. It was the worst part of being a widow. In fact, in some respects perhaps it was the only part that was really hard to bear. Now she was answerable to no one. There was a certain degree of sympathy and respect for a widow, the last one of her generation alive in her family.

Of course all that could change . . . now that Samuel Ellison had arrived from America. Who in all the green earth could have imagined that that would have happened? Alys had had a son. Edmund had never known that. He would have been . . . she stopped. She had no idea how he would have felt about it. It hardly mattered now. In fact, there was only one thing which did matter, and control over that was fast slipping away from her.

Where was Mabel? What was the use of bringing a maid all the way from Ashworth House if the woman was not there when she was needed? The old lady reached out and yanked on the bell rope at the side of the bed so hard she was fortunate it did not come away in her hand.

It seemed forever until Mabel came, but when she did she was carrying a tray with hot tea. She set it on the small table by the bed, then opened the curtains and let in the sunlight. There was a sort of sanity in it, a reassuring, pedestrian business in the very ordinary sounds of the day: footsteps, horses' hooves in the street, someone calling out, a bucket dropped, a girl somewhere laughing.

Perhaps she would find a way to keep control of it after all?

It was eight days since Caroline had come back from the theatre saying Samuel Ellison had turned up.

Breakfast was satisfying, if a meal taken in near silence, and alone except for Caroline, could be said to be satisfactory. Caroline was even more self-absorbed than usual. Sometimes she looked thoroughly miserable, which was very unbecoming in a woman of her age, who had little to offer except good temper, knowledge of how to behave in any company whatsoever, and the ability to run a household. Since Caroline had no household to speak of, and she no longer mixed in public society, an equable nature was her only asset.

Her mood this morning was one of excitement and unattractive smugness, as if she knew something amusing which

167

she refused to share. That was even more unbecoming. It was bad enough in a young girl, who could not be expected to know better, and had to be taught. In a woman with grandchildren it was ridiculous.

The reason for her satisfaction manifested itself in the middle of the afternoon. Samuel Ellison arrived yet again. Caroline had not the sense to put him off, even after all Mariah had said, and it seemed he was totally insensitive to all hint or suggestion, however plain. This time he brought flowers and a box of Belgian sweetmeats. They were ostensibly for her, but she knew perfectly well they were really for Caroline; etiquette forbade he be so open about it.

The old lady accepted them in a matter-of-fact manner, and even considered having the maid take them up to her room straightaway so Caroline would not have them at all. She did not do it, and then was annoyed with herself for her failure of nerve. It would have served them both right.

Before tea was sent for and he was made thoroughly welcome, the old lady considered excusing herself. A headache or any other such thing would have served. Certainly neither Samuel nor Caroline would have tried to persuade her to stay. They might be only too delighted were she to retreat. It would leave them unchaperoned, of course. But would they have the decency to care? She could not even rely on that. Family honor required she remain, and so did a certain sense of self-preservation. At least if she was present she might exercise some degree of control over events. Samuel would hardly speak about her if she was sitting right in front of him. Yes, painful as it was, it was definitely better to stay. She could not afford the luxury of running away.

After the usual exchange of pleasantries, Caroline asked Samuel about his early days in New York.

"I cannot imagine what it must have been like for you and your mother, completely alone in a city teeming with immigrants, many of them with nothing but hope," she said earnestly.

"Hope, and a will to work," he answered. "To work all day and as much of the night as one could stay awake. They spoke a hundred different languages . . ."

"Babel," the old lady said distinctly.

"Absolutely," he agreed with a smile towards her. Then he looked again at Caroline. "But it is amazing how much you can understand what people mean when you share the same emotions. We all feel hope and fear, hunger sometimes, exhilaration, the sense of being miles away from anything familiar—"

"I thought you were born there!" the old lady said.

"I was," he agreed. "But for my mother it was a terrible wrench to leave all that she was used to and begin again, with nothing, and among strangers."

Mariah could have kicked herself. How incredibly stupid of her? She had found a dangerous situation and turned it into a disaster. Ice gripped her stomach. She gulped as fear overcame her. Did her face show it? Did he know?

He looked as perfectly smug and bland as usual. She did not want to meet his eyes.

Caroline was talking. For once, the old lady was glad of it.

"I cannot say how much I admire her courage," Caroline said warmly. "It is both frightening and uplifting at once to hear of such people. I admit it makes me feel as if I have done very little."

Dear Caroline! How dare she be so perceptive? How dare she put so exquisitely into words the compassion between Alys and other women, Alys and Mariah herself.

The room seemed to blur around her. Her face was hot, her hands and stomach cold.

"Thank you," Samuel said softly, his eyes on Caroline's face. "I think she was marvelous. I always thought so . . . but then I loved her." He blinked quickly. "But I'm sure much happened here that was extraordinary and exciting too. I seem to have talked endlessly about myself." He shook his head a little. "Please tell me something about England in all these years. I daresay your news of us was more than ours of you. We tend to be rather absorbed in our own affairs. I am American by birth . . . just . . . and by upbringing, but I'm English by heritage." He leaned back in his chair and turned to face Mrs. Ellison. "What was it like here at the heart of things when I was growing up in New York, out on the edge of the world?"

He was waiting for her to answer. She must do so, take control of the conversation. Remember all the things that were going on outside in the city, in the country. Think of nothing in the house, nothing of history. That should be easy enough.

She told him all manner of things as the memories came to her. He listened with apparent interest.

"Actually, it was the year before the old king died and the new one was crowned," she resumed with an effort. "And the Duke of Wellington resigned."

"I didn't know dukes could resign," he said. "I thought it was for life."

"Not as duke," she said contemptuously. "As prime minister!"

Samuel colored. "Oh . . . yes, of course. Wasn't he the general who fought at Waterloo?"

"Certainly he was," she agreed. She made herself smile. This, after all, was as safe a subject as possible. "Most people alive now have never known war," she boasted. It was a staggering thought. She found herself smiling, lifting her chin a little.

Samuel was watching her, his face alight with interest, waiting for her to go on.

But that was her youth, a time it was painful to think of. It was another life, another person, when she had been a girl full of hope and an innocence which was unbearable to look back on, knowing what came after. It had not occurred to her until this moment to wonder what secrets too awful to touch lay in other women's lives, behind their composed outward faces. Maybe none. Maybe she was as alone as she felt.

The silence grew heavy. She became aware of outside sounds, beyond the windows, horses in the street. It was Caroline who broke the tension.

"All I know of the reign of William IV was to do with the Irish. Tens of thousands of people left Ireland for America. You will have known some of them, I daresay."

There was a sharp compassion in his eyes. "Of course. I

couldn't count how many of them fetched up in New York, haggard faced, their clothes hanging off them as if they were made of sticks underneath, their eyes full of weariness, trying to hope, and yet not hope too much, and homesick."

"Your mother must have felt like that too," Caroline said gently, and it was clear in her face how vividly she was imagining how that unknown woman felt, trying to put herself in her place and understand.

Samuel must have seen it. His smile was touched with grief.

Mariah tried to imagine it. She knew nothing of Alys, except that she had gone. Edmund had never described her. Mariah did not know if she had been beautiful or homely, fair or dark, slender or buxom. She knew nothing of her personality or tastes.

But Alys had gone. That was the one thing that rose like a mountain in her mind, and it made her as different from Mariah as if she had been of another species. That was why she had hated Alys all these years, and envied her, why it choked in her throat to say she admired her, because it was the truth.

Did she want to know more about her? Did she want to be able to see her in the mind's eye as a real woman, flesh and blood, laughter and pain, as vulnerable as anyone else? No— because then she would have to stop hating her. She would be forced to think of the differences between them and ask herself why she had stayed.

Samuel was talking about her. Caroline had asked him. Of course—Caroline—it was always Caroline!

". . . I suppose a little taller than average," he was saying. "Fair brown hair." He smiled a little self-consciously. "I know I am prejudiced, but I was far from the only one who thought she was beautiful. There was a grace about her, a kind of inner repose, as if she never doubted what she held dearest, and she'd fight like a tiger to protect it. She could get terribly angry, but I never heard her raise her voice. I think she taught me more than anybody else what it means to be a gentleman."

171

There was nothing to say that sounded appropriate, and Caroline held her peace.

Mariah knew the familiar bitterness that rose up inside her. How could Alys have been such a perfect lady? Wasn't she broken inside as well, broken and crying like a hurt child, alone in the dark? Why was her anger only a fleeting thing, acted upon and then forgotten, so that she kept her temper and behaved with such sublime dignity . . . and was loved? Mariah's anger was deep, inward, lacerating until there was no dignity left, and she seldom ever tried to keep her temper these days. What had made Alys so golden, so bright and brave? Was she just a better woman? Was it as simple as that? What had given her the courage?

". . . but I want to know more about all of you," Samuel was saying, looking earnestly at Caroline, then at Mrs. Ellison.

"It is you I really care about. Where did you live? What happened to you? Where did you go and what did you do? What did you talk about to each other? You are my only link with a father I never knew. Perhaps I need to know more of him to understand myself?"

Mariah drew in her breath sharply, and it caught in her throat, making her choke. It was several moments before she could speak.

"Nonsense!" She coughed violently. Caroline was staring at her. "What I mean . . ." She tried again: ". . . is that you are who you are, regardless of your father." This was terrible. She must say something that would not make him suspicious. Her mind raced futilely.

Caroline came to the rescue.

"Papa-in-law was very charming," she said gently, as if she thought the old lady's coughing were to hide emotion—as it was—she thought of grief, not cold, gripping fear. "He was tall, about the height you are, I should think," she went on. "And he dressed beautifully. He had a gold watch, and he wore the chain across his waistcoat. He liked very good boots, and always had them perfectly polished till you could see your reflection in them." There was a faraway look in her eyes. "He did not smile very often, but he had a way of listening that gave you his complete attention. You never felt as if he were merely waiting for you to stop so he could say something, without being rude."

It was all true. Mariah could picture Edmund as Caroline was speaking. She could almost hear his voice. It surprised her that after all this time she could recall it so perfectly. In her mind she imagined his step across the hall, brisk and firm. Whenever she smelled snuff she thought of him, or felt the faint scratch of good tweed. He used to stand in front of the fire, warming himself and keeping the heat from other people. Edward had done just the same. She wondered if Caroline had noticed it as she had, and if it had annoyed her as much. She had never said so, but then one did not.

Caroline was talking about Edmund again, telling Samuel some of the stories he used to enjoy, and how he sang sometimes, and how fond he was of the girls, Sarah, Charlotte, and Emily, especially Emily because she was so pretty and she laughed easily when he teased her.

Was that really how Caroline remembered him, how she had seen him when he was drunk? Why not? It was true, it was all exactly true. What did anybody really know of anybody else?

And Samuel sat there listening with his eyes on Caroline's as if he believed every word of it.

"Your mother must have spoken of him," Caroline exclaimed ingenuously. "Whatever her reasons for leaving, she knew he was your father, and therefore you had to care about him." She did not add that he must have asked her, but the implication hung in the air between them.

Mariah could hear her own heart beating. She was holding her breath, as if that could somehow stop him from answering. This was her worst nightmare come back, no longer a dream but as real as tea and toast, the maid's footsteps on the stairs, and the smells of soap and lavender or the morning newspapers. It would become part of life, as inescapable as the past, only worse, because the wound had healed over. This would be a second time, without escape ever, and she had not the strength anymore. The first time you don't know what is

173

coming, and ignorance shields you. This time she did know, and the fear before would be as bad as the fact, and the morning afterwards. Except there would be no afterwards. It would never stop. As long as Caroline knew, it would be there in her eyes every time they met.

And she would tell Emily and Charlotte, and that would make life unbearable. Emily might tell Jack. The old lady could picture the pity and then the revulsion in his wide, dark-lashed eyes.

Samuel was talking about his mother again, about Alys. His face was lit with the same tenderness as before, his eyes shining.

". . . people made the mistake of thinking that because she carried herself like a lady that she hadn't the courage to speak out or stick to her beliefs," he said urgently. "But I never knew a woman with more courage."

Mariah cringed inside as if he had struck her. He knew! He must know. It was there in his words, just under the surface. If it was true of Alys, then it was true of Mariah. He would know that, anyone would. People don't change.

What possessed Alys to have told him? How could she?

Mariah imagined telling Edward! Her face burned at the very idea of it. Would he have ever believed her? If it repelled him as it did her, then he would have been unable to accept it, and he would have considered her not only mad but dangerous.

But then if that same hideous seed were in him, he would have believed, and he would never have looked at her in the same way again. The image of "mother" would be gone and that other terrible one would replace it.

And that is how Caroline would be now. The old lady refused to think about it. Every shred of dignity, of human worth or value, would be stripped from her abjectly, and leave her grotesquely naked, as no living thing should be. It would be better to be dead. Except that she had not the courage. That was at the core of it, she was a coward—not like Alys.

Samuel was still talking about Alys, how beautiful she was, how brave, how everyone admired her, liked to be in her

174

company. She was different, breathtaking, unbearably different, and the knowledge of it was like a red-hot knife twisting in an old wound, gouging deeper till it touched the bone.

They were still talking about the past, Caroline recounting some anecdote that had happened years before. She made it sound as immediate as yesterday. It could not go on. It was only a matter of time before the truth was said. That must be prevented—at any cost.

But nothing the old lady said now would make the slightest difference—the only means of stopping this conversation would be to make it necessary for Samuel to leave. If she retired from the room, surely he would go? He said he admired his mother so much, he would attempt to behave like a gentleman.

"Excuse me," she interrupted, rather more loudly than she had intended. "I feel a little faint. I think if you will ring for my maid, Caroline, I will retire to my room. At least until dinner. I shall see how I feel then." She forced herself to look at Samuel. "Pardon me for ending your visit so abruptly. I have not the good health I used to."

Caroline looked crestfallen. "I am sorry, Mama-in-law. Would you like a tisane sent up?" She reached for the bell as she spoke.

"No, thank you. I think a little lavender will suffice. It is one of the disadvantages of age, one has not the stamina one used to have."

Samuel rose to his feet. "I hope I have not bored you, Mrs. Ellison. It was very thoughtless of me to have remained so long."

She stared at him and said nothing. The man seemed impervious to suggestion.

The parlormaid opened the door, and Caroline asked her to send the old lady's maid to assist her upstairs.

Samuel took his leave—he had no alternative. But even as she was climbing the stairs slowly, not having to ape the stiffness or fumbling hands on the banister—they were all too real—the old lady could hear Caroline inviting him to return

175

and resume their conversation, and his acceptance. It was that which finally sealed the decision in her mind.

Since she had said she was ill, she was obliged to remain upstairs for the remainder of the afternoon, which was irritating because she had nothing to do and would either have to lie down and pretend to be resting, which would leave her thoughts free to torment her, or else create some task or other and affect to be busy with it. She did not want to face her decision—not yet.

Mabel was a good woman, both competent and tactful, which was the only reason she had survived in the old lady's service for so long. She made no comment on the situation, simply brewed her a chamomile tisane, without asking, and brought her a lavender pillow. Both were refreshing, and had she suffered from the headache she professed, they would have helped her immensely.

She lay on the bed for nearly an hour, quite long enough to have recovered, then, feeling lonely and oppressed with useless thoughts and memories, she went to the small upstairs room where the maids mended the household linen and did a little dressmaking as was necessary. Most reasonably well-to-do women had three or four bought gowns for afternoon wear, the same again for evening, and they had their maids sew the others. It was cheaper, and if the maid was good, quite as effective. She knew Mabel was making something for her, because it was a permanent state of affairs. Emily was generous with supplying fabric, beads, braid, and other trimmings.

"Are you feeling better, ma'am?" Mabel asked, looking up from her needle. "Can I get you anything else?"

"No, thank you," the old lady said, closing the door behind her. She sat down in the other chair. Mabel resumed stitching. It was growing dusk outside and the lamps were lit. The gaslight caught in the silver needle, making it look like a flash of light itself, weaving in and out of the cloth, in the thimble. Mabel was getting old too. Her knuckles were swollen, rheumatic. She did not walk as easily as she used to either. As always, the cloth she sewed was black. The old lady had worn black ever since Edmund died. Like the Queen, she was conspicuous in her mourning. It had seemed the right thing to do at the time. Grief was an acceptable emotion, very appropriate. Everyone understood and sympathized. It was so much better than guilt, although to onlookers it could appear the same. She could weep, retreat to privacy, or ask for anything, which was freely granted. She was the center of attention and no questions were asked.

She very easily fell into the habit of being "bereaved." There never seemed a suitable time to come out of black, and then it was too late. People assumed she was devastated by Edmund's death. It became impossible to do anything but agree. She told people what she wanted them to believe, which in time she tried to believe herself. It was better that way.

Now Samuel Ellison had turned up out of God knew where, and everything was crashing in ruins.

Mabel was threading black beads onto her needle, stitching them on the bosom of the new dress. Why in damnation should Mariah wear black for the rest of her life for Edmund's sake? He must be laughing in whatever hell he had gone to. It had never suited her, and did so even less now that she was old and sallow-skinned. And to put rouge on her face would make her look like a painted corpse. A painted corpse! That was how she felt, dead inside but still hurting, and ridiculous.

She wanted to tell Mabel to throw it away, make something of another color—maybe purple; that was half mourning. But lavender would not suit her either, in fact it would look even worse.

She was afraid to change. Everyone would ask why, and she did not want to mention Edmund at all, let alone offer any explanations. So she sat in silence, idle-fingered. Her head ached.

She did not go down to dinner. She dreaded listening to Caroline wittering on about Samuel Ellison, and far worse, she might talk about Edmund, ask questions, bring back memories. Of course, what Caroline recalled of him was the face everyone knew, the one the old lady herself had perpetuated deliberately. She could talk about his kindness, his charm, his ability to tell a story and bring it to life. She could recall Christmas, when they walked together through the snow to church on Christmas Eve, how he sang the old songs with such a rich voice.

Her throat ached. Tears spilled and ran down her cheeks. If only it could all have been like that!

Who was wrong? Was it she? Was she the one who was different, out of step, cold, stuck in some childish fantasy of the world, a woman who had grown old but had never grown up?

Then that was how it would be. She could not change now.

But this was unendurable. She would rather be dead.

Mabel came to her room and removed the dinner tray, the food half eaten. She said nothing. But then she could not. She had served the old lady for twenty years. They knew all kinds of intimate things about each other, physical things, habits, footsteps, a cough, the texture of skin and hair. And yet at heart they were also strangers. The old lady had never asked what Mabel thought or hoped for in life, what kept her awake at night, and Mabel had no idea now what dread clutched inside her mistress like a cold hand.

She could not go on like this. She must do something, now, before it was too late. Caroline must never know. She was left with no choice. All the old panic and despair were back, the familiar darkness inside her, eating away at her heart, closing her in, unutterably alone.

Damn Samuel Ellison for coming from America, where he was safely out of her life. Damn Alys for being beautiful and brave and in control of everything. She had gone—just left. But there was nowhere for Mariah to go. She was not young and healthy with a lovely face. She was old, stiff, bone-weary, and terrified. What would so-lovely, so-clever Alys do if she were here now?

She would do something! She would not sit waiting for the ax to fall like some helpless rabbit. Then not only would the old lady be despised for what was known, she would despise herself for letting it happen. That was the worst of it, the self-loathing.

But how could she stop it?

* * *

It took all the resolve she possessed to go down to the breakfast table. But she could not spend the rest of her life in her bedroom. She had to appear sometime. Joshua would be present at this hour of the day, and that would prevent Caroline from chattering on and on endlessly about Samuel Ellison, and somehow she would contrive to speak to him alone. She must. She dare not leave it any longer.

The usual greeting and enquiries dealt with, she forced herself to take tea and toast.

"Have you heard from Thomas lately?" Joshua said, turning to Caroline.

"Not for over a week," she replied. "I imagine he is very busy with the death of that man found at Horseferry Stairs. It was mentioned in the newspapers again. It seems he was a very famous society photographer."

"Delbert Cathcart," he said, taking more toast and reaching for the apricot preserves. "He was brilliant."

"One wonders why anyone should wish to kill him," Caroline continued, pushing the butter dish across the table for Joshua. "Envy? Perhaps jealousy over some private matter?"

"Do you mean a lover?" he asked with a smile. "Why are you being so delicate?"

She flushed very slightly. "That sort of thing," she conceded.

It was an opening. The old lady did not hesitate.

"When people practice immorality it very often ends in disaster," she said distinctly. "If people would remember that, we should be able to get rid of half the misery in the world!" She was startled to hear the bitterness in her own voice. She had meant it for Caroline, but waves of loathing were thick in it as well, carrying a passion she would rather not have revealed.

Joshua was staring at her. He had heard it and was puzzled. She looked away.

"It may simply have been robbery," Caroline said calmly. "The poor man was out late, and what was intended merely to take his watch or money became more violent than expected. Perhaps he fought."

"Are you suggesting he brought it upon himself?" Mariah

179

demanded. "He fought, so he deserved to be murdered?" She did not want this line of thought. "Sometimes your ideas of right and wrong confuse me." She aimed that remark at Caroline.

"I am not talking about right or wrong," Caroline said impatiently. "Only about probability."

"That should not surprise me," the old lady retorted. She did not explain what she meant. Their looks of confusion satisfied her.

The meal continued for some time in silence.

"Warriner has withdrawn his bill," Joshua said finally.

Mariah had no idea what he was talking about, but from his expression she deduced that it displeased him intensely. She did not ask.

"I'm sorry," Caroline said quietly. "I suppose it was to be expected."

Joshua grimaced. "Part of me says it is providence. They should wait for a better time. The other part says it is cowardice and we should make our own time. We could wait forever."

Mariah's curiosity was piqued. On a different occasion she would have asked what they were taking about. Now other matters were crowding far too urgently in her mind. She must contrive to speak to Joshua alone. One thing he had said was true—one must make one's own time. One might wait for other people to offer it forever, and still fail.

Her mind raced. What excuse could she make for speaking with Joshua alone? She could hardly ask him for financial advice. She obtained that from Jack. A family matter she would have spoken about to Caroline, a loss or a threat of any sort she would have called Pitt for. A chore she would have called a servant to do. She barely knew Joshua. She had never hidden her disapproval of him personally and of the marriage in general. What reason could she use?

Maybe she could get Caroline to leave? A domestic duty. But what? Anything usual she would leave until Joshua was gone.

She must go herself, and then catch Joshua in the hall. Not very satisfactory, but she could not wait for something better.

She stood up, placing her napkin across her plate. She was leaving half her tea, but that could not be helped.

"Excuse me," she said, her voice a little high-pitched. It was ridiculous. She must control her nerves. "I have a small errand to do." And without struggling for further explanation, she went. No one commented. They were not curious as to what she was doing in such a hurry. This realization made her feel bitterly alone.

She must govern her thoughts. This was a time for action. Soon Joshua would leave and she must take the opportunity to catch him alone. If Caroline came into the hall to wish him good-bye, she would have no opportunity, unless she actually went outside altogether. It would appear excessive. There would be no way in which she could claim it was an accidental encounter. But she could not afford to wait another day. Samuel Ellison must not come back to the house! Once he spoke it would be too late forever. It could never be withdrawn. One cannot undo knowledge.

She went to the front door and opened it. The air was brisk, the sun warm, smelling of dust and horses. In the park a hundred yards away the leaves were beginning to turn. The grass was still damp. An errand boy was whistling. There was a woman on a bicycle, wearing most unsuitable clothes, traveling far too quickly. Mariah envied her. She looked so completely free, and happy.

She turned her attention back to her task. How long would he be? She had not actually made certain that he was going out at all this morning, but he usually did, not early like most men, because he had been late the previous evening. The whole household rose late.

She paced back and forth on the pavement, feeling more and more conspicuous. Then suddenly he was there, coming down the path, and she had had her back to him and not seen. She turned and hurried towards him.

"Mrs. Ellison." He looked startled. He seemed about to say something, and then decided against it.

She must seize the chance, no matter how awkward it was

to find the words or how foolish he thought her. Her survival depended on it.

"Joshua! I . . . I must speak with you . . . in confidence."

"Is something wrong?" he asked, catching her emotion.

"Yes," she said hastily. "I fear it is. But it may be addressed, and more damage prevented."

He did not look sufficiently alarmed. How should she phrase it so as to be believed? She had rehearsed this through the restless hours of the night, but still it did not sound right yet.

"What is the matter?" he asked her, quite gently, without alarm.

She wanted to be away from the front door, in case Caroline should chance to look out one of the windows and see them. She started to walk, and he moved with her, keeping step. She must begin.

"It is Samuel Ellison," she said, finding herself oddly breathless. "No doubt you know he has been calling quite regularly at the house, in the afternoons. He stays for far longer than merely a social call."

"He is family," Joshua replied. "Is that not natural enough?"

"Natural, maybe." She heard the sharpness in her voice and tried to steady it. "But he is . . . behaving in an unfortunate manner."

"Really?" There was no change in his expression.

This was worse than she had expected. Damn him for being so obtuse. Now she would have to be too frank. Why couldn't the man use his imagination? He was supposed to be an actor. Couldn't he think?

"He is overfamiliar!" she said sharply.

"With you?" His eyebrows rose as if he found the thought of it incredible. "Well, if you feel he is rude and you cannot curtail it yourself, you had better ask Caroline to speak to him."

"Not with me!" she said. She only just avoided adding "you fool!" "With Caroline! He very obviously finds her attractive and feels no need to disguise it. It is . . . it is worse than unsuitable—it is cause for concern."

He stiffened slightly. "I am sure Caroline is quite able to

182

remind him of appropriate behavior," he said, a little coolly. "He is American. Perhaps over there manners are freer."

"If he is anything to go by, then they are very free indeed," she said with a note of desperation. "I speak because I am concerned for Caroline's reputation. And for your welfare . . ." For heaven's sake, could he not see what she was saying? Was he totally stupid? Or perhaps he did not care? What a terrible thought . . . it filled her with ice, as if someone had opened a door onto midwinter. Maybe theatre people behaved that sort of way and expected others to. Immorality might mean nothing to him.

No! That could not be true. It must not be.

Joshua smiled very slightly, a small curve of the lips. "I am sure Caroline will rebuff him, gently, if he should trespass. But thank you for speaking on her behalf. I'm glad you are there, which will assure no one has room to speak ill of her. Good morning." And with a nod of his head, he passed her and continued on his way towards the end of the street, where presumably he was going to look for a hansom.

The old lady stood on the pavement alone, furious and defeated. But it was temporary. It must be! She could not afford to surrender. Samuel Ellison would be back, and next time, or the time after, he would finally say something which Caroline would understand, some thread which she would unravel until it reached the truth and nothing was left anymore, nothing safe or clean, no light, nothing but the darkness consuming everything.

She turned and walked back up the path, climbed the steps and went into the house. Her mind raced. She had tried, and it had not been enough. She had been delicate, subtle, laying no blame except upon Samuel, and it had not worked.

She crossed the hall past the housemaid carrying one of those new sweeping machines. Time had been when there were half a dozen maids, and carpets had been sprinkled with damp tea leaves and swept and beaten two or three times a week. Households had been run properly then!

She went upstairs to her room and closed the door. She

must be alone to think. There was no time to waste. Whatever she did, it must be today. Another visit could bring ruin.

There was still only one way she could think of to ensure that Samuel Ellison never returned. If Joshua would not be told and believe her, then he must be shown in such a way he could not disbelieve. He had left her no choice.

The question now was how to achieve it. There were many details to be considered with great care. She could afford no mistakes. Since she had tried and failed that morning, there was now only one chance left. It must succeed.

She sat by the window in the autumn sun and worked it out to the least detail. The timing must be perfect. She knew what the cost would be. She regretted it would be so high. If Joshua left Caroline she would be alone, reputation ruined and without means of her own, but Emily would see that she was not homeless. She would be provided for to that extent. If she were to live in Ashworth House it would be highly uncomfortable, but it was large enough that Caroline and Mariah would be able to avoid each other. If necessary one of them could live in the hall in the country. Probably Caroline, since she would be socially ostracized. It was a pity, it was not what Mariah would have wanted, but survival made it necessary. There was no decision to consider.

It was best to begin immediately. Long thinking might weaken her resolve. Now that the times for everything had been planned precisely, written in a neat, crabbed hand, but unwaveringly, there was nothing else to prepare. She already knew Caroline's plans for the next two days. She would be in this evening, and Joshua would be at rehearsal. It was perfect, as if it were meant to be.

She wrote the first letter.

Dear Samuel,

You can have little idea how intensely I have enjoyed your company and the friendship you have offered me. You have brought into my life much that I had not even realized I was missing so deeply. Your stories of America are not only thrilling, but far more than that, you have the eyes to see beauty where other people might miss it, to see laughter and to feel compassion in a rare and wonderful way, which wakens in me an appreciation of life I hardly knew I possessed.

Was that too strong? Or not plain enough? Surely he would understand? She had seen Caroline's handwriting often enough over the years on household accounts and invitations for the cook that it was easy to copy. They had never written letters to each other; there had been no occasion. The style she had to invent. But then Caroline had not written to Samuel Ellison either, so he would not know differently.

He must not mistake her meaning. She must leave no doubt or the whole plan would fail. There was only this one chance. It was win or lose everything.

She continued:

Before you leave London and go to see the rest of the country I should like to visit with you as often as you can spare the time. I shall miss you extraordinarily when you return to New York. Life will seem so pedestrian again.

Surely that was forward enough, even for an American?

Please call upon us this afternoon, at about five o'clock, if you are at all able. I realize I am behaving with unbecoming urgency, but I can talk with you as I can with no one else. You are family, a link with the past which for me is gone everywhere else I turn. We have so much in common which no one else shares. As you may have observed, and I am sure you have, I find my mother-in-law difficult to speak with, except about trivialities.

Should she add anything about loneliness? No. It was explicit. She must not sound hysterical, it might put him off, and that was the last thing she wished—unless it were

185

completely. And she doubted she could do that. This was her only chance, like one throw of the dice. Win—or lose it all.

I hope to see you,
Yours most affectionately,

Caroline

Should she read it over? Or would she lose her nerve and fail at the last minute? No. Fold it up and post it. Now.

Or maybe she should read it?

She hesitated, sitting with it in her hands.

Once it was gone it was irretrievable.

But the situation was irretrievable anyway. It had been, even since Samuel Ellison had come through the door.

She folded it, put it in the envelope, addressed it, and attached the stamp.

She stood up and walked downstairs and out of the front door into the warm sun. The pillar box was at the end of the street. The post would be collected in half an hour. If Samuel returned to his hotel in time, he would have it long before five o'clock.

Again she hesitated, standing with it in her hand next to the red pillar box.

But if she did not post it he would come in an afternoon, perhaps with other people there, and the conversation would turn to Alys, as it had every other time. Caroline would ask about her, and it would all come spilling out, now or tomorrow, or the day after. Here on the hot pavement in the bright sunlight she was cold as remembered pain filled her, the struggle, the anger swelled back like a tide, the helplessness, the knowledge she could not fight, could not escape, could not refuse, could not even slip into the mercy of oblivion. She had tried that, tried to die, but one did not die of misery.

She let go of the letter and heard it thump on the others lying inside the box. It was done. Now to return home and carry out the rest of the plan. Alys would have done something like this—to protect herself.

Then there was nothing to do but wait. Caroline had already said that she did not intend to go out. Perhaps she was hoping Samuel Ellison would call. That was possible.

The old lady spent a wretched day. She thought it must be the most tense and miserable time of her life. She had no more excuses to remain upstairs unless she pretended to be ill, and she did not want to behave in any way other than usual, in case it aroused suspicion. No one must ever know what she had done.

But she could hardly bear to look at Caroline. Her own thoughts consumed her. Perhaps it would be easier if she called on someone else, but she must be there in case he came early, or should Caroline change her mind and decide to go out. She might need all her wits to counter such a thing.

This afternoon would make up for all the years of the past when she had done nothing but endure, like a coward. It would wipe all that away, cancel it as if it had never been. She would be rid of it. The thought of that freedom was like a crushing burden lifted. She would not despise herself anymore, nor feel that boredom of shame like a stone inside her.

She would have liked to talk about something trivial, to keep her thoughts occupied, but she could think of nothing, and it would be out of character. She and Caroline never chatted in friendly, inconsequential fashion. So she sat in silence while Caroline wrote to Charlotte in Paris, and there was no sound in the room but the flames in the hearth, the occasional fall of ash as the coals collapsed, and the scratch of Caroline's pen over the page.

Then suddenly it happened. The maid was at the door.

"Mr. Ellison has called, ma'am. Shall I say you are receiving?"

Caroline looked surprised. "Oh! Yes, please tell him we are." She was smiling. She looked very elegant in her afternoon dress, and there was a slight flush to her cheeks.

The door opened again and Samuel came in, his eyes going straight to Caroline. He could not keep the pleasure from his face. He barely glanced at Mariah.

"How nice to see you," Caroline said courteously. "It is a little late for tea. Would you care for some other refreshment?"

"Thank you," he accepted, coming farther into the room. "I hope it is not an inconvenient hour?" At last he acknowledged the old lady. "Good afternoon, Mrs. Ellison."

This was going extremely well. She could hardly have orchestrated it better. She rose to her feet.

"If you will excuse me," she said, grasping her stick. "I shall return directly." And without further explanation she left the room. She must send the other letter immediately. It was already written. There was an all-purpose manservant. He would deliver it if she gave him the necessary cab fare. She had that ready also.

She went up to her room and fetched the letter. She knew it by heart. It was very simple.

Dear Joshua,

Will you please return home the moment you receive this. Do not hesitate. The situation is serious, and only your presence may avert disaster.

I am very sorry,

Mariah Ellison

She took the envelope and several shillings and gave them to the manservant.

He looked startled.

"Will you take this to Mr. Fielding immediately, please," she requested. "It is most urgent, a matter of the utmost importance."

" 'E's in rehearsal, ma'am," he protested. " 'E won't want to be interrupted."

"Of course he won't," she agreed. "But he will want even less the disaster which will happen if you do not deliver this to him at once and see that he reads it. If you have any loyalty to him at all, do as you are told!"

"Yes, ma'am." Looking puzzled and unhappy, he obeyed.

Mariah went back upstairs, checking the clock on the landing, wondering how long she would have to wait.

Perhaps she should go downstairs again, in case Samuel

was aware of being unchaperoned and left? Or Caroline perceived the impropriety of it and asked him to go.

She turned and walked back, still uncertain.

She stood at the top of the stairs and saw the parlormaid go across the hall with a salver with a decanter of whisky and a glass. Excellent! At least he would remain until he had drunk that.

She would go down in five minutes, or maybe ten. How long would it take the servant to go to the theatre, and Joshua to read the letter and come back? He would come, surely? If he didn't it would only be because he already suspected something and did not care. That was not true. He was certainly an actor, but he was a decent man, gentle, unusually honest. She had noticed that about him. He had unfortunately liberal ideas about some things, but he was essentially loyal and kind. He would care very much. No one could be betrayed without pain.

She refused to think of that. She was stupid to have allowed her mind to wander to such thoughts.

She watched the clock. Eight minutes, and she could not bear the tension. She went down the stairs again slowly, gripping the banister. She reached the bottom and crossed the hall.

What if he had mentioned the letter, even shown it to Caroline, and she had denied it? What if they had guessed the truth, and he was at this moment telling her all about his mother and why she had gone. The hall swam around the old lady. She struggled for breath.

She could not go in. She couldn't bear it! There was nowhere to run. Her heart was pounding so violently her body shook. She could hear it in her ears.

She stood there paralyzed. Seconds ticked by. Or was it minutes?

She had to know. Nothing could be worse than this. It was as bad as knowing, and yet every so often there was this hope so sharp it was like sickness, leaving her dizzy. Knowledge, even despair, would be worse.

She walked towards the withdrawing room door and opened it. It was like a dream, like moving underwater.

Samuel was sitting in the chair Joshua usually chose, and Caroline was very upright in the one opposite. Her color was high, and they both turned rather quickly as they heard the door.

Mariah looked at Samuel. She did not want to meet Caroline's eyes. He did not look any different. He seemed puzzled, but not contemptuous, not angry, certainly not knowing. He did not understand . . . not yet.

The old lady took a deep breath and let it out slowly.

"I have . . . a slight . . . headache," she said with difficulty. She had meant it to sound casual, quite natural, but she had not the control of her voice she had wished.

Samuel murmured something.

"If you don't mind," she went on. "I shall go into the garden for a little while. I shall be just around the corner. The air might do me good." And without waiting for either of them to reply, she crossed the room and went out of the French doors onto the small patch of grass, and down the steps out of sight.

It was another ageless fifteen minutes before she heard the voices and came back up the steps to eavesdrop at the French doors.

Joshua was standing just inside the withdrawing room. Samuel was by the fireplace and Caroline was in between them. Even from where she stood, Mariah could see the color high and bright in Caroline's neck and staining her cheeks.

"Caroline, please leave us," Joshua said softly. From his tone and his gestures he was repeating himself.

She said something, a protest. She had her back to the window, and Mariah did not hear her words.

Joshua did not answer but stood very still, his face cold, eyes steady.

Caroline walked to the door and went out, closing it behind her.

"You were made welcome in my home, Mr. Ellison," Joshua said in a tight, low voice. "But your behavior in visiting so frequently, and spending your time alone with my wife, is inappropriate and is compromising her reputation. I

190

regret I must ask you not to call again. You have left me no room to do anything else. Good day, sir."

Samuel stood perfectly still, his face scarlet. Once he made as if to speak, hesitated, then walked past Joshua to the door. Again he seemed about to say something.

"Good day, sir," Joshua said again.

"Good day," Samuel answered, and opened the door.

It was done, accomplished. Samuel Ellison had left and he would not return. He had been prevented from saying anything.

But Mariah did not feel any sense of elation. She was cold in the afternoon sun, and she could not bear to go into the withdrawing room. She turned away and walked all the way around to the areaway and in at the scullery door, through the kitchen without looking to right or left, and up to her own room, where she sat on the bed with the tears running down her face.

9

CAROLINE STOOD at the top of the landing, confused and wretched. The whole scene with Samuel had been acutely embarrassing, and she had no idea what had produced the change in his attitude. He had been friendly and open from the beginning, much less formal than an Englishman would in the same circumstances. She had found it refreshing and not in the least out of place. She had not misunderstood it for forwardness, and she felt that she had responded only appropriately.

Then today he had arrived at an unusual hour and behaved as if she had invited him—more than that, as if there had been something peculiarly intimate about her invitation, and urgent.

She racked her brain to think of anything she could have said which could be so misinterpreted, but nothing came. She had listened to all his stories with interest, perhaps more than courtesy demanded. But they were extraordinary and fascinating to her. Anyone else would have done the same. It was immeasurably more than drawing room chatter. And he was a relative turned up from nowhere, a brother-in-law she had not known she had. At a glance, before he spoke, he was so like Edward, perhaps she had offered a friendship more instant and natural than was normal, but surely she had not implied anything else.

Had she?

She was touched by guilt as she realized how much she had enjoyed his company. No, not just his company, the way he had flattered her by liking her so much, by the unspoken suggestion that he found her equally interesting, charming, attractive. It was such a welcome contrast to Cecily Antrim's subtly patronizing air that she had reveled in. It made her feel feminine, in control of herself and the situation again.

Now it was completely out of control, out of even her attempts to understand what had gone so disastrously wrong.

What did Joshua believe she had done? Why had he come racing home from a rehearsal in the middle of the late afternoon and in such ice-cold anger commanded her to leave the room, and then seemingly ordered Samuel from the house? Did he really not know her better than to believe she had . . . what? Had an assignation of some sort, here in her own house? In his house! That was absurd! It was only the merest coincidence that Mrs. Ellison had not been in the room with them the entire time, as usual. And the old lady missed nothing; she was as quick as a ferret, and twice as vicious.

Should she try to explain? Samuel had left, but her courage failed at the thought of going down to Joshua. She had never seen him really angry before, and it hurt her more than she could have imagined. No, *hurt* was the wrong word. It frightened her. Suddenly she caught a glimpse of what she might lose, not to Cecily Antrim but because of her own behavior, something stupid, unintentionally immoral, she had done. It would not be that he had found Cecily more alluring, more exciting, but that he found Caroline contemptible, not to be trusted to behave with honor, with inner cleanness of spirit.

That cut to the heart.

And it was not true. Not really. If it was true at all, it was by omission, carelessness, misunderstanding . . . never intent.

She went down the first step, but Joshua came out of the withdrawing room and went straight across the hall and out of the front door without looking back. He had not even tried to speak with her. It was as if he no longer cared what she thought.

A new kind of darkness had begun, a pain inside she could not believe would ever heal.

She turned and went back up to her room, not her bedroom, which she shared with Joshua, but her sitting room upstairs, where she could be alone. She could not eat dinner, and she certainly could not face the prying, jubilant eyes of the old woman. She had warned her this would happen. She would be triumphant now that it had.

Caroline went to bed a little after ten o'clock. Joshua had not come home. She had thought for a moment about whether she wanted to wait up for him, however long it would be, but she dreaded the confrontation. What would she say? It might only make things worse. He would be tired. They could neither of them pretend that nothing had happened.

She might have considered sleeping in the spare bedroom, and perhaps he might also, but Mrs. Ellison was in it, so that was impossible.

Of course the worst possibility was that he would not come home at all. That was too painful to hold in her mind. She thrust it away. This might be the death of trust . . . for a while, even a long while . . . but it could not be the end of the marriage. He could not believe she had done anything but be indiscreet, surely?

She lay in the dark longing for sleep, starting at every sound in case it was his footsteps. Eventually, about midnight, she drifted into oblivion.

She woke again with no idea what time it was, and knew instantly that he was there beside her. He had come in and gone to bed and to sleep without disturbing her, without speaking or touching her.

She lay listening to him breathing. He was on the far side of the bed. She could barely feel the weight or the warmth of him. He was as separate from her as if they were strangers, together by chance in the crowd in some public place. She had never felt more crushingly alone.

Part of her wanted to wake him now and end the terrible tension, provoke a resolution, for better or worse. Her stomach was sick at the thought of what the worst would be. Could he really think that of her? Did he not know her better than that? She remembered the moments of tenderness, the laughter, the quick understanding, the vulnerability in him, and the hot tears filled her eyes.

Don't wake him now. It would be childish. Wait. Perhaps in the morning it would be better, there would be some sense in it. He would speak to her and explain. But when she woke, headachy and still tired, he was already gone and she was alone.

The old lady also slept little, in spite of her triumph. Nothing would warm the coldness inside her. She drifted in and out of nightmare. She was alone in an icy swamp. She cried out and no one heard her. Blind, inhuman faces peered and did not see. Hate. Everything was drenched and dark with hate. Guilt brought her out in a sweat, and then froze, leaving her shuddering under the bedclothes.

When Mabel finally came at half past eight with hot tea, the old lady had dozed into a fitful sleep again and was actually grateful to be startled into wakefulness in a sunlit room and see the familiar, plump figure of the lady's maid, whose ordinary face held no alarm and no accusation.

The tea had never been more welcome. Even almost scalding as it was, it was clean and fragrant and it eased her dry mouth and pounding head. She had no desire to get up and get dressed and face the morning, but to lie there in bed alone with her thoughts would be unendurable.

"Are you all right, Mrs. Ellison?" Mabel said with concern.

"I . . . I didn't sleep well. I think I may have to remain upstairs."

"Oh dear." Mabel looked suitably sympathetic.

The old lady wondered suddenly what Mabel really thought of her. Was she anything more than the source of a good position, someone to look after until she died, because Mabel was secure in Ashworth House, always warm enough, always well fed and treated with respect? Did she have any personal feelings for her? Perhaps it would be better not to know. They might be of dislike. And if she were to think of it honestly, she had given Mabel very little cause to feel anything else. One did not treat servants like friends; they did not expect it or want it, it would be embarrassing. But there were always degrees of consideration, and of the occasional word of thanks. Usually a lady's maid could expect as part of her remuneration to receive her mistress's clothes when they were past her best use of them. However, since Mariah had worn black for the last quarter of a century, that was of less value to Mabel than might have been foreseen. But she never complained, at least not as far as the old lady knew.

"Thank you," she said aloud.

Mabel looked startled.

"For your care," the old lady said tartly. "Don't look like that at me, as if I'd spoken to you in Greek!" She moved to get up, impatiently, and a stab of pain brought her up with a gasp.

"Would you like a doctor, ma'am?" Mabel asked helpfully.

"No, thank you, I would not! Here, give me your arm." She took it and hauled herself heavily out of bed and stood up, steadying herself with difficulty. She really did feel unwell. She had had no idea her plan would leave her with this kind of reaction. She should have felt the weight lifted, not added to. After all, Samuel Ellison was gone. She was safe. She had achieved what she wanted to—no, needed to. It had been a matter of survival.

He had threatened to destroy her, unwittingly perhaps, but destroy her nevertheless.

But that did not relieve the darkness. In fact, it hardly seemed even to matter.

She dressed with Mabel's help. Pity about the black. There would be nothing decent for Mabel to inherit when the time came. Perhaps that would not be long. What was she clinging to life for? She was old, worn out and unloved. Maybe she would wear something lavender or dark blue.

"Mabel!"

"Yes, Mrs. Ellison?"

"I want three new dresses . . . or perhaps two new dresses and a suit . . . a skirt and jacket."

"I'm making one now, ma'am. Is that three including that?"

"Not that one!" she said impatiently. "Three more. Put that aside for now. I want one in dark blue, one in lavender, and . . . and one in green! Yes . . . green."

"Green! Did you say 'one in green,' ma'am?"

"Are you losing your hearing, Mabel? I would like a green dress, a dark blue one, and a lavender one. Unless you don't care for lavender, in which case make it something else . . . burgundy, perhaps."

"Yes, Mrs. Ellison." The incredulity was high in her voice. "I'll fetch some designs for you to look at."

"Don't bother, just do whatever you think is becoming. I trust your judgment." Heaven forfend she chose something outlandish and the old lady lived long enough that she had to wear them! But an unbecoming dress was really the least of her worries now. Yesterday it would have been merely irritating, two weeks ago it would have been a major catastrophe. Now it was nothing at all. "See to it," she added firmly. "I shall give you the money immediately."

"Yes, Mrs. Ellison," Mabel said quietly, her eyes wide.

But it was a wretched morning. It was impossible to concentrate on anything, not that she had any tasks of importance to do. She never had. Her entire life was a round of domestic trivialities that did not matter in the slightest.

She did not want to spend the morning with Caroline. She could not bear to see her, and sooner or later she would be bound to say something about yesterday's disastrous events. What answer was there? She had thought she could cope with it, be evasive, or even tell Caroline she had brought it upon herself. But now that it was accomplished, she felt nothing but a black despair—and a weight of guilt that was like a physical pain.

She busied herself doing small domestic chores, to the considerable irritation of the maids. First she gathered several pieces of used string and undid the knots, all the while instructing the youngest maid how to do it herself in the future.

"Never throw away good string!" she said imperiously.

"It's full o' knots!" the girl pointed out. "I can't get them undone! It's more'n me fingers is worth!"

"That is simply because you don't know how," the old lady pointed out. "Here. Fetch me a wooden spoon. Quickly!"

"A wooden spoon?" The girl, who was perhaps thirteen, was nonplussed.

"Are you deaf, child? Do as you are told! And quickly! Don't stand there all day."

The girl vanished and returned in a few moments with a large wooden spoon. She offered it, handle first.

"Thank you. Now watch and learn." The old lady took the first piece of knotted string, placed it on the table in front of her, and, turning the knot over as she went, struck it hard several times with the spoon. Then she took a tiny pair of scissors from her pocket and inserted the points into the middle of the knot. Gradually she eased it open. "There you are!" she said triumphantly. "Now you do the next one."

The girl obeyed with enthusiasm, pounding the knots and gouging them undone. It was a considerable victory.

Next she taught the child how to clean the cane stand in the hall with lemon juice and salt, then how to shine the brass in the withdrawing room with olive oil, and then sent her to find beer from the servants' hall and have Cook set it on the hearth for a few minutes to warm it. With that, she instructed her how to clean the dark wood of the mantel.

"I'd teach you how to clean diamonds in gin," she said tartly, "if Mrs. Fielding had any diamonds!"

"Or any gin," the child added. "I never met anyone afore wot knows so much!" Her eyes were wide with admiration. "D'yer know 'ow ter get rid o' scorch marks an' all? We got a terrible one on the master's shirt yesterday, an' the mistress'll be proper tore up w'en she knows."

"If she were any use she'd know how to get it out herself!" Mariah said with satisfaction. Here at the back of the house she could not hear every carriage that passed, or footsteps coming and going. She would not see Caroline, or Joshua if he came home. She would not have to hear them, the confusion, the pain. "Vinegar, fuller's earth, washing soda and a small onion chopped fine," she went on. "You should know that! Can't throw out a good piece of linen just because there's a scorch mark on it. Make a paste, spread it on the stain, and let it dry. Brush it off the next day."

" 'Ow much vinegar?" the girl asked.

"What?"

" 'Ow much vinegar, please, ma'am?"

She took a deep breath and told the girl the proportions.

The rest of the morning passed with other minor duties, excuses to fill the time. She ate no luncheon. It was as if her throat had closed.

By mid-afternoon she could no longer avoid Caroline without some very good excuse. She considered saying she was ill, or even that she had fallen downstairs and was in too much pain to remain out of her bed. But then Caroline would send for the doctor, whether she wanted it or not, and that might provoke all sorts of worse things. She would be proved a liar. No. Far better she exercise courage and self-mastery. She was going to have to for the rest of her life. This afternoon was an excellent time to begin.

She changed into a suitable black bombazine afternoon dress with jet beading on the bodice, and put on a smart brooch she had not worn for thirty years. It was not a mourning brooch, with a carefully preserved coil or braid of hair. It was a handsome crystal piece with pearls.

She went down to the withdrawing room, and there was no one there.

Caroline's morning began equally wretchedly, but she was looking for something to do to keep her mind from turning over and over the same miserable thoughts when she half overheard the one manservant they kept talking with the housemaid.

"How could I?" he said indignantly. They were standing by the sideboard in the dining room and she was regarding the silver with distaste. "That old devil sent me out in a rush like the house was on fire. Had to go. She said it was urgent, life an' death, as you might say."

"Sent you?" she said with her eyebrows raised. "Where?"

"To fetch Mr. Fielding, of course," he replied. "And he came home hotfoot, and threw out that American gentleman that's been here so often. Then went right back out hisself."

"Pity." She shook her head. "He was very nice spoken, but I s'pose he was here a bit much, like. Anyway, I've got no time to stand here gossiping, and neither have you. You'd best get those knives done now, and quick, or Cook'll be after you. You're all behind!"

"So would you be, if you'd been all the way to the theatre an' back!" he retorted, picking up the knives and going out, leaving the door open.

Caroline stood still, her mind racing. Joshua had not come home by chance. The old lady had sent for him, knowing Samuel was there. Why? And what had she said?

What else had she done? Had she somehow caused Samuel to come at five in the afternoon, uninvited? And then he had behaved as if Caroline had summoned him.

As she stood in the hall, her thoughts racing, there was a certainty growing in her mind which she did all she could to suffocate, drive out of existence. She must learn the truth, and that must be from Samuel himself.

If only Charlotte or Emily were there, she would take one of them with her. As it was she would have to go alone. She dreaded it so much it must be done immediately, before she could think about it and lose her courage. Joshua would never understand. This might make it all even worse. He would think she was chasing after Samuel, after he had forbidden him the house.

And what would Samuel himself think? That made her cold to the pit of her stomach.

Yet to leave it as it was would be worse. There was no point in asking the old lady. She would never tell the truth.

She put on her hat and coat, informed the parlormaid she was going out, and left.

The journey was terrible. Half a dozen times she nearly lost her nerve and told the hansom driver to take her home again, but the knowledge of the days and weeks ahead of loneliness, of never being able to understand or tell Joshua the truth, was enough to spur her on.

She arrived at the hotel where Samuel was staying and went to the desk. She asked for him and was told he was in the lounge. She allowed the bellboy to conduct her through.

Samuel was reading the newspaper. There were three other men in the room, all equally absorbed. She forced herself to be calm and walked over to him.

He glanced up, then recognized her, and the color burned up his face.

It was too late to run, as she would have. For a moment she could hardly breathe.

He stood up. "Good morning, Mrs. Fielding," he said stiffly.

She could feel her face flame. "Good morning, Mr. Ellison. I am sorry to intrude on your time in this way, most particularly after our last parting." That was an extraordinary understatement of events. "But there are too many things that I do not understand, and I fear my mother-in-law may have been meddling with the intention of causing trouble. I do not yet know why."

He looked confused and more than a little embarrassed. "I . . . if . . . of course. If you believe it will help?"

"I do." She sat down without waiting to be invited, smoothing her skirt self-consciously. She was intensely aware of his presence within a few feet of her. She wondered if he felt as aware of her.

"I'm sorry." He apologized for the oversight in his manners, then sat down sharply himself.

This was dreadful.

They both started to speak at once, she to ask why he had called. She never knew what he was about to say.

They both stopped.

"I'm sorry . . ." He colored deeply, but he did not move his eyes from her face.

She looked down at her hands. "Why did you come yesterday afternoon? I had the impression you thought I expected you."

"You had the impression?" His voice rose in disbelief.

"Yes." She avoided looking up. "Was I mistaken?"

She heard the crinkle of paper and saw it in front of her. It was held in his hand, pushed forward.

She read it with horror that crawled over her skin and left her cold. She found her voice hoarse when she tried to speak.

"I didn't write that!" Dear God, he had to believe her. And yet her first thought was to pray that Joshua had not seen it. He would be so hurt, so . . . betrayed. "I did not write that!" She looked up and met his eyes. She was angry now, not for herself but for Joshua. "It was my mother-in-law who sent the manservant for Joshua to come home. I believe it was she who wrote the note to you as well." She kept it in her hand and stood up. "I am very sorry. Please believe me, I am! I like you, I enjoy your company, but whatever I had felt, I would never have written a letter like that. I apologize that you were misled by a member of my family, and for the embarrassment it has occasioned. But I am about to go home and address the matter." She did not ask if she could keep the letter. She had no intention whatsoever of giving it up. "Thank you for seeing me," she added. She was about to say something about a good day, and abandoned it as absurd. She glanced at him once again, then turned and left.

Mariah was sitting alone in the withdrawing room telling herself that the danger had passed, and she had only done what was necessary, when the door opened and Caroline came in. She looked very pale and there were shadows around her eyes. The pain in her face needed no explanation.

At that moment the old lady would have given all she possessed to have undone yesterday, but she knew nothing could ever be undone. A last thought flickered out somewhere inside her, and the darkness was complete.

"We are not at home," Caroline said to the maid, somewhere behind her. "Not to anyone. Do you understand?"

"Yes, Mrs. Fielding, not to anyone."

"Good. Now, do not interrupt us."

"No, ma'am."

Caroline closed the door and faced the old lady.

"Now!" she said grimly. "You are going to explain this!" She held out the slightly crumpled letter in her hand.

The old lady stared up at her. There was no yielding in her face, her eyes did not waver, no softening.

"Explain?" she repeated through dry lips.

"Don't pretend you don't know," Caroline said grimly. "Samuel received this letter inviting him to call yesterday. It is a highly suggestive letter, and he came expecting . . . Heaven knows what! Then you sent Joseph to the theatre to fetch Joshua so he would arrive and misread the situation." She held up the letter. "Someone used my name. That could only have been you."

Denial sprang to the old lady's lips, and she saw in Caroline's face that she would not be believed. There was a kind of finality in the moment. A black void of hate opened up in front of her. There was nothing left to lose now. The pen was not where she had expected it. It was not the past after all, it was the present, the loss now. It was the knowledge of having destroyed it all herself.

"I am waiting!" Caroline said sharply. "This requires an explanation. Why did you send Samuel this letter in my name?"

Could she disclaim any knowledge? Say she sent the letter to prevent Caroline from becoming involved in an affair and ruining her marriage? Would Caroline believe her? No. It was a travesty, and they both knew it.

The ultimate nightmare was real at last. This was the moment when the truth would begin. She might delay it, push it before her in bits and pieces into the future, but in the end it would all be known. It would be clearer to tell it now, like a quick kill. There was nothing left to lose, it was only the manner of it that was in question.

Caroline was still staring at her, implacable.

The old lady took a long, deep breath.

"Yes, I sent him the letter in your name to get him here. I knew he would come, for you . . ."

At any other time Caroline's blush would have given the old lady satisfaction. Now she barely noticed it.

"I assume you will tell me why," Caroline said coldly.

"Of course." The old lady gulped air and felt it painful inside her. "I intended Joshua to find you together and throw him out, and forbid him ever to come here again."

Caroline sat down as if her legs had given way, her skirts all squashed around her.

"Why? What has he ever done that you should even dislike him, let alone do something . . . so . . ." She was lost for words, and her voice trailed off helplessly. She looked as if all understanding had fled from her.

There was no alternative. Caroline had to know. It would only be harder if she left it. Now was the time. Half a century of secret pain was about to be opened up without comfort or mercy.

"Because he knows. He must!" the old lady said hoarsely. "I thought I couldn't live with that. Now I am going to have to."

"Knows?" Caroline shook her head a little. "Knows what? What could he possibly know that would be worth . . . that?"

Finally the nightmare was real, something no longer private. It was fixed inescapably, dragged from the darkness of the inner soul and spread wide open. Even if the old lady could forget it, even for a day, others would always remember. Somehow she had lost control of it.

Caroline leaned forward in her chair, crushing her skirt further. "Mama-in-law! What is it you think Samuel knows?" She moistened her lips. "Were you not married to Father Ellison?"

The old lady wanted to laugh. That would have been shameful—of course it would—and it would mean both her children would be illegitimate. But somehow it looked almost trivial compared with what she would have to tell Caroline.

"Yes, I was married to him. He divorced Alys perfectly legally, and I knew of her existence. My father saw to all that."

"Then what?" Caroline demanded. "It obviously has to do with Alys, or Samuel could not know about it."

"Yes it has. It has to do with why she left. Have you never wondered why she did something so extreme, so dangerous, and both legally and socially unacceptable?"

"Yes, of course I have," Caroline said instantly. "But I could hardly ask. I assumed she ran off with someone, and then he abandoned her, and of course she would not then go back to Grandpapa. She must have left before she knew she was with child. No one could doubt Samuel is Grandpapa's."

"That is what one would assume," Mariah agreed very quietly. "It is not what happened."

There must have been something in her voice which struck Caroline in a new way, more deeply, and with a stab of tragedy. She barely moved, but there was a gentleness in her eyes, an attention which no longer made judgments.

"Why did she go?" she said in little more than a whisper.

This was the moment. It was like plunging into black, stinking water, ice-cold to take the breath away.

"Because he forced her into unnatural practices—painful, degrading things no human should do . . ." It was like hearing someone else's voice.

Caroline drew in her breath as if she had been struck. Her face was white to the lips, her eyes hollow. She started to speak, then faltered and fell silent. She began to shake her head in short, sharp little movements.

"I thought you wouldn't believe me," the old lady said quietly. "No one would. It is not something you can tell . . . not anyone . . . not ever."

"But . . . but you didn't know Alys!" Caroline protested. "Samuel didn't tell you . . ." Again she stopped. She stared fixedly into the old lady's eyes. In all the years they had known each other they had never met in a look so honest. Caroline took in a long, shaking breath and let it out in a sigh. "You mean . . ." She put her hand up to her lips as if to stifle the next words. "You mean he . . . you . . ."

"Don't say it!" Mariah pleaded. This was absurd, futile. She ached to be believed, and here she was begging Caroline not to give words to the truth.

"Un . . . natural?" Caroline struggled with the word.

205

Mariah shut her eyes. "I believe men do it to each other . . . at least some men do. It is known as sodomy. It is more painful than you can imagine . . . against your will. It is your pain which . . . which gives him pleasure." The rage and humiliation of it poured back over her, bringing her body out in sweat. "He made me strip naked, on my hands and knees, like an animal—"

"Stop it!" Caroline's voice was high and shrill. "Stop it! Stop it!" She put up her hands, palms outward, to push it away.

"You can't imagine your father-in-law like that, can you?" Mariah whispered. "Or me? Together on the floor like dogs, me weeping with pain and humiliation, wishing I could die, and him more and more excited, shouting, unable to control himself until he was finished."

"Stop it!" Caroline moved her fingers to her mouth. "Don't!"

"You can't listen?" The old lady was shaking so violently with the memory of it she could hardly speak without stuttering. "I l-lived with it . . . for years . . . all my married life. He died of a stroke like that, naked, on the floor, without his clothes. I'd prayed for him to d-die . . . and he did! I crept away from him and washed myself—he often made me bleed—then went back to look at him. He was still dead, lying on the floor on his face. I washed him, and put his nightshirt on him before I called anyone."

There was horror in Caroline's eyes, but denial was slowly being replaced by the beginning of pity.

"You always said . . . you said you loved him . . ." she began. "He was so . . . such a wonderful man . . . you said you were so happy!"

The old lady felt the bitter heat of shame in her cheeks. "What would you have said?" she asked. "The truth?"

"No . . ." There were tears in Caroline's voice. "Of course not. I don't know . . . I don't know what I would have done. I can't imagine it . . . I can't . . . I don't know. It . . ." She did not say it was not true, but it was there in her voice, her face, the stiff, tight angle of her shoulders.

"You can't believe it!" It was a challenge, laying bare her

own humiliation and her cowardice all those years. No one would believe that Alys left, her courage, her dignity, and Mariah remained, to be used like an animal.

"I . . ." Caroline stopped, lifting her hands helplessly.

"Why didn't I go . . . as Alys did?" The words were torn out, like barbed wire. "Because I am a coward." There it was, the lowest ugliness of all, the loathing, the self-disgust, not just that she had been reduced to bestiality, her human dignity stripped from her, but that she had stayed and allowed it to go on happening. She made no excuses. There were none. Whatever Caroline thought of her, it could not equal the contempt she had for herself.

Caroline looked at the old woman's face, tight and crumpled with pain and years of bitterness. The self-hatred was naked in her eyes, and the despair.

She rejected the idea. It was obscene. And yet it made a hideous sense. Part of her believed it already. But if it was true, it shattered so much of her world, the ideals and the people she had trusted. If behind the self-composed manner, the smile and the Sunday prayers, Edmund Ellison had been a sexual sadist, submitting his wife to humiliating cruelties in the secrecy of their own bedroom, then who, anywhere, was what he seemed? If even his familiar face hid ugliness so appalling her imagination refused to grasp it, then what was safe . . . anywhere?

And yet looking at the old woman in front of her, she could not push the truth of it away. Something terrible had happened to her. Something had precipitated the years of anger and cruelty she had exercised on her family. The hatred she seemed to feel for the world, anyone and everyone, was really for herself. She saw the worst in others because she saw it in her own heart. And for years she had despised her inability to fight against it, to defend her humanity from degradation and pain. She was a coward, and she knew it. She had submitted, and endured, rather than run away into the dangerous and unknown as Alys had done, alone, penniless, with nothing but her courage and her desperation. No wonder Samuel admired his mother so profoundly.

Mariah had stayed with her husband, living with it, night after night, putting on a brave, smooth face every day, then going up to her bedroom knowing what would happen . . . and it had, year after year, until he had finally died and set her free. Except that she was not free, she was as much imprisoned as when he had been alive, because the memory and the loathing were still there, locked inside her.

"Did you really think Samuel would tell anyone?" Caroline said gently, not knowing why these words came to her lips.

There were tears in the old lady's eyes, although no one else would ever know whether they were grief, rage or self-pity.

"He knew . . . at least . . ." Suddenly her eyes were hollow with doubt. "I think he did. He might have told, but I couldn't live with the uncertainty . . . if he . . ."

Caroline waited.

The old lady sniffed. "I'm sorry for what I did to you. You didn't deserve that. I . . . I wish I hadn't."

Caroline reached forward and very tentatively touched the ancient hand lying on the black skirt. It was stiff and cold under her fingers.

"There are many kinds of courage," she said softly. "Running away is one of them. Remaining is another. What would have happened to Edward and Suzannah if you had gone? You could not have taken them with you over to America. It would be illegal. The police would have come after you."

"I could have tried!" The words were angry, grating.

"And made it worse for yourself," Caroline pointed out. "To go was brave—but to stay and make the best of it you could for your children, that was brave too."

A tiny spark lit in the old lady's black eyes, a flare of hope.

They had cordially disliked each other for years, living under the same roof, circling around each other with chill, occasionally open, hostility. Now all that seemed unimportant. This was a consuming reality which overrode all the past. The moment was now, in a new light, with new knowledge.

"No, it wasn't. I was afraid to go." The old lady said the words carefully, looking at Caroline all the time.

Caroline spoke honestly. It was not difficult, which surprised her.

"Perhaps Alys was afraid to stay?"

The old lady hesitated. It was obvious she had not thought of that. In her mind Alys had always been the one who was brave, the one who did the right thing. This was hope from a quarter she had never expected.

Caroline smiled very faintly, just an instant. "It takes strength to endure and tell no one, never to run away, simply give up. Did you ever allow Edward or Suzannah to know?"

The old lady stiffened. "Of course not! What a monstrous question."

"You hid it from them for yourself . . . but for them also."

"I . . . I hid it . . ." The struggle for honesty was so plain it was painful. "I don't know. I hid it for myself. . . . I couldn't bear my children to know I had . . . I had been . . . to see me like . . ." At last the tears spilled over onto her cheeks and she began to shudder uncontrollably.

Caroline was horrified. For a moment she was paralyzed. Then pity swept away everything else. She could not like the old woman—there was too much cruelty, too many years of criticism and complaint to forget—but she could feel the wrenching sorrow inside her, the guilt and the self-loathing, the unbearable loneliness. She leaned forward and put her arms around the old woman's shoulders and held her gently.

They stayed like that, motionless, neither one of them speaking, until Caroline felt a kind of peace settle over them, perhaps no more than a temporary emotional exhaustion. Then she let go, and sat back in her own chair for a moment.

Was there something else she should say of comfort, or honesty, something which if left silent now could not be re-caught later? Should they agree on some story to tell Joshua? He had to know.

For a moment she was cold, frightened.

She looked at the old woman in front of her, head still bent, face hidden. How could she explain the letter? It had to have been someone in the house using her name. She and Samuel had never been seen together in public, except at the theatre the night they met. No woman in Samuel's life, presuming there was one, could be jealous enough to do such a thing. Caroline was his brother's widow. Who more natural for him to call on in a strange city?

But she must explain yesterday to Joshua. That was insistent, at the front of her mind.

She looked at the old lady, and pity ground hard with a unique pain, but she had brought that upon herself; her own actions had made it inevitable. Caroline was not going to wound Joshua, and herself, to save Mariah Ellison. She could not believe Alys could have told her son something so terrible. But even if he knew, Samuel had not behaved towards them as if he knew. Joshua would remain. What should she say?

Her own decision was made. She rose to her feet and went quietly out of the room, closing the door. In the hall she saw the maid.

"Mrs. Ellison would like a little time alone," she said to the girl. "Please see that she is not disturbed for a while, half an hour at least. Unless, of course, she rings for you."

"Yes, ma'am."

Caroline went upstairs deep in thought. It would be very difficult to tell Joshua. Perhaps she could avoid the details. She had never kept a secret from him before. She had been used to discretion all her married life with Edward, but Joshua was different . . . or he had been, before this.

Perhaps she could tell him that there was an agonizing, humiliating secret but not what it was? Maybe he would not ask.

She crossed the landing to her bedroom. She had no particular purpose in going there, simply to be alone. Her mind was in far too much turmoil to be concentrated on any household task, and there was none outstanding that mattered.

She closed the door and sat down in the dressing chair with its pretty chintz flowers. She loved this room. It was what she had wanted for years, in Edward's time, but he would have disliked it. He would have found the flowers too large, too bright, and the whole thing not dignified enough.

She tried to remember him clearly, bring back his presence into her mind, everything that was good and gentle about him, the reality of his feelings. How he had grieved for Sarah. He had disliked Pitt so much, to begin with. He had never really come to know him well. But then like a lot of men, he had loved his daughters deeply, even if he had not often shown it, and no man was good enough to marry them and care for them as they should have been. Emily's first husband had had the money and the breeding, but Edward had always worried that he would not necessarily be faithful to her.

And of course Pitt had no money to speak of, and no social background at all. How could he ever give Charlotte all Edward thought she was worthy of?

And how Dominic had treated his beloved Sarah was an old pain best forgotten now. Sarah was dead, and nothing could retrieve that.

Then her thoughts skipped to Edward himself, and Mrs. Attwood, whose lovely face Caroline could still picture quite easily, even after all these years. She remembered exactly how she had felt when she had first realized she was Edward's mistress, not the invalid widow of an old friend, as he had claimed. She had discovered a part of Edward she had not known. What else might there have been that she never knew?

She was beginning to feel a coldness inside her. Her hands were trembling. She had been totally duped by her father-in-law. She had seen him only as the dignified man she met in the withdrawing room, or presiding at the dining table, saying the family prayers. The other man, the creature Mrs. Ellison described, was a monster living in the same skin, and she had neither seen nor felt anything of him at all. How could she be so utterly blind, so insensitive?

What else was she blind to? It was not only that she had been wrong about her father-in-law, it was that she had been so wrong about herself! All that cruelty, that misery and humiliation, even physical pain, had been there behind the daily masks, and she had seen nothing of them.

In who else's face had she seen only what she wanted to? What had Edward asked of Mrs. Attwood that he had never asked of Caroline? How much did she really know about anyone? Even Joshua . . . ?

* * *

She did not feel in the least like going out that evening, but it was the first night of Joshua's new play. Normally she would be there, whatever the circumstances. Not to go would make a statement she could never retrieve.

She ate a light supper alone—the old lady remained upstairs—then she dressed with great care in a magnificent royal blue gown. She added the cameo pendant that Joshua had given her, and a long velvet cloak, then took the carriage to the theatre, feeling cold, shivering and uncertain. Joshua could not be more afraid of this evening than she was. He could not have as much riding in its success or failure.

For a while the buzz of excitement carried her along and she had no chance to think of anything other than greeting friends and those who wished her well. They congratulated her for Joshua and were filled with anticipation of the audience's reaction. She desperately wished him to succeed, to be praised, and yet not to portray any of the disturbing passions she saw in Cecily Antrim.

At last the lights dimmed, the audience fell silent, and the curtain rose.

The play was superb, subtle, intelligent, and funny. Many times she found herself laughing aloud. During the first interval she glanced across and saw Mr. and Mrs. Marchand, smiling and at ease. She was too far away to read their expressions in detail, but their gestures made their pleasure evident.

Suddenly Caroline was aware of hurt, even defensiveness. She did not want them to be disturbed; she liked them and understood them, she wanted their friendship and perceived both its values and its limitations. And yet complacency was a kind of death. Something that did not stir thought, awaken new emotions or challenge preconceptions was agreeable, but no more than that. And she knew that Joshua would despise himself if that was all he did. He did not wish merely to entertain. That was at least in part why he admired Cecily Antrim so profoundly. She had the courage to say what she believed, whether one agreed with it or not.

The second act was swifter moving, and it was almost over

before she realized there were deeper emotions drawn from her than in the first, and becoming more complex. It was painful, and it was also a kind of relief. She began to think again of Mariah Ellison and how the sudden knowledge of her suffering and anger over all these years had changed her own life.

Twenty-four hours ago she would not have believed that civilized people would even think of the things the old lady had said Edmund Ellison had forced on her most nights of her married life. And yet even sitting here in this exquisite theatre, watching drama so perfectly performed, acted, pretended with consummate skill, surrounded in the half dark by hundreds of exquisitely dressed people, she did believe it. That darkness might lie behind any number of these calm, smoothly groomed faces. She would never know.

She thought of the old lady sitting in growing terror every time Samuel called, then at last planning her terrible, destructive escape. Had she thought that if Joshua left Caroline, threw her out for immorality, just what that would mean? Surely she had. And yet she had known nothing but bitterness and humiliation in marriage, and she could not live with the thought that her family, to whom she had perpetuated the lie for so many years, would at last know that.

What terrible isolation, what loneliness and fear all the time that Caroline had never guessed, horror that had never entered her imagination.

Perhaps some of these things needed to be said, emotions stirred and disturbed, painful questions asked, so a thread of understanding could be woven between people who would never experience for themselves the things that tortured others who sat only a few feet away.

She leaned forward to watch the third and final act of the play.

Afterwards she went backstage to his dressing room, as she always did after a major performance. She was as nervous as if she herself was about to step out in front of the audience and she did not know her lines.

She had rehearsed a dozen times what she was going to say

213

to him, but what if he would not see her? What if he would not listen? She would have to make him . . . insist. She could be as determined as Cecily Antrim or anyone else. She loved Joshua, wholly and completely, and she was not going to lose him without fighting with every skill and strength she possessed.

The dressing room door was closed. She could hear laughter inside. How could he laugh, when he had left her in the morning without speaking?

She knocked. She would not go in uninvited. She might see something she would prefer not to. That thought was like ice inside her. It made her feel sick.

There were footsteps and the door opened. Joshua stood there in a robe, half changed from his costume. He looked startled, then his face softened a little. He pulled the door wide without saying anything. There were two other people inside, a man and a woman.

Relief flooded over Caroline, and guilt. He had not been alone with anyone.

They were actors she knew from other plays, and they welcomed her. She congratulated them all on the performance, quite honestly. She could hardly believe how normal her voice sounded.

They seemed to talk endlessly. Would they never leave? Could she say anything to suggest they did? No . . . that would be unforgivably rude.

Then the words were out. "I'm so glad I came, it was so much richer than I could have guessed," she said distinctly. "There is something about a first night that can never be repeated exactly. And I nearly didn't." She avoided Joshua's eyes. "My mother-in-law is staying with us at the moment, and she was not at all well today. Something . . . happened . . . which distressed her more than I would have thought possible."

The others expressed their concern.

"Should you be home early?" the man asked.

Caroline looked at Joshua at last.

"Is she ill?" he said. His voice was unreadable.

The other two excused themselves, graciously, and left.

"Is she?" Joshua repeated.

214

"No," Caroline replied. He was tired, and the mood was too fragile between them to play with words. "She did something wicked, and today I discovered it, and when I faced her she told me why."

He looked puzzled. He did not really want to know. He tolerated the old lady because he felt he should, perhaps for Caroline's sake.

"Wicked?" he said dubiously.

She must continue. "Yes, I think so. She wrote a very forward letter to Samuel Ellison, inviting him to call yesterday afternoon, and signed it with my name." Why did he not say something? She hurried on. "When he arrived she deliberately left the room, which she has never done before, then sent Joseph to fetch you."

"Why?" he said slowly. "I know she disapproves of me because I am an actor and a Jew, but as much as that?"

The tears stung her eyes and she felt her throat ache. "No!" She wanted to touch him, but it would be wrong now. He might see it as pity. "No! It has nothing to do with you. She is afraid that Samuel knows something about his own mother which was true about Mariah also, something dreadful, of which she was so ashamed she could not bear anyone else to know. She worried that he would tell me, and so she wanted you to throw him out so he would never return. Then her secret would be safe. She was so terrified of it she did not care if she ruined my happiness. She would do anything to stop me knowing, and of course the rest of the family as well. She felt she could not live if we did."

He stared at her in amazement. He was very pale, but it was not anger in his face, it was horror.

"I know what it is," she said quietly. "And I think I can forgive her for what she has done. If you don't mind, I would rather not tell you what she suffered, but I will if I must."

His face relaxed. He was too tired, perhaps too shaken to smile, but there was a gentleness in him she did not mistake.

"No," he said softly. "No, I don't want to know. Let her keep her secret."

The tears spilled down her cheeks and she found herself

215

sniffing and swallowing hard. "I love you," she whispered, and sniffed again.

He stood up and reached out a little tentatively. Suddenly she realized how much he had been hurt. He had doubted . . . feared.

She put her arms around him and held him so hard she felt him wince. "I'm sorry I didn't behave so you knew that," she said into his shoulder.

His arms tightened until he was holding her just as closely as she held him. He did not say anything, just moved his lips over her hair, slowly.

10

P*ITT AND TELLMAN* still pursued the matter of Henri Bonnard and his quarrel with Orlando Antrim. Frankly, Pitt was not certain that they would learn anything useful from it, even if they were to discover the entire truth of the matter. If Bonnard had disappeared of his own volition it might well be worrying, and extremely irritating to the French Embassy, but it was not a police matter. The only real connection with Cathcart's death was photography. Their resemblance to one another was coincidental and he could see no importance in it. He was perfectly certain that the body found at Horseferry Stairs was Cathcart and that it was Bonnard with whom Orlando Antrim had quarreled.

"Do you think it was really about pictures?" Tellman said dubiously as they rode in a hansom towards Kew, where they had been told the camera club was photographing interesting foliage in the tropical glasshouses. "Would anyone really commit murder over a photograph? I mean," he added hastily, "a photograph that wasn't of somebody doing something they shouldn't."

"I doubt it," Pitt admitted. "But I suppose it could have been the start of a quarrel which got out of hand."

Tellman sat forward morosely. "I think I'm just getting to understand people and know why they do what they do, then I get on a case like this, and I feel as if I know nothing."

Pitt looked at his angular shoulders and dour, lantern-jawed face and saw the confusion in him. Tellman had such

217

set ideas about society and people, about what was just and what was not. They sprang from the poverty of his youth, the underlying anger that fueled his desire to change things, to see labor rewarded and find some greater equality among people who worked and those who, as far as he could see, did not and yet possessed so much. Investigating the private tragedies of their lives constantly upset his preconceptions and obliged him to feel a pity and an understanding he did not wish to, where it would have been so much easier, and more comfortable, simply to have hated.

Now the photographs, which these privileged young men obviously cared about so much, seemed to him both beautiful and trivial, but not a comprehensible motive for murder.

Pitt was inclined to agree with him. But at the moment they had little better to pursue. No one in the area where Cathcart lived had observed anything helpful, and Lily Monderell was telling nothing more about the photographs she had removed and sold almost immediately at such an excellent profit. Once again they were back to photographs. It seemed the motive lay somewhere within them.

They traveled the rest of the way to Kew Gardens and went in to find the tropical house, a magnificent tower of glass containing giant palm trees with fronds more than a yard across, exotic ferns, trailing vines with flowers, and bromeliads blooming in pale, lustrous colors.

Tellman drew in his breath deeply, smelling the heat and the damp, the rich humus. He had never experienced anything like it before.

Pitt saw the photographers first, balancing their tripods carefully on the uneven surfaces of the earth, angling cameras up to tangled vines or intricate patterns of branches, trying to catch the light on the surface of a leaf. He knew they would be furious to be interrupted. He also knew that unless he forced his way into their attention he would stand waiting until the light faded at the end of the day.

He approached a fair-haired young man with a keen face, at that moment shading his eyes as he stared at the crown of a soaring palm.

Pitt craned his neck upward and saw a tracery of vines across the roof, erratic circles and curves against the geometry of the paned glass. It was a pity to interrupt, but necessary. Beauty and imagination would have to wait.

"Excuse me!"

The young man waved his other hand to ward off the disturbance.

"Later, sir, you may have my entire attention. Come back in half an hour, if you would be so good."

"I'm sorry, I have not half an hour to spare," Pitt apologized. He meant it. "I am Superintendent Pitt of the Bow Street station, and I am investigating the murder of a photographer."

That captured the young man's concentration. He abandoned the palm and stared at Pitt with wide blue eyes. "One of our club? Murdered? My God . . . who?"

"Not one of your club, Mr. . . ."

"McKellar, David McKellar. You said a photographer?"

"Delbert Cathcart."

"Oh!" He seemed vaguely relieved. "Oh yes, of course. I read about that. Robbed and thrown into the river, so it seems. I'm terribly sorry. He was brilliant." He colored faintly. "I'm sorry, I didn't mean that to sound callous. Of course a death is terrible, whoever's it is. From his point of view, I daresay his talent is irrelevant. But I know nothing about it. What could I tell you?"

"On the morning Mr. Cathcart was killed there was a quarrel between Orlando Antrim, the actor, and Mr. Henri Bonnard of the French Embassy," Pitt explained.

McKellar looked startled.

"Do you know anything about it?" Pitt pressed. "It was apparently on the subject of photographs."

"Was it?" McKellar seemed perplexed but not entirely at a loss, as he might have been were the subject to make no sense to him at all.

"Do people quarrel over photographs?" Pitt asked.

"Well . . . I suppose so. What has that to do with poor Cathcart?"

"Do you sell your pictures?" Tellman said suddenly. "I

mean, is there money in it?" He glanced around at the cameras and their tripods.

McKellar colored a little more deeply. "Well, sometimes. It—it helps funds, you know. Costs a bit, all this stuff. Not that . . ." He trailed off and stopped, standing a little uncomfortably.

Pitt waited.

"I mean . . ." McKellar fidgeted. "Look, I think I may be speaking a trifle out of turn, you know? I've just sold the odd picture here and there, that's all."

"Of vines and leaves?" Tellman said incredulously. "People pay for that?"

McKellar avoided his eyes. "No . . . no, I shouldn't think so. Mostly a nice picture of a young lady, perhaps a few flowers . . . more . . . more personal, more charm, that sort of thing."

"A young lady with perhaps a few flowers," Pitt repeated, raising his eyebrows a little. "And a gown, or not?"

McKellar looked wretched. "Well, I daresay. Sometimes . . . not." He met Pitt's eyes and this time he was quite vehement. "Just a bit—artistic. Not vulgar!"

Pitt smiled. He carefully avoided Tellman's glance. "I see. And these sales supplement your funds for the expense of films and so on?"

"Yes."

"And do the young ladies in question receive part of this profit?"

"They get copies of . . . of one or two of the pictures."

"And are they aware that the rest are sold—to be bought, I presume, by the general public?" Pitt enquired.

McKellar was silent for a moment. "I . . . I think so," he said unhappily. "I mean . . . the reason's clear, isn't it?"

"Perfectly," Pitt agreed. "You wish to make some money in order to finance your hobby." His voice was colder than he had meant it to be.

McKellar flushed bright pink.

"And where are these photographs sold?" Pitt pressed.

"Sergeant Tellman will take down the names and addresses of all the dealers you have business with."

"Well . . . I . . ."

"If you can't remember them then we'll accompany you to wherever you have the information, and take it from there."

McKellar gave up. He swallowed convulsively. "It's all quite innocent, you know!" he protested. "Just . . . just pictures!"

In the afternoon Pitt and Tellman began visiting the dealers in postcards.

To begin with, all they saw were pretty pictures of a variety of young women in fairly conventional poses, their gentle faces looking out at the camera, some awkwardly self-conscious, others boldly, with a smile, even a challenge. There was nothing to be offended by, except the possibility that they had been denied a share of the profits. But then, considering the cost of cameras, film, development and so on, the profits were probably extremely small. The postcards themselves sold for a few pence, and they were of a good quality. The greatest gain from them was the pleasure in the creation and the possession.

"Is that all you have?" Pitt asked, without hope of learning anything further that was of value; it was a matter of habit. They were in a small tobacconist and bookseller's in Half Moon Street, just off Piccadilly, its shelves crowded, wooden floor creaking at every step. The smells of leather and snuff filled the air.

"Well . . ." the dealer said dubiously. "More the same, others much like these. That's all."

There was something in the way he said it, a directness that caught Pitt's attention. He was not certain it was a lie, but he felt it was.

"I'll see them," he said firmly.

Several dozen more cards were produced, and he and Tellman went through them fairly rapidly. They were of a wide variety, some quiet country scenes with pretty girls in the foreground, some almost domestic, some artificial and carefully posed. Many had a kind of innocence about them and were obviously amateur. Pitt recognized the round form and the type of foliage and patterns of light and shade he had seen the young men of the camera club study. He thought he even recognized parts of Hampstead Heath.

There were others more skilled, with subtler uses of light and shade, effects less obviously contrived. These were taken by enthusiasts with more practice and considerably more ability.

"I like the round ones," Tellman observed, fingering through the cards. "I mean I like the shape of the picture. But it does waste space, and on the whole I'd say the square ones were better, in a way. Sort of different, not like the girl you might meet in the street, more like . . . I don't know—"

"Square ones?" Pitt interrupted.

"Yes, here. There's half a dozen or so." Tellman passed over four of them.

Pitt looked. The first was well done but ordinary enough. The second was very good indeed. The girl had dark, curly hair blowing untidily around her face and she was laughing. In the background was a distant scene of the river, with light on the water and figures out of focus, no more than suggestions. She looked happy, and as if she was ready for anything that might be fun, the sort of girl most men would love to spend a day with, or longer. The photographer had caught her at the perfect moment.

The next was equally good but extremely different. This girl was fair, almost ethereal. She gazed away from the camera; the light made an aureole of her hair, and her pale shoulders gleamed like satin where her gown had slipped a little low. It was a brilliant mixture of innocence and eroticism. She was leaning a little on a pedestal, either of stone or plaster, and there was a vine growing around it.

It stirred a memory in Pitt, but he could not place it.

The last picture was of a very formal beauty reclining on a chaise longue. He had seen a photograph of Lillie Langtry in a similar pose. Only this girl was looking directly at the camera and there was a slight smile on her lips, as if she was aware of a hidden irony. The longer he looked at it the more attractive it became, because of the intelligence in her face.

Then he remembered where he had seen the pillars in the photograph before, because the chaise longue came from the same place. They belonged to Delbert Cathcart; Pitt had seen them in his studio.

"These are very good," he said thoughtfully.

"You like them?" the dealer asked with interest, scenting a possible sale. "I'll make you a fair price."

"Did you buy them legitimately?" Pitt said, frowning a little.

The man was indignant. "Of course I did! Do all my business fair and legal."

"Good. Then you can tell me where you bought these. Was it from Miss Monderell?"

"Never 'eard of 'er. Bought 'em from the artist 'isself."

"Did you? That would be Mr. Delbert Cathcart."

"Well . . ." He regarded Pitt nervously.

Pitt smiled. "Actually, it is Mr. Cathcart's murder I am investigating."

The man blanched visibly and swallowed. He shifted his weight from one foot to the other. "Oh? Yeah?"

Pitt continued to smile. "I'm sure you would be eager to help as much as possible, Mr. Unsworth. I think if you have these pictures of Mr. Cathcart's then you may have others as well, worth more money, perhaps. And before you make an error by denying that, I must advise you that I can very easily remain here to talk to you about the matter while Sergeant Tellman goes to fetch a warrant to search your premises. Or I could call the local constable to wait, and Sergeant Tellman and I could both go—"

"No . . . no!" The thought of a constable in uniform was enough to settle Unsworth's mind completely. It would be very bad for custom, particularly among those gentlemen who had rather private tastes. "I'll show you the rest meself. 'Course I will. A bit o' color in life is one thing, but I draw the line at murder. That's quite diff 'rent—quite diff 'rent. Come wi' me, gents. This way!" He led the way up rickety, twisting stairs.

The pictures that he had in the room above were a good deal more explicit than those in the front of the shop. Many women had abandoned gowns altogether and were posed with little more than a few wisps of fabric, a feathered fan or a posy of flowers. They were handsome women in early or middle youth, with firm, high breasts and rich thighs. Some of the poses were more erotic than others.

"All quite harmless, really," Unsworth said, watching Pitt guardedly.

"Yes, they are," Pitt agreed, conscious of Tellman at his elbow exuding disapproval. In his opinion women who sold themselves for this kind of picture were of the same general class as those who sold themselves in prostitution, only these girls were young and well fed and far from any outward sign of poverty or despair.

Unsworth relaxed. "Y'see?"

Pitt looked at them more carefully. He saw half a dozen or so which could have been Cathcart's. The quality was there, the subtlety of light and shade, the more delicate suggestion of something beyond the mere flesh. One woman had a bunch of lilies in her hands half obscuring her breasts. It was a highly evocative mixture of purity and license. Another woman with rich dark hair lay sprawled on a Turkish carpet, a brass hookah behind her, as if she was about to partake of the smoke from some pungent herb. The longer he looked at it, the more certain Pitt became that it was Cathcart's work. The symbolism was there, the skill of suggestion, as well as the practiced use of the camera itself.

But none of these, good as they were, were worth the price of Lily Monderell's teapot, let alone the watercolor.

"Yes, I see," he said aloud. "Now how about the others, the expensive ones? Do you bring them to me, or do I have to look for them myself?"

Unsworth hesitated, clearly torn as to how much he could still hope to get away with.

Pitt turned to Tellman. "Sergeant, go and see if you can find—"

"All right!" Unsworth said loudly, his face dark, his voice edged with anger. "I'll show 'em to yer meself! Yer an 'ard man! Wot's the 'arm in a few pictures? Nobody's 'urt. Nobody's in it as doesn't wanter be. It ain't real!"

"The pictures, Mr. Unsworth," Pitt said grimly. He would not argue realities of the mind with him.

Ungraciously Unsworth produced the pictures, slamming them down on the table in front of Pitt, then stood back, his arms folded.

These were different. Innocence was gone completely. Pitt heard Tellman's intake of breath between his teeth and did not need to turn sideways to know the expression on his face, the revulsion, the hurt inside. Some of them still possessed an art, albeit a twisted one. In the first four the women were leering, their bodies in attitudes of half ecstasy already, but vulgar, totally physical. There was no suggestion of tenderness, only appetite.

He flipped through them quickly. He would rather not have looked at all. Each one of these women had not so long ago been a child, searching for love, not lust. They may have been used rather than cared for, they may have been lonely or frightened or bored, but they had still been outside the adult world of selfish, physical use of one person by another merely to relieve a hunger.

Except, of course, for those who long knew abuse from the very people who were supposed to protect them. And looking at some of these sad, worldly eyes, that might have described a few of them. There was already a self-disgust in some that was harsher than any of the physical degradations.

Others were worse again, mimicking pain inflicted for pleasure, with the implication that it held some kind of secret joy reached only by breaching all the barriers. Some were obscene, some blasphemous. Many women were dressed in mockery of those in holy orders, nuns with skirts torn open, hurled to the ground, or over the banisters of stairs, as if rape

225

was on a level with martyrdom and a kind of religious ecstasy was achieved by submission to violence.

Pitt felt a sickness churn in his stomach. The moment he looked he wished he had not seen them. How did one erase from the mind such images? He would not want it to, but the next time he saw a nun this would return to him, and he would be unable to meet her eyes in case she saw what was in his mind. Something was already soiled for him.

And there were others equally ugly, some involving men also, and children. Satanic rituals were suggested with emblems of death, sacrifice. In two or three the shadow of a goat's head, goblets of blood and wine, light shining on the blade of a knife.

Tellman gave a little grunt. It was a short sound, barely audible, but Pitt heard the distress in it as if it had been a scream. He wished there was a way he could excuse them both, but there was not.

Among the pictures he recognized one beautiful face, not a young one, not lovely with the untouched flower of youth, but older, the beauty that of the clean sweep of throat and cheek, the perfect balance of bone delicate yet strong, the halo of fair hair. It was Cecily Antrim, dressed as a nun, her head back, her arms tied by the wrists to a wheel, her body bent over it. A man knelt in front of her, his face reflecting ecstasy. It was a curious picture, half pornographic, half blasphemous, as if the two, in the figure of the priest, came together. It was a powerful and profoundly disturbing image, far less easy to forget than those which were simply erotic. This raised questions in the mind as to the nature of religious practice and the honesty or dishonesty of what purported to be service of God.

Pitt looked at a few more, another dozen or so. He was almost at the bottom of the pile when he saw it. He knew from the stifled gasp beside him that Tellman had seen it at the same instant.

It was Cecily Antrim again, in a green velvet gown, lying on her back in a punt, surrounded by drifting flowers. Her knees were half drawn up. Her wrists and ankles were very obviously manacled to the boat. It was the parody of Ophelia again, making it seem as if the imprisonment of the chains was what excited her, and the beginning of ecstasy was sharp and real in her face.

"That's disgusting!" Tellman said with a half sob. "How could any woman like that sort of thing?" He was glaring at Pitt. "What kind of idea does that give a man, eh?" He jabbed his thin finger at the shiny card. "A man looking for that is going to . . . to think . . . God knows! What's he going to do, tell me that?"

"I don't know," Pitt said quietly. "Maybe he's going to think that's the sort of thing women like. . . ."

"Exactly!" Tellman's voice cracked. "It's revolting. It's got to be stopped! What would happen if some young lad came in here?"

"I don't sell to young lads," Unsworth cut in. "That sort of thing's only for special customers, ones I know."

Pitt swung around on him, his eyes blazing, his voice raw. "And of course you know exactly what they do with them, don't you! You know that every one of them is safely locked up by some sane and responsible person who treats his own wife like a precious friend, a lady, the mother of his children?" His voice was getting louder and he could not help it. "No one ever feeds his own dreams with them and then acts them out? No one ever sells them on to curious and ignorant boys who don't even know what a naked woman's body looks like and is aching to find out?"

He remembered his own first awakenings of curiosity with surprising sharpness, and his ideas, his realizations of boundless, terrifying and wonderful possibilities.

"Well . . ." Unsworth spluttered. "Well, you can't hold me responsible for . . . I'm not my brother's keeper!"

"Just as well for him! The way you're going about it he's on that high road to that misery where he destroys everything he sees because he no longer believes in the possibility of worth. No, Mr. Unsworth, perhaps it is people like Sergeant Tellman and me who are his keeper, and we are now going to set about doing exactly that. You have a choice. You can either

227

give us a list of your clients who buy these pictures—a complete list . . ."

Unsworth shook his head violently.

"Or," Pitt continued, "I shall presume you have these here for your own pleasure, and since one of them is evidence in a murder, that you are protecting the person who committed it . . ."

Unsworth gasped and waved his hands in denial.

"Or that you committed it yourself," Pitt finished. "Which is it to be?"

"I . . . eh . . . I . . ." Unsworth ground his teeth. "I'll give you a list. But you'll ruin me! You'll put me in the workhouse!"

"I hope so," Pitt said.

Unsworth shot him a venomous look, but he went and fetched a piece of paper and a pen and ink, and wrote a long list of names for Pitt, but no addresses.

Pitt read through the names and saw none he recognized. He would get a list of members of the camera club and compare them, but he held little hope that there would be any in common.

"Tell me something about each of these men," he said grimly to Unsworth.

Unsworth shook his head. "They're customers. They buy pictures. What do I know about them?"

"A great deal," Pitt replied without shifting his gaze. "If you didn't, you'd not risk selling pictures like these to them. And I want a list of the men who supply these pictures as well." He watched Unsworth's face. "And before you deny that too, one of these pictures prompted the murder of Cathcart. The murderer saw it, and laid Cathcart's body in the exact image." He was satisfied to see Unsworth pale considerably and a sweat break out on his brow. "Coincidence would be unbelievable," he went on. "Especially since Cathcart took the photograph. I need to know who else saw it. Do you understand me, Mr. Unsworth? You are the key to a murder which I intend to solve. You can tell me now . . . or I can close down your business until you do. Which will it be?"

Unsworth looked at him with hatred, his eyes narrow and dark.

"You tell me which picture it is, I'll tell yer 'oo brought it an' 'oo I sold it to," he said grudgingly.

Pitt indicated the photograph of Cecily Antrim in the punt.

"Oh. Well, like yer said yerself, Cathcart brought me that one."

"Sole rights?" Pitt asked.

"Wot?" Unsworth hedged.

"Do you have sole rights to the picture?" Pitt snapped.

"Wake up an' dream! O' course I don't!"

It was a lie. Pitt knew it from the fixed steadiness of his eyes.

"I see. And you wouldn't know the names of the other dealers who have it because you wouldn't have sold it to them?" Pitt agreed.

Unsworth shifted his weight again. "That's right."

"So tell me all you can about those people you did sell to."

"That'd take all day!" Unsworth protested.

"Probably," Pitt agreed. "But Sergeant Tellman and I have all day."

"Maybe you bleedin' 'ave—but I 'aven't. I've got a livin' ter make!"

"Then you had better start quickly, hadn't you, and not waste your valuable time in arguing," Pitt said reasonably.

But even though they spent several hours in the small upstairs room and the shop was closed for business all the time, they learned nothing that appeared to be of use in guiding them any further in Cathcart's murder. They left as it was growing dusk and went out onto the gaslit pavements with a heavy feeling of oppression.

Tellman drew in a long breath, as though the foggy air—with its slight damp, the smell of horses, wet roads, soot and chimneys—was still cleaner than the air inside the closed shop.

"That's poison," he said quietly, his voice husky with misery and rage. "Why do we let people make things like that?" It was not a rhetorical question. He wanted and needed an answer. "What good are we doing if we can only arrest people after they do things wrong, if we can't stop them?" He jerked

229

his head back towards the shop. "We could arrest someone if they put poison in a sack of flour."

"Because people don't want to buy sacks of flour with poisons in them," Pitt answered him. "They want to buy these things. That's the difference."

They walked in silence for a while, crossing the street amid rumbling drays and wagons, fast-moving carriages, light hansoms, all with lamps gleaming. The sound of hooves was sharp, the hiss of wheels, the smell of fog in the nostrils and an increasing chill as darkness closed in. Wreaths of mist shrouded the lamps, diffusing the light.

"Why do they do it?" Tellman demanded suddenly, striding out to keep up with Pitt, who, in his own anger, had unconsciously been going faster and faster. "I mean, why does a woman like Miss Antrim let anyone take pictures like that? She doesn't need the money. She isn't starving, desperate, can't pay the rent. She must make hundreds as it is. Why?" He waved his arms in a wild gesture of incomprehension. "She's quality! She knows better than that!"

Pitt heard the confusion in him, and more than that, the disappointment. He understood it sharply. He felt it also. What perversity led a beautiful and brilliant woman to such degradation?

"Was she blackmailed into it, do you suppose?" Tellman asked, swerving to avoid banging into a lamppost.

"Maybe." He would have to ask. He half hoped that was the answer. The weight of disillusion inside him was heavier than he would have imagined. A dream had been broken, a brightness was gone.

"Must be," Tellman said, trying to convince himself. "Only answer."

For Caroline it was not quite the end of the matter with Samuel Ellison. She had liked him very much, not for his resemblance to Edward, or because he liked her or found her attractive, but for his enthusiasm and for the gentleness and the complexity with which he saw his own country. She did not wish to part from him with anger remembered.

She looked across the breakfast table. She and Joshua were alone. The old lady had remained in her room.

"May I write to Samuel and tell him that we have solved the mystery of the letters, and we apologize for the mischief caused? I cannot quite see how to do it without telling him the reasons, and I would prefer not to do that."

"No," he said clearly, but his eyes were soft, and he was smiling. "He still behaved a trifle improperly. He admires you, which shows excellent taste, but he was too forward about it. . . ."

"Oh . . ."

"I shall write to him," he continued. "I shall tell him what happened, as much as I know. I cannot tell him the old lady's reason because I don't know it. And I shall apologize for her appalling behavior, and invite him out to dinner . . ."

She smiled, delight flooding through her.

". . . at my club," he finished, looking amused and a trifle smug. "Then I shall take him to the theatre, if he accepts, and introduce him to Oscar Wilde. I know him passably well, and he is a very agreeable fellow. I am not having him here. Mrs. Ellison may be a mischief-making woman, but Samuel is still too fond of my wife for my peace of mind."

Caroline felt the color burn up her cheeks, but this time it was pleasure, sharp and delicious. "What an excellent idea," she said, looking down at the toast on her plate. "I am sure he will enjoy that enormously. Please give him my best wishes."

"Certainly," he replied, reaching for the teapot. "I shall be happy to."

After Joshua left, Caroline went upstairs and asked if Mrs. Ellison was well. She was told by Mabel that so far she had not arisen, and it seemed she had no desire to get up today. Mabel was concerned that perhaps the doctor should be called.

"Not yet," Caroline replied firmly. "I daresay it is no more than a headache and will pass without treatment—except what you can give, of course."

"Are you sure, ma'am?" Mabel asked anxiously.

"I think so. I shall go and see her."

"She didn't want to be disturbed, ma'am!"

"I shall tell her you said so," Caroline assured her. "Please don't worry." And without arguing the point any further, she went along the landing to the old lady's room and knocked briskly on the door.

There was no answer.

She knocked again, then opened it and went in.

Mrs. Ellison was sitting propped up against the pillows, her gray-white hair spread around her, her face pale, with dark shadows under her eyes, making the sockets look enormous.

"I did not give you permission to come in," she said tartly. "Please have the decency to leave. Do I not even have the privilege of being alone in the house?"

"No, you don't." Caroline closed the door behind her and walked over to the bed. "I came to tell you that I spoke with Joshua yesterday evening . . ."

Mariah stared at her, misery draining her face of all life.

Caroline wanted to be furious with her, but pity overtook justified anger and every shred of the satisfaction in revenge that she had expected.

"I told him you had written the letter to Samuel. . . ."

Mariah winced as if Caroline had struck her. She seemed to grow smaller, huddled into herself.

"But I did not tell him why," Caroline went on. "I said it was something that had hurt you greatly, and he did not ask what it was."

There was total silence in the room. Slowly Mrs. Ellison let out her breath and her shoulders sagged. "He didn't . . ." she whispered with disbelief.

"No."

Again there was silence. Caroline searched for words to tell her that the wound would heal, the damage was not irreparable after all, but perhaps it was unnecessary.

Mrs. Ellison started to say something, then stopped. Her eyes did not move from Caroline's face. She was grateful, it was there somewhere in the depths, but to put it into words would make it real, a solid thing between them, and she was not ready to yield that yet.

Caroline smiled briefly, then stood up and left.

She did not see the old lady again that day.

In the evening, when Joshua had left for the theatre after a very brief supper, the maid announced Inspector Pitt, and Caroline was delighted to see him. The pleasure of having Joshua at home during parts of the day was paid for in far too many lonely evenings.

"Thomas! Come in," she said with pleasure. "How are you? My dear, you look awfully tired. Sit down." She gestured to the big armchair near the fire. "Have you eaten?" She was very aware that with Charlotte in Paris he too was alone. He looked even more crumpled than usual and had a forlorn air about him. It was not until he had done as he was bidden and the gaslight caught his face more closely that she realized he was also deeply unhappy.

"Thomas, what it is? What has happened?"

He gave a very small smile, rueful and a trifle self-conscious.

"Can I be so easily read?"

It had been a day of honesty. "Yes."

He relaxed into the chair, letting the warmth seep into him.

"I suppose it's Joshua I really wanted to speak to. I should have realized he wouldn't be here at this hour." He stopped.

She could see he wanted to talk about something. Whatever it was that had distressed him, he needed to speak of it, and Charlotte was not there.

"I can tell Joshua when he comes home," she said almost casually. "What is it about? The theatre, I presume. Is it to do with the murder of the photographer?"

"Yes. It is really not something to discuss with a woman."

"Whyever not? Are you embarrassed?"

"No." He hesitated. "Well . . ."

She thought bitterly of what her mother-in-law had told her. Whatever Pitt had to say, it could hardly be more obscene than that, or more intimately degrading.

"Thomas, I do not need to be protected from life. If you are afraid I cannot keep a confidence, then—"

"That is not it at all!" he protested, running his hand through his hair and leaving it even more rumpled. "It is simply . . . intensely unpleasant."

"I can see that much in your face. Do you believe that Cathcart's murder has something to do with the theatre?"

"I think it may. He certainly knew Cecily Antrim . . . very well."

"You mean they were lovers?" She was amused at his delicacy.

"Not necessarily. That would hardly matter." He stretched out his legs a little more comfortably. His face was contorted. It was obviously still difficult for him to say to her what it was that filled his mind. She thought of herself this morning trying to find words to tell Samuel about Mrs. Ellison, and she waited.

The fire flickered pleasantly in the grate. There was no other noise in the room except the clock.

"I found photographs of Cecily Antrim in a postcard shop," he said at last. "We didn't tell the newspapers how Cathcart was found, except that it was in a boat." He avoided her eyes and there was a faint color in his cheeks. "Actually, he was wearing a green velvet dress . . . pretty badly torn . . . and he was manacled by the wrists and ankles . . . into a sort of obscene parody of Millais's painting of Ophelia. Flowers thrown around . . . artificial ones." He stopped.

She controlled her amazement with difficulty, and an idiotic desire to laugh.

"What has that to do with Cecily Antrim?"

"There were several obscene or blasphemous pictures of her in the shop," he replied. "One of them was almost exactly like that. It couldn't be a coincidence. It was the same dress, the same garlands of flowers. It looked to be even the same boat. He was killed, and then placed in exactly that pose. Whoever did it had to have seen the photograph."

A cold prickle ran through her. "You think she was involved?" She thought how it would hurt Joshua. He admired her so much, her courage, her passion, her integrity. How could such a woman lend herself to pornography? It could not be for something as paltry as more money. Surely it had to be a willingness in the mind?

Pitt was looking at her, watching her face, her eyes, the hands now closed tightly in her lap.

"Were there a lot of these pictures?" she asked. "I mean, could they have been sold to many people or used for blackmail?"

"Some of the activities portrayed were . . . illegal." He did not elaborate, but she guessed his meaning.

"The shop's owner gave me a list of his customers," he went on. "But there is nothing to say it is a complete list. We'll investigate it." His face was sad and tired in the gaslight. "Some of them will be dealers who sell them on. God knows where they'll end."

She felt tired herself, a little beaten by the cruelty and the squalor that she had quite suddenly encountered, invading her warm, bright world with dirt she could not dismiss. Most of all it was in the old lady's wounds, so deep they had become woven into her nature. But this that Pitt told her of was part of the same thing, the same sickness of the mind and heart that took pleasure in pain.

"The trouble is," Pitt went on quietly, "they could end up in anyone's hands—young people, boys keen to learn a little about women . . . knowing nothing . . ."

Caroline could see in his eyes that he was thinking of himself long ago, remembering his own first stirrings of curiosity and excitement, and crippling ignorance. How appalling it would be for a boy to see something like the brutality Mrs. Ellison had described, or the pictures Cecily Antrim had posed for. Young men would grow up seeing women like that . . . willingly chained—just as young Lewis Marchand would have thought of her, twisted and repellent in her desire for pain, her acceptance of humiliation.

Was that blush in his face for anything he had conjured out of *Hamlet*, the taunting of Ophelia from Shakespeare's text . . .

or from Delbert Cathcart's photograph? She had no moral choice but to go to the Marchands and warn them. The misery that could follow did not allow her the luxury of evading it, however embarrassing it might be.

"You must stop it, if you can," she said aloud. "Thomas, you really must!"

"I know," he replied. "We've taken all the pictures, of course. But that won't prevent him from buying more. You can't ever prevent it. A man with a camera can photograph anything he pleases. A man with a pencil or a paintbrush can draw whatever he likes." His voice was dark, his lips delicate with revulsion. "Almost all we can do is see he doesn't display them publicly. Unless the people photographed are abused, then of course we could act on that." There was no lift in his voice, and she knew he felt beaten.

She thought of Daniel and Jemima, their innocent faces still looking at the world with no idea of cruelty, no knowledge of the ravages of physical appetite or how it could become so depraved that it consumed all honor or pity, or in the end even preservation of self.

She thought of Edmund Ellison, and Mariah in her youth, terrified, crouching in the dark, waiting for the pain which would come, if not tonight, then tomorrow or the next night, and the next, as long as he was alive.

If anyone had done that to one of her own daughters she would have killed him. If someone did it to Jemima, or Daniel, she would now, and answer even to God, without regret.

She did not know what connection the pictures had to the act, whether they prompted it, excused it, excited it—or replaced it. She was confused and tired, and uncertain how to help. She was sure only that, above all things, she needed to help.

She sat in the silence with Pitt. There was no sound in the room but the fire and the clock, and neither of them felt compelled to break the understanding with words that were unnecessary. It was a long time before they at last spoke of Charlotte in Paris, her ecstatic account of her visit to the Latin

Quarter, breakfast at Saint-Germain, poets in pink shirts and another day of a leisurely walk under the horse chestnut trees along the Champs-Élysées.

11

T*HE OLD LADY* did not come down to breakfast the following morning either. Caroline lost her taste for toast and preserves, even though the apricots were delicious.

Joshua looked up. "What is it? What's wrong?"

She had told him nothing so far. He was absorbed in his own work. She knew by now how exhausting the first few nights of a new play were. Everyone worried how it would be received, how the audience would react, what the critics would say, whether the theatre bookings would remain good, even what others in the profession would think. And if all those things went well, then they worried about their own performances, and always about health, most especially the voice. A sore throat, which was merely unpleasant to most people, to an actor was ruinous. His voice was the instrument of his art.

At first she had found it difficult to understand and know how to help. She had experienced nothing like it in her life with Edward. Now she knew at least when to remain silent, when encouragement was appropriate and when it was not, and what to say that was intelligent. It was the one area in which Joshua had no patience with less than honesty. He could not bear to think he was being patronized. It was at those moments she caught a rare glimpse not only of his temper but of his vulnerability.

"Thomas was here yesterday evening. Of course he is

238

missing Charlotte . . . and the case he is on is giving him concern."

"Doesn't it always?" He took another slice of toast. "What good would he be if it didn't worry him? I'm sorry about Cathcart, he was a brilliant photographer. I suppose Thomas is no nearer finding out what happened?"

How much of the truth did he want to know? Not all of it—not until he had to.

"I don't think so. You didn't know him, did you?"

He was surprised. "Cathcart? No. Just by repute. But I know his work. Everyone does . . . well, I suppose people in the theatre do more than most." He looked at her narrowly. "Why?"

She was not as good at deceiving him as she intended. He sensed she was telling him less than she knew, though he did not know what it was. She hated the feeling of concealment, the barrier she was creating between them, but to have told him would be a small selfishness, exposing him to unhappiness just for her own peace of mind. And he had already been hurt so deeply by Samuel Ellison, even if it was healed now.

She made her smile more spontaneous, more direct.

"Poor Thomas is trying hard to learn about him because it seems such a personal crime, a matter of hate or ridicule. If you know anything about him other than reputation it might help." That sounded reasonable, like herself.

He smiled back and resumed his breakfast.

She made her excuses and went upstairs. The matter of Lewis Marchand had to be addressed, but not until that afternoon. Mrs. Ellison should be seen now.

As yesterday, she was still in bed.

"I am not receiving visitors," she said coldly when Caroline went in.

"I am not a visitor," Caroline replied, sitting on the edge of the bed. "I live here."

The old lady glared at her. "Are you reminding me that I have no home?" she enquired. "That I am dependent upon the charity of relations in order to have a roof over my head?"

"That would be quite unnecessary," Caroline answered her

levelly. "You have complained about it often enough I could hardly imagine you were unaware—or had ever forgotten."

"It's not something one forgets," Mrs. Ellison retorted. "One is never allowed to, in a dozen subtle ways. You will learn that one day for yourself, when you are old and alone and everyone else of your generation is dead."

"Since I have married a man young enough to be my son, as you never tire of telling me, I shall be unlikely to outlive him at all, let alone by long," Caroline pointed out.

The old lady stared at her, her eyes narrow, her mouth tight shut in a thin, miserable line. She had been bested at her own game, and it thoroughly disconcerted her. She was not sure how to retaliate.

Caroline sighed. "If you are still not well enough to get up, I shall send for the doctor. We can tell him whatever you please, but whether he believes you is another matter. It is not good for you to lie there. Your system will become sluggish."

"I am perfectly able to get up! I don't want to!" Mrs. Ellison glared at her, daring her to argue.

"What has wanting got to do with it?" Caroline asked. "The longer you delay it, the more difficult it will be. Do you wish to cause speculation?"

The old lady raised her eyebrows. "What is there to speculate about? Who cares what I do or do not do?"

Caroline did not speak. All sorts of thoughts crowded her mind, how close the old lady had come to destroying the happiness she held so precious. She still cringed inside at the memory of her own misery and the fear which had darkened everything inside her.

"Please go away. I am exhausted and I prefer to be alone." Her face was set in a mask of loneliness and despair, shutting out Caroline and everyone else. "You don't understand. You have not the faintest idea. The least you can afford me is the privacy of suffering without being stared at. I do not want you here. Have the decency to go."

Caroline hesitated. She could feel the other woman's pain as if it were a living thing in the room, but beyond her power to touch. She longed to reach out and give it some comfort, some beginning of healing, but she did not know how to. For the first time she realized how deep it was. The scars were woven through Mariah Ellison's life, not only for the humiliation itself but for how she had dealt with it over the years. It was not just what Edmund had done to her but what she had done to herself. She had hated herself for so long she did not know how to stop.

"Get out of my room!" the old lady said between her teeth.

Caroline looked at her, lying hunched up in the bed, her gnarled hands gripping the covers, her face blind with misery, the tears running down her cheeks. Caroline was helpless to do anything about it, even to reach out to her, because the barrier between them had been built over the years, reinforced with a thousand daily cuts and abrasions until the scars were impenetrable.

She turned and went out, closing the door behind her, startled to find that the tears were thick in her throat also.

She went to call on the Marchands as early as it was decent to do so, perhaps even a little earlier. Mrs. Marchand was surprised to see her but appeared to be delighted. They sat in the heavy, comfortable withdrawing room for several minutes, making idle conversation, before Mrs. Marchand became aware that Caroline had some purpose in coming other than to find a pleasant way to fill an otherwise empty afternoon. She stopped in the middle of a sentence about some small event and what people had said about a particular soiree.

Caroline was aware that she had not been listening. Now that she was faced with putting into words what she feared, it was much harder than she had imagined. She looked at Mrs. Marchand's wide blue eyes, her direct, almost challenging stare and her pretty features. She was so sure of her world, of its conventions and its rules. She had conscientiously taught them to her son. Caroline was certain it had never crossed her imagination that he would venture outside its values. She cared almost as passionately as her husband about censorship so the innocent would not be tainted. She would have put fig leaves on all the great classical statues, and blushed to look at the Venus de Milo in the presence of men. She would have seen in it not naked perfection but the indecent display of a woman's breasts.

"Are you quite well, my dear?" Mrs. Marchand asked with concern, leaning forward a little, her brow furrowed. "You look a trifle pale." Of course, what she meant was "You are not listening, what is disturbing you so much you have forgotten your usual manners?"

There would never be a better opening. She must take it.

"To tell you the truth, I have been worried lately on a number of matters," she began awkwardly. "I am so sorry my attention wandered. I had no wish of being so . . . discourteous."

"Oh, not at all," Mrs. Marchand disclaimed immediately. "Can I help, even if it is only to listen? Sometimes a trouble shared seems a little lighter."

Caroline looked at her earnest face and saw only kindness in it. This was going to be worse than she had expected. Mrs. Marchand was so vulnerable. It occurred to her to invent something, evading the link altogether. Perhaps she was quite wrong. Maybe Lewis's remarks about Ophelia, the look she had seen in his eyes, was only her own imagination, fueled by Mrs. Ellison's story and what Pitt had told her.

But what if it were not? What if Lewis had Cathcart's photographs, lots of them, images which could twist his dreams and cause untold pain in the future—to him, and to some young girl as unknowing as Mariah Ellison had been half a century ago?

"My son-in-law is a policeman, as you know . . ." She ignored the slight flicker of distaste and plunged on. "He is working on a matter at the moment to do with a photographic club . . ." That was a ridiculous euphemism! She swallowed and plunged on. "From something Lewis said when I was here the other day, I believe he may have stumbled on a piece of information which could help. May I have your permission to speak with him?"

"Lewis?" Mrs. Marchand was incredulous. "How on earth could he? He is only sixteen! If he had seen anything . . . wrong . . . he would have told me, or his father."

242

"He could not know it was wrong," Caroline said hastily. "It is merely information. I am not even sure if I am correct. But if I am, then it would greatly serve justice if he would tell me. I don't believe it would be necessary for him to do more than that. Please, may I speak with him . . . confidentially, if that is possible?"

Mrs. Marchand looked uncertain.

Caroline nearly spoke again, then changed her mind. To press too hard might awaken suspicion. She waited.

"Well . . . yes, of course," Mrs. Marchand said, blinking several times. "I'm sure my husband would wish Lewis to be of any help he can. We all would. A photographic club? I did not know he was interested in photography."

"I don't know that he is," Caroline answered quickly. "It is just that I think he may have seen a particular photograph, and he could tell me where, and I would tell Thomas without mentioning how I learned."

"Oh. I see." Mrs. Marchand rose to her feet. "Well, he is upstairs with his tutor. I am sure we could interrupt them for something so important." She rang the bell for the maid, and Lewis was sent for.

He arrived within minutes, having been going over some of the more abstruse irregular Latin verbs, from which he was delighted to be distracted. He went quite willingly with Caroline into the library and faced her with interest. Anything she had to say, however tedious or pedestrian, had to be better than the eccentricities of the past tense of words he would never in his life have any cause to use. It had been explained to him many times that it was not the practicality but the mental discipline of the exercise which benefited him, but he remained unconvinced.

"Yes, Mrs. Fielding?" he said politely.

"Please sit down, Lewis," she replied, sitting herself in the worn, leather armchair in front of the fireplace. "It is kind of you to spare me your time. I would not have interrupted you were it not an issue of great importance."

"Of course, Mrs. Fielding." He sat opposite her. "Whatever I can do."

243

She wished now that she had had sons as well as daughters. She had no acquaintance with sixteen-year-old boys. Her own brothers had been older than she, and their adolescence had been an impenetrable mystery to her. But there was no retreat now, except complete failure . . . cowardice. She could hardly send Pitt to do this, although he would certainly have been better at it. He was not the one who had heard Lewis's remarks about Ophelia or seen the look in his eyes.

She must somehow continue to be direct enough to allow no misunderstanding, and yet spare him as much embarrassment as possible. She had no desire to humiliate him, and no need to. It might even destroy the very purpose for which she had come. Looking into his earnest young face, polite, not really interested, smooth-cheeked still, guileless, she had no words ready that would be subtle.

"Lewis, I did not tell your mother the whole truth; that is up to you, if you wish. The matter my son-in-law is investigating is very serious indeed . . . it is murder."

"Is it?" He was not shocked or alarmed. There was a quick flare of interest in his blue eyes. But then he almost certainly had no conception of what that word meant in reality. He would know the facts, not the loss, the horror, the fear that it brought, the sense of pervading darkness.

"I'm afraid so."

He straightened up a little, and his voice lifted. "What can I do to help, Mrs. Fielding?"

She felt a twinge of guilt for what she was about to do, and also the certainty that she must destroy in him the illusion of adventure that filled him at the present.

"When I was here a few days ago and we were speaking, you made a remark from which I now believe you might know something of use," she said.

He nodded to indicate he was listening.

"In order for you to help," she went on, "I need to tell you something about this crime . . . something which is not known to anyone except the police and the person who committed the murder . . . and to me, because I was told by the police. It is confidential, do you understand?"

He nodded more eagerly. "Yes, yes, of course I do. I won't tell anyone, I swear."

"Thank you. I am afraid this is very distressing. . . ."

"That's all right!" he assured her, taking a deep breath and sitting very stiffly. "Please don't worry about it."

She wanted to smile, but it would have been too easily misunderstood. He was so very young, and unaware.

"The murdered man was struck on the head," she began solemnly, watching his face. "Then he was dressed in a green velvet gown . . . a woman's gown . . ." She saw him flinch and a look of incomprehension fill his eyes. "Then he was laid in a small, flat-bottomed boat, a punt, and his wrists and ankles were chained to the boat."

The color drained out of his skin, leaving him white. His breathing was audible.

"And it was scattered with flowers," she finished. "Only his knees were drawn up a little, in a parody of pleasure." There was no need to go on. It was painfully apparent from the scarlet of his cheeks and the hot misery in his eyes that he had seen the picture and it was indelible in his memory.

"Where did you see it, Lewis?" she said softly. "I need to know. I'm sure you must realize that the murderer also saw it, and it is not the kind of picture that is easily found."

He swallowed, his throat jerking.

"I think you know that," she went on. "It is carefully posed. It is not the way women really behave, it is a pretend thing, for people who take pleasure in hurting others. . . ." She saw him wince but she did not stop. "There are people whose appetites are sick, who are not capable of fulfillment in the way most of us are, and they do these sorts of things, cruel and terrible things, regardless of how they torture others." She stopped, realizing she was thinking more of Mariah and Edmund Ellison than of the picture of Cecily Antrim, but they were closely intertwined in her belief. "Where did you see the picture, Lewis?"

He started to shake his head. He was having difficulty controlling his voice, and above everything he did not want to humiliate himself by weeping in front of a woman he barely knew. He felt cornered. There was no way of escape.

"I would not ask you if it were not connected with murder, Lewis," she said gently. "The man who took that photograph is the one who is dead. You can see why it is so important to know everybody who has seen it."

He gulped. "Y—yes. I . . . I bought it from a shop. I can tell you where it is . . . if you want?"

"Yes, please."

"In Half Moon Street, off Piccadilly, about halfway along. It's a shop that sells books and tobacco, and that sort of thing. I don't remember the name."

She nearly asked him how he knew of it. Such pictures would not be in the window. But she was afraid of pursuing too far and losing his cooperation altogether. It did not matter.

"That's all right," she said instead. "I'm sure they'll find it."

He kept his eyes lowered. She had the feeling there was something else he wanted to say. And almost as important to her as finding the information for Pitt was reaching out to this boy and making him believe that what he had seen was an aberration, not the way normal people thought or felt. He had seen the Ophelia picture, she had no idea what other pictures he might also have seen. But how could she do it without betraying his trust to his parents, whose rigid ideas had led him to such a way of learning what very little he knew of women and intimacy?

"I suppose they had other pictures as well?" she said.

He avoided her eyes. "Yes."

"Were they similar—of women?"

"Well . . . sort of." His face was scarlet. "Some . . . were . . . men . . . doing . . ." He could not say it.

She ignored it, for both their sakes. "Would you prefer to see something a little . . . gentler?" she asked. "Something more like the kind of woman one day you would like to know yourself?"

His eyes flew open and he stared at her in utter dismay.

246

"You . . . you mean . . . decent women . . . ?" He blushed crimson and stammered to a halt.

"No, I don't," she said, trying not to be embarrassed herself. "I mean . . . I'm not sure what I mean. Decent women certainly don't have photographs like these taken. But we all need to know certain things about men and women." She was floundering. "This sort of thing . . . what you've seen . . . is very ugly, and has more to do with hate than with love. I think you need to begin at the beginning, not at the end."

"My parents would never allow that!" He said it with absolute conviction. "My father hates . . ." He gulped. "Pornography. He has spent his whole life fighting against it. He says people who make that and sell it should be hanged!"

She did not argue. She knew it was true.

"If you will allow me to mention these pictures, I think I may be able to persuade them."

"No!" His voice was shrill with desperation. "Please don't! You promised you wouldn't tell!"

"I won't," she said instantly. "Unless you give me permission." She leaned towards him earnestly. "But don't you think, in the long view, it would be better? One day your father is going to have to tell you certain things. Aren't you ready for it to be soon?"

"Well . . . I . . ." He was obviously acutely uncomfortable. He looked everywhere but at her. A moment ago she had been a friend; now, overwhelmingly, she was a woman.

"You already know," she concluded, then wished she had not. Perhaps he did not know? Perhaps it was his burning imagination which had driven him to buy such pictures? Then, seeing his agonized face, she was certain he did not know. He was confused, hideously embarrassed by his ignorance and his curiosity, and so self-conscious he was crimson to the tips of his ears.

"I think you should speak to your father yourself," she said gently. "What you feel is common to all of us. He'll understand exactly." She hoped to heaven that was true. She was far less certain of Ralph Marchand now than she had been even an hour ago. She stood up and left the room without saying anything more.

She had dealt as well as possible with the issue of the photographs. She would send the address of the dealer to Bow Street for Pitt, then she would have to face Mrs. Ellison again. This could not go unresolved indefinitely.

But the damage was so deep, how did she reach it? It had years ago become part of the old lady's character, the anger was consumed into her view of everything. She had hated herself and everyone else for so long she did not know how to stop. If the hatred was removed, would there be anything left?

It was a cool, clear autumn day, the streets full of hazy sunlight, traffic moving swiftly apart from the occasional crushes at corners, where everyone seemed to be a rule to themselves. At a glance she could see a score of people walking, as she was, simply for the pleasure of it. She was not yet ready to look for a cab. Perhaps that was as much because she dreaded returning home as anything to do with the weather.

The situation could not continue like this, day after day. Emily would be home in just over a week. It must be dealt with before then. Which raised another question she had been avoiding. What should she tell Emily, or Charlotte?

She smiled and nodded to two women passing her. She was sure she had met them somewhere but could not think where. They had the same polite, slightly confused looks on their faces. Presumably they were thinking exactly the same.

She could hardly tell Emily nothing. She had to offer some explanation for the change in the old lady. And whatever she told Emily she would have to tell Charlotte also.

She pictured Edmund Ellison as she remembered him. He was her father-in-law, a relation by marriage, but to her daughters he was Grandfather, a relation by blood, in a sense part of who they were. That made it different. They would find it far harder to bear.

And what thoughts would it awaken about Edward also? It had disturbed Caroline herself, made her view certain memories differently, and she had known him intimately. She had all the knowledge with which to dismiss all doubts, see them for the slander they were.

Honesty was not the only thing that mattered, surely?

She wished there was someone else she could speak to, someone whose advice she could ask, without laying upon that person a burden it was unfair to ask someone to carry. She certainly could not ask Joshua, especially not now, with a new play just beginning. Even at any time it would not be right. He had not been warned before. He had no experience of this kind of family problem in all its complicated ugliness and ever-widening circles of pain.

She could not even ask Charlotte, and certainly not Pitt. It was really not a problem she wished to discuss with a man at all, let alone one a generation younger than herself and with whom she had a continuing family relationship.

A hansom carriage and four swept by with a crest on the door, liveried coachman on the box and footman behind. It was a pleasure to watch them.

Lady Vespasia Cumming-Gould—that was the answer. Of course she might not be in. She might consider this something of an impertinence, a familiarity not warranted by their very slight acquaintance. But on the other hand, she might help Caroline as she had helped Charlotte so many times.

She hailed the next hansom and gave the driver Vespasia's address. It was quite an acceptable hour for afternoon calls.

Vespasia received Caroline with both interest and pleasure, and did not indulge the pretense that it was merely a usual courtesy call.

"I am sure you did not come to discuss society or the weather. You are plainly concerned about something," she said when they were seated alone in the light, furnished sitting room looking into the garden. It was one of the most restful rooms Caroline had been in, the sense of space and air and the cool tones were calming, and she found herself sitting more comfortably in the chair. "I hope nothing is going badly with Charlotte?"

"No, far from it," Caroline assured her. "I believe she is enjoying herself enormously."

Vespasia smiled. The light was silver on her hair and warm on her face, which was beautiful as much because of her age as in spite of it. All the lines were upward, the faint prints of time left by courage and laughter, and an inner certainty no one had seen waver.

"Then you had better tell me what it is," she offered. "I have instructed my maid that I am not at home to anyone else, but I have no taste to play games with words. I have reached the age when life seems too short as it is; I do not wish to spend any of it uselessly . . . unless it is fun? And from your face, this is not so."

"No, I am afraid it is not. But I should greatly appreciate your advice," Caroline admitted. "I am not sure what I should do for the best."

Vespasia looked at her steadily. "What have you done so far?"

As succinctly as possible, Caroline told her of meeting Samuel Ellison at the theatre and of his visits to the house and Mrs. Ellison's increasing tension.

Vespasia listened without interruption until Caroline reached the point where she had retrieved the letter and confronted Mrs. Ellison and demanded to know the truth. Then she found it unexpectedly difficult to repeat the obscenity of what the old lady had finally recounted.

"I think you had better tell me," Vespasia said quietly. "I presume it was extremely unpleasant, or she would hardly have gone to such lengths to keep it concealed."

Caroline looked down at her hands, locked together in her lap.

"I did not know people behaved in such ways. I have always disliked my mother-in-law. I have never admitted that before, but it is true." She was embarrassed to confess it. "She is a bitter and cruel woman. All my married life I have watched her look for ways to hurt people. Now I find myself sorry for her . . . and angry with myself because I can't think of any way to help. She is dying of rage and humiliation, and

I can't touch her. She won't let me, and I can't break the barrier." She looked up. "I ought to be able to! I'm not the one who has been abused and degraded!"

Vespasia sat silently for so long Caroline began to think she was not going to reply. Perhaps Vespasia was too old to deal with such things and she should not have trespassed.

"My dear," Vespasia said at last, "wounds such as you imply can sometimes be healed, if they are reached soon enough. A gentle man, a tender man, might have taught her differently, and she would have learned what love can be. In time she might have put the past to the back of her mind, where it could do no more harm. I think for your mother-in-law it is far too late. She has hated herself so long she can find no way back."

Caroline felt herself go cold, her hands stiff. It was not what she wanted to hear.

"It is pointless to blame yourself for not being able to ease her pain," Vespasia went on. "It is not your fault, but more to the point, self-blame will help neither of you. I do not mean to be harsh, but it is a kind of self-indulgence. The most you can do for her is to treat her with some nature of respect, and not allow your new knowledge of her to destroy what little dignity she has left."

"That's not very much!" Caroline said angrily. "That sounds like self-preservation."

"My dear," Vespasia said gently, "I have found that when something very dreadful happens, and has to be faced, it is wisest to consider the matter in the most practical terms. What is fair or unfair no longer really matters, only what is or is not. It is a waste of energy you will desperately need to expend anger on injustice you cannot alter. Concentrate your attention on the pain you can reach, and weigh very carefully what is the most likely result of your actions and if it is what you wish for. When you have made the wisest judgment you can, then do it. Let the rest take care of itself."

Caroline knew Vespasia was right, and yet she could not help a last protest. "Is that really all? I feel so . . . there ought to be . . ."

Vespasia shook her head very slightly. "You cannot heal

her, but you can allow her time and room to heal herself . . . a little . . . if she wants to. After these years of anger it would take a miracle . . . but miracles do happen from time to time." She gave a very slight smile. "I have seen a few. Never give up hope. If she can believe that you have hope, she may learn to have it herself."

"It doesn't sound a great deal," Caroline said reluctantly.

Vespasia moved very slightly, the light silver on her hair.

"The damage done by that kind of abuse is very, very deep. The physical is nothing, in comparison. It is the wound to the faith, to what one believes of oneself, that may be irrevocable. If you cannot love yourself, and believe you are worth loving, then it is impossible to love anyone else." She gave a tiny shrug, the sun shimmering on the silk of her gown. "When Christ commanded us to love our neighbor as ourselves, the 'self' part was just as important. We forget that at a terrible price."

Caroline considered it for several minutes. She thought also of Pitt, and the photographs of Cecily Antrim, and young Lewis Marchand's face. In stilted words she told Vespasia about that also.

When she had finished, Vespasia was smiling.

"That must have been very difficult for you," she said with approval. "Please do not chastise yourself over what you cannot change. There is a limit to what any of us can do, and sometimes we take the blame for things far beyond our power to affect. We each have our own agency to choose how we will react to our circumstances. We cannot take that from anyone, nor should we wish to, even if we have the arrogance to believe we know better than they do how they should behave or what judgments they should make. We may beg, plead, argue, we may pray—and we should—but in the end the only person anyone can change is themselves. Please be content with that. It is all you will receive, I promise you. And it is all you should. It is sufficient."

"And what about the pictures?" Caroline asked. "We talk very freely about not censoring art. But the people who say that don't think of the damage they can do. If they had seen young Lewis Marchand's face, they wouldn't have thought their freedom worth so much. They aren't the people with children . . . they . . ." She stopped, realizing how wrong she was. "Yes, they are . . . at least Cecily Antrim is." She frowned. "Am I old-fashioned, repressed, backward-thinking? She would say I am boring and getting old!" The words hurt as she said them. Spoken aloud they were even worse than silent in her mind.

"I am not getting old," Vespasia replied vigorously. "I most assuredly have arrived there. It is not as bad as you may fear . . . in fact it has distinct pleasures. Go and read your Robert Browning, and have a little more faith in life, my dear. And so far as being boring is concerned, kindness and honesty are never tedious. Cruelty, hypocrisy and pretentiousness always are . . . excruciatingly so. A fool may not be interesting, but if he or she is generous and interested in you, you will find you like him, however limited his wit."

"Why would Cecily Antrim pose for such pictures?" Caroline followed her thoughts. "When Joshua finds out he is going to be so distressed . . . I think . . ."

Then suddenly she was terribly afraid he would not be, it would be she herself he thought out of step, critical, imprisoned in old thought.

Vespasia was looking at her very steadily, her eyes silvergray in the soft light of this clear, uncluttered room. The sun was bright on the grass beyond the windows, the trees motionless against the blue sky.

Caroline felt transparent, all her thoughts, her fears, naked.

"I think you are being a trifle unfair to him," Vespasia said frankly. "Of course he will be hurt, and wish to judge her more kindly than may prove possible. Disillusion cuts very deep. He will need you to be sure of yourself. I think you should consider long and carefully what it is you hold most dear, and then do not let go of it."

Caroline said nothing. She already knew that was true; Samuel Ellison had taught her that.

Vespasia leaned forward a fraction. It was just a slight gesture, but it gave an impression of closeness. "You are older than he is, and it troubles you." That was a statement, not a question. "My dear, you always were. He chose you for who you are. Don't destroy it by trying to be someone else. If he loses a friend he has admired in this miserable business, he is going to need you to be strong, to remain honest and fight for the values you have represented to him. Years are accidents of nature; maturity is very precious. He may very much need you to be older than he is . . . for a little while." The flicker of a smile touched her mouth. "The time will come when you can reverse the roles and allow him to be stronger, or wiser, or even both! Just be subtle about it, that's all. Sometimes when we most need help, we least like to know we are receiving it. Set your own doubts aside for a little while. Fight as you would for your children, without thought for yourself. Just don't lose your temper. It is terribly unbecoming."

In spite of herself, Caroline laughed.

Vespasia laughed also. "May I lend you a pen and paper? Then you may send a note to Thomas to give him the address of this dealer. I shall have my coachman take it to Bow Street. I confess I find it most irritating that Charlotte has gone to Paris. I have no idea what Thomas is doing, and I am bored to doll-rags!" She gave a self-deprecating shrug, pulling the dove-gray silk of her gown. "I have become addicted to police life and I find society infinitely tedious. It is merely a new generation of people doing exactly what we did, and convinced they are the first to think of it. How on earth do they imagine they came into the world?"

Caroline found herself overtaken with laughter; the blessed release of it was marvelous. The tears ran down her cheeks and she did not even try to stop, she had no desire to at all. Suddenly she was warm again, and surprisingly hungry. She would like tea . . . and cakes!

While Caroline was worrying about Mariah Ellison and trying in vain to think of some way to comfort her, Pitt was sitting at the table in his kitchen reading the latest letter from Charlotte. He was so absorbed in it he let his tea go cold.

Dearest Thomas,

I am enjoying my last few days here in a unique kind of way. It has been a marvelous holiday, and no doubt the moment I leave I shall wish I could recapture it better in my memory. Therefore I am looking at everything especially closely, so I can print it in my mind ... the way the light falls on the river, the sun on the old stones ... some of the buildings are quite frighteningly beautiful and so steeped in history. I think of all the things that have happened here, the people who have lived and died, the great battles for liberty, the terror and the glory ... and of course the squalor as well.

I wonder, do other people come to London and look at it with the same bursting sense of romance? Do foreigners come to our city and see the great ghosts of the past: Charles I going calmly to his death after years of civil war, Queen Elizabeth leaving to rally the troops before the Armada, Anne Boleyn ... why is it always executions? What's the matter with us? Riot, bloodshed and glorious deaths ... I suppose it is the ultimate sacrifice?

By the way, talking about ultimate sacrifice, well, not ultimate I suppose ... but a young French diplomat, Henri Bonnard by name, has just made a conspicuous sacrifice on behalf of his friend. It is in all the newspapers, so Madame says. Apparently he is posted in London and has come back to Paris to testify in this case I was telling you about—the man who said he could not have killed the girl because he was at a nightclub at the time? Well, so he was—the Moulin Rouge! And the diplomat was with him— all night. It seems they went there quite respectably, like anyone else, then stayed over when the most infamous of the dancers—La Goulue—was doing the cancan—without her underwear, as usual—and then went on to even more disreputable pursuits. But together! He swears to it— very reluctantly, I might add. His ambassador will not be pleased. All Paris is laughing about it today—I imagine London will know of it by the time you read this. At least some of London will, the people the ambassador cares about. Poor Monsieur Bonnard, a high price to pay to rescue a friend. I hope he does not lose his job.

We are going to the opera tonight. It should be great fun. Everyone will be dressed in the latest fashion. It's just like London, the very best courtesans parade at the back and pick up custom, only of course I'm not supposed to know that!

All this is marvelous to watch, but nothing on earth could persuade me to live this way permanently. It is the best thing of all to know that I shall be home in a few days, and with you all again.

I don't suppose you have heard from Gracie? I don't think she is sure enough of her writing yet, and of course Daniel and Jemima wouldn't think to write. I hope they are building sand castles, finding crabs and little fish in the rock pools, eating sweets, getting wet and dirty and having an unforgettable time.

I imagine you are working hard. The case you describe sounds macabre. There must be a tragedy behind it. I hope you are eating properly, and finding where I put everything you will need. Is the house horribly silent without us all? Or wonderfully peaceful? I trust you are not neglecting Archie and Angus? I don't imagine they will allow you to.

I miss you, and shall be happy to be home soon,

Yours always,
Charlotte

He read it again carefully, not that he had missed any part of it but that it gave him a sense of her nearness. He could almost hear her quick footsteps down the passage and half expected her to push the door open and come in.

It also finally solved the question of what had happened to Henri Bonnard. He found himself smiling at that. It was a pleasant thought, among the other miseries, that he had gone for the most generous of reasons. He hoped the ambassador in London viewed Bonnard's loyalty to his friend as a quality far outweighing the indiscretion of having attended a nightclub of exceedingly dubious reputation. Even if it was as sordid as gossip would have, it was still the sort of thing young men did, even if largely out of curiosity and a certain bravado.

Was that what he and Orlando Antrim had quarreled about? Orlando had been trying to persuade him to go? It seemed finally he had acquiesced.

Pitt finished the last of his tea, grimacing at its coldness— he liked his tea as hot as he could bear it—and stood up, forgetting that Archie was on his lap.

"Sorry," he apologized absently. "Here, Archie, have some more breakfast. I hope you realize you'll go back to rations when your mistress comes home? There'll be no extras then. And you'll have to go back to your own bed as well . . . you and Angus!"

Archie wound around his legs, purring, leaving white and ginger hairs on his trousers.

Pitt had no alternative but to confront Cecily Antrim with the photographs. He would have liked to avoid it so he could keep his illusions about her and imagine in his mind that she could produce an explanation which would make it understandable and somehow not her fault. She had been blackmailed into it to save someone else, anything that would not mean she was a willing participant. That was not a great leap of the imagination. Some of the other photographs had certainly been blackmail material, had any of the people in them gone on to a more respectable position or career. And the money so obtained would explain Cathcart's style of life, and Lily Monderell's.

But he could not so easily imagine Cecily Antrim as anyone's victim. She was too vibrant, too courageous, too willing to follow her own beliefs even to destruction.

He found her in the early afternoon in the theatre rehearsing for *Hamlet*. Tellman was with him, reluctant to the last step.

"Shakespeare!" he said between set teeth. He made no further remark, but the expression on his face was eloquent.

As before they were allowed in grudgingly and had to wait in the wings until a suitable break came when the person

257

they wished to see was not necessary to the performance. To-day they were rehearsing Act V, in the churchyard. Two men were digging a grave and speaking of the suicide who was to be buried in it, even though it was hallowed ground. After a little joking, one departed, leaving the other alone, singing to himself.

Hamlet and Horatio entered, this time in costume. It was not long until the first night, and Pitt noticed immediately how much more polished they were. There was an air of certainty about them as if they were absorbed in the passions of the story and no longer aware of direction, let alone of the world beyond.

Pitt glanced at Tellman and saw the light reflected in his face as he listened, the words washing over him, not in familiar cadence as they did for so many, for Pitt himself, but heard for the first time.

" 'Alas poor Yorick!—I knew him, Horatio; a fellow of infinite jest, of most excellent fancy . . .' "

Tellman's eyes were wide. He was unaware of Pitt. He stared at the plaster skull in Orlando Antrim's hand, and saw the emotions within him.

" 'Now get you to my lady's chamber,' " Orlando said with irony hard-edged in his voice, harsh with pain, " '. . . and tell her, let her paint an inch thick, to this favor must she come; make her laugh at that,—Pr'ythee, Horatio, tell me one thing.' "

" 'What's that, my lord?' " the other actor enquired.

Tellman leaned forward a little. His face was like a mask, not a muscle moved, nor did his eyes ever leave the small pool of light on the stage. The words poured around him.

" 'To what base uses we may return, Horatio! Why may not imagination trace the noble dust of Alexander till he find it stopping a bung-hole?' "

Someone moved in the wings. A look of annoyance crossed Tellman's face but he did not turn to see who it was.

" 'Imperious Caesar, dead and turned to clay.' " Orlando spoke the words softly, filled with centuries of wonder and music, as if they wove a magic for him.

" '. . . Might stop a hole to keep the wind away:

O, that that earth which kept the world in awe
should patch a wall to expel the winter's flaw!
But soft! But soft! aside—Here comes the king.' "

And from the wing moved a slow, sad procession in somber, magnificent garments. Priests, the coffin of Ophelia followed by her brother, then the king, and Cecily Antrim, beautiful as Gertrude. It was extraordinary how she could hold one's attention, even when the scene was not about her at all. There was a light in her face, a force of emotion in her that could not be ignored.

The drama played itself out, and neither Pitt nor Tellman moved until it was over. Then Pitt stepped forward.

Tellman was still transfixed. In a space of less than fifteen minutes he had glimpsed a new world which had thrown aside the old. The still water of his preconceptions had been disturbed by a wave whose ripples were going to reach to the very outer edges, and already he felt it.

Pitt walked alone across the stage to Cecily Antrim.

"I apologize for interrupting you, but there is a matter I need to discuss which will not wait."

"For God's sake, man!" Bellmaine shouted in outrage, his voice raw-edged with tension. "Have you no soul, no sensibilities at all? The curtain goes up in two days! Whatever you want, it can wait!"

Pitt stood quite still. "No, Mr. Bellmaine, it cannot wait. It will not take a great deal of Miss Antrim's time, but it will be even less if you permit me to begin straightaway, rather than stand here and argue about it."

Bellmaine swore colorfully and without repeating himself, but he also waved his hands in dismissal, indicating the general direction of the dressing rooms. Tellman remained rooted to the spot, spellbound for the next scene.

Cecily Antrim's room was filled with rails hung with velvets and embroidered satins. A second wig rested on a stand on the long table beneath the mirror amid a clutter of pots, brushes, bowls, powders and rouges.

"Well?" she asked with a wry smile. "What is it that is so

urgent that you dare to defy Anton Bellmaine? I am consumed with curiosity. Even a live audience would not have kept me from coming with you to find out. I assure you, I still do not know who killed poor Delbert Cathcart, or why."

"Nor do I, Miss Antrim," he replied, digging his hands into his coat pockets. "But I know that whoever it was saw a particular photograph of you which is not available to most people, and it mattered to him very much."

She was intrigued, and the smile on her mouth was too filled with amusement for him to believe she had any idea what he was going to show her. The laughter went all the way to her clear, sky-blue eyes.

"There are scores of photographs of me, Superintendent. My career is longer than I wish to admit. I couldn't begin to tell you who has seen which." She did not say he was naive, but her voice carried the implication quite plainly, and it entertained her.

He did not like what he had to do next. He pulled out the postcard with the Ophelia travesty and held it out.

Her eyes widened. "Good God! Where did you get that?" She looked up at him. "You are quite right . . . that is one of Delbert's. You are never going to say he was killed for that. That's preposterous. You can probably buy them from half a dozen back street shops. I certainly hope so. It will have been a lot of discomfort for nothing if you can't. The wet velvet was revolting on the skin, and abysmally cold."

Pitt was stunned. For a moment he could think of nothing to say.

"But it is effective, don't you think?"

"Effective." He repeated the word as if it was in an unfamiliar language. He looked at her vivid face with its fine, delicate mouth and wonderful bones. "Yes, Miss Antrim, I have never known a picture to have more effect."

She heard the emotion in his voice.

"You disapprove, Superintendent. That may be just as well. At least you will remember it, and it might make you think. The image that has no power to disturb probably has no power to change either."

"To change?" he asked, his voice a little hoarse. "To change what, Miss Antrim?"

She looked at him very steadily. "To change the way people think, Superintendent. What else is worth changing?" Her expression filled with disgust. "If the Lord Chamberlain had not taken off the play you came to, then Freddie Warriner might not have lost his nerve, and we would have started a bill to make the divorce laws more equal. We wouldn't have succeeded this time, but maybe the next, or the one after. You must begin by making people care!"

He drew in breath to make a dozen replies, then saw her smile, and understood what she meant.

"If you can change thought, you can change the world," she said softly.

He pushed his hands farther into his pockets, his fists clenched tight. "And what thought was it you intended to change with this picture, Miss Antrim?"

She seemed faintly amused. He saw the flicker in her eyes.

"The thought that women are content with a passive role in love," she replied. "We are imprisoned in other people's ideas of who we are and what we feel, what makes us happy . . . or what hurts. We allow it to happen. To be chained by your own beliefs is bad enough, heaven knows; but to be chained by other people's is monstrous." Her face was alight as she spoke. There was a kind of luminous beauty in her, as if she could see far beyond the physically jarring image on the paper to the spiritual freedom she was seeking, not for herself so much as for others. If it was a lonely crusade, she was prepared for it and her courage was more than equal to it.

"Don't you understand?" she said urgently to his silence. "Nobody has the right to decide what other people want or feel! And we do it all the time, because it's what we need them to want." She was close to him. He could feel the warmth of her, see the faint down on her cheek. "We feel more comfortable, it feeds our preconceptions, our ideas about who we are," she went on fiercely. "Or else it is what we can give them, so we decide it is what they want. They should be grateful. It is for their good. It is for somebody's good. It is what is

261

right or natural . . . or most of all, it is what God wants! What monumental arrogance that we should decide that what is comfortable for us is what Almighty God wants. And we should make it so."

"All of the pictures?" Pitt asked with the very faintest sarcastic edge to his voice, but he had to struggle to find it. "Some of them seemed blasphemous to me."

"To you?" Her marvelous eyes widened. "My dear, pedestrian Superintendent. Blasphemous to you! What is blasphemy?"

He jammed his hands farther still into his pockets, straightening his arms. He could not allow her to intimidate him because she was beautiful and articulate and supremely sure of herself.

"I think it is jeering at other people's beliefs," he replied quietly. "Making them doubt the possibility of good and making reverence appear ridiculous. Whose God it is doesn't matter. It isn't a question of doctrine, it's a matter of trying to destroy the innate idea we have of deity, of something better and holier than we are."

"Oh . . . Superintendent." She let her breath out in a sigh. "I think I have just been bested by a policeman! Please don't tell anyone . . . I shall never live it down. I apologize. Yes, that is what blasphemy is . . . and I did not mean to commit it. I meant to make people question stereotypes and look again at us as individuals, every one different, never again say 'She's a woman, so she feels this . . . or that . . . and if she doesn't, then she ought to.' Or 'He's a priest, he must be good, what he says must be right, he doesn't have this weakness, or that passion . . . if he does he's wicked.' " Her eyes widened. "Do you understand me?"

"Yes, I understand you, Miss Antrim."

"But you disagree with me. I can see it in your face. You think I shock people, and it is painful. I am breaking something, and you hate breakage. You are here to keep order, to protect the weak, to prevent violent change, or any change that is not by consent of the masses." She spread her hands wide—strong, beautiful hands. "But art must lead, Superintendent, not follow. It is my work to upset convention, to defy assumptions, to suggest that disorder out of which progress is born. If you were to succeed . . . entirely . . . we would not even have fire, let alone a wheel!"

"I am all for fire, Miss Antrim, but not for burning people. Fire can destroy as well as create."

"So can everything that has real power," she responded. "Have you seen *A Doll's House*?"

"I beg your pardon?"

"Ibsen! The play—*A Doll's House*!" she repeated impatiently.

He had not seen it, but he knew what she was talking about. The playwright had dared to create a heroine who had rebelled against everything that was expected of her, most of all by herself, and in the end left her husband and home for a dangerous and lonely freedom. It had created a furor. It was condemned passionately by some as subversive and destructive of morality and civilization. Others praised it as honest and the beginning of a new liberation. A few simply said it was brilliant and perceptive art, most particularly since it was written with such sensitivity and insight of a woman's nature—by a man. Pitt had heard Joshua praise it with almost the same burning enthusiasm as Cecily Antrim now showed.

"Well?" she demanded, the light in her face fading with exasperation as she began to believe she was confusing him.

"There are some differences," he said tentatively. "One chooses to go to the theatre. These pictures are on sale to the public. What if young people are there . . . boys who know no better . . ."

She waved it aside. "There are always risks, Superintendent. There can be no gain without a certain cost. To be born at all is to risk being alive. Dare it! Shame the devil of the real death . . . the death of the will, of the spirit! Oh . . . and don't bother to ask me who saw that picture. I would tell you if I could . . . I am deeply sorry Delbert Cathcart is dead—he was a great artist—but I can't tell you because I haven't the slightest idea!" And with that she turned and walked out of the door, leaving it wide open behind her, and he heard her footsteps dying away along the passage.

He stood alone in the dressing room and looked around at the trappings of illusion, the paint and the costumes which help the imagination. They were wrought with skill, but they were a minuscule part of the real magic. That sprang from the soul and the will, the inner world created with such passion it poured through and no material aids were needed to make it leap from one mind to another. Words, movement, gesture, the fire of the spirit made it real.

He looked at the photograph again. How many people were chained by other people's beliefs of them? Did he expect Charlotte to be something that was not her true nature or what she really wished? Then he thought back to his first meeting with Caroline. In some ways she had been imprisoned . . . but by family, society, her husband—or herself? The prisoner who loves his bonds is surely also responsible for their continuance?

He would rather Jemima, with her sharp, inquisitive mind, did not ever see a picture like this . . . certainly not until she was at least Charlotte's present age.

What kind of a man would she marry? That was a preposterous thought! She was a child. He could see her bright little face in his mind's eye so easily, so vividly, her child's slender body, but already growing taller, legs longer. One day she would marry someone. Would he be gentle with her, allow her some freedom, and still protect her? Would he be strong enough to wish her happiness in whatever path it lay? Or would he try to make her conform to his own view of what was right? Would he ever see her as herself, or only as what he needed her to be?

So much of him agreed with what Cecily Antrim was trying to do, and yet the picture offended him—not only because he had seen it mimicked in death but because of the innate violence in it.

Was that necessary in order to shatter complacency? He did not know.

But he would have to send Tellman to establish beyond

doubt where Cecily Antrim had been on the night of Cathcart's death, even though he did not believe she had killed him. There had been no fear in her, no shock, no sense of personal involvement at all.

He would also send Tellman to find out precisely where Lord Warriner had been that night, just in case his love for her was less casual than it appeared. But that was a formality, simply something not to be overlooked. She had posed willingly for the picture; in fact, from what she had said, it had been her idea. She wanted them sold. The last thing she intended was for such a performance to be without an audience.

He pushed the picture back into his pocket and went to the door. He found his way out past piled screens and painted trees and walls, and several pieces of beautifully carved wood, to the stage door.

———— 12 ————

CAROLINE RETURNED HOME with new heart and went straight upstairs before she could think better of it. She knocked on the old lady's door, and when there was no answer, she opened it and went in.

Mrs. Ellison was lying half reclined in bed. The curtains were pulled to keep the light out and she looked asleep. If Caroline had not seen her eyelids flicker she would have believed she was.

"How are you?" she enquired conversationally, sitting on the edge of the bed.

"I was asleep," Mrs. Ellison replied coldly.

"No, you weren't," Caroline contradicted her. "Nor are you going to be until tonight. Would you like to come to the theatre with us?"

The old lady's eyes flew open. "Whatever for? I haven't been to the theatre in years. You know that perfectly well. Whatever should I do there?"

"Watch the play?" Caroline suggested. She smiled. "And watch the audience. Sometimes that can be more fun. The drama on the stage is seldom the only one."

Mariah hesitated for just an instant. "I don't go to the theatre," she said sullenly. "It's usually nonsense they are performing anyway: cheap, modern rubbish!"

"It's *Hamlet*."

"Oh."

Caroline tried to remember Vespasia's words.

266

"Anyway," she said honestly, "the actress who plays the queen is very beautiful, talented and frightfully outspoken. I am terrified of her. I always feel as if I shall say something foolish, or naive, when I see her afterwards, which we will because Joshua is bound to go and congratulate her. They are great friends."

The old lady looked interested. "Are they? I thought the queen in *Hamlet* was his mother. She's hardly the heroine, is she!"

"Joshua likes older women. I thought you had appreciated that," Caroline said dryly.

Mrs. Ellison smiled in spite of herself. "And you are jealous of her." It was a statement, but for once there was no edge of unkindness to it, rather something that could even have been sympathy.

Caroline decided to tell the truth. "Yes—a little. She seems to be so certain of herself . . . of everything she believes in."

"Believes in? I thought she was an actress!" Mariah hitched herself a little higher in the bed. "What can she believe in?"

"All sorts of things!" Caroline pictured in her mind Cecily's passionate face, her vivid eyes and the fire in her voice. "The absolute evil of censorship, the freedom of the mind and will, the values of art. . . . She makes me feel terribly old-fashioned . . . and . . . dull."

"Poppycock!" Mrs. Ellison said vehemently. "Stand up for yourself. Don't you know what you believe in anymore?"

"Yes, I think so—"

"Don't be such a milksop! There must be something you are sure of. You can't live to your age without having at least one certainty. What is it?"

Caroline smiled. "That I don't know as much as I thought I did. I gather facts and make judgments about people and things, and so often there is one thing more that I didn't know, and if I had it I would have changed everything." She was thinking of the old lady and Edmund Ellison . . . but there were other things too, stretching back over the years: issues, decisions, stories only half known.

Mrs. Ellison grunted, but some of the anger had drained out of her.

"Then you are wiser than this woman, who imagines she knows so much," she said grudgingly. "Go and tell her so."

Caroline did not ask again if the old lady would come. They both knew she would not, and to have made the offer again would have broken the fragile thread of honesty between them.

She stood up and went to the door. Her hand was on it when the old lady spoke again.

"Caroline!"

"Yes."

"Enjoy yourself."

"Thank you." She turned away.

"Caroline!"

"Yes?"

"Wear the red dress. It becomes you."

She did not look back and spoil the moment by making too much of it. "Thank you," she accepted. "Good night."

Caroline dressed very carefully for the first night of *Hamlet*. She hesitated some time before having her maid put out the red dress the old lady had mentioned. It was actually a rich wine color, very warm, but definitely dramatic. She was uncertain about being so conspicuous. She sat in the chair in front of her looking glass and stared at her own face while her maid dressed her hair. She was still slender—she had not lost her shape at all—but she knew all the signs of aging that were there, the differences between her skin now and how it had been a few years ago, the slight blurring of the smooth line of her jaw, the fine lines on her neck, not to mention her face.

She had not Cecily Antrim's glowing vitality, the confidence inside which gave her such grace. That was not only youth, it was part of her character. She would always command attention, admiration, a kind of awe, because she carried part of the magic of life in her mind.

Caroline still felt dull compared with her, sort of brown . . . compared with gold.

She thought of what Vespasia had said, and Mariah Ellison. But it was the thought of Mariah's despair which finally made her sit up with a straight back, almost jerking the pins out of the maid's hands.

"I'm sorry," she murmured, wincing.

"Did I hurt you, ma'am?"

"My own fault. I shall sit still."

She was as good as her word, but her thoughts still raced, wondering how she should conduct herself, what she should say to be honest, generous and yet not gushing. She cringed inwardly at the picture of appearing to seek favor, push herself forward with too much wordiness in praise she could not mean because she did not really know what she was talking about. They would listen from good manners, wishing she would stop before she embarrassed everyone further. Her face was hot merely imagining it.

Every instinct was to retreat into quiet dignity, say very little. Then she would appear to be sulking, and make herself even more excluded.

Either way Joshua would be ashamed for her. And suddenly it was not about how she felt at all, but how miserable he would be that mattered, and how the change would spill over into all their lives afterwards.

The maid was finished. It was beautiful; Caroline had always had lovely hair.

"Thank you," she said appreciatively. Now she was ready for the dress. She hated having to go alone, but Joshua's own performance would not be over until shortly before the end. Thank goodness *Hamlet* was such a long play. He would be there in time for the last act.

The theatre was so crowded she had to push her way forward, nodding one way and another to people she knew or thought she recognized. She was quite aware, several times, of smiling graciously at complete strangers whose looks wavered in confusion for a moment, then dutifully smiled back.

She made the deliberate decision to treat that as a joke. She refused to be self-conscious.

She found her way to the box Joshua had reserved for her. It was far easier not to come too late and thus disturb no one else, even if she might feel rather more lonely sitting there so obviously by herself. She spent the time watching others arrive. It was such a parade of character. At a glance she could see status, income, social aspiration, confidence or lack of it, taste, and so often what a woman thought of herself. There were those who were diffident, dressed in somber colors, dark blues and greens, modest and well cut. She wondered if they would rather have been more daring, had they had the nerve. Was the sobriety their own choice, or due to fear of displeasing their husbands—or even their mothers-in-law? How much did anyone dress to conform with what others expected?

And there were those in vivid colors, aching to be noticed. Was her own red dress like that, a dramatic gown to disguise an undramatic woman?

No. As Vespasia had said, she was free to choose to be whatever she wished. If she were undramatic, overshadowed by Cecily Antrim, then that was her own decision to retreat, to conceal her beliefs in order to please others and conform to what they expected of her. There was no need to be offensive, too forceful; there was never excuse to be intentionally or carelessly unkind. But she could be true to her own values.

And she liked the red dress. It became her coloring and lent a certain glow.

And of course there were those young girls in pale colors, looking innocent and virginal, self-conscious, but fully intending to be looked at.

Almost everyone she saw was acting, in their own way, as much as most of the players would be. It was only that the story line was obscure. The onlooker saw only one scene.

The lights dimmed at last and there was a breathless expectation. The curtain rose on the battlements at Elsinore. Caroline found she was nervous for Orlando Antrim. This was by far the largest role he had ever played. But then Hamlet was surely the largest role anyone would play. Was it not every actor's dream?

From the moment he entered in the second scene, she sat forward a little, willing him to succeed, to remember all his lines, to pour into them the passion and the grief and the confusion the role demanded.

At the very first he seemed hesitant. Her heart sank. Would he, as always, be overshadowed by his mother, who seemed to dominate every stage on which she stepped?

Then the others left, except Orlando. He stepped forward into the light. His face was pale, even haggard, although presumably it was from paint. But the gestures of his body no one else could have imposed upon him, nor the agony in his voice.

" 'O, that this too too solid flesh would melt,

Thaw, and resolve itself into a dew! . . .

Or that the Everlasting had not fix'd

His canon 'gainst self-slaughter!' "

He gave the whole speech without hesitation. It poured from him so naturally it sounded as if he must have been the first to say it, not as learned and rehearsed, not brilliant acting, but torn from a young man's soul.

" 'But break, my heart—for I must hold my tongue!' "

For a moment after the curtain descended there was silence. The stalls forgot they were an audience; they had seemed more like unseen, individual intruders in someone else's tragedy.

Then suddenly they remembered and the applause boomed like thunder roaring around the vast space, filling the high ceiling.

From then on there was an electricity in the air, a charge of emotion so high the entire performance was lifted. The tragedy unfolded relentlessly; the doomed relationships progressed from one step to the next as if no one had the power to prevent them. Hamlet's pain seemed a palpable thing in the air; the king's duplicity, Polonius's wise counsel fell on deaf ears, but its words had become familiar down the ages, and Bellmaine's marvelous voice filled the heart and the mind. For those moments he dominated the stage. Even Hamlet was forgotten.

  " 'This above all: to thine own self be true,
  And it must follow, as the night the day,
  Thou canst not then be false to any man.' "

  Ophelia drifted helplessly into madness and death, an innocent sacrifice to others' ambition, greed or obsession. Joshua
tiptoed in and sat down silently, merely touching Caroline's
shoulder. Queen Gertrude wrought her own fate, still blind to
it to the very last sip of the poisoned cup.
  In spite of the skill and the personality of every actor on the
stage, Hamlet towered above them all. It was his pain, and in
the end his light extinguished, which left them in darkness
when the last curtain came down.
  As Caroline rose to her feet to applaud, Joshua beside her,
there were tears running down her cheeks and she was too full
of emotion even to think of speaking.
  When at last the applause had faded, the house lights were
blazing again, and people began to gather themselves to
leave, Caroline turned to Joshua.
  There was a mixture of joy and sorrow in his face. The joy
was by far the greater, the excitement and the admiration, but
she saw the faint shadow also, and knew in her heart how he
would love to have played Hamlet himself, to have had a gift
that far transcended mere talent and soared to genius. He
knew that he had not. His art lay in wit and compassion, in
making people laugh, often at themselves, and feel a new
gentleness toward one another. In years to come he might
play Polonius, but he would never be Hamlet.
  She tried to think what to say that was honest and held no
trace of condescension. That would be unbearable for him,
just as it was for her.
  The silence needed words, and she could not find them.
  "I feel as if I've never really seen *Hamlet* before," she admitted. "I would never have thought anyone so young could
have such a comprehension of—of betrayal. His rage with
the queen was so raw . . . and so close to love as well. Disillusion can destroy you." She thought of Mariah and Edmund
Ellison. How does one go on when dreams are shattered so

totally there is nothing left to rebuild? How does one continue living with things soiled beyond retrieval?

She longed to share that with Joshua. She knew, looking at his face now, that he would feel only tenderness for Mrs. Ellison—no judgment, no revulsion.

But was it a breaking of trust to speak of it? The old lady would certainly know, because she would see it in his eyes, hear it in his voice. And she would be looking for it. She would be waiting for Caroline to betray her.

Then Caroline must keep silent. Maybe one day she would allow it, and then it would be all right.

"Are you going to speak to Cecily?" she said aloud.

His face broke into a smile. "Oh yes! I wouldn't miss it. She was good—but he was better! This is the first time she has been eclipsed by anyone, except perhaps Bellmaine—long ago, when she was just beginning. She will be feeling . . ." He lifted one shoulder very slightly. "A great mixture of pride in Orlando . . . surely one has to be proud of one's children. . . ."

She remembered with a stab that he had no children, and he was far too young to regard either of her daughters in that light. He might have had children, if he had married someone younger. She forced that thought away. This was no time for pity of any sort, least of all self-pity, or for doubt where he had given her cause for none.

"It's not always easy," she replied frankly. "You can envy them their youth, and be exasperated by it. And you agonize for their mistakes, especially when you can see them even at the time. And of course you never cease to feel guilt for everything they do that turns out badly. Every flaw of character is directly attributable to something you did . . . or failed to do, or did the wrong way, or at the wrong time."

He put his arm around her. "Come! We'll go and congratulate Cecily . . . and commiserate with her—or whatever seems best." But he was smiling as he said it, and the faint lines had eased out from around his mouth.

The dressing room was already crowded when they arrived, but this time Orlando was not there. He was the center now, not peripheral to his mother's star.

Cecily stood with her back to the dressing table and the looking glass. She was still wearing the gorgeous gown from the last act. Her face was radiant, her fair hair spreading a halo around her. At first glance Caroline thought she was miscast as Hamlet's mother; she looked too young, too vibrant. Then she remembered with a jolt that Cecily was in life Orlando's mother, so she could not be wrong, except to the imagination.

Lord Warriner was not there this time. It was as if he had chosen deliberately to distance himself from the theatre for a while, or at least from Cecily. Two other minor players stood at the edge of the center looking tired and happy. A woman in a black gown and a magnificent diamond necklace was enthusiastic, and a middle-aged man with ribbons on his chest was agreeing with her.

Cecily saw Joshua almost immediately.

"Darling!" She came forward, arms wide to embrace him. "I'm so glad you could be here. Did you catch the end?" She allowed him to kiss her on both cheeks before she stepped back and acknowledged Caroline. "And Mrs. Fielding . . . Caroline, isn't it? How generous of you to come as well."

"Generosity had nothing to do with it," Caroline replied with a smile she hoped was warmer than she felt. "I came because I wished to . . . for myself . . . from the beginning. And I am delighted I did. It is by far the best *Hamlet* I have ever seen."

Cecily's eyes widened. She hesitated only a moment. "Really? And have you seen so many?"

Caroline kept her smile sparklingly in place. "Certainly. From the schoolroom onward. Almost every actor who is remotely suitable has played him at one time or another, and some who are not. I daresay I have seen twenty or more. Your son brought a new life and truth to it. You must be very proud of him."

"Of course. How kind of you to say so." Cecily turned back to Joshua. "He was rather marvelous, wasn't he? It is the strangest sensation to see your own child begin his first

274

stumbling performance, then progress to minor parts on stage, and ultimately have the whole theatre at his feet." She gave a slight laugh. "Can you imagine how I feel?"

Caroline saw the shadow in Joshua's face only for an instant. A week ago she might have felt crushed by it for her own inability to give Joshua children. Tonight she felt only anger that Cecily should have chosen to defend herself by hurting him this way.

Before Joshua could reply she stepped in.

"It is always surprising to find one's children have grown up," she said sweetly. "And that quite suddenly they can outshine you in the very area in which you thought yourself always superior . . ."

Cecily's face froze.

"But of course you are thrilled for them," Caroline continued blithely. "How could one not be? Apart from Lady Macbeth, all Shakespeare's tragedies seem to be based around men as the protagonists. But I am sure you could be unsurpassable by anyone in some of the great roles in classical Greek drama. I for one would queue all night for a ticket to see you play Clytemnestra or Medea."

There was total silence in the room. Everyone was staring at Caroline.

No one had heard the door open and Orlando come in.

"Clytemnestra!" he said distinctly. "What a brilliant idea! How extraordinarily clever of you, Mrs. Fielding. Mama has never done the Greeks. That would be a whole new career, and superb! And there is also Phaedra!" He turned to Cecily. "You are too old for Antigone, but you could always do Jocasta . . . but Mrs. Fielding is right, Clytemnestra would be the sublime vehicle for you. Who would want Gertrude after that?"

Cecily looked at Caroline, her head high, her eyes bright.

"Perhaps I should be obliged to you, Mrs. Fielding. I admit, I am surprised. I should never have thought of you as being so . . . liberal in your views of art. You must tell me, why do you think I might do Clytemnestra well?" She laughed. "I hope it is not merely because she has adult children?"

275

Caroline looked back at her with just as much bright candor.

"Of course not, although that does make a difference to one's life. But I was thinking of the fact that she is central to the play, not secondary. She is the character whose passions drive the plot. And she has been profoundly wronged in the sacrifice of her daughter. Her murder of her husband is not a sympathetic action, yet it is one most mothers would identify with. It needs an actress of extraordinary power to carry the audience with her and neither play to their pity and lose her own dignity, nor yet become unattractive because of her power and her willingness to take the ultimate step." She took a deep breath. No one had interrupted her by so much as a movement.

She plunged on. "It should leave one emotionally wrung out and yet deepened in experience, and perhaps with more compassion and understanding than before." Unwittingly the old lady came to her thoughts again. Horror for endless pain could change one's own life immeasurably, cast so much in a different view.

For the first time Cecily looked at her directly and without any mask of emotion. "You are most surprising," she said at length. "I could have sworn you had not a revolutionary idea in your head, much less your heart. And here you are recommending that we stir up the complacent society out there by making them feel Clytemnestra's passions!" She smiled. "You will provoke letters to the *Times* and thunder from the Archbishop, not to mention disfavor from the Queen, if you suggest that to murder your husband can even be acceptable!" The edge of mockery was back in her voice again.

She swiveled around. "Joshua darling, you had better be careful how you treat your wife's daughters!" She gestured to Caroline. "You do have daughters, don't you? Yes, of course you do—one of them is married to that policeman with all the hair. I remember him. For heaven's sake, darling, don't sacrifice them to the gods, or you may end your life abruptly with a knife in your heart. There sleeps a tiger inside that calm and dignified-looking wife of yours."

276

"Yes, I know," Joshua said smugly. He placed his hand very lightly on Caroline's arm just for a second, but it was a gesture of possession, and Caroline felt the warmth ripple through her. The door opened and Bellmaine came in, still dressed in his Polonius robes, the smudges of greasepaint on his face lending him greater gravity rather than detracting from it.

"Wonderful!" he said radiantly. He spoke to all of them, but it was Orlando his eyes rested on. "Wonderful, my dears. You surpassed yourselves. Cecily, you had Gertrude to perfection! I had never seen her in such a sympathetic light before. You made me believe in her unawareness of what she had done—until it was too late—a woman caught in the mesh of her own passions. I wept for her."

"Thank you," she accepted graciously, smiling at him, but there was a curious brittleness in her stare. "If I can move you to tears for Gertrude, I feel as if I can do anything."

Bellmaine turned to Orlando. His expression softened to one of pure joy.

"And you, my dear boy, were sublime. I hardly know what to say. I feel as if I have never really seen *Hamlet* before tonight. You have taken me along a new path, shown me a madness and a sense of betrayal that transcend the magic of Shakespeare's words and take me into a reality of feeling that has left me exhausted. I am a different man." He spread his hands as if he could say no more.

Caroline knew exactly what he meant. She too had been shown a new and wider experience. She found herself nodding her agreement. It was born of honesty; she could do no less.

Cecily turned to her, an edge to her voice. "So you are happy to be harrowed up in such a way, Mrs. Fielding? I thought from your previous visit that you were in favor of at least some censorship. Excluding the irresponsibility of shouting 'Fire' where there is none, and causing a panic, or of advocating crime or falsely speaking of someone else, would you agree that the limiting of ideas is an unmitigated evil? Art must be free if man is to be free. Not to grow is the beginning of death, albeit slow death, perhaps taking a generation or more." She looked very directly at Caroline. It was a challenge no one in the crowded room mistook. Perhaps it was made because of Orlando's success, a need to assert herself. One did not give up center stage easily.

Everyone was waiting for Caroline.

She glanced at Joshua. He was smiling. He would not step in and take away her chance to answer. She must speak honestly. She hoped he would not be disappointed in her, or embarrassed, but to say other than what she believed would lay a foundation for misery later. She thought of her daughters, of Jemima, of the old lady sitting hunched up in bed at home.

"Of course not to grow is death." She felt for the right words. "But we grow at different speeds, and sometimes in different ways. Don't try to make the argument in general as justification for doing it your way in particular."

"You have been preparing this!" Cecily said quickly. "You will give me a game for my money after all. So what are you going to censor . . . in general and in particular? You have already said you will allow husband murder in Clytemnestra, a child murder in Medea, and a man to marry his mother and beget children upon her in Oedipus. Great heavens, my dear, what can it be you disapprove of?"

Caroline felt her face flush hot.

"These are all tragedies, and depicted as such. One feels a terrible pity for the protagonist, an insight into how such things could have come about, and perhaps an admiration for the courage or the honesty with which in the end they meet their fate—good or bad."

"So it is all right, so long as the values are kept?" Cecily said with wide eyes.

Caroline saw the trap. "Whose values?" she asked. "Is that not what you are going to say?"

Cecily relaxed in a smile. "Exactly. If you are going to answer me that it is society, civilization, or even God, then I will ask you whose God? Which part of society? Mine? Yours? The beggar's in the street? The old Queen, God bless her? Or Mr. Wilde . . . whose society is certainly different from most people's!"

"That is your own judgment," Caroline replied. "But the

values we adopt will be the ones the next generation will live by. I am not sure if anyone can decide for you. But no one can relieve you of the responsibility for what you say, in whatever form. And the better you are at it, the more beautiful or powerful your voice, the greater the burden upon you to use it with wisdom and a great deal of care."

"Oh my God!" Cecily said, a trifle too loudly.

"Bravo!" Orlando gave a little salute of praise.

Caroline turned to look at him. His face startled her, it was so full of emotion, his eyes wide, his lips slightly parted, a kind of rigidity in his body.

Joshua was staring at her.

Bellmaine stood motionless, but his face was filled with amazement and a kind of painful relief it was impossible to interpret. Caroline was startled to see his eyes filled with tears.

"The greatest power sometimes lies in not doing a thing," she finished; her voice suddenly dropped, but she would not leave the rest unsaid. "It is so easy to use a skill simply because you have it, and not look two . . . three steps ahead to see what it will cause. People listen to you, Miss Antrim. You can move our emotions and make us reconsider all kinds of beliefs. That is very clever. It is not always wise . . ."

Cecily drew in her breath to say something in rebuttal, then looked at Joshua's face and changed her mind. She turned to Caroline with a dazzling smile.

"I apologize for having thought too little of you." She said it with utmost sincerity. There was no doubting that she meant it. "I think I should have listened to you rather better. I promise I shall in future." She turned to the others filling the room. "Now, shall we send for the champagne and toast Orlando? He has deserved all the praise we can give . . . and all the rejoicing. Tomorrow all the world will be congratulating him. Let us be the first, and do it tonight!"

"More than all," Bellmaine agreed fervently. He raised his hand. "Orlando!"

"Here, here, Orlando!" everyone responded eagerly. Only

Orlando himself seemed still bemused. Caroline looked across at him and wondered how exhausted he was. His young face was pale, and his eyes still held the look of Hamlet's haunted madness. It was not a role one could assume so wholly, live its passions and be destroyed by them, and then cast it off as if it had been a garment and not a skin.

She would have liked to comfort him, but she had no idea how. This was his world, not hers. Perhaps all great actors felt like this? Could one give such a performance merely on technique and skill, rather than by also pouring oneself into it until it became, for a time, one's own reality?

She looked to Joshua, but he was speaking to one of the other actors and she could not interrupt.

There was a knock on the door, and someone came in with champagne and a tray of glasses.

On the way home through the quiet streets, sitting beside Joshua in the hansom, Caroline was tired, but there was a degree of peace inside her that she had not felt in a long time. She realized now, with surprise, how long it had been. She had spent far too much time looking in the mirror and seeing what she disliked, being frightened of it, and projecting onto Joshua emotions born of that fear.

He had been very patient in enduring her self-centeredness. Or perhaps he had not noticed? That was a far uglier thought. Could she hurt so much, and he be oblivious to it?

Of course! Why not? She had been oblivious to his feelings. Had she for an instant wondered how hard it was for him to be the newcomer in her family, to see her children and grandchildren and know he could never have his own? They might learn to love him, but that was not the same. There was an essence of belonging that . . . that what? Mariah Ellison belonged, and she had lived all her adult life imprisoned in an icy hell of loneliness beyond anything Caroline could imagine. She had glimpsed its horror, but she had no concept of what it would do to her over time. Time was a dimension one could not create in the mind; it was change, exhaustion, the slow dying of hope.

She understood so much more of why the old lady had become the person she was, but what had made Edmund Ellison seek his pleasures in cruelty? What devils had crawled into his soul and warped it out of human shape?

She would never know. The answer was buried with him, and best let go now, left to drift into the darkness of the past and become covered over with other memories.

"He was brilliant, wasn't he?" Joshua's voice came softly out of the shadows beside her. Through the weight of her cloak and his coat she could feel his body stiffen.

"Oh yes," she agreed honestly. "But I wonder if it will make him happy."

He was silent for several minutes before finally asking her, "What do you mean?"

She must word this exactly as she meant it, no carelessness, no fumbling for the right way and missing it.

"He conveyed a dreadful understanding of Hamlet's pain," she began. "As if he had looked at a kind of madness and seen its face. I am not sure if I believe one can portray that simply from imagination. Turn one horror into the image of another, probably, but not call it up without a kind of experience, some taste of its reality. It was still there in him long after the curtain had fallen."

They were moving faster through the darkness, only occasional lights from other vehicles moving past and disappearing.

"Do you think so?"

There was no denial in his voice.

She moved closer to him, so slightly only she was aware of it.

"What my mother-in-law told me made me see many things I had not understood before. One of them is the kind of damage that cruelty can inflict, especially when it is held secret where it cannot heal. To be clever is a great gift, and certainly the world needs its clever people, but to be kind is what matters. To be clever or gifted will make people laugh, and think, and perhaps grow in certain ways; but to be generous of spirit is what will bring happiness. I would not wish anyone I loved to be a success as an artist if it meant that he was a failure as a human being."

He reached out his hand and slid it over hers, gently, then tightened it.

The hansom swayed around a street corner and straightened again.

He turned in his seat and leaned forward. Very gently he kissed her lips. She felt his breath warm on her cheek, and put up her gloved hand to touch his hair.

He kissed her again, and she clung tighter to him.

13

P*ITT RECEIVED CAROLINE'S LETTER* with the address of the second seller of photographs and postcards, also in Half Moon Street, and with a deep anger inside him, he went with Tellman to see the man.

"No!" the man protested indignantly, standing behind his counter and staring at the two policemen who had intruded into his place of business and were already costing him good custom. "No, I don't sell no pictures except proper, decent ones as yer could show to a lady!"

"I don't believe you," Pitt said tersely. "But it will be easy enough to find out. I shall post a constable here at the door and he can examine every one you sell. And if they are as good as you say, then in four or six weeks we'll know that."

The man's face went white, his eyes small and glittering.

"And then I'll apologize to you," Pitt finished.

The man swore venomously, but under his breath so the words were barely audible.

"Now," Pitt said briskly, "if you will take another look at this picture you can tell me when you got it in, how many copies you have sold and to whom, Mr. . . . ?"

"Hadfield. . . . An' I can't remember 'oo I sold 'em ter!" His voice rose to a squeal of indignation.

"Yes, you can," Pitt insisted. "Pictures like that are sold only to people you know. Regular customers. But of course if you can't remember who likes this sort of thing, then you'll just have to give me a list of all of them, and I'll go and question them—"

"All right! All right!" Hadfield's eyes burned with fury. "Yer a vicious man, Inspector."

"Superintendent," Pitt corrected him. "It was a vicious murder. I want all your customers who like this sort of picture. And if you leave any out, I shall presume you are doing it to protect them because you know them to be involved. Do you understand me?"

"O' course I understand yer! D'yer take me fer a bleedin' fool?"

"If I take you at all, Mr. Hadfield, it will be for accessory to murder," Pitt replied. "While you are making me a list, I shall look through the rest of your stock to see if there is anything else that might tell me who killed Cathcart and who knew about it . . . possibly even why."

The man flung his arms out angrily. "Well, there y'are! Seein' as I can't stop yer. An Englishman's 'ome not bein' 'is castle, like, anymore, yer'd best 'elp yerself. Cheap way o' getting yer 'ands on pictures an' lookin' at 'em for nothin', if yer ask me!"

Pitt ignored him and began to go through the drawers and shelves of pictures, postcards and slim volumes of drawings. Tellman started at the other end.

Many of them were fairly ordinary, the sort of poses he had seen a hundred times before in the last week, pretty girls in a variety of flattering clothes.

He glanced at Tellman and saw the concentration in his face, and now and again a slight smile. Those were the sort of girls he would like. He might well be too shy to approach them, but he would admire them from a distance, think them attractive and decent enough.

He bent back to the task, and pulled out a new drawer with small books in it. He opened the first one, more out of curiosity than the belief that it would be relevant to Cathcart's death. They were drawings in black and white. There was a kind of lush, imaginative beauty about them, and the draftsmanship was superb. They were also obscene, figures with leering faces, and both male and female organs exposed.

He closed it again quickly. Had they been more crudely drawn, they would have been less powerful and less disturbing. He had heard that nature could become so distorted as to do this to people, but this was not the representation of the tragedy of deformity, it was a salacious artistic comment on appetite, and he felt soiled by it. He understood why men like Marchand crusaded so passionately against pornography, not for the offense to themselves but the strange erotic disturbance to others as well, the degrading of all emotional value. In some way it robbed all people of a certain dignity because it touched upon humanity itself.

He did not bother to open the other books of drawings. Cathcart dealt only in photographs. He moved to the next drawer of cards.

Tellman grunted and slammed a drawer shut.

Pitt looked up and saw the distress in the sergeant's face. His eyes were narrowed and his lips drawn back a little as if he felt an inward pain. In spite of all his experience, this confused him. He expected something higher of artists. Like many of little learning, he admired education. He believed it lifted men above the lowest in them and offered a path out of the trap of ignorance and all the ugliness that went with it. This was a disillusionment he did not expect or understand.

There was nothing for Pitt to say. It was a private distress, at least for the moment better not put into words. In fact Tellman would find it easier to deal with if he did not even realize Pitt was aware of it.

The next drawer of pictures was much the same as the last, pleasant, a few rather risqué, but nothing more than the art of young men seeing how far they dare go in putting their fantasies into expression. Some were the usual rectangular professional plates, slick, showing the same, rather repetitive use of light and shade, angle or exposure.

There were also several of the round pictures which held considerably more individuality, although they were also less skilled. Sometimes the form was not as sharp, the balance less well disposed. These were the amateur ones, taken by the likes of the camera club members he had interviewed.

One or two of them were good, if a trifle theatrical. He recognized poses that seemed to be taken directly from the stage. There was a fairly obvious Ophelia, not like Cecily Antrim but alive and disturbingly frantic, on the borders of madness. And yet it was a fascinating picture. She looked no more than twenty at the most, with dark hair and wide eyes. Her lips were parted and faintly erotic.

A few more were rather Arthurian, reminding him of the pre-Raphaelite painters, definitely romantic. Something in the background of one of them caught his attention, a use of lighting rather than a specific article. In the center was a young girl kneeling in vigil. On the altar were a chalice and a knight's sword. It made him think of Joan of Arc.

In another a woman in despair leapt to her feet as if fleeing from a mirror, presumably intended as the Lady of Shalott.

A third came from the classical Greek theatre, a young girl about to be sacrificed. The same length of carved wood was used in all three, very cleverly. It gave them a richness of texture as the light and shade accentuated the repeated pattern.

Pitt had seen it before, but it took him a moment or two to remember where. Then it came to him. He had passed by it as he had gone from Cecily Antrim's dressing room to the back door.

"Where did you buy these pictures?" he said aloud.

Hadfield did not even look up from the list he was writing. "What's the matter now?" he said wearily. "What crime are you trying to tie them up with?"

"Where did you get them?" Pitt repeated. "Who brought them to you?"

Hadfield put down his pen, splattering ink over the page, and swore. He came over to Pitt irritably and stared over his shoulder at the photographs.

"I dunno. Some young photographer who thinks he can make a few bob. Why?" His voice was laden with sarcasm. "What terrible offense ter 'umanity and civilization can yer see in these? Got a dirty mind, you 'ave. Looks as innocent as a cup o' tea ter me."

"Who brought them to you?" Pitt repeated, a steel edge of anger to his voice, although it was misery he was feeling inside. He did not want the answer he was almost certain would come.

"I dunno! Do you think I ask the name and address of every young amateur who comes here with an 'andful o' pictures? They're good pictures. Nothin' wrong wif 'em. I bought 'em. Fair sale. Nothin' more ter say."

"Describe him!"

"Describe 'im! Yer crazy, or summink?" He was thoroughly aggrieved. " 'E was a young man wot fancies 'isself as a photographer, an' 'e in't bad."

"Tall or short? Dark or fair? Describe him!" Pitt said between closed teeth.

"Tall! Fair! But there's nothin' wrong wif 'em! You can find pictures like this all over London . . . all over England. Wot's the matter wif yer?"

"Did he see your other pictures? Like the one of Ophelia chained up in the boat?"

The man hesitated. In that instant Pitt knew that it was Orlando who had brought the photographs, and that he had seen Cathcart's picture of his mother. Until then Pitt had been clinging to the hope that it had been Bellmaine, or even, by some obscure chance, Ralph Marchand, pursuing his crusade against pornography.

"Sergeant Tellman!" Pitt turned sideways, his voice sharp.

Tellman stood up, letting the postcards fall onto the floor.

"Yes sir?"

"Go and find the nearest constable to stand guard here. I think we should continue this discussion at Bow Street."

"All right!" Hadfield snapped. " 'E could 'ave! I dunno!" What was his name?"

"I'll 'ave ter look at me records."

"Then do it!"

Muttering under his breath, Hadfield went back to his

desk, and it was several silent, painful minutes before he returned, waving a piece of paper. There was no name on it, simply the amount of money, a brief description of the photograph, and the date—two days before Cathcart's death.

"Thank you," Pitt said quietly.

Hadfield's face conveyed the words he did not dare to say.

Pitt wrote him a receipt in exchange for the photographs he was sure were taken by Orlando Antrim, also the sales receipt with its date.

Outside the air seemed cold.

Tellman looked at him questioningly.

"Orlando Antrim," Pitt answered. "He was here two days before Cathcart's death. If he saw that picture of his mother, and perhaps some of the others, how do you suppose he felt?"

Tellman's face was pinched with misery, and there was an emotional conflict in him that was painfully apparent. "I don't know," he said, stumbling a little as he stepped off the pavement onto the road to cross. "I don't know."

Pitt tried to imagine himself in Orlando's place. Cecily was an actress. It was her profession to portray emotion in public and behave in such a way as to stir any of a score of passions. He must be used to it. But could anything make this acceptable to him?

Pitt could see the grotesque picture of Ophelia in his mind's eye so clearly there was no need to pull it out of his pocket to remind himself. It was a woman bound by literal, physical chains, but appearing to be in a paroxysm of sexual ecstasy, as if the bondage she experienced excited her as no freedom could. It suggested that she hungered to be overpowered, forced into submission. It was lust that lit her face as she lay there, knees apart, skirts raised. There was nothing of tenderness in it, certainly nothing that could be thought of as love.

If Pitt had seen his own mother like that, for any reason at all, it would have revolted him beyond measure. Even now, striding along the footpath at an increasing speed, he could not allow his mind to touch such an idea. It polluted the very wellspring of his own life. His mother was not that kind of woman. His intelligence told him she had loved his father. He had heard them laughing together often enough, long ago, and seen them kiss, seen the way they looked at each other. He knew the nature and the acts of love.

But that picture had nothing to do with love, or the things men and women do in private in generosity, hunger and intimacy. It was a mockery of them all.

Of course the world was full of people whose ideas were different, whose acts he would have found offensive if he had considered them. But within one's own family it was different.

Had he seen Charlotte portrayed that way . . . he felt the blood rise in his face and his muscles lock, his fists clench. If any man were ever to speak coarsely to her he would be tempted to violence. If anyone actually touched her Pitt would probably strike him and consider the consequences afterwards.

For anyone to think of Jemima in that way, and then use her so, would break his heart.

Cecily Antrim had such profound understanding of so many different kinds and conditions of people, how could she fail to grasp the distress any man must feel to see his own mother in such a way? Had she no conception of the grief and the confusion that had to follow?

He thought of Orlando. If he had seen that picture, or any of them, he would have walked away from the shop like a blind man; the world of footpath and stones and sky, soot in the air, clatter of people, smell of smoke and drains and horses would make no mark on him at all. He would be consumed by the inner pain, and perhaps hatred.

And above all, he would be asking the same question Pitt was—Why? Was any cause worth fighting in such a way? Pitt could ask it, and still be hurt by the disillusion over a woman whose glorious talent he had admired, who had made him think, and above all, care about her on the stage. How infinitely more must Orlando have felt?

Pitt had been convinced from the beginning that Cathcart's death was a crime of passion, not simply escape, even from the life-draining clutches of blackmail. That would induce hatred and fear, but there was more than either of those in the way Cathcart had been laid in the mockery of Millais, the exact replica, a soul-deep injury that could not be undone.

"D'you think he knew who took that picture?" Tellman's voice, which cut across Pitt's thoughts, was harsh, yet so quiet he barely heard it.

"No," Pitt replied as they both stopped at the next curb while a heavy wagon rolled past, horses leaning forward into the harness, the wheels rumbling over the cobbles. "No. He saw it two days before Cathcart's death. I think it took him that long to find out." He started forward across the street. He did not even know where he was going; at the moment he simply needed to put in a physical effort because he could not bear to keep still.

"How could he do that?" Tellman asked, running a couple of steps to keep up. "Where would he begin? He can't have asked her. In fact, if I were in his place I couldn't even have spoken to her."

"He's an actor," Pitt replied. "I presume he is better at masking his feelings than either of us." He walked a few yards in silence. "He would know it was a professional photograph . . . the square exposures. Professionals don't use the round ones. No good except in daylight. And he'd hardly have the film manufacturer develop them, which is what the amateurs do."

Tellman grunted with profound disgust. His emotions were too raw to find words. He walked with his shoulders tight and hunched, his head forward.

"He'd have started to consider the different professionals it might be," Pitt continued with his thoughts. "He'd do it very discreetly. He would have been thinking of murder already . . . or at the very least a confrontation. Where would he begin?"

"Well, if he's trying to keep it secret, he'll hardly ask anyone," Tellman retorted. "Not that you would ask anyone about pictures like that anyway."

"He'd narrow it down to professional photographers who use that kind of scenery," Pitt answered his own question. "He'd study them for style. He takes photographs himself. He knows how an artist puts things one way, then another, trying to get exactly the right effect. It's like a signature."

"So how would he see the style of Cathcart's photographs?" Tellman turned to look at him. "There must be dozens! How would he even know where to look?"

"Well, he did!" Pitt pointed out. "He found him in less than two days, so whatever he did was effective."

"Or lucky."

Pitt shot him a sideways glance.

Tellman shrugged.

"Exhibition," Pitt said abruptly. "He'd look to see if there was an exhibition of photography anywhere. Wherever he could see the largest collection of different people's work."

Tellman quickened his pace a trifle. "I'll find out! Give me half an hour and I'll know where there are any."

Nearly two hours later Pitt and Tellman stood side by side in a large gallery in Kensington, staring at photograph after photograph of lovely scenery, handsome women, magnificently dressed men, animals and children with wide, limpid eyes. Some of the pictures were hauntingly beautiful, a world reduced to sepia tints, moments of life caught forever, a gesture, a smile.

Pitt stopped in front of one. Ragged children huddled together on a doorstep in some alley, dresses with holes in them, trousers held up by string, no shoes. And yet the childish curves of their cheeks held a timeless innocence.

In others sunlight slanted across a plowed field, bare trees filigree against the sky. A flight of birds scattered in the wind, like leaves thrown up.

He was looking for style, use of water, someone who saw symbolism in ordinary objects. Of course Pitt knew he was looking for Delbert Cathcart. Orlando had had no idea of who he was trying to find, or why the man would have used his mother. Had he believed it was blackmail, some kind of force or coercion that had made her do it? He would have to believe that. Anything else was unbearable.

He looked at Tellman, who was standing a few yards away,

unaware that he was blocking the view of a large woman in lavender and black, and her dutiful daughter, who was quite obviously bored silly and longing to be almost anywhere else. Tellman was staring at a photograph of a young girl, a housemaid, caught momentarily distracted from beating a rug slung over a line in an areaway. She was small and slight with a humorous face. Pitt knew she reminded him of Gracie, and he was startled that anyone should think of her as a subject for art. He was proud that ordinary people were considered important enough to be immortalized, and it confused him because it was unexpected and made him self-conscious. They represented his own life caught and displayed for its interest, its uniqueness.

He stopped sharply and turned away, only just missing bumping into the large lady. He muttered an apology and rejoined Pitt. "This isn't getting us anywhere," he said quietly. "Can't learn a thing from this lot."

Pitt forebore from making any comment.

The next room was more useful, and in the one after they saw some pictures which Pitt knew immediately were Cathcart's. The light and shade, the accentuation of focus, were all similar to the work he had seen both in Cathcart's own house and in those of his clients. There were even two with the river for background.

"That's his," Tellman said bluntly. "But how would Antrim know that? It doesn't prove anything, except that Cathcart's work is exhibited. You'd expect it to be."

"We've got to prove the link," Pitt said unnecessarily. "Antrim found out who he was. This is probably how."

Tellman said nothing.

Pitt looked carefully at the other pictures until he had found several more showing water, two with small boats, one with a garden and half a dozen using artificial flowers, and one with a long velvet gown.

"Who took these?" Tellman asked.

"According to the card there, Geoffrey Lyneham."

"Wonder if Antrim went to see him?" Tellman thought

aloud. "Or if he went to Cathcart first? If he did it will be harder to prove, seeing as he can't tell us anything, and Mrs. Geddes doesn't know or she'd have said so."

"He went to Lyneham first," Pitt assumed. "And probably somewhere else as well. It took him two days to find Cathcart. I don't think he waited any longer than he had to."

"I wouldn't!" Tellman said with narrowed lips. "Where do we find this Lyneham?"

It was late afternoon and already growing dusk, the gas lamps coming on in the streets and the air crisp and cold when they went up the stairs of Geoffrey Lyneham's house in Greenwich. Wood smoke drifted on the damp air from a bonfire in someone's garden nearby, and the smell of earth and leaves was sweet.

Lyneham was a small man with a sharp, intelligent face. He was at least fifty, probably more, his hair white at the temples. He was startled when Pitt told him who they were.

"Police? Why? As far as I know I haven't infringed any laws."

Pitt forced himself to smile. None of the horror was Lyneham's fault, and he would very much sooner discuss the matter in the warmth of Mr. Lyneham's sitting room by the fire than out there on the step.

"It is a matter of importance, sir," he replied. "About photography."

"Ah!" Lyneham's face lit with instant enthusiasm. He pulled the door wide and stood back. "Come in, gentlemen, come in! Anything I can tell you. I should be delighted. What is it you would like to know?" He led the way inside, to the sitting room, still waving his hands energetically, leaving Tellman to close the front door and follow behind.

"I saw several of your photographs in the Kensington exhibition," Pitt began courteously.

"Oh yes . . . yes?" Lyneham nodded, waiting for the inevitable comments.

"Excellent use of light on water," Pitt said.

Lyneham looked startled. "You like that? I find it most interesting to work with. Gives the whole thing an extra dimension, don't you think?"

"Yes . . ."

"Funny you should say that," Lyneham went on, standing with his back to the fire. "Young fellow here a couple of weeks ago, said almost exactly the same."

Pitt felt his stomach tighten. He tried to keep his face blank.

"Really? Who was it? Maybe someone I know."

"Said his name was Harris."

"Tall, fair young man, about twenty-five?" Pitt asked. "Very dark blue eyes?"

"Yes, that's right! You do know him," Lyneham said eagerly. "Most interested, he was. Keen photographer himself. Very good eye, judging by his remarks. Amateur, of course." He waved a deprecating hand. "But very keen. Wished to know what localities I thought best, and that kind of thing. Asked about the use of boats. Bit tricky, actually. They tend to move about. Any wind and you're sunk, so to speak. Essence of good photography, light, focus, and position."

"Yes, I see. And what localities did you recommend? Or is it a secret of your profession?"

"Oh no, not at all! Norfolk Broads, myself. Lovely light in East Anglia. Don't have so many painters there for no reason, you know?"

"Always the Broads?" Pitt asked, although he was certain he had the answer.

"Personally, yes," Lyneham replied. "Got a house up there. Makes it easy, convenient for taking advantage of the weather. Moment's notice, and there you are. Damned nuisance if you have to go a distance from home and trust to chance. Can get rained on just as you arrive. Carting tripods and things around, very heavy . . . awkward. Much better to have it right there to hand. I've got some lovely shots of swans. Beautiful creatures. Light on white wings."

"I can imagine," Pitt agreed. "Never on the Thames?"

Lyneham pushed out his lip and shook his head. "No, not personally. Some people have—very well too. Fellow called

John Lawless, does some excellent work. Specializes in pictures of children and the poor. People washing, people playing, pleasure boats and so on." His face darkened. "And of course poor Cathcart. He actually had a house on the river. Opportunity right there." He frowned. "Why do you want to know, sir? Has this to do with Cathcart's death?"

"Yes, I am afraid it has," Pitt admitted. He produced a theatre bill with Orlando's picture on it, and showed it to Lyneham.

Lyneham looked at it only a moment, then up again at Pitt. "Yes," he said quietly. "That is the young man. I hope he is not seriously involved. He was such a . . . a decent-seeming fellow."

"What was his mood? Please think carefully."

"Upset. Very upset," Lyneham said unhesitatingly. "Oh, he hid it well, but there was obviously something that troubled him. Didn't say what, of course. But I really can't imagine anyone killing another man over photography—even passionate about it as some of us are. He just wanted to know about styles, that kind of thing . . . nothing else. And he never mentioned Cathcart."

"I'm sure he didn't. I don't believe at that point he even knew his name. Where did you direct him, Mr. Lyneham?"

Lyneham looked at him very steadily, his eyes troubled, his mouth pinched a little.

"To the exhibition in Warwick Square," he replied. "Prints, but very good. I thought there he would get the chance to see some of the best uses of water, light and so on. Did I . . . contribute to the . . . crime, sir? I regret that profoundly."

"No," Pitt assured him. "If he had not learned from you, then he would have from somebody else. Don't chastise yourself for ordinary civility."

"Oh dear." Lyneham shook his head. "Oh dear. He seemed such an agreeable young man. I'm so sorry!"

Pitt and Tellman arrived at the exhibition in Warwick Square just before it closed for the night. It took them only twenty minutes to walk around the half dozen rooms used

and see the array of photographs. Those which mattered were
e pictures of women, stretches of water and the use of symbols and romanticism.

"That's like what's-his-name's paintings, isn't it?" Tellman said presently, nodding towards one photograph of a girl sitting in a rowing boat, her long hair loose about her shoulders, flowers drifting in the water.

"Millais," Pitt supplied. "Yes, it is."

"Except she's alive, and sitting up," Tellman added.

"Same flavor." Pitt walked away. It would not be difficult for Orlando Antrim to have found Cathcart's name here. It was written out on a neat placard under half a dozen of the photographs, with his address underneath it, in case anyone should wish to purchase his professional skills. All the pictures were powerful, characteristic, and one of them even used the same velvet gown with its unique embroidery, but untorn, and on a slender girl with long, dark hair.

Pitt tried to imagine how Orlando had felt when he knew at last not only who had taken the photograph, but exactly where he lived. Seeing that same dress he can have had no doubts left. What would he do then?

"It's it, isn't it?" Tellman made it a statement, not a question. "Poor devil." His voice was thick with pity.

"Yes," Pitt agreed quietly.

"Do we need to ask if anyone saw him?"

Pitt pushed his hands deep into his pockets. "Yes."

There was a guard on duty, to make sure no one damaged any of the exhibits, and perhaps that they did not steal them. He remembered Orlando Antrim, although of course he did not know his name. It was sufficient.

Outside in the cold, walking to find a hansom and go home for the night, Pitt tried to put himself in Orlando's place. What would he do? His mind would be in turmoil; the wound would hurt intolerably, the sense of betrayal. He might not blame Cecily. He would still be fighting to excuse her. She must have been frightened or coerced into such a thing. It could not be her fault. It had to be Cathcart's.

He knew where to find him. Now he would have to resolve

in his mind what he meant to do about it. He intended to harm him, perhaps already to kill him. He would be careful.

He would find out all he could about Cathcart—but discreetly now. He might have searched for what was more or less public knowledge from newspapers, advertisements for photographic skills. He might even have made an appointment to be certain of finding Cathcart at home. If he had, he had destroyed the record of it.

"Tomorrow we'll have to find if he asked anyone local about Cathcart and his habits," Pitt said aloud.

"And where he got the weapon," Tellman added. "Someone may have seen him. I suppose it's just a matter of being thorough."

"Yes . . . I suppose it is." There was no pleasure in it, no satisfaction in the solution, only a sense of tragedy.

Tellman did not bother to reply.

Pitt spent a restless and unhappy night. The house seemed cold without Charlotte and the children, even though he had kept the kitchen stove alight. It was a sense of darkness, and he expected no more letters from her because in a couple of days she would be home, the weather across the Channel permitting. He had not actually put words to it in his mind until now, but he would be glad when she was safely on land again in England. And Gracie would be back with the children two days after that. The house would be bright and warm again, full of the sounds of voices and footsteps, laughter, chattering, the smells of wax polish, baking, clean laundry.

In the meantime he had to follow the steps of Orlando Antrim and find the proof of exactly how he had murdered Cathcart, and then, when he had it, go and arrest him. There was an anger against Cecily Antrim inside him like a stone, heavy and hard. Her arrogant certainty that she knew best how to pursue her cause, without thought for the consequences, had destroyed her son. He was angry with her for what she had done and because she also woke in him a terrible pity. Could Pitt ever, unthinkingly, pursuing what he believed to be justice or truth, do the same to his own children? His emotions were as strong, perhaps their consequences as profound.

He met Tellman in Battersea, at the far end of the bridge, just after nine o'clock. Tellman was there before him, a forlorn figure standing in the early morning river mist, his coat collar turned up, his hat pulled forward and down over his eyes. Pitt wondered if he had had any breakfast.

"I've been thinking," Tellman said as he heard Pitt's footsteps and looked up. "He didn't need to ask about where he lived; he knew that already. And he wouldn't want to be too open in trying to find out about the household."

"Household?" Pitt asked.

"Yes!" Tellman was impatient, shivering a little. "You don't go attacking someone if you think there's a resident manservant that'll come to his rescue, or even a maid who'll remember you, maybe scream the place down. First thing, he'd go and see if there are near neighbors, and how he's going to get there and away again."

"Yes, you're right," Pitt agreed quickly, increasing his pace. He was wondering if Orlando had intended to use the dress and the chains right from the beginning, or if it had been an inspiration only when he realized they were still there, but he did not say so aloud.

"And what weapon did he mean to use?" Tellman went on morosely as they walked together along the road towards the river and Cathcart's house. "Or did it go too far and turn into murder?"

Pitt had not wanted to face that question, but it was inevitable. "The time he chose the weapon would answer that."

"We don't know what it was," Tellman reminded him. "It's probably at the bottom of the river by now anyway. That's what I would have done with it, wouldn't you?"

"Unless I dropped it by mistake, in the dark," Pitt replied. "I should have asked Mrs. Geddes if there was anything missing." He blamed himself. That was an oversight.

"We could still do that. We know where she lives." Tellman was half offering.

It should be done. Pitt accepted.

"Right!" Tellman squared his shoulders. "I'll meet you at the Crown and Anchor at one." He set off at a smart pace, leaving Pitt to pursue the less-clear objective of tracing Orlando's investigation into Cathcart's daily life and domestic arrangements.

He turned and went back towards the Battersea Bridge Road, away from the river and the soft mist curling up from it with the smell of the incoming tide. Autumn was in the air, and the smells of turned earth, wood smoke, chrysanthemums, the last mowing of the grass. When Orlando had come this way did he really think only to quarrel with Cathcart and then walk away? Why? He had no threat against him, no way to stop him from doing such a thing again as often as he wished to, until Cecily was no longer worth photographing, if that time ever came.

He would not have trusted to finding a weapon when he got there, he would have obtained it first. Pitt reached the center of the village, the shops and public houses, places where Orlando might have made enquiries or purchased something to use as a weapon.

It must have been something of considerable weight to land a blow sufficiently hard to kill a man. A length of plumbing pipe would do, or perhaps the handle of a garden implement.

He walked past a chemist's shop with blue glass bottles in the window, and a grocer's, and crossed the street. There was a small row of houses opposite a milliner and glovemaker. On the near side was a wine merchant. Would Orlando ask there? A bottle was an excellent weapon.

All Orlando had really needed to know was if Cathcart had any resident household staff. Laundry could be done easily enough by a woman who went in every day. Cooking was another matter.

Pitt had an advantage. He knew the answers already. There was only Mrs. Geddes. Orlando might have wasted much time before he had learned that. Also, Pitt did not have to be discreet.

He tried the laundry, the dairy, the greengrocer and the butcher. No one remembered anybody answering Orlando's description. He might have been there, he might not. They could not say.

He was at the Crown and Anchor before one, and had a glass of cider waiting for Tellman when he arrived.

"Nothing missing," Tellman said with a nod of thanks. He drank thirstily, looking towards the open door to the kitchen, from which drifted the smell of steak and kidney pudding. He was very partial to a good suet crust, as was Pitt himself. "Going to get some?" There was no need to specify what he meant.

In the early afternoon they started to consider where Orlando would have found or purchased a suitable weapon.

"Well, it won't have been something you'd think of as meant for harm," Tellman said, shaking his head. He looked profoundly unhappy, in spite of his excellent meal. "Who'd have thought people that clever would end up murdering someone?" he said miserably. "They've got a kind of . . . magic . . . in their minds. It really had me . . ." He stumbled for words to express the wonder he had felt, the excitement and awe at the world it had allowed him to glimpse and wooed him to enter. He had been more than willing to go. He would certainly not admit it to anyone at the Bow Street station, but he might one day go and watch a whole Shakespeare play, right from beginning to end. There was something about it. In spite of the fact that they were kings and queens and princes, the feelings in them were as real as those in the people he knew from day to day, it was just that they knew how to put them into those wonderful words.

Pitt knew no answer was necessary. He understood Tellman's feelings. He shared them.

They went first to the ironmonger's. It seemed the obvious place to start. The entire shop was crammed with every conceivable piece of equipment for the house, from watering cans to jelly molds, carriage foot warmers to chop covers and game ovens. There were gas lanterns, jelly bag stands, corkscrews and table gongs, toast racks, cake baskets, sardine boxes, butter coolers. There were also spades, forks, scythes, baby perambulators and a newly invented torpedo washer, which claimed to launder linens better than ever before. There were tin baths, carpenter's tools and an array of knives for every purpose imaginable. He saw trussing needles, larding pins, turnip scoops, egg whisks, meat saws and a heavy ceramic rolling pin.

The words were out before he had time to reconsider.

"That's a nice piece. Have you sold any of those lately?" He picked it up and felt the solidity of it. It was a perfect weapon, round, hard, heavy, and easily handled.

"That's the last one I got, till more come in," the ironmonger replied. "You're right, sir, it's a good one. That'll be ninepence to you, sir."

Pitt was quite sure it would be ninepence to anybody, but he did not say so. He might have bought a new rolling pin for Charlotte, but not this one.

"Did you sell one about two weeks ago?" he persisted.

"Probably. We sell a lot of those. They're very good quality." The man was determined to do business.

"I daresay," Pitt replied with a sudden wave of anger and unhappiness. "But I'm a police officer investigating the murder of Mr. Cathcart, about a mile away from here, and I need an answer to my question. Did you sell one of those exactly two weeks ago to a tall, young man, probably with fair hair?"

The ironmonger paled visibly. "I—I didn't know there was anything wrong! He seemed . . . very quiet, very nicely spoken. But, no, not fair hair, as I recall, rather more . . . sort of . . ."

"His hair doesn't matter!" Pitt said impatiently. "Was he tall, slender, young . . . about twenty-five?" Although Orlando could have disguised that too, if he had thought of it.

"I . . . I can't remember. I sold one that day, though. I know that because I keep very close watch on my stock. Never run out of any household ironmongery if I can help it. If it can be bought, it can be bought here at Foster and Sons."

"Thank you. You may be required to testify to that, so please keep your records safe."

"I will! I will!"

Outside on the footpath Tellman stopped and stared at Pitt, his face somber.

"There isn't much more to do, is there." It was a statement, almost a surrender. "He could have spent the time till dark in any one of the pubs around here. If you want I'll go to all of them and ask, but I reckon we don't need to know, now that we've got the rolling pin."

"No . . . not really," Pitt agreed. He smiled and straightened his shoulders a little. "We'd better go and see if we can find it, although it's probably in the river. It would be proof. We'll go through the crime, see what must have happened."

Tellman pulled his coat collar up and they set out back to the house on the river, walking silently. They must do it before dark, and there were only a couple of hours left.

Mrs. Geddes had been sent for and was at the house waiting, her face full of mistrust as she watched them enter the hallway and solemnly begin the reenactment of the murder, Pitt taking the part of Orlando, Tellman of Cathcart.

Of course they had no idea of what conversation there might have been between the two men, or what reason Orlando had given for his visit. They began from a point which was incontestable.

"He must have stood here," Tellman said, thin-lipped, placing himself near the pedestal where the vase had been smashed and the alternative set in its stead.

"I wonder why?" Pitt said thoughtfully. "He had his back to Orlando when he was struck, which makes me wonder how Orlando disguised the pin. No one goes to visit carrying a rolling pin, even wrapped in brown paper."

"Say he'd just bought it . . . on his way?" Tellman suggested, frowning with dislike of the thought even as he said it.

"A young actor?" Pitt raised his eyebrows. "Don't see him as a pastry cook, do you?"

"A gift?"

"For whom? A young lady? His mother? Do you see Cecily Antrim rolling pastry?"

Tellman gave him a sour look. "Then he must have had it disguised somehow. Maybe rolled in papers, like a sheaf of pictures or something?"

"That sounds more probable. So if Cathcart were standing where you are, and Orlando here"—Pitt gestured—"then Cathcart unquestionably had his attention on something else, or he would have noticed Orlando unwrap his pictures and

302

take out a rolling pin, and he would have been alarmed . . . it's an act without reasonable explanation."

"Then he didn't see," Tellman said decisively. "He was going somewhere, leading the way. Orlando was following. He hit Cathcart from behind . . . we know that anyway."

Pitt went through the motion of raising his arm as if to strike Tellman. Tellman crumpled to his knees, rather carefully, to avoid banging himself on the now-bare wooden floor. He lay down, more or less as Cathcart might have fallen.

"Now what?" he asked.

Pitt had been considering that. They had little idea how long Orlando had been there, but knowing what he had done, he had had no time to hesitate for more than a few minutes.

"If you think you're going to put me in any dress . . ." Tellman began.

"Be quiet!" Pitt snapped.

"I . . ." Tellman started to get up.

"Lie down!" Pitt ordered. "Privilege of rank," he added ironically. "Would you rather change places?"

Tellman lay down again.

"Where were the green dress and the chains kept?" Pitt said thoughtfully. "Certainly not down here!"

"Up in the studio, most likely," Tellman replied, his face to the floor. "With all the other stuff he used in his pictures. What I want to know is, how did Orlando know that the punt was here and not somewhere else? It could have been anywhere, any lake or river. Could have been miles away—in another county, for that matter."

Pitt did not answer. His mind was beginning to reach for a new, extraordinary thought.

"Do you suppose he went upstairs first?" Tellman went on. "Maybe saw the chains and the dress in the studio?" He did not say it as if he believed that himself.

"And then came down, and Cathcart was going up again, ahead of him, and Orlando killed him?" Pitt said almost absentmindedly.

Tellman rolled over and sat up, scowling. "Then what do you think?"

"I think he certainly didn't wander down the garden, in the dark, to see if there was a boat moored in the river," Pitt replied. "I think he had been here before, often enough to know that these things existed, and exactly where to find them . . ."

"But he hadn't," Tellman said decisively. "He had to ask where it was . . . from the pub landlord. We know that."

"Or there was someone else here as well," Pitt answered. "Someone who did know . . . someone who finished the job that Orlando only started."

"But he came alone!" Tellman climbed to his feet. "You think there was someone else here the same night . . . also bent on murdering Cathcart?" His tone of voice conveyed what he thought of that possibility.

"I don't know what I think," Pitt confessed. "But I don't think Orlando Antrim murdered Cathcart in a passion of fury over the way Cathcart used Cecily, then set about searching the house to see if he could find the clothes and the chains, and the boat, to make it a mockery of the photograph. For one thing, there was no sign of a struggle when Mrs. Geddes came in in the morning, which means that if he searched, he put everything back where he found it . . . exactly. Does that sound like a man in a murderous rage to you?"

"No. But Cathcart's dead," Tellman said reasonably. "And someone put him in that dress and chained him in the punt, then scattered all the flowers . . . and I'd swear anything you like it was someone who hated him . . . and hated him because of Cecily Antrim."

Pitt said nothing. He had no argument.

"And we know Orlando was here, and he bought the pin," Tellman went on.

"We'd better go and look for it," Pitt said miserably. "Before it gets dark. We've only got just over an hour."

Together they trudged down the path towards the river, watched from the side door by Mrs. Geddes.

They were sodden wet, covered in mud, and it was beginning to grow dusk when Tellman slipped on it at the edge of the bank, swore, and pulled it out, washing it in river water and holding it up in angry triumph. "So he didn't throw it after all," he said with surprise. "Maybe he meant to and dropped it."

They were obliged to get the ironmonger from his dinner to identify it. He came to the door with his napkin tucked into the tip of his waistcoat and a considerable reluctance in his manner. He eyed the rolling pin with disgust.

"Yes, that's one o' mine. Put my mark on 'em, in blue, I do. See?" He pointed to a tiny blue device on the end of the pin near the handle. "Is that the one what . . ." He would not say it.

"Yes, it is. You sold it to a tall, young man on the afternoon of Cathcart's death?"

"Yes."

"Are you certain?"

" 'Course I am. Wouldn't say so if I weren't. My books'll show it."

"Thank you. Sorry to have disturbed your supper."

"Now what?" Tellman asked when they were outside in the dark again. "Is it enough to arrest him?" He sounded tired and doubtful.

Pitt was doubtful himself. He had no uncertainty that Orlando Antrim had seen the photograph of his mother and reacted with extreme distress. He had searched for the photographs and gone to the house and found Cathcart. He had purchased the rolling pin. But the dressing of the corpse in green velvet, and chaining him on the punt with the flowers strewn around, did not follow so easily.

Could there have been two people there other than Cathcart? If so, then who? He knew coincidences happened, but he did not like them. Most things had a cause, a line of circumstances connected to each other in a way which could be understood, if you knew them all and considered them long enough.

"Can we arrest him?" Tellman pressed.

"I don't know." Pitt shook himself a little.

"Well, it had to be him," Tellman said pointedly. "He was here, we know that. He had plenty of reason to kill Cathcart.

He bought the weapon and we've got it. What else is there—apart from working out how he knew where to find the dress and the chains?"

"And the boat," Pitt added.

"Well, somebody did." Tellman was exasperated. "You can't argue with that! If it wasn't him, who could it have been? And why? Why would anybody else do all that with the boat and the flowers? Wouldn't they want to get away as quickly as possible? Just leave him where he was. Why dress up a dead man . . . that somebody else killed . . . and risk getting caught?"

"Not a lot of risk," Pitt argued. "Bottom of a garden by the river in the middle of a foggy night. Still, he must have cared passionately about something to have bothered."

They crossed the road, still walking slowly, heading back towards the bridge.

"Maybe it was someone he blackmailed, after all?" Tellman suggested. "Or more like, someone who hated that kind of picture and the way it makes people think."

Pitt thought of Ralph Marchand. It was believable, very easily, but another idea was also forming in his mind, uncertain, perhaps foolish, but becoming clearer with each step.

As soon as he saw a hansom he hailed it, and to Tellman's sharp stare of astonishment, he gave not the address of the theatre but that of the medical examiner.

"What do you want with him?" Tellman said incredulously. "We know how he died!"

Pitt did not answer.

When they arrived, he told the cab to wait and ran up the steps of the building and in through the door. To his intense relief he found the surgeon still there. He knew the one question he wanted to ask.

"Was there any water in Cathcart's lungs?" he demanded.

The surgeon looked startled. "Yes, there was a bit. I was going to tell you next time you were by." His eyes narrowed. "Doesn't make any difference to your case."

"But did he actually die of the blow to his head or of drowning?" Pitt insisted, fidgeting with impatience.

Tellman watched with what might have been a dawning comprehension. His eyes were steady, and he stood motionless in the cold room, his nostrils slightly flared with distaste at the pervasive odor, real or imagined.

The surgeon stared at Pitt, shifting his weight. "Clinically, I suppose the drowning got to him before the wound, but it's academic, Pitt. He would have died of the blow anyway . . . or exposure, in his injured state, sodden wet and left out in the river like that. It's murder any way you look at it at all. What's your point?"

"I'm not sure," Pitt said honestly. "Thank you. Come on, Tellman." He turned on his heel.

"Theatre now?" Tellman asked, racing to catch up with him as he strode down the steps and swung back up into the hansom.

They rattled through the dark, gaslit streets without speaking again, Pitt leaning forward as if by effort of will he could make the horse go faster.

He was out of the door almost before they came to a stop, leaving Tellman to pay the driver and follow behind him. He raced up the steps and into the foyer, brandishing his card and calling out who he was, pushing past the usher and swinging the door wide into the back of the auditorium.

He saw with a flood of relief that the stage was still lit, although it was the very end of the final act. Gertrude and the king were both already dead, and Laertes; Polonius and Ophelia were long since gone, he by accident, she the suicide of drowning. Hamlet, Fortinbras, Horatio and Osric were left amid a sea of corpses.

There was the sound of a shot.

" 'What warlike noise is this?' " Hamlet asked, swinging to face it. He seemed as taut as a wire, his nerves stretched to breaking.

Osric answered him.

Hamlet turned back towards the audience, his eyes wide with agony, staring straight ahead to where Pitt stood in the center of the aisle.

" 'O, I die, Horatio;
The potent poison quite o'er-crows my spirit
I cannot live to hear the news from England;
But I do prophesy the election lights
On Fortinbras; he has my dying voice;
So tell him, with the occurents, more and less,
Which have solicited.' "

His voice was hoarse, cutting to the soul. " 'The rest is silence.' " He crumpled and slid forward.

There was such utter stillness the audience might not have existed, except for the tension in the air like a storm.

" 'Now cracks a noble heart,' " Horatio said through a throat thick with tears.

" 'Goodnight, sweet prince,
And flights of angels sing thee to thy rest!' "

Fortinbras and the English ambassadors entered and the last, tragic words were spoken. Finally the soldiers carried off the bodies to the somber familiarity of the Dead March. The curtain descended.

A complete silence filled the auditorium, thick, crackling with emotion, then the applause erupted like a sea breaking. As if impelled by a single force, the entire audience rose to its feet. Above the thunder of clapping, voices could be heard shouting "Bravo!" again and again.

The curtain rose and the full cast lined up to take the call, Orlando in the center, Cecily radiant at his side, and Bellmaine looking ashen, as if Polonius had risen from the grave to acknowledge his praise.

Pitt walked down the aisle and along in front of the orchestra, through the side door towards the back of the stage. Tellman joined him, but still they had to wait. The applause went on and on, drowning out every other sound. It was impossible to speak above it for almost a quarter of an hour.

Finally the curtain fell for the last time and the players turned to leave.

Pitt stepped onto the stage. He could afford to wait no longer. Tellman was on his heels.

Orlando faced him. He looked haggard and utterly exhausted. He took a step forward, but he was shaking.

"You've come for me." His voice was clear and soft. "Thank you for letting me finish."

"I'm a policeman, not a barbarian," Pitt replied just as softly.

Orlando walked towards him, his hands held as if ready for manacles. He did not once look at his mother.

"What is going on?" Cecily demanded, looking one way then the other. "Superintendent, what do you want here? This is surely an inappropriate time. Orlando has just performed perhaps the greatest Hamlet there has ever been. If you still think there is anything to ask us, come tomorrow . . . about midday."

"You don't understand, Mother," Orlando said, still without turning to her. "You never did."

She started to say something, but he cut across her.

"Mr. Pitt has come to arrest me for murdering Cathcart. Although I didn't put him in the river. I don't know how that happened, I swear."

"Don't be ridiculous!" Cecily moved forward at last. This time she addressed Pitt, not her son. "He's exhausted. I don't know why he should say such a thing. It's absurd. Why should he murder Cathcart? He didn't even know him!"

Orlando turned slowly towards her. His face was bloodless, his eyes dark ringed as if he had come to the end of a terrible journey.

"I killed him because I hated him for what he had made you into. You are my mother! And when you debase yourself, you debase me also . . ."

"I don't know what you're talking about!" she protested. And to judge from her wide, frank eyes, Pitt believed she still did not perceive what she had done.

It was Bellmaine who told her. He moved past Orlando, close to Pitt but turned to her. "You made your crusade without thinking what it would do to those who loved you, Cecily," he said in a low, painful voice. "You had pictures taken of yourself that would shock people into thinking what you wanted them to. You woke new and powerful emotions, hurling them out of their safety of heart into the ways you wished them to be, because you thought it was good for them. You didn't stop to think, or to care, that in doing it you were destroying what they might have held too dear to lose without tearing them apart, breaking them inside." There were tears in his throat, and a terrible grief. "You broke your son, Cecily. The mind might tell him pornography is all right if it breaks down old prejudices, but the heart can't accept." His voice cracked. "The heart only says, 'That's my mother! The source of who I am!' "

At last the horror reached her. Understanding spread through her with unspeakable pain. As if she had been crippled inside, she turned her eyes to Orlando.

He did not answer. His face was eloquent enough; all the anger, and the loss and the pain, were there in his haggard features. He swiveled away from her and held out his wrists to Pitt.

"No." Bellmaine touched him with intense gentleness. "You struck him, but you did not kill him. I did that."

"You?" Cecily demanded "Why?" But there was already the beginning of a terrible realization in her.

"Because I hated him for blackmailing me," Bellmaine said wearily, "over a photograph I posed for years ago . . . when I needed the money. Shown now, it would have ruined me. An actor counts on image. But mostly to protect my son . . ."

"Your son . . ." Pitt began to ask, then he looked at Cecily, at Bellmaine, and at Orlando, and saw it in their faces. Orlando had his mother's hair and eyes, but there was a resemblance to Bellmaine also. And acknowledgment was in Cecily's silence.

Orlando had not known. That also was only too apparent.

"How did you know Orlando had gone there?" Pitt asked.

Bellmaine shrugged. "Does it matter now? I knew he was greatly distressed the evening before. I did not know why. Then on the day of his death, Cathcart sent me a message to tell me not to go to his house to pay my usual monthly dues to him because he had a new client coming, someone who had made the appointment that day. A young man called Richard Larch."

"Who is Richard Larch?" Cecily demanded, but there was no anger in her, no spirit. The fire inside her was quenched.

"The first role Orlando ever played," Bellmaine answered. "Don't you even remember? I knew then—at least, I feared. I've seen the Ophelia picture as well. That's why I dressed him . . ." He swallowed and seemed to stagger a little. He regained his balance with difficulty. "That's why I dressed him that way and sat him in the boat. He was still alive, but I knew he wouldn't last in the cold . . . and the water. There was . . ." He gasped. "There was a kind of symmetry in it. I was a good Hamlet myself, thirty years ago. Not as good as Orlando. Cecily was my Ophelia then."

Pitt saw the sweat break out in his gray face and understood. He was glad he had had no time to prevent it.

Bellmaine fell forward onto his knees.

" 'O, I die, Horatio,' " he said hoarsely. " 'The potent poison quite o'er-crows my spirit . . . The rest is . . . is . . .' " He did not finish.

Cecily closed her eyes and the tears ran down her white cheeks.

Orlando did not go to her. He looked at Pitt for a moment, then bent over the motionless body of his father.

" 'Good night, sweet prince,' " he whispered. "May flights . . ."

But he too could not complete his line. This cut the heart too deep.

Silently Pitt turned and left, Tellman behind him, his face wet with tears.